Praise for It's the Way of Love Story:

"Thrilling...Sexy...Inspiring...This book shakes the foundations of the quantum holowave, entangling the reader in a delightful mesh of heart-and mind-bending adventure."
--*The New Star Supernova*

"A true tour-de-force of the future, and a key period in our past...Hager succeeds in taking the reader on a whirlwind journey. But behind it all is a simple story, a love story, a deep and moving tale of two lovers, kept apart by so many forces, yet never thwarted. And the basic story of how one true love can lead to a great and mighty Way."
--*The Boulder Creek Bloghorn*

"This is dangerous literature. It reveals key links between states of existence, masked in the crowd-pleasing format of the romantic novel. It is sure to create subtle currents of consciousness striving to illuminate dark recesses of our collective dream. The power of pure consciousness cannot be underestimated."
--*The New Cali Call*

"The work in question can be traced through 27 independent holopaths, creating a quantum ripple with a positive vibration esponent rating of 144, easily the most significant of the early 21st century. The strange attractor fractal derived through it's impact in holospace displayed heretofore unseen synchronistic reflections and refractions on the quantum weave screen."
--*DatArch Prime Excelsior*

Also by M.C. Hager
Published by 1earthpress

BOOM! Backstage Pass

Coming in 2013:
It's the Way of Love: The Agappa
It's the Way of Love: Guide Book
Mother of the Forest: How the West was Saved.

Praise for BOOM! Backstage Pass:
"Hager's novel (BOOM! Backstage Pass) is not just some silly
backstage expose...Aside from juicy gossip about high-tech
celebs and rock-stars, the book is filled with flashes of what
life was like at the beginning of the dotcom boom...The novel
illuminates the cross-pollination of many different facets of
Silicon Valley in ways that only a longtime insider can do. For
example....just as there's a rhythm that flows through the
entire behind-the-scenes concert operations, there's a similar
rhythm that buckles in, out, and through the spider web of
intersections between venture capital culture, high-end audio
proliferation, Zen, computer hardware, chaos theory fractals,
rock music, backstage passes, Bluetooth and the
Rosicrucians...Everything is an organic, interconnected whole,
with the Tao flowing through it."
                              --Gary Singh, Metro Silicon Valley

"*BOOM! Backstage Pass* should be required reading for
anyone interested in the media or the stage."
                              --Steve Hilla, Union Technician

It's the Way of Love Story

≥ ∞ ✝ ☪ ☯ ॐ ✡

Romance and Adventure
In Times of Trouble

By M.C. Hager

1earthpress

www.1earthpress.com
www.itsthewayoflove.com

1earthpress

FIRST 1EARTHPRESS TRADE PAPERBACK EDITION

Copyright © 2011 by Mark C. Hager

All rights reserved.

Published in the United States by 1earthpress (www.1earthpress.com), a division of 1earth Media Consultants Group, Inc. (www.1emcg.com)

Library of Congress Cataloging-in-Publication Data

Hager, M. C.
It's the Way of Love Story: Romance and Adventure in Times of Trouble/ by M. C. Hager

Library of Congress Control Number (LCCN): 2011962471

ISBN-13: 978-0-9832857-1-7
ISBN-10: 0983285713

Printed in the United States of America.
Cover art by Mark C. Hager
Cover photo courtesy of: photostock / FreeDigitalPhotos.net

12   11   10   9   8

To the Source of All Love, most particularly those manifestations closest to me -- my wife Rockelle and three sons. Thank you for being a part of this story with me.

To my parents, brothers and sisters, all the rest who are part of the team and this growing community, thanks for all that you do, and may you all take something of value away from this work of love...

Special thanks to Babaji and Sita, for your inspiration, and Marion "Sun" Lundell, for your special editorial help, and Nick Herbert and Al Lundell, for your intellectual contributions.

CONTENTS

AUTHOR'S NOTE: A CREATION STORY

This novel was projected back into the past from a year in the latter half of the 21st Century, using a technique developed by certain specialists known as Data Archaeologists, or DatArchs for short. Massive changes have occurred in this timeline, and great knowledge has been discovered by many great minds working in tandem. Great pressures often create great advances, and the last several decades have been some of the most stressful in human history. This stress has led some big thinkers in my time to determine that certain thoughts and concepts needed to be seeded into the minds of the early 21st century. Concepts and ideas form the bifurcation points of major movements in history. The DatArchs have figured out how to trace delicate lines of thought throughout time, and certain renegades have developed a technique to send fully conceived works back in time by encoding holographic word strings in the greater quantum fabric of an individual consciousness. The impact can be carefully tracked and analyzed by fluctuations in the quantum warp and woof.

It was determined that we could send this story back to an earlier version of myself, and at risk of my own sanity, we have succeeded. The first and most far-reaching of the expressions was to be a romantic adventure novel, the results of which you are holding in your hand. The nature of quantum consciousness is such that nothing is ever exact, but certain effects can be quantified and tracked. The DatArchs had the audacity to claim that the story really did not matter, that all that was necessary was that certain carrier frequencies of love be coded into the text. I knew the story had to be a good one. I chose the standard hero quest, but this time it had to be a woman and a man. I did not think there had to be a villain per se, but there had to be major events challenging them, helping them grow.

Almost all cultures have stories of civilization-changing natural events, from global floods to fire falling from the skies. In all of the stories a heroic family plays center role, and God, in some form or another, plays a personal part. So many stories of the last couple centuries, novels, plays and movies, have included great evil powers or even the devil as a main character. Few include any God as a character, yet almost all of the world disaster myths do. The nature of this God is a key part of the Way of Love. The Way holds that our universe is suffused with consciousness, and this consciousness loves all life, particularly conscious life. It loves conscious life so much that It comes to that life in whatever form expected and acceptable to that life. Thus a Christian finds Christ, a Buddhist sees Buddha, and a skeptic studies a cold world devoid of mystical mystery. These ancient catastrophe stories also included helpers from the animal kingdom, from the dove of Noah to hummingbird helping the Ohlone to the top of Mt. Ummunum. These were already a part of our tale.

We believe that there are many potential futures and many potential paths, and this is a communiqué from one potential timeline back to a critical juncture in our past. In our timeline there has been a major direct democracy movement, and this facilitated some changes that might seem strange to a reader in the early part of the century. An interconnected community where everyone votes on everything can make some drastic changes rather quickly. One was to change over to a base-twelve number system based on the Agappa. Major debates were held where the merits of a system that combined numbers and time, from seconds to the seasons, with the geometry of the circle. Some compared it to a Unified Field Theory. The Agappa is a symbol made with twelve spheres that also is a system of numbers. It has also been turned into a series of 12 single-hand gestures, with the "Agappa" meaning 12 flashed by the hand looking as the fusion of "peace" and "hang-loose," two other hand gestures.

The sphere symbols correlate with certain shapes which have come to represent the number, as well as philosophical names reflecting what was considered to be a metaphorical representation of each number. The Agappa is also a creation story in its form, and a map to higher states of consciousness. It is a love story. Agape is the concept of unconditional universal love. It is a lifeforce that underlies all of existence. It has many names in many languages: chi, prana, manna, and many others, for all represent a basic force that came from a big bang and blossomed out into the universe as we know it, all out of love.

1. ONA, UNITY, was whole, longing for love, became

2. DUA, POLARITY, was creative, gave birth, became

3. ATRUA, TRINITY, was expansive, became

4. KATERO, QUATERNITY, was crystallizing, became

5. PENTERO, PHYSICALITY, was solid, became

6. EXORTO, MORTALITY, was transition, became

7. FAMMO, COMMUNITY, was persistent, became

8. TEMMO, ETERNITY, was cyclical, became

9. NONNO, MENTALITY, was aware, became

10. ADEKKA, SYNCHRONICITY, was timely, became

11. AMANNA, CAUSALITY, accomplished, became

12. AGAPPA, DIVINITY, was everything, became…
And so we come to our story.

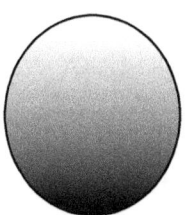

Ona (1) Freed

The dust swirled in the early summer air, but Lucky Star did not care. Few things bothered her, and even she never really knew why. Except when someone hurt the cows, of course. Then she lost all composure. But the cows were well today, lowing and happy, although a calf was limping somewhere out in the pasture. At least, according to Buck Smith when he had rushed up to the ranch house that afternoon. Buck always looked for any excuse to get Lucky out in the field on horseback, and he knew she could not resist the report of an injured calf. They had spent half of their childhood on horseback in the fields, but lately Lucky had been evasive, and Buck sensed the change. Certainly things had changed quite a bit since Lucky had returned from veterinary school a few years back. She brought a lot of new-fangled ideas that could prove risky, Buck thought, but he did not have it in him to disagree with her. Something about her was always right.

There was something more going on here. A certain Consciousness was already with them, reaching out to each of them in their own particular way. Something lived in everything, in the land, in the water, in the sky, and beyond, and it was almost doggedly pursuing them, somehow training them for what lay ahead.

Buck was rather preoccupied with the particularly painful consciousness of the beautiful form in front of him. Lucky gripped the horn lightly and her faded Levis squeaked in the saddle. She rode ahead of Buck, naturally taking charge of the situation, even though Buck was supposedly leading her to where he saw the injured calf. Her sun-bleached hair blew about below her hat, and she seemed to look everywhere but back at Buck. He could not take his eyes off her. Lucky was carrying the burden of leadership like any woman in a similar position, working twice as hard as most men. Buck had been following her around for years, but he did not mind the subordinate position, if only because it afforded him the best view of her tight ass in the saddle. In the last couple of years she had grown curves that elicited a warm rush through his body when he saw her, but she remained as aloof as always. Buck was as handsome as they come, and he had many girls chase him over the years, and one or two caught him, briefly. Many boys chased Lucky, too, but they never caught her. In dejection they spread rumors that she was gay, but she was even less interested in girls. Buck could not believe that any woman so beautiful was not meant to eventually settle down and have children, so he sat back patiently in the saddle and waited, following her around wherever she went.

They rode through the clouds of dust which seemed to purposely swirl around Lucky and right into Buck's face. He choked and coughed but she rode on ahead nonchalantly. She had taken control of the ranch midway through veterinary school when her father Bud had suffered a stroke. The Lucky Star Ranch near Freedom, California, had been one of the last free-range dairy ranches in the area. Bud had maintained it that way even when the big dairy conglomerates started taking control of everything, even with the drop in the price of milk and mounting economic pressures, because, he said, grass fed milk just tasted better. Even he began to doubt his position, however, when it came to paying Lucky's tuition, and some said the stress led to his stroke. He had decided to sell the whole thing and be done with it, but Lucky had convinced him to let her take it over. Lucky's mom, Belle, was a retired nurse, so Bud was well cared for, but she was from a city family and never had taken to life on horseback. She tried to protect him from stress and often complained to Lucky about all the changes.

Bud, Buck, and the other ranch hands had their doubts, and they protested openly when she implemented new so-called "natural" methods in caring for the animals. When she slapped an "Organic" label on the cartons and their sales and profits shot heavenward, however, they stopped complaining. Now they had more cash for tools and supplies than ever, and Lucky hardly discussed her ideas with the hands, much less asked for their opinions.

Most of the hands were old-school, and they openly had difficultly listening to a woman with new ideas. Some of them would smirk and move slowly when she asked for something, and she tolerated little of the sort. She would fire a hand for seemingly small offenses when it came to her cows, and it had become a nearly desperate situation for good hands were scarce and running a two-thousand head dairy ranch was no small operation. Every morning they had to be separated and herded into milking barns, a significant task that was not relished by the hands who had worked other larger automated dairy farms where the cows were continuously confined. In such operations the work amounted to keeping care of the machinery. Lucky kept her father's early version milking machines, because milking a thousand cows was nearly impossible by hand with so few workers, but she still insisted on going to each cow individually, caressing it and assuring it, because, she claimed, giving milk was an act of love, and no cow could love a machine.

It certainly seemed that love is what kept the ranch running. The pool of hands had quickly shrunk when Lucky had taken over, and may have disappeared altogether had it not been for Buck and Pico Martinez, a dedicated hand who kept appearing with new "friends" to replace old hands. At

Bud's insistence, each new hire had to absolutely have at least a green card, which seem to cause Pico some consternation, but he and Lucky helped the uncarded ones get legal. Even with the total crew now numbering 20, Lucky, Buck, and Pico still did most of the work. But things were getting easier. The cows sensed the change, too, and seemed to approve. They would naturally respond to Lucky, and they could often be found waiting at the milking barns in the morning when the hands came to let them in. They seemed to sense why Lucky and Buck were out this afternoon as well, and they slowly parted and started walking toward a calf in the distance. Lucky took the cue and nudged the horse to move more quickly. She and Buck galloped up to about ten feet from the calf, and dismounted.

The calf stood as if in shock, and made no move as if to run. It was a young female, and blood was trickling down from her back left foot, which she held off the ground. Lucky crossed to the back of her saddle and opened her veterinary bags. She pulled out a syringe and a suture kit.

"Look at that, a young girl," she lamented. "She'd a been eaten by the coyotes tonight for sure." She approached the calf and it bleated half-heartedly, knowing instinctively that Lucky meant relief from its troubles. "Now, now, girl, it's okay," Lucky intoned as she stroked the calf's neck. She sought to reassure and calm the frightened animal before she even looked at the injured leg. Buck started to come around to hold the animal.

"Just a minute," Lucky said as she held back Buck with one hand while still stroking the calf with the other. Buck stopped immediately, only pretending to oppose the press of her soft yet firm touch. She lingered for a moment, then sensing no real resistance, gave both hands to the calf, tenderly stilling its nerves. "There now girl, you're all right. I'm here." The calf responded almost immediately and its fervent bleating became a faint guttural moan. Lucky motioned to Buck to now come around and take hold of the calf, and he knelt down and lightly locked the calf into place. As soon as Lucky took hold of the leg, the calf started to bleat again and struggled against Buck, but he was firmly immobilized.

"Oh my, just look at that!" Lucky exclaimed as she examined the bloody hoof. A short length of barbed wire was twisted in and around the two halves. "Nasty barb wire! I thought we got rid of all that crap!" she said as she pulled out a syringe of anesthetic.

"We did," Buck insisted. "I told Pico to make sure he got all the pieces."

"He did," Lucky affirmed. "This looks like an old piece, probably covered with tetanus." Her hands deftly delivered the shot, and the calf struggled violently, knocking Buck in the chin, but he held firm. Lucky gently reassured the calf and waited for her to settle down. Slowly the anesthetic took effect and the calf grew calm. Quickly Lucky grabbed wire cutters and removed the wire and held it up momentarily for Buck to see.

"Look at that evil shit," she said and then wrapped it in plastic and deftly threw it in the bag. She grabbed a water bottle and flushed the wound, and took out a brush and started to scrape vigorously. "I'm sorry sweetie, I can't let any germs stay in there."

"Have you named her yet?" Buck asked. Lucky had individually named every cow at the ranch for the last 25 years ever since she could talk."

"Linda Govinda," she said lyrically.

"She's going to be 'Gimpy' now," Buck quipped.

"Don't let her hear that!" Lucky gasped, protecting the sensitive pride of the young animal.

"Sorry, I meant...'Lindy," Buck recovered weakly.

"Lindy?" Lucky asked. "Okay, we'll take it." She finished her cleaning and took out a pair of clippers, quickly removing dead tissue and hair from around the wound while holding the calf's leg between her own. She bathed it with alcohol and patted the inside spaces with gauze. The anesthetic had taken affect and the calf was calming down. It released an occasional quizzical cry as Lucky worked expertly to dress the wound. After cleaning she prepared a few quick sutures, all with the calf's hoof protruding from between her thighs. Buck knew not to joke as she struggled and the strain pulled her jeans deep between her legs. This was a serious and difficult moment. Sensing a bit of attention from behind Lucky made a half dozen lightning stitches and was almost done.

"Bring me the crazy glue!" she barked out, perhaps a bit too harshly. Buck went to the bag and pulled out a tube of crazy glue. This was an old trick for Buck now, one of many from that early on brought plenty of questions and jeers from other ranch hands. But the first quickly healed cow silenced most of the complaints, and now no one questioned any of Lucky's seemingly unusual methods. She daubed the hoof dry with a bit of gauze, took the tube of glue and poured it liberally over the new stitches. She had discovered that the super glue helped to keep hoof injuries from getting infected.

"Did I ever tell you how super glue was created?" Lucky asked as she waited for the glue to dry on the hoof between her legs.

"As stitchless sutures?" Buck remembered.

"That's right, stitchless sutures, for the medical industry," Lucky affirmed. "Very good, you remembered. I find it is perfect for hooves, and nails," she said, grimacing at her dirty fingers.

"How do you use it on wet tissue?" Buck asked.

"You have to dry it. Most tissues, without blood, are dry. Works best on the outside, skin and stuff, you know."

"You may be the first bovine plastic surgeon," Buck supposed.

"You'd be surprised what vets have done, over the years," she maintained. "Vets have to be everything, surgeons, pediatricians, epidemiologists, podiatrists, nutritionists..."

"Plastic surgeons..." Buck added.

"Plastic surgeons, yep," Lucky agreed. "Psychologists..."

"Psychologists?" Buck wondered.

"Yes, psychologists," Lucky insisted. "Vets that have no concern for the psychology of an animal are likely to do more harm than good. Old-school types might have rode in, roped Lindy here, thrown on a few stitches with no anesthetic, maybe sterile, and then rode out, leaving Lindy in shock and more stressed than from the injury."

"That's just common sense," Buck claimed.

"It may be sense but it's not too common," Lucky said.

"Uncommon sense, then," Buck supposed. "Maybe that's what you got."

"Maybe uncommon, but not much sense myself," she figured.

"You're just being modest," Buck believed. "No one else seemed to know what it took to turn this ranch around."

"I'll tell you who else knows...the cows," she claimed. "That's right, the cows. Less than half of what I know came from some book. Most of it came from these cows themselves," she said, gesturing out over the herd. Several heads rose from grazing as if acknowledging the reference. "Look how happy they all look, and, I'll tell you, happy cows make more milk."

"Now you're starting to sound like that commercial," he said, with a wry smile.

"Don't get me started," she said with a frown. "You know as well as I do that those commercials are a lie. Most cows in California are not happy, all cooped up in factory farms in their own excrement. I tell you, I think they spied on our cows for research for that commercial, cause we gotta be the only ranch that raises dairy cows this way."

"There's Pete Capitanich," Buck proposed.

"Ol' Pete is a dear and a great and knowledgeable man," she conceded. "But seven dairy cows, even holistically cared for, hardly make a commercial dairy ranch."

"You didn't say commercial dairy ranch," Buck defended himself.

"Well I meant it," Lucky continued. "Ol' Pete doesn't count."

"How can you say that? Of course he counts," Buck touted. Ol' Pete was a dear friend from the Croation community in nearby Watsonville. He had a diverse farm on the edge of town, claiming his family had been practicing organic agriculture since before there was a name for it. He had made his money packing apples then bought his retirement property. He was a dear friend of Lucky and Buck but his was a small mixed farm as opposed to the Lucky Star Ranch which was one of the largest operations of its kind around.

"Well of course he counts as a PERSON," Lucky stressed. "But I doubt they went by his lot to research dairy cows."

"But you think they came to our ranch?" Buck questioned.

"You never know. We have the happiest cows around," Lucky said.

"I think Ol' Pete's cows are happier. Better feed." Pete was able to virtually spoil his cows with mixed greens from his various gardens. Lucky Star used organic feed to supplement grazing, but it was mostly just alfalfa and hay.

"There's nothing wrong with our feed, and I meant happy cows on a commercial dairy lot," Lucky defended her operation.

"Well you didn't specify," he demurred.

"The commercials themselves implied commercial dairy farms," she continued.

"Okay, I'll give you that. Those commercials do look a lot like the Lucky Star," he admitted.

"That's all I'm saying, sheesh!" She gently put the calf's foot down and turned around to face Buck. "Now I know a happy cow. Listen, Lindy, don't you worry about that foot. It will be fine, hear me?" They both looked down at Lindy, who was standing motionless right in the same spot. "Any other situation that calf would have bolted as soon as you let go."

"I know," Buck conceded. "Maybe there is something to this psychology for animals stuff."
"You bet there is. Get along, girl," Lucky said to Lindy, gently prodding her on the back. The calf started slowly and bleated again, casually looking through the crowd for its mother. It lumbered slowly along and found its way into the herd, disappearing with hardly a limp. The ease was a wave that passed through the mass of animals as Lucky and Buck watched with a brief moment of satisfaction. The clouds mingled with the dust and turned the light a lotus blue. There was a Consciousness there, initiating them. They were beginning some journey that led to a destination beyond their understanding as of yet.

There was a moment, there, between them, like many moments before, but different this time. A new presence, a glimmering hope appeared between them. They did not talk about it, as they turned and headed back to the main ranch house, just like they never talked about any of the other moments they had shared. The moments were not about words. But they shared them, and they remembered them, as the images floated by on the blue lotus light.

Something had begun, well, maybe long ago, but now they knew they were on a journey, they were going somewhere, and it was a place where things were possible, where you could do it the right way and not get bothered. There might be problems, injuries, bumps on the road of life, but there was something there that would get them through it all. Yet, Lucky wondered, was it the same something? There was a comfort, a promise, a compromise, that surrounded them, including them, yet Lucky knew there was something else, something more. She felt the pull of Buck's desires, a certain gravity, yet she longed for levity. She had so long grown accustomed to Buck's presence that she could imagine no other man as her partner, yet she felt there was something more. She had considered women, and had found more than one attractive, but ultimately found the prospect unfulfilling. In the end she disregarded it all as unnecessary longings, but her heart registered the reality.

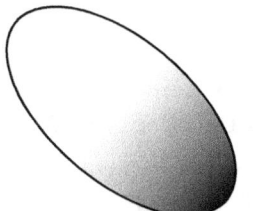

Dua (2) Tied

Bud pulled himself up over to the coffee table and grabbed the remote control. Nothing good on but nothing good was better than nothing, he figured. His recent stroke had reduced his capacity for doing many things, but had not decreased his sense of being. This was perhaps the most frustrating part. So many people, upon sensing his new limitations, assumed some sort of concurrent diminishment of consciousness, as if some dimmer switch had been turned down in his mind. Many treated him as a child, like much of the help around the ranch, who had previously treated him with awed respect before. He could not seem to communicate that his mind was still as sharp behind the new cloud in his brain. He felt things as acutely, he new things as always, but he had never been a great communicator, and now his main weakness had become a complete deficiency. The whole situation served to isolate him, like a cow with encephalitis in a holding pen. Yet Bud was from old self-sufficient stock. He had no use for depression or complacency, and he moved on. Only Lucky seemed to understand him, and they had grown closer than ever, somehow moving together to a different plane.

His cognitive difficulties had oddly had a liberating effect on him. He began to realize, as his memory failed, his speech faltered, that he was not these things after all. He began to sense that he could give up the whole package and yet still, somehow, be around, more liberated than ever. Things did not matter to him so much anymore. But no one understood. Even Belle, who tried to show the most sympathy of all, did not seem to understand. She instead spent her time trying to protect Bud from what she feared were indignities and keeping him as comfortable as always. She sensed many things that she also could not communicate, and harbored a great and abiding faith in Christ. Somehow her faith made her worry all the more about her damnably unChristian family. Her prayers were no small catalyst for the mystical events that were about to transpire.

At first Bud resented Belle's protective efforts and shot her harsh glances, but he soon realized that he could not communicate his reasons and Belle was doing her best with it all, so he just stared at the ground. He counted the seams of the old wood floor. Belle was trying to shield him from the ranch issues as much as possible. She had protested mightily to Lucky as her daughter had pushed through such drastic changes after Bud's stroke. She felt Lucky should change as little about the Ranch as possible until Bud's condition stabilized. Belle even sided with one of the earlier hands who had complained that Lucky was endangering the Lucky Star Ranch itself. Lucky and Bud would get into intense debates over each change, and Belle would get severely distressed over the tension she imagined was being created in Bud. In a way it was therapeutic for Bud as a last tie to the Ranch business, but Belle was probably right in that the stress was not good for him, and so for both of their health he began to withdraw from the discussions. After a while Belle stopped resisting any of Lucky's choices, and now merely tried to shield him from all Ranch business. Bud, however, could not really keep his nose out of any of it, even something as small as a wounded calf.

"So... you find it?" Bud asked Lucky as she came in from her ride with Buck. Without a glance Buck had ridden off to the cottage he shared with his aging mom down in Freedom, the next town from Corralitos.

"Yes I found HER," Lucky affirmed.

"What was it?   Co...co...co...yot..r..uh...rot foot?" he squeezed out.

"Neither," she answered. "Damn barbed wire, a short bit caught in her hoof..."

"What?!" He started to get up, as if to reach to his old home vet kit. He fumbled out for his boots. "I thought you got r...r...rid a that."

"We did," she insisted. "It was an old piece..."

"Lucky..." Belle interrupted. "We are about to have dinner. Where is Buck? Did you chase him off?"

"D...DON'T interrupt!" Bud stammered. "The c...c...calf..."

"I'm sorry I don't mean to interrupt, Dear," Belle soothed, "but I am getting dinner ready and I'm sure our vet daughter has taken good care of the calf. Right, Lucky?"

There was a pause where several things went unspoken. Bud counted grains in the wood.

"Yes, of course, Mom," Lucky acquiesced. "The calf is fine. I stitched her up and she trotted off."

"Anti-b...biotics?" he asked.

"No, Dad, I told you, we're holding back on drugs these days..."

"Whata? Fwup! Nothe..." Bud worked up. "Outbreak of rot foot decimal...decim...DE...CIM...ATE... the herd!"

"Bud, please! Sit down!" Belle implored.

"Mom's right Dad," Lucky assured him, "The calf will be all right. No hoof rot. I will clean it every day, I promise."

"Oh all right," Bud sat down. He had never really noticed the grain of this floor before. That spot looked like that Japanese wave painting. It really was calming for him as he traced his escape along wooden lines.

"Now, where were we? Oh yes, where is Buck anyway?" Belle asked, concern her eternal veil.

"He rode off toward home," Lucky said nonchalantly.

"Did his mother need something? I thought he was going to stay for dinner," Belle pouted.

"He didn't say," Lucky said, following her dad into the grain.

"I declare, girl," Belle declared, "You will regret being so dismissive to that man, someday."

Lucky frowned. "How do you know what I'll regret? I'll regret nothing, no matter what."

"I didn't mean to offend your pride, dear," Belle demurred. "I just mean that good men like that don't hang around forever."

"He has a good job here," Lucky missed the point. "I don't think he'll move on to another ranch."

"That's not what I mean, Dear," Belle said coyly. "He has special feelings for you right now, but they may not last."

"Exactly," Lucky said as if it was proving her point.

"What do you mean by that?" Belle asked.

"Feelings, Mom! What are they? Do they last?"

"They can. Look at me and your father," she said, gesturing toward Bud who had now become so entranced with the grain that a small stream of drool had found its way down his cheek. "Okay, maybe we are not so spectacularly romantic, but we have been there for each other." They laughed as Belle reached over with a handkerchief and wiped Bud's chin.

"What?!" Bud snapped out of trance as the two women laughed. "Oh...thank you."

"I know, you and Dad are perfect, Mom. How can I ever find a love that can compare to what you guys share?"

"You don't find a love, you build it," Belle claimed.

"A love is not a ranch, Mom," Lucky said. "Times are different out there these days. Women don't have to be tied to some man to have a life. We don't have to have some man around to succeed in everything."

"A love is not a ranch, dear," Belle quipped back. "I know you can run this place all by yourself, but to have a family you need a man."

"I have a family. You, Dad, the animals..." Lucky pleaded. What was the more she needed?

"That is not a suitable family for a pretty young lady," Belle maintained, wishing for anything a bit more normal.

"Well it is all the family suitable for me right now," Lucky was adamant.

"You don't know what you want," Belle continued.

"I know what I don't want," Lucky persisted.

"You are too young to know what you will want in life," Belle maintained.

"Who knows how old I am?" Lucky wondered.

"I think I have a good idea," Belle pointed out.

"No, I mean, who knows how old my soul is? Who knows how many lives I might have lived?" Lucky pondered.

"I believe in resurrection, not reincarnation," Belle nearly recited. "I am a babe in the arms of my Lord."

"Well maybe that's good for you, Mama, but maybe not for me," Lucky surmised. "I don't feel like a babe in anyone's arms."

"You will always be my baby," Belle claimed.

"Oh yeah, a baby..." Lucky was getting angry. "A baby who took over this ranch, brought it back from the brink of bankruptcy, running the management and the labor, all the while receiving attacks and threats for daring to do things the right way, and all this time barely getting the begrudging support of my own parents whose asses I am saving, because I am some kind of child..."

"Now honey, I didn't mean to offend you by calling you my baby," Belle teared up, "but I did hold you in my arms, and I can never forget that."

"Yes I know Mama, I'm sorry," Lucky softened. "It's just that I feel different. I don't feel like I am your baby. I feel like I am the only adult around here. I can't do things the way they've always been done if they're being done wrong. If it's bad for life, if it's bad for the earth, it's bad for us. Divide, conquer, and multiply just doesn't add up anymore."

"You will feel differently when you have your own baby in your arms," Belle contended. "Then you will understand me. I truly understood the Madonna and Christ child when I held you in my arms."

"Ma, I wish I could tell you why, but my god may not be a child, or a man nailed to a cross," Lucky confessed.

"I may not understand all the things you believe about God," Belle conceded, "But there is a lot more to the church than you realize, too. Christ is not an idol, he is an eternal spirit that stretches across the heavens."

"Okay, now we may be getting closer to where we agree, but I think there may be some aspects of my god that you may not like," Lucky challenged.

"There is only one God," Belle resolved.

"I think I believe that," Lucky went along, "But that one God must be really big, so infinitely big that He must be many many things, including maybe a She, and everything is circles within circles, like an onion..."

"Now don't blaspheme," Belle warned. "God's an onion?"

" Why not? How can anything be blasphemous in universe that is part of a God that is All?" Lucky pressed.

"God allows many things that are not of Him, out of love for us that we might come to Him of our own free will," Belle reaffirmed.

"So might not such a compassionate God have us come back time and time again until we get it right?" Lucky pressed.

"It does not mention reincarnation in the Bible," Belle maintained.

"But it does," Lucky insisted. "Does it not say that John the Baptist was Elijah, and that Jesus was Elisha?"

"That's different," Belle believed.

"Why?" Lucky demanded.

"Because..." Belle deliberated, "because that was a long time ago, and saints are different, and they may have been speaking poetically."

"Oh Mom, that's ridiculous," Lucky huffed. "Those are three separate arguments that just don't make sense. Even the clearest evidence from the Bible itself can be explained away by you."

"I just don't believe the Bible supports New Age ideas like reincarnation," Belle stonewalled.

"The idea of reincarnation is ancient!" Lucky exclaimed.

"And it...keeps...coming back..." Bud interjected. Lucky laughed but Belle barely heard the joke.

"Now don't upset your father, you know how he doesn't like all this radical talk..." Belle sheltered him.

"NO...no..." Bud stammered. "I have lived...many lives...in this lifetime. I see no problem with lives...before this one..."

"Oh thank you, Daddy," Lucky hugged him. "I am glad you agree with me."

"No..." Bud corrected her, "...I see no...problem."

"Still, you have an open mind," Lucky gave him.

"Yeah...brains...leak out." Bud managed through a wince.

"Now now, dear," Belle maternalized,   "I told you not to upset him."

"I am...not...upset," Bud stood his ground.

"Well then I'm upset, then," Belle realized. "I don't see why we have to resist the order of things."

"Who's resisting what?" Lucky questioned. "I am trying to match the greater flow of things, rather than just do what's easy."

"Path of...least...resistance," Bud winked.

"You got it, Pop," she kissed him.

"I think you both got it, in the head," Belle complained.

"Ah Mama," Lucky embraced them, "You know we couldn't do it without you."

"And...we wouldn't...want to," Bud admitted.

"Well..." Belle acquiesced with a smile, "...seems nobody else suitable is allowed to step up and into this family, so each of us will do it all until then."

"I have to do it all twice a day," Lucky joked.

"I have...to do it all... twice...an hour," Bud moaned as he stood up, and they laughed.

"My old man," Belle nursed, "do you need a hand?"

"Nah...nah.." he grunted as he made his way down the hall. "Some of my b-business...I can still...handle...myself."

"You should let him do as many things as possible by himself," Lucky advised.

"You don't know Bud like I know him," Belle pointed out. "It's like we can still read each other's minds. You know, you shouldn't spurn Buck the way you do."

"I don't spurn Buck. You don't know Buck like I know him. It's like we..." she stopped herself.

"It's like what?" Belle asked.

"Well...nothing," Lucky paused.

"It seemed like something," Belle mused.

"Well...maybe..." Lucky considered.

"Maybe what?" Belle pondered.

"Maybe something..." Lucky allowed.

"Maybe something like...?" Belle persisted.

"Maybe something like we could..." Lucky almost.

"...read each other's minds?" Belle jumped.

"Sort of..." Lucky admitted.

"I knew it!" Belle proclaimed. "I knew there was some sort of spark between you two."

"Well, whatever, but I don't know it," Lucky resisted. "I don't know anything for sure."

"Give it time," Belle said, her smile fading only slightly. They seemed to be at odds, they seemed to believe different things, but they were so much the same, so much the same that they were loved so much the same way, and they loved so much the same way. But they were different, too, and they all loved their differences, and the Universe knew it, and continued to work through them all towards some great event. The hills whispered of it.

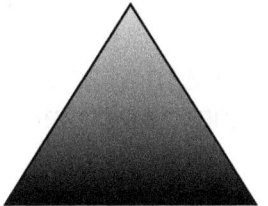

Atrua (3) Certified

Lucky lived in her dreams the way others lived in their clothes. The azure sky hung over a lotus pool amidst an emerald sea of cattail. Down the grassy hill towards the horizon stretched a line of cattle moving past Lucky. As they passed her, Lucky pridefully wielded a gun that left the rump of each with a large stamp that read "CERTIFIED: 100% ORGANIC." The stamp was not a brand, but some sort of henna stain that let off a grapevine smell. There was a beat to the stamping, and some strange syncopated rhythm emerged from the background merged with a nearby flute. With each new pass, Lucky beamed with pride at the implications of the stamp. That marking, more than the brand of olden days, signified something special for the entire life of that animal. It implied health, harmony, and truly happy cows. She smiled deeply with the satisfaction that this symbol really indicated goodness, something authentic and real. She was so engrossed in thought that she did not see a different sort of cow coming up in the line. She did not even notice until she had shot the label that it was not a cow at all, but was Buck, naked and crouching. The last image before she awoke was Buck standing, proud and naked, wearing his stamp like an ornament.

When she hit the alarm she imagined the label gun again, but the rest was lost in the transition to the waking day. However, she could not get rid of the image of Buck with the big label, which was as her Unconscious self intended. It was an appropriate image for the day, as she and Buck were going up to Santa Cruz to the headquarters of the California Commission of Organic Farming. So appropriate did the image appear that Lucky completely missed any deeper meaning of the image, but she still held it in her head with a perverse fascination. Seeing Buck nude was no big deal for her. They were comfortable with their sexuality as those raised their whole lives around animals usually are. But on a ranch, there are things much more intimate than sexuality. Emotions, sensitivities, feelings, these things were more rare, more precious. There was something more precious to Lucky in that image of Buck, burnished with her label. She would relish it in her mind for a moment and then reject it as an artifact of the conversation with her mother. Nothing seemed to take the sensuality out of a situation for a girl like Lucky than a mother's approval. At this point Lucky's mind pushed into some more hardcore creative vision just to secure an imaginary mother's scowl, possibly involving a bridle or sadle, but then it became just too involved, so Lucky just let it go altogether.

"Not that there isn't enough to be thinking about," she thought to herself as she walked out to the ranch building, finally clearing her mind of the image. She came around to the back loading dock, and Buck was there leaning against his new pickup, his eyes gleaming and proud. It was a small S10 of the type she had suggested for fuel efficiency. The image from the dream immediately jumped into her head and she could not hold back a short explosive chuckle.

"What?" Buck was hurt. "Don't you like it?"

"No, you're beautiful," Lucky started. "I mean, it's beautiful."

"Took me a long time to save up for this," Buck's mind took a second to catch up. "Wait a minute, I'm beautiful?"

"Sure, you look like some Chevy commercial," Lucky continued chuckling.

"Well it can't be that funny," he prodded. "What's got you going?"

"Nothing, nothing, come on, we've got to get going," Lucky prodded back. "We don't want to be late." Lucky jumped in the car and stared ahead with a subtle message of leaving the subject behind, but a certain way her mouth curled at the sides told Buck that there was more mirth that could be teased out of this one. He started his new truck with pride which brought back the dream image naturally for Lucky. Buck sensed his opportunity and continued his casual press as they started winding down Freedom Boulevard.

"Maybe I want to be a part of the laugh," Buck suggested.

"Oh, you're a part of it. A big part," Lucky jumped in, making herself laugh again.

"I knew it! Tell me," he insisted. "Is it about my truck?" he asked, stroking the dash with pride.

"No!" she insisted with a bigger laugh.

"What is it? You said I should get a truck like this!" Buck was frustrated. "Why can't I ever get your stamp of approval about anything?"

Lucky screamed as the flood of mirth overwhelmed her defenses. She finally let it all come out in a lengthy stream of guffaws.

"Okay, now you have to tell me or you're just psycho," Buck concluded.

"No, no, listen," Lucky tried to squeeze out some words through the laughter. "Your truck is fine, it's wonderful, you're wonderful, it's not that..." she tried to dismiss it all.

"So what is it?" Buck delved. "Stamp of approval?" Lucky burst forth with a new stream of glee.

"Yes, yes, that's it..." she managed. "Stamp, stamp, oh..." She let herself have one more unrestrained stream of guffaws. Gradually, she slowed down.

"Are you done yet?" Buck inquired. "You have to tell me what it is, now."

"Okay, okay, it was just this dream I had," Lucky allowed.

"A dream? Tell me about it." Buck insisted. They had an old tradition of exchanging dream stories and casual interpretations and it would have violated their old playful dream trust not to tell.

"Okay, okay," her resistance collapse in giggles. "There was a long line of cows that I was branding as "100% CERTIFIED ORGANIC" and then you came along, totally nude, and I stamped your ass before I could stop myself," she deteriorated into one long giggle.

Buck finally joined her in the laugh. "Well that says something, right?" he insisted. "You did give me your stamp of approval," he said proudly.

"My mom would probably think so, but I'm not so sure," Lucky said with only slightly less mirth.

"Come on, face it," Buck continued. "Your unconscious mind has given me the nod."

"Maybe, but my conscious mind still has doubts," she ribbed him.

"Oh, thanks," he mocked mock despair. Then mocking cheer, he changed the subject. "So what do you plan to accomplish today?"

Lucky sighed and switched emotions. She sensed that there was some inflection in Buck's question, but she was ready to move on to another subject, any subject.

"The CCOF is the world's pre-eminent organic certification organization, and it's based right up here in Santa Cruz," she informed him. "I've set up an appointment with the executive director to discuss some issues around organic classifications of Dairy."

"Gonna straighten them out, eh?" he queried.

"They allow transition feed to be given to dairy cows," she began. "It's become a dump for huge amounts of sub-food grade not-quite-organic transition grains, totally undermining the whole point." Lucky not only fed her cows organic grain when they needed it, she encouraged various plants in their free range that the cows seemed to like. Blackberries, dandelions, and chamomile were favorites, and many were plants she could not name because the cows had no name for it, but they pointed it out to her, and she learned ways to encourage mixed flora. The fact that she thus had to give her cows less grain led her to stay competitive with those organic dairies that used transitional feed.

"You think you can change them?" Buck wondered. "It sounds like there is a lot of money behind transitional grains.

"The money is in 100% organic," Lucky insisted, "and everything else is a losing business, I'm telling you."

"I believe you, I know you have a canny way of knowing things," Buck admitted. "But these guys will want real facts and figures."

"I have the real facts and figures, even if I don't repeat them to all you guys all the time anymore. You all let me know a long time ago that you did not want to hear all of my facts and figures."

"Hey, don't lump me in with those guys," Buck said, knowing that they were both talking about the other ranch hands. "I've always respected what you've had to say. I'm just trying to help you prepare for these guys."

"Well, you know I have the facts and figures..."she persisted.

"You're right. I'm sorry," Buck understood. "Perhaps what I should have said is that I fear that these men might be biased despite all your facts and figures."

"Thank you. Yes, you may be right, but I think they may have come into this business with a slightly more open mind then most," she hoped. There was an intuitive sense that this particular hope did not matter. Lucky had been working through dashed hopes for years. They shared these thoughts and others as they rolled over the hills in unspoken reverie. Buck and Lucky could often communicate better in silence than with words. When the need to make complete sentences was abandoned, thoughts could swirl and float like red tail hawks that would momentarily catch their gazes as the scenery passed by. Certain thoughts could be expressed in silence that never came out in words. There were those thoughts that seemed too mundane or inappropriate to speak, like Buck wondering if he had locked the gate when they left, and why that made him think of Lucky's bra, with its black strap peeking out from under the shoulder of her lavender top.

There were other thoughts that could not be spoken, because there were no right words. Something between them, or through them, or with them, they could not tell, because it kept changing. One instant it gave them new hope and excitement, and the next it seemed to highlight a growing sense of distance. It was not that they were growing apart, for they truly felt closer than ever, but it was something of immense size that accentuated the distance between everything. Like a tiny raft adrift in the sea that might as well have been a leaf, their very perspective was shrinking in the midst of a vast expanse.

They gazed over the golden hills that held patches of oaks like pubic hair between the sensual rounds. Gradually the oaks gave way to the conifers of North County, and the very pace of life seemed to change. The height of the redwoods held some secret of persistence, and the mood was more of determination rather that the lazy sporadic oaks of South County. Everything closed in, and thoughts were more specific and targeted. It was enough to spark a return to verbality for Lucky and Buck.

"I don't care what they think, really," Lucky reaffirmed. "But I've got to at least make a point."

"I know, I know," Buck nodded. "Can't fault a soul for trying." He would not say it, because he was still so unsure of her feelings, but that was one of the reasons he loved her.

He stopped mentioning his feelings a while ago, figuring she probably knew already, which she did. But one of the few things he would do is reserve the words until a time when she would really appreciate them, if that ever came. For a man like Buck it was so hard to talk of such things, feeling vulnerable and all, and to keep letting out such valuable gems of his emotions seemed a little like tossing pearls before swine. Not that he considered Lucky any sort of domestic animal, but he did sense that she did not give his feelings the proper respect.

Lucky sensed this too. His feelings were actually more precious to her than she could explain, but she could not bring herself to openly admit it. This was one of the things that they could not truly understand about each other, one of the few areas where there was a real disconnect. If only Buck could know how she truly felt, this may have helped him through the long dry emotional expanse, but she could just not let him know. Oddly, if she let him know, she felt that this would be to betray him. She knew what kind of man he was, she knew firsthand the honor, and the humble pride, the strength, but she feared if he knew it would lead him towards deeper feelings that she might not be able to reciprocate. But like any young woman she was drawn, irresistibly drawn though she resisted.

This was the heart of what he could not understand about her, but Buck did understand. He understood that there was something inherently contradictory about it all, and his experience said contradictions did not stand. His experience said contradictions folded soon or later under the pressure of relentless reality, for something in them was a lie. Unlike some of the fancy philosophers that he imagined walked the streets of cities like San Francisco and New York, he did not entertain thoughts that the universe was riddled with paradoxes. In his country education he had learned contradictions died fast, like a fawn born without a leg. There may be something hard and severe about the world, but it was clear. Lines were drawn fast and bold, and any anomalies just pointed out what you would not or could not understand. His quaint philosophy might not earn him any Nobel or Pulitzer Prizes, but it had won him countless moments of survival where others might have perished of pathos.

They spoke little about these things. How could they? But they shared their thoughts, and they agreed with each other. Silent agreement may not have seemed like much, but how many more passionate relationships were built on much less? Many older couples had struggled for years to get to this point, providing some comfort as the more heated passions faded, but many more never found it. Lucky and Buck knew they had something special, and they would not let it go, could not let it go, but they could not shake the feeling that something was missing. It was a different something for both of them, but they both felt the same gap. It was a gap that seemed to taunt them, to goad them on. They were not some old couple relaxing into a comfortable sunset. Somehow they were starting where others finished. They were blazing a new trail, as if they had left the old highway of romantic love long ago, and were now pushing into what lies beyond. It was all uncharted, so they could not say if they were lost, but they somehow knew that they were making their way.

They drove into the town of Santa Cruz, a former sleepy seaside tourist town that had become a hotbed of progressive politics ever since the founding of UCSC in the '60's, or so some of the longtime residents thought. Others felt there was something in the air that preceded the University, a feeling of being on the edge, either of paradise, death, or both. Certainly the geology was unusual. It was perched on a small portion of the Pacific Plate, the tectonic section of the planet whose edge of volcanoes and faults had been called "the Ring of Fire." As Lucky briefly thought of this, she pictured a giant wedding ring, blazing away. She understood the irony of this image, and let it fade and snuff out.

Santa Cruz was the only major section of the country, excluding Hawaii, that was not on the North American Plate, and was separated from the rest by the formidable San Andreas Fault. Certainly its citizens were separated from the rest of the country, and many considered themselves on the cutting edge of new ideas and thoughts. It was certainly only a short drive from Silicon Valley, and had often been called Silicon Beach, but such a moniker was considered to geeky for the decidedly more surf oriented locals. Most residents would claim to be more interested in sun and good food than silicon, and thus it was no mystery why the headquarters of the first organic certification organization would be located there. Lucky and Buck drove into the Old Sash Mill, a former agricultural station next to the railroad tracks that had become a gentrified shopping complex. Perhaps the headquarters of the California Certified Organic Foundation was the last reminder of its agricultural roots, but the CCOF was certainly was a bit of a transitional institution itself. As the most respected organic certification organization in existence, the CCOF seal had become a gold standard for organic products worldwide.

Certainly the reception that Lucky and Buck got from the director was not exactly what they expected. Todd Evans had been a pioneer in the organics movement, and surprisingly he was very familiar with the Lucky Star ranch, and had been a long time supporter. His overtly positive reaction brought short Lucky's expected prolonged debate.

"Oh, I am very in favor of stronger standards for organic dairy," he assured them.

"Would you be willing to review our research into the effects of truly humane dairy practices, and consider publishing the results?" Lucky asked.

"I would gladly publish your results," he replied, "And I will lobby our board to incorporate those results into our certification process."

"Well, that's wonderful!" Lucky rejoiced. "Another step forward."

"Wait a minute," Buck was cautious. "There has to be some catch. What's the deal?"

Lucky was afraid that Buck was being too confrontational, and she sensed that she could trust Todd. "There doesn't have to be a catch. This man has been doing great work in the organics field for years."

"I'm not saying anything against him, but I just think..." Buck persisted.

"No, no, it's all right," Todd calmed them. "I'm afraid your friend is right, there is a catch."

"I knew it," Buck nodded.

"What?" Lucky wondered.

"Well," Todd began, "we here at the CCOF are committed to the most stringent standards of organic labeling that we can justify, but we are about to be pre-empted."

"What do you mean?" Lucky asked.

"We have weathered some massive attacks in our support of organics in the past, but our success may now be our undoing," Todd explained.

"How can that be?" Lucky was perplexed.

"The USDA has decided to get into the game, and they are likely to advance much less stringent standards than the CCOF," he continued. "We have reason to believe they will support the use of certain synthetics in organic agriculture."

"Ah, I get it," Buck understood.

"But what does that matter? The CCOF will still be the gold standard," Lucky insisted.

"No..." Buck realized.

"Why not?" Lucky was in denial.

"USDA certification pre-empts any state or local certification," Todd further explained. "This may be our death knell. Let me put it this way, I'm putting out my resume. Got any leads?"

"Oh no! I mean, yes, I will help anyway I can," Lucky offered. They finished the rest of the meeting on a positive and active note, but there was definitely a different feeling about it all now. As Buck and Lucky left Santa Cruz, they thought about how things can turn out so differently than expected. Often one thinks of two possible contradictory outcomes, but how often it turns out to be a third totally unexpected option that comes to pass. Here they had been more positively received than they could have hoped, but yet they left with a feeling of defeat. The feeling did not last for them, though. Instead it just hardened their sense of resolve, of taking the battle to the next level. In a way, the strangeness of it all served to take them beyond such battles. Maybe such battles were mere skirmishes a larger war. Perhaps their cause of the day was just another distraction, or some small act in a much bigger play. They had to keep doing what they were doing, but maybe the battle was not theirs to win or lose. Maybe to just do what they could do was to win. Certainly, even with the best of luck, they would be only footnotes in the larger drama of history. Yet, in their silent drive home, this realization was a victory of sorts, because no one could keep them from doing the best they could do. In a sense, they could not lose. As they shared this realization they became more hopeful than before, seeing that they were now free to win the bigger personal battles of their lives. Maybe life was not about battles at all, and looking at it as such was the only way to lose. If life was instead just a big lesson, a big realization, than nothing could stop them. Together they knew this was true, and they came back to the Lucky Star like secret returning champions.

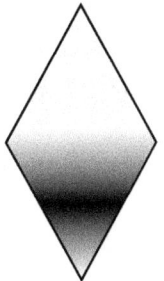

Katero (4) Fried

How many more moments, days, years, Bud wondered as he traced the lacey wood lines along the old floor. How many until the blur made such distinctions irrelevant. Belle shuffled around the kitchen making fried chicken, talking about everything because somewhere she had heard that regular communication staved off dementia. He hoped it worked for her. He could still think clearly. So clearly it scared him. Was he meant to keep a crisp front row seat to view his own decline? More clear than ever, in fact so clear that some things were only now beginning to make sense. Had he really drowned out so many revelations over the years with his own incessant voice? Must have. What did he miss? Now he heard everything, even Belle's never ending chatter.

"I just know she feels something for him," she went on. "She's so stubborn she would have galloped off somewhere else if she didn't."

"Can't put her...'n no corral," Bud managed.

"Well, she won't be a spring philly for much longer," Belle continued. There was a pop, and bits of grease flew up onto Belle's hand. She hardly noticed, did not bother to wipe it off. Years had taught her to waste no energy on such momentary concerns. She kept her eyes on the horizon. "And I just want to see a little colt or two before you and I are put out to pasture."

"Im..ni..inim.." Certain letter combinations, like 'i' and 'n,' caused Buck the most trouble, but he persisted. "I'm...in...pasture now."

"Don't be silly," Belle worried. She did not understand his new philosophical bent. "We got too many good years to quit yet."

"Not quitting...like pasture," Bud tried to explain. If he could only really explain what he understood now. He had spent too many years looking only at the dirt under his nose. He had labored, scrimped and saved, driven himself harder than any of his hands. What had it gotten him? He looked down at his hands. They were cracked like the dry gorge on the back forty that led down to the San Andreas Fault. Those were some quakes that had fissured his skin, countless sledge blows on fence posts, pick strikes on hard earth, cracking flesh and soil at the same time, precious little salve to grease the shocks.

What had he been working for? He had never really stopped to ask himself that before. He had grown up with hard work covering him like his dark curly hair, only now it had all turned gray. He knew now though. Even if he could not explain it to his beloved Belle or Lucky, he knew why he had worked so hard. He worked because now he could rest peacefully, he could settle into his pasture and feel all right about it. He felt no desperate drive, no devil nipping at his heals. That was for kids like Buck and Lucky, younger folk that thought they had time to burn and energy to spray out aimlessly like those old sprinkler units they used to use before they switched to drip. No, he liked his pasture, and he was thankful it was green.

"Maybe you should try that new vitamin Lucky was talking about," Belle suggested. "She says it works wonders for aging minds. She's even talking about adding to her special cow formula."

Bud nodded. Gestures could still be easy for him, but he had an ongoing stream of nods and shakes and shrugs that most people just ignored. Lucky and Belle tried to understand, they knew when he was answering them, but they also noticed that he seemed to answer questions that they had not asked. This also worried Belle, thinking he might be hearing voices in his head that nobody else heard. Lucky had a closer idea, Bud knew. She seemed to understand that life was an ongoing conversation and that he was somehow getting the right answers. He knew things like he did not before. He could not really talk well, but he knew better what to say.

"Love...you," he said to Belle with a straightforward simpleness that he could never really muster before. He knew his love would make her forget her worry.

"Oh, sweetheart," Belle melted and gushed. "I love you too. You know, every moment is so precious, how is it that I could love you so much more after 53 years? Think of it, 53 years...not many kids these days will ever reach that. So many hardtimes, but how love won out each time..." She dove right into reverie like a warm pond. The water was nice, and Bud gladly joined her. She swam, he floated, but they both enjoyed the soft coolness. "You were always so handsome, so strong, yet so kind. Thank you for that. People sometimes only saw your hard crust, but you were always soft with me at home, and I thank you for that."

"Hard...in bed," Bud protested.

"Oh, Bud, I didn't mean like that," she blushed. "I mean a soft heart, like I always hoped and prayed I could find. Papa thought different, but I knew. He didn't want me to be with a farmer. He thought you would work me to death, but I knew better. From the beginning, you gave me nothing but life."

"More kids...given you more kids," Bud lamented.

"No, no, honey, we don't know what that was," Belle reassured him.   There had been an unknown something, many years ago, and they stopped being able to have kids. "It might have been me. Barren like Sarah, but we got Lucky, you know. Think of the Martins in town. Six children and not one worth spit. I give 'em all up for one Lucky." She was certain and Bud nodded.   They had been on the farm long enough to know that quality was premium and quantity became a commodity, driving value down.

Just then, as if on cue, Lucky came in, burnt and seemingly depressed. She had been out in the fields doing one of her least favorite jobs. Although they were strictly a dairy farm, aged cattle were a regular issue, and had to go somewhere.   The regular market for aged dairy cattle was to slaughterhouses for dog food.   They were notoriously unpleasant places, particularly for the cows which would be held in place with metal hooks as they were killed with high voltage electricity. Lucky's method of humane euthanasia for her animals had been one of the greatest targets of denigration by the hands and by other dairy farms, and even originally from Bud. It involved elaborate procedures that involved what seemed to some like near funereal rights, and added cost without the typical easy dollar of the slaughterhouse. Although she had been working with certain companies on developing a line of organic dog food, such markets were slow to develop and had yet to materialize. Although Lucky had developed certain treatments and supplements that extended a cows milking prime much longer that usual, and although she kept her dairy cows long after when others would have sent them away for declining production, she still had to face the killing of her cows on a regular basis, and it was never easy for her.

Belle and Bud new already her state and her pains, and so they tried to help her immediately. Although they had built a beautiful new solar powered house for Lucky closer to the cows, she still regularly came back to the old ranch house for dinner.

"There you are, dear. Here, sit down," Belle motioned to an empty chair at the table. "I made you some of that textured vegetable whatever for you that you like." Belle was able to set a table with grace and efficiency, giving each person exactly what they liked and how they liked it. Sometimes she thought that only the angels noticed, but that was enough.

"Thanks, ma," was all Lucky could manage.

"All...done?" Bud asked.

"Done...until the next time," Lucky allowed a sense of resignation to permeate her presence. Belle took it in like so many other things, with concern. Bud could not help but feel a little consternation, hoping to have long ago instilled Lucky with a farmer's sense of the inevitable. Lucky sensed this without him having to speak it, and they had a nonverbal argument that consisted of eyebrows and various grunts and breaths between bites. Belle's concern was accentuated by the exchange that she too could sense was going on.

"Why don't you two just let it out rather than have it spoil our supper?" she finally let out.

"Good money..." is all Bud could manage.

"Somebody having money problems?" Lucky retorted.

"Not money...emo..mo...tional attach...ment," Bud tried to shoot out.

"This day and age we don't view emotional attachment as a problem, Dad," Lucky lashed out.

"To animals, not people," Bud came back, a little sternly. As Bud got a little upset his communication ability improved with the adrenalin that shot into his system.

"Are you questioning my methods?" she pressed him, knowing that he could no longer do that with all the success she had had. She did not have to mention the reality that the Ranch probably would have gone under already without her changes. They were about the only family-owned dairy farm in the area. Bud was very particularly aware of this.

"No, not methods, just emo...mo...motions," Bud slipped back into his regular state.

"Well, emotions are part of my methods, okay," Lucky basically stopped the argument with that one. There were all sorts of things that Bud did not understand about her methods and so emotions just might well play a major part in them. Lucky did not want to oppose her father, and she sensed that he backed down, but there was something that she herself did not understand about her own methods. All along she had insisted on the strictest scientific training. She knew that she would need it to bolster her decisions with all the criticisms she was likely to draw with any proposed changes. But she was essentially guided by her intuition, by an inner sense of what was right or wrong, and sometimes she pushed into areas where science had never ventured. For all of the vaulted research into various methods of killing, science had mostly focused on the most efficient methods, rather than the right methods. Make appropriate judgments of what should be done was often not a consideration with science. It required the scientists to provide the answers of what should be done and instead focused on what could be done. Propriety was an area that was too vague and unspecific for science, meaning that it was not impossible to figure out but very difficult. Most scientists just avoided the issue, either out of laziness or because the profit motive secretly superseded moral questions. Lucky knew there believed that profit would ultimately follow doing what was right, and she certainly was not lazy.

"I'm sorry, Dad, I know that you have strong reasons for thinking that way," she softened. "But I know that there is a better way, I just can't figure out what it is." Lucky had perfected a painless death for her cows, but there always seemed to be something missing. They looked at her plaintively as she administered the injections, understanding and accepting but somehow expecting something more. It was this unspoken moment of some promise unfulfilled that left her so disturbed after each killing.

"Keep...looking," her Dad encouraged her. It was this ability of his to accept her leanings and encourage her in disagreement that kept her going. Although she was rebellious and strong-headed, any persistent resistance by Bud would have her collapse in resignation. She would eventually find her own way, but they had both long ago realized that Bud could help along the whole process by this for of quiet acceptance.

"Thank you, Dad," she got up and kissed his head, making him blush a little. "I love you so much, you know..."

"Old codger...like me..." Bud tried vainly to dismiss the affection.

"Oh, look at you two," Belle joined in on the reconciliation. "All at each other and now simply gushing." She feigned being upset. "What about me, Mrs. Steadfast, don't I get any love?"

"All..of it," Bud said as Lucky jumped up to hug them both.

"Oh, Ma, we do everything we do for you, you know," Lucky assured her.

"Really? I thought it was the other way around," Belle jested. There was a certain mock disagreement that was the height of love for them. They could take whatever leftovers and compost them into something rich and fertile. Belle had started to clean up the remnants of their feast when there was a light tap on the door. Belle went over to open the door and reveal an old but gentle looking man with a knowing sparkle in his eye standing at the door. Belle did not bat an eyelash.

"Come in you must be hungry let me get something," Belle gushed as she led him to the table. She had taken seriously the Biblical admonition that a stranger at the door may be an angel, and she had always insisted on giving strangers at least a good meal. Bud was tolerant, and Lucky took an instant interest in the stranger. He was dressed in simple clothes that could be modern, but they had no labels of any kind and hardly appeared to even have seams. His exact age was hard to pin down, but he had a definite unthreatening air.

"Thank you, Ma'am," he said. "I will accept whatever you have to offer when given in love."

"Well how about a mess of chicken and dumplings smothered in love?" she offered.

"Yes, thank you, and I have something to offer in return," he suggested mysteriously. Belle spread out a veritable feast almost immediately and the stranger devoured it with graceful ease.

"What have you brought for us?" Lucky asked with piqued curiosity.

"A message for each of you, Lucky," he said, purposefully pronouncing her name.

"Okay, that's kind of creepy, what is it?" Lucky pressed.

"Lucky!" Belle admonished her. "He's our guest." Bud customarily remained silent but cautious with strangers.

"Well, how did you know my name?" she asked.

"Let's just say a Star let me know," he said, which could easily have been a reference to her dairy brand or the sign at the entrance of the ranch. She was, after all, fairly well known.

"Okay, Mr. Mysterioso, all due respect, what is the message?" she pushed further.

"I bring great tidings," the stranger said. "My Master comes. He is the husband to the Goddess of Fortune, but he must extract the true costs that all must pay."

"Hey, we don't need riddles, what's up really?" Lucky demanded, being forward but in a playful way.

"I cannot speak riddles," he said. "Sometimes the simplest truth sounds like a riddle."

"Oh really?" Lucky played the skeptic. "Well, where are you from, anyway? What is your name?"

"I come from a far off land," he said. "My real name you could not pronounce, but you may call me Uriel."

"I knew it! An angel, right?" Belle got excited.

"Merely a servant and a messenger," he replied humbly.

"What's the message, again?" Lucky asked.

"Great tidings! My Master comes, but he often comes in unexpected garb," he added.

"More riddles," Lucky complained.

"Simple statements," he claimed. Before he could say more there was an explosion in the kitchen with a flash and lots of smoke. Belle and Lucky ran in and Bud followed behind. When they returned, the door was open and the stranger was gone.

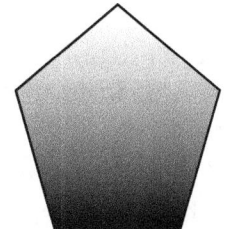

Pentero (5) Allied

Buck ran his horse in a particularly aggressive way through the slough at the edge of the ranch property. Only when he saw the thistle and nettles through which his mare dutifully charged did he slow his pace a bit. Somewhere out in the distance was the cow Lindy, the same one they had saved about a year before when it had gotten a bit of wire in its hoof. Now it was a spirited yearling and Buck thought somehow it had inherited a stubborn streak and tendency to roam from Lucky.

"Cow and woman just the same" He fumed to himself. "Always causing me trouble." He wanted to push his horse harder, to take it out on the trail, but he resisted. He knew that all his frustration was his own to work out. Certainly his horse had done him no harm. Luck, he had called her, and, yes, there was an irony in that, but he knew she was as loyal and responsive as the best mare could be. They settled into a gentle trot and circled around the old trail. He knew he was following Lindy, every once in a while he could see a hoof print in the dust, but even these would not have been enough to track her. Buck and Luck somehow just knew, and they just kept at it. Buck had been doing more of the general chores around the ranch as Lucky had become more and more involved with her political and veterinary activities. He had become the day to day tender of the ranch, and he knew that Lucky was envious of that. He had taken over all the jobs where you could get lost in the routine of it all and get philosophical, whereas she had immersed herself in the hectic mental world of management.

"Serves her right," he thought to himself. He had always thought that she had too eagerly plunged into big issues, sometimes at the expense of the little ones. He felt that he was one of the little issues, and he suspected that she knew that somehow he would always be there. Yet, he knew he saw something that she did not. He looked around and really saw something. Maybe he could not describe it well, maybe he could not ace a college test and remake the ranch in a blaze like she had, but he could sense something in the little things that brought him contentment, patience, and wisdom. He had to think this because it eventually brought him peace and gave him faith that she would come around some day. It was a message that he received. It was in the wind, in the dust, in the rustling of the rattlesnake grass. As he looked out over the golden hills he saw a shimmer move against the wind. He heard a buzz where there were no bees. It was an old voice that told him everything was okay. This was the voice that he had learned to trust. He just listened, sat back in the saddle, and felt better.

There was another dusty print, and one too many broken stalks. The sky was bluer than blue, and the gold stood out like some technicolor spasm when he looked from one to the other. He knew the grass was old and dry and brittle, but it was brimming with life. Seedpods stood ready to pop next to empty sheaths, and he let his mind drift to an old scene. He was passing an Ohlone acorn grinding spot, and the jagged rocks stood out like sunspots against the rounded earth. In his mind he saw baskets, and brown women full of soul and mirth as they winnowed the tall grass. Seeds jumped with gaiety into their intricately woven baskets, and they sang a song in a lost language but he understood it. He saw another print, but this one was different, more rounded, almost hairy. These details might not seem like much to most people, but to someone who grew up on a ranch small details could mean the difference in anything. He had seen thousands of hoof prints in his time, but he had never quite seen one like that. He could still hear the song drifting over the breeze and he decided to continue on, following something like a scent but more of a feeling.

There was a change in the light, and he might have considered that it was due to something like the atmosphere or the angle of the sun, as many would, but he had seen too many sunsets to believe that. There was a strange iridescence to the air, a sparkly something that made him both excited and trepidatious.

"Where is that cow," he said to himself. "She's never gone this far." The scenery had become unfamiliar, something he had never experienced in these environs before. He thought he had gone up and around every ravine for miles, yet these were different. He was following an faint animal trail at this point, hardly a parting in the tall dry grass, yet man and horse both knew this was the right direction. Many ravines stuck out into the dry hills like fingers probing a lover's body, and many held the magic gift of small streams. He stopped and dismounted to give his mare a chance to drink, and he looked around at his surroundings. Alder, cottonwood, and redwoods crept out of the shadows, and a large brown rock showed ancient fading pictographs, positively convincing Buck that he had never been here before. More strangely, it appeared as if no other man had been here since the pictographs were carved. All of the redwoods were old growth, and usually in this area one would find at least a stump or two. All of the plants and stones had that settled look that indicated an undisturbed area, no signs of erosion or encroachment anywhere.

Buck remembered various stories he had heard since a child of strange portals in these mountains, strange areas that seemed to evade everything but the accidental encounter. He had unusual feelings like this before in these hills, times when even his horse had been spooked, but now Luck was as calm as a babe in the arms of its mother. There was a caress in the breeze and the mare looked at him as if to say, "Relax, we're okay."

Buck could never sit still for much, and this place, this little trip, was a mystery that he had to solve. He looked around in the soft mud for more clues, and saw more of the rounded hairy hooves going up a dry side ravine. He tied Luck to a branch and followed the narrowing trail up between the big trees and rocks, expecting to find Lindy stuck in a dead end. Slowly the walls closed in, almost to the point where he could stretch out his two hands and touch both sides at once. He knew cows, and this was unusual for them to come into an area so confined where a predator like the many cougars common in this area could easily corner them. Pretty soon he came to an area that was so narrow that he had to turn sideways to pass comfortably, and he knew that a cow would never come through such a narrow passage unless it was being forced or chased. He looked down to verify that he was still following tracks and as he did he noticed a strange thing. The tracks changed midstride, even mid-track, into those of a child or small woman. He rubbed his eyes and then looked more closely, and sure enough, the tracks that continued were most definitely human.

Contrary to the claims of most skeptics and debunkers, most people will generally try to come up with every mundane answer that they can to an unusual observation. Buck twisted his brain to come up with some answer for what he saw that did not violate the known laws of physics. Perhaps some woman had been riding a cow up here. No, then were did the cow go? Surely he would have seen other tracks exiting back since there was no other way out. Maybe someone had been wearing strange shoes in order to trick him, like those old hoaxters that would put on Bigfoot boots and run around in the woods to fool tourists. Maybe, but as he looked closer he noticed the depth of the prints dropped as they changed, as if they were made by something significantly lighter. Maybe they had been carrying a pack with weights that they had discarded somewhere. But, there was nowhere nearby to hide it, and the tracks hardly veered at all. And back a ways he could make out distinct rear and fore hooves. Had someone been walking on all fours with strange hoof-like gloves and boots? Now that image was so absurd that Buck was forced to realize the ridiculousness of the entire line of thought. What would have been the motive of such a ruse, and who could have done such a thing? Lucky! Sure, if anyone could cook up such an elaborate con it would have been her, and she certainly was known for unfathomable motives.

Despite obvious contradictions and incongruities in this conclusion, Buck held onto it like a log in a rushing river. He bounded up the twists and turns of the gully certain that he was about to catch up with Lucky, and in his delusion he imagined that she had cooked up this whole scheme as some sort of indirect was of telling him how she truly felt about him. He became so lightheaded with anticipation and exertion that he almost failed to notice the song drifting though the ravine. It was similar to the one he had heard earlier, but it hardly sounded like a voice at all. It was almost like a bird, or a flute, or wind blowing through some cave hidden in the cliffs. He slowed his pace, becoming more careful in the difficult terrain and the dimming dusk. His thoughts settled, and he even stopped thinking about Lucky, which he almost never did, or, rather, his thoughts of her changed. He always felt a warmth in his heart when he thought of her, and often something a bit lower, and this warmth was still there, but it was moving up his body. His heart knew what he wanted, and now his throat joined in the expression, becoming softer and tight all at once. He face flushed, but a lighter shade than embarrassment, and he thought he felt a finger pressed to his forehead, then a palm on the top of his head.

The walls of the ravine were coming together so closely that the floor almost disappeared, and Buck had to carefully place one foot in front of the other. Overhead the walls closed in as well, and he found himself having to duck and squeeze. Just as he was about to have to turn around, the space becoming too tight and the light disappearing, he noticed a strange glow on the rock where his passage took a turn up ahead. Getting down on all fours he pushed through the last couple of yards. As he rounded the bend he was abruptly spit out of the hole on to a sandy bottom. He stretched out, sensing significantly more space around him, but hesitating to get up abruptly, because he sensed something there with him, something like a wild animal. On the sand in front of his face he could see faint shimmers like a light bouncing off a stream, but he knew there was little water here. He was in the dry bed of a ravine that only saw water at certain times in the winter. And the song was still there, although it was still indistinct, even though it seemed to be coming from somewhere close.

He kind of just stayed there, flat on his belly, seemingly content to just watch the grains of sand in the strange light, as if that particular mystery was as much as he wanted to face right now. He sensed that the answer was there right in front of him if he just looked up, but he knew by the strangeness of it all that it was something that he had never encountered before, and he was most comfortable right now just thinking about the light on the sand. He was obviously in a small box canyon, an opening in the normal system of gullies. Perhaps there was a silver fir or bull pine up on the hill that was reflecting the alpen glow in a particular way. Well, no, that would be a different color, more reddish really. Maybe there was some plane reflecting lights or the sun somehow. No, that could not be it because then it would have faded out a while ago when the plane passed. Maybe there was...no, there could not be, way up here...

"Are you ever going to look up, my dear friend?" came a voice with that same flute-like quality that he had heard in the song. "It was hard enough to get you up here, to have you just lie there staring at grains of sand." She finished with a gentle laugh, for it was indeed a woman that had spoken, although there was definitely something more than human about her.

Buck slowly raised his eyes, realized why he had been so slow to look up before. Something in his soul realized the great beauty that was before him, the awesome sacred presence that had permitted him to draw near. She leaned lightly on a stone at the other end of the gully where it came together to form a solid wall. She wore a dress of the purest buckskin that was so white that it seemed to shine with a light of its own. It was adorned with an intricate array of porcupine quills and pendants of abalone shell, and these had caused the glistening light on the sand that had mesmerized Buck before. He noticed that her feet were bare, but they showed no trace of wear or dust, as if she had been floating over the ground. He examined her lower body not with sexual desire but out of reverence, keeping his eyes averted. He also knew he would be forever changed when he looked up. Even her toes had a transformative power for him, their gentle nature curves and otherworldly perfection. He knew that her face would transform him, and her eyes particularly would hold something that his spirit would barely be able to witness, something his soul would barely be able to contain.

He wanted to keep staring at her feet, to keep his gaze respectfully down for however long he could, forever, if necessary. But she drew him up, she pulled on him, as she had pulled him into this gully. He could feel it, like gentle hands on his cheeks lifting his head. Slowly he allowed his eyes to rise, trying to hold the reverence in his mind as he looked up, as if he could somehow taint the brilliance with his simple glance unless he maintained proper respect. As he was drawn into the whole of her, as his eyes were forced by the flood of her will to encompass her, he felt a shift deep within. He knew then many things. He knew he had holding back. He had been holding back his love, holding back his heart from life, from Lucky. But now it was beyond Lucky. Who was Lucky? Who had she been? Who had he been? No one, nothing, not ever, as he stared at HER everything else disappeared.

Her dark skin still blazed with its own radiance, though her buckskin dress wrapped around her like clouds around the sun. Her clothing was simple and natural, yet it had an otherworldly quality about it, as if it had been made by a million tiny hands, each stitch a ritual of love and harmony. The abalone seemed to be in constant motion, though there was no wind, hardly a breath. Buck could not speak, could not hardly think, but all he knew was this love that arose within him. It was not a sexual love, although she was the most physically beautiful woman he had ever seen, and he probably could easily been coaxed into arousal had that been her intention. Yet that was apparently not her intention, for she held his attention with that degree of shy coyness, direct yet self-effacing in a maddeningly enchanting sort of way.

"Who...are you?" Buck asked, although he figured he should or did probably know already.

"Right here, right now, for you, I am White Buffalo Calf Woman," she answered.

"But, I don't understand," Buck searched his brain. "Isn't that an Indian...uh, Native American myth? Sioux, right?"

"The Lakotan people are very dear to me, and I to them," she acknowledged.

"But, why appear to me, then?" Buck asked.

"I am of this land, Turtle Island," She said, touching the stone around her. "You are very much of this land. I appear in a form that is most enchanting for the beholder."

"Well, you got that part right, then," Buck affirmed.

"I have loved you for a very, very long time," she remembered. "I could tell you of great heroic feats you accomplished for this land, in a time you don't recollect. You devoted yourself to my service for as long as the rivers flow and the grass shall grow." She caressed the grasses that sprung with some heroic magic of their own from the sparse cracks in the rock.

"I...know, somehow. How?" Buck wondered, his throat tightening with realization.

"The spirit never forgets," she informed him. "We are Wakan, and that reaches beyond the forgetfulness of the grave.

"But, how...why?" he managed before breaking down in tears and falling at her feet. "Why? Why don't we remember? Why don't they see, all those people, going on with things, destroying things, why don't they know." He was suddenly racked with sobs, but she knelt down and grasped his arms, brushing the sand from his cheeks and pulling him into her embrace.

"But, how?" he wondered in amazement. "Are you real? Are you not a vision?"

"Is the grass not real?" She asked. "Though it sprouts one summer and is gone the next, no one doubts its reality. I am with you always." She held him close, and let him relax into her warmth. He inhaled deeply of her scent, permitting himself to feel her hair on her back, and the soft push of her breasts against his chest. He held her like he would never let go, and she let him. He drank her into his being, etching her reality into his deepest memories. He held on as deeply as he could, for although he knew she told the truth that she was with him always, he knew he was being permitted something very special that he might never experience again. By being flushed through all his self, by sensing her in every way, he knew he would never doubt again, never lose her again, at least not in this life.

"That is why I came to you here now, in this way," she informed him. "Never doubt again, I am with you. I can take many forms, and I ALWAYS do." As she said this, for some reason he thought of Lucky again, for this first time since he had been chasing her. "You cannot truly love another, without loving me. Let yourself love, but you know I AM a shy one. I am not easily pursued. Even when you think you are chasing me, like into this canyon, it is I who have been chasing you."

"I see that now," he admitted, still holding her firm. "I never could have found you, but you found me." He breathed her in, deeply holding her in his lungs. He did not want to, but he knew he had to let her go. He took one more moment to etch her in every cell of his memory, in every corner of his mind and his heart. Than slowly, gracefully, he pulled away, bringing her hands to his lips. "I thank you, thank you, so much, for saving me."

"Know this, my dear love, every moment that you let your heart and spirit be touched, you save yourself," she touched the center of his chest. "You save yourself, and the part of me that resides in you, and many, many around you."

"Thank you, again. This is so much, almost too much," he gestured to her and the sacred spot. "What am I to do with all this?"

"You are already doing it," she reassured him. "Have faith and strength. There are always trials and tribulations while in a body."

"Why? You are in a physical body now, you have trials and tribulations?" he pressed.

"Yes," she assured him, "Even now, for a brief time, in this body, I feel them. I feel an urge, a very deep desire, to stay, to be with you, to embrace you. But, I cannot."

Buck was touched and filled with compassion. "Don't let me draw you in, you have done so much already. You have shown me so much more in such a brief time."

She smiled. "Don't worry for me. I can now come and go as I please, but such dense sensation is not without danger even to one such as I. However, it is a gift to be able to come to you, to touch you and feel you." Something began to change in her. He might have said that she began to fade, but she became more bright. It was if the world around her had begun to fade.

Buck momentarily lost composure. "Take me with you! I am ready! I don't want to stay." He dove down at her feet, but they had already become buffalo feet, and he momentarily jumped back, startled.

She giggled. "Like an old trick your grandmother used to wean you. She put snakeskin on her breast and you stopped reaching in."

"Yes, I'm sorry." He regained himself. "Thank you."

"Remember, I am always with you, but if you wish to see me you must come to where I am," she informed him. "Do not struggle. It will happen in due time."

"I...understand," he tried. "I will persevere."

"YES," she said or more like fluted birdlike. She was now more wisps of whispers and reflections than anything else. In her, he could suddenly see many things, and a white buffalo running into a mouth opening in the space of the stone all around.

"Thank you again," he thought, for he knew that was enough. He looked around. The light had returned to normal. The last rays of the setting sun painted the rocks overhead a pretty scarlet, but it seemed dull and flat. He looked back down at sand, wondering if it had all just been a vision, but there he saw the same half-prints of a woman and a buffalo, and that was enough for him. As a man of the land he had learned to accept enough as enough. He made his way back by himself, but not alone. She had been right. He could still feel her. Now he knew that she had always been there for him, but now he had a stunning full-body image to accompany the feeling.

"Now back to being just a ranch hand," he said to her in his head. "I guess I can do it."

"You know you can do it," he thought he heard her say. He accepted that too. They wove back through the narrow canyon, observing in wonder this hidden little sacred spot that he had never seen before in his years of exploring these mountains. He still saw the occasional track, and this made him smile. As he came back to where he had tied Luck, he saw Lindy grazing peacefully next to his mare.

"So there you are," he said in amazement. "I bet you were in on this too, weren't you?" Lindy lifted her head and lowed lightly. "Yeah, I bet. Now, are you ready to go?" He mounted Luck and thought of throwing a rope around Lindy, but just to see he started off back towards the ranch, and Lindy followed faithfully. They road back through slough and dust colored red by the last rays of the sun, and it certainly seemed a lot closer than when he had first gone out. When road up the hill past the milking sheds he saw Lucky's truck in the driveway. He tied up Luck to put Lindy back in the barns and Lucky came running out.

"My, my, where was she this time?" she demanded of the both of them, a bit stern.

"Oh, far," Buck said simply, his calmness unshaken.

"Well, where? Tell me all about it," she pressed.

"I'm sorry, I...can't," gently kissing her forehead in dismissal. "Well, what about you? What do you have to say for yourself?" she asked Lindy, but the cow just walked past into the stall with an air of disinterest. "Oh! Cow and man just the same, always causing me trouble."

Buck hardly seemed to hear or react. Instead he went over to Luck and gave her a caress that seemed much more affectionate than the kiss he had given Lucky. "Thank you," he said to the mare. "You stayed with me all the way." He led her back over to the horse stables. Lucky could tell there was something going on, something new that had entered them all. She knew them all too well. And though it aggravated her and teased her in her present state after a day of management duties, it maddened her most because it stirred deep feelings that she had been trying to resist. He was so damned sexy when he seemed cocky and self-content. What was it about men, no, what was it about her feelings that turned right when he seemed disinterested? It was all part of what made her want to avoid the whole mess. These feelings were too chaotic and uncooperative, something she had learned to avoid in the business of running a ranch, but they pushed through her like a herd into new green pastures after a rain.

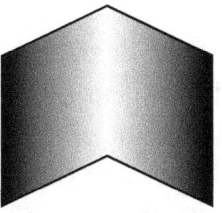

Exorto (6) Teased

Lucky had a new gelding and she pushed him hard. There was no mercy in her, she was out for a gallop. She had her reasons, of course. She wanted to test it, to see what it could do. This was a necessary part of training a horse to be a good working ranch animal. She would occasionally let it canter, but only while she scanned around, and then should would push it again. Up steep slides, through rock fields, plowing into water and making it swim to the other side. She had resisted the temptations to name it yet, to get personalized with it, even to look at is as something more than an "it." But this was because, she reasoned, she was not sure yet if it was any good, if she would keep it.

The horse performed perfectly, admirably, taking every prod with gusto and executing each maneuver. This just fired Lucky more, and she pushed the animal harder, thinking it cocky for not bending under her pressure. She jumped an oak branch, and then dove straight down another hill. This part of the Santa Cruz Mountains was surprisingly diverse and rugged, from rolling hills to redwood filled canyons, and the two seemed to range over the whole gamut. The pace was frantic, almost desparate, and both horse and rider knew that something was being worked out here beyond physical endurance. Emotions were thick but neither let up, both seemingly intent on proving that they were beyond the scope of any mere challenges. But there did not seem to be an end to the obstacles, and frail flesh, no matter how determined, always had a limit against an endless flood.

They pushed headlong into a dense chaparral slope, both getting covered in scratches. A family of quail were flushed out and flew in their faces, seeming to call out in complaint. In with the sounds that now surrounded them came out something different, the sound of a flute echoing with a delicate yet seemingly random precision. They both heard, and the horse understood something, but Lucky ignored it. They galloped on, through dust, twigs, and blood, at an unimaginable pace, put the music came closer. It circled them, and the horse was growing cautious, but Lucky pushed harder, thinking she had found a weakness. They burst out of the chaparral into a creek and ran on top of the water to the other side, following no trail anymore, but the music stayed ahead of them.

Suddenly the music stopped, and a long golden stick reached out behind a rock into their path. Lucky did not see it, but the horse did, and it stopped cold. Lucky went flying head first into some thistles and burrs, and was out cold. A figure blue like the sky draped in gold came over and lightly touched her on the forehead. Instantly she awoke, and gasped at the brilliance of the figure before her. She was awake, but she thought she was dreaming, or that she had been dreaming, or perhaps she finally understood that life is a dream. The colors around her were more brilliant than her eyes could contain, but she was given the capacity to truly see. There was a transcendent ease and grace in His presence that had Lucky transfixed.

"Who...are you?" she asked.

"I am that I am," He responded.

"Do you have a name?" she clarified.

"Many, some say 9 billion, but that is a severe underestimation," was His response. "In this form, I am known as Krishna, but you may call me Govinda."

"I'm sorry...I am not sure I believe in you," she apologized.

He laughed, and the rippling tones were a blessing to all things within a resonant range. "I am fortunate that My existence does not require belief," He assured her.

"But, excuse my impertinence," she demurred, "I believe in God, but how can you be one individual cultural identity?"

"Indeed, I am not," He smiled. "But the limitations of an individual's perception require that I circumscribe my appearance. I come in this form for it best embodies that which you need to learn."

"In an infinite universe how can necessary knowledge be limited to one form?" she persisted.

"No more questions until you have heard the answers already given," His response was playfully stern. "You push a perfectly fine steed too hard for nothing but your own uncertainties. I am here now to reflect this back to you. Ready yourself to run with me!" He raised His staff.

"Wait," she stalled. "What if I don't want to race?"

He laughed again. "I give you no choice." He staff came booming down to the ground, and a massive earthquake instantly shattered the hillside. The sand and stone immediately liquefied and Lucky found the ground disappearing beneath her.

"Come! Catch Me!" He cried as his jumped over a boulder. Lucky jumped onto the same boulder just to save her life, but then it started sliding down the hill. She watched Govinda gracefully leap to another, and she followed him. Each stone was in motion, and she realized she would have to pursue just to avoid being crushed. She caught on and decided to leap right at Him quickly to try to end the game, but He joyfully slipped right out of her grasp.

"Good!" He laughed again. "Keep up." He danced and twirled, taunted her and halted right under her fingers, but just as she tried to grasp him he seemed to slip out like blue-golden dust. She pushed harder and faster, and soon they were flying over the terrain faster than she had ever believed she could run. Still, no matter how she drove herself and dove at Him, He remained ever outside of her grasp. It was just as if He exactly matched and superseded whatever effort she put out. Then she had a revelation, and she no longer tried to grasp at Him. Instead, she tried to drive into the space just ahead of where He was going. As she did she felt a momentarily press of his flesh like cool lightening right before he ran even further past.

"Better!" He exclaimed. "Now you are getting it!" He spun in the air in a perfect pirouette and flew ahead. Now she tried to grasp ahead of Him again, but this time she only got a corner of golden cloth before it was torn out of her hand. "Go faster in your mind, in your heart."

"Faster?!" She could hardly imagine going any faster. She was already bounding from rock to log to sand to stream to mud faster than she had ever thought she could go. Finally, she stopped trying to catch Him, and tried to just match His pace. Soon she was bounding right beside Him, and she put out her hand in His general direction. He reached out and took it, and her heart melted in bliss. For a few moments they were running hand in hand and then he took firm grasp and began to spin her around.

"Now you have it!" He declared. "But is that good enough? Think of your poor horse!" He spun her faster and faster and then flung her far ahead. She tried to keep her footing, to maintain some balance, but she was going too fast. As she flew ahead she realized that she was coming back towards where she began. Finally she flew into the weeds and hit the ground, and she was out cold.

She awoke to hot breath and soft whiskers, and as she opened her eyes her horse was nudging her in the cheek.

"Oh, it's you," she said as she rolled over. She was in pain but her whole body was electric with the remembrance of bliss. "Well, you are a good horse, aren't you. A good tiding, too, I'd say. That's what I'll call you, Tiding. How about that?" she asked him as she swung up on to his back.

She picked her way back towards the ranch, and at first she thought she was lost, because everything seemed different. Rocks were tossed about like pebbles, and trees were snapped like toothpicks. She founds herself completely dazed, disoriented, and doubting what had happened. She was beginning to think it was all some seismic dream when she noticed the footprint. In the middle of a large boulder was what looked like the imprint of a foot etched with a lotus-leaf pattern. She stopped to look more closely, and felt the presence of her Friend. Also, off to the side, she could see her own print, looked smeared and hurried, but definitely identifiable.

She returned to her trip home with a sense of pleasant resolve, realizing that the reality of her experience was somehow beyond the day to day existence to which she was accustomed, even on the ranch on its best days. As soon as she realized that the landscape was the same one significantly changed, she was able to make her way by navigating by changed but familiar landmarks. As she came around a new hill that had pushed aside an old one, she noticed the black plume billowing into the sky, its mushroom shape signifying a fire that had just escalated into a new size, and though things were changes she new immediately it was coming from the ranch.

She immediately pushed Tiding into a gallop and made the remaining distance in seconds. The scene that greeted her was something out of her nightmares. The ranch house was up in flames many stories high, providing the bulk of the smoke cloud she had seen from afar. The hands, including Buck, Belle, and Bud had abandoned the house and were desparately trying to put out smaller fires that had begun in the stables and the milking barns. Pico was releasing the cows and the horses out into the pasture, and they were racing with abandon, wild eyes, trampling over each other in desperation. Many cows were still in the barns, and so she raced to the other end from Pico to begin the release on the other side. She burst into the barns to hear pandemonium as the animals panicked and flickering red illuminated the smoke. Men were spraying the sides with water and hacking away at the edges of burning wood. Lucky used all of her instincts and training to calm the animals and lead them orderly out the doors. They generally followed her dutifully but frantically as she opened each stall. Somehow at some point she lost her footing, and though the animals keep pushing out, mercifully they kept from trampling her. As the last one made it out she allowed herself a breath and looked around. Smoke was still everywhere but there was no more red flickering, and she thought hopefully that the worst was over. She looked down at herself and she was covered with mud, ash, and cowdung, and she looked up and said with a rough tinge in her voice, "What was all that about?"

Just then, as if on cue, the floor began to rumble and the walls shook. She could see sunlight streaming intermittently through the slats of the boards as they were pulled apart by the quake, and the bright lines through the smoke reminded her of some rock concert effect.

Voices yelled outside to come out, and Lucky ran out to the front towards the ranch house as the shaking stopped. Dust and smoke hung in the air like some whisper of violence just passed. Buck was dousing some spot in the ranch house, and the rest of the buildings seemed to be safe. Bud and Belle were over to the side, embracing, Bud trying to console Belle who was crying. Lucky ran over to them and hugged them both, overjoyed to see them alive. They were a bundle of burnt clothes, mud, flesh and ash, and they all started to cry together.

"We can rebuild," Bud said, "We've done it before," he managed through the tears, referring to a fire in 1952 that had brought down most of the ranch house.

"But the things we can't replace," she mourned. "Our wedding photos, Lucky's baby pictures..."

"Ma, it's okay," Lucky consoled her. "We are all still alive, that's what counts."

"I know, I know, it's just...how could this happen?" Belle wondered. Her family had come out to California in the thirties, and so she had never experienced a large earthquake before.

"Ma, it happens," Lucky reasoned as she let go of the embrace. "Many are probably worse off than we are."

"I know, I know, I just...am shocked that this could happen...so fast," Belle reasoned.

"I know, I am shocked too," Lucky confessed. "I wonder why..." She was cut off by another aftershock that ripped through the ranch, causing another part of the house to fall over. Belle started crying and screaming.

"Stop it! Stop it!" she yelled out, as if she could command the very earth beneath, and the shaking obediently stopped. Belle continued shaking and crying.

"Now, now dear, it's okay. Lucky, go get Buck and tell him to get out of there," Bud said with a clarity driven by the adrenalin. He stayed and rocked Belle gently back and forth as Lucky ran towards the house.

Buck abruptly came around the corner carrying a box. He was the dustiest of them all, soot black all over as he finally looked up and saw Lucky running towards him. "Oh thank goodness, there you are," he said, striding towards her with full arms. "I wanted your Mom to see this." Lucky embraced him around the box and planted a kiss on his cheek.

"Well, gee, you're going to make me want an earthquake every day."

"That's nothing," Lucky dismissed her gesture. "Thank you so much for everything."

"Well, just part of my job, really," he downplayed it all.

"What about your home and folks?" Lucky asked with real concern.

"I don't know yet, I'm worried too," he acknowledged.

"Well why don't you go find out?" she asked.

"I'm about to, I just wanted to show this to your Ma," he informed her. "I pulled it out right at the beginning and didn't have time to tell her. Come with me." They walked over to Belle and Bud still embracing. "Uh, Sir, Ma'am? I thought you might like to see this."

Belle looked up and immediately gasped. "Oh, my hero!" she cried as she ran over to Buck and jumped in his arms, and gave him a big kiss.

"Well, this might turn out to be a good day for me after all," he said, blushing. Belle immediately opened the box and started to pull out picture after picture, many old and brittle but still intact. Her and Bud as two young lovers, Lucky as a swaddled babe, picture after picture.

"They're all here!" she exclaimed with delight. "Buck, I swear I would marry you right now if I wasn't already married!"

"Hey!" Bud protested.

"I'm just saying..." she was delighted. " But Buck, what about your home, your Ma?"

"I know, I know, I have to get going," he nodded. "That felt like the epicenter was real close."

"It was," Lucky said knowingly. "I know exactly where it was." Her words trailed off into a rumble as another shock rocked the valley.

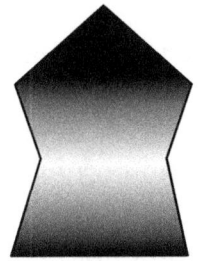

Fammo (7) Eased

Buck came up on horseback to the makeshift emergency center that had formed around Lucky's house. Her new clean place, so often abandoned and empty for the older more homey houses of the ranch, had become control center for the ranch and surrounding area. The solid new construction survived unscathed, but the aftershocks caused them to prefer to stay in tents outside, just to be safe. Fortunately the late October weather remained warm and dry, permitting the mass camping experience that it had become for many.

"There you are!" Belle was the first to see him and call out as he rode up. "What's the news? How are you and yours?" she asked with a tinge of desperation, everyday mundane questions becoming dire interrogations in the aftermath of a major disaster.

"My house is fine, Ma is fine," he reassured her. "The chimney is a bit crooked. Ma won't go inside, cause of the aftershocks, but we are basically untouched."

"Oh, thank God," Belle exclaimed. "Every little bit of good news is a miracle right now."

"What about the rest of town?" Bud asked clearly, having remained amazing sharp since the earthquake.

"Not good, I'm afraid," Buck broke the news. "Watsonville and Santa Cruz are in ruins. The Bay Bridge and

880 in Oakland have collapsed, and they fear hundreds may have died."

"Good lord, we have been lucky," she said as her daughter came around the corner. Lucky was tired and dirty, worn and exhausted after working through the night tending to injuries to animals and people.

"Oh, Buck, good," she managed. "How is your Ma?" She wanted to rush into his arms, but resisted, more out of fatigue than anything else, although also fearing she had led him on the day before with the kiss on the cheek. The wear and tear of the last couple of days had left her beyond philosophical concerns amidst the dirt, bandages, blood and dust. She was experiencing a depression that seemed to match the elation of the experience she hardly remembered from the day before. Somewhere behind it all was a form of shock reflecting the strange impression that this whole event had been predicated on some sort of display for her directly. Bud and Belle wandered off to leave the two of them alone.

"She's fine. Our place is fine. Every where else is messed up, though," Buck reported. "Damage was clear up past San Francisco, even though they are saying that the epicenter is down here near Loma Prieta. In fact, they are calling it that, now, the Loma Prieta Earthquake."

"I believe it," Lucky said, perhaps a little too pointedly.

"You said something like that yesterday," Buck caught on. "Where were you yesterday, anyway?"

"Right up in that area," she answered with enough deflection to take both of their minds off the more mysterious issues. "I never felt anything like that before. I was thrown right to the ground."

"Well I'm glad you're okay," he responded. "How is the ranch?"

"We're doing better than you would think. Only the house was destroyed. The herd is calming down, although not many are giving milk yet," she added with a distressed tone.   Cows were known for drying up after a big shock. Another rumbler came through, shaking everything a bit, but at this point Buck and Lucky hardly reacted.   "These aftershocks are pretty much keeping everyone on edge. What news from Santa Cruz?"

"Well, it's not good." Buck shook his head. "And I have some particularly sad news. The coffee roasting company collapsed, and they think Robin was inside."

"Robin Ortiz?!" Lucky asked in shock about the girl that would serve her coffee every time she would go up to the town for business. "What are they doing to rescue her?"

"They're doing everything they can," Buck claimed.

"Well, maybe that's not enough," she protested.

"Look, there are almost 40 buildings down in Santa Cruz, more crumbling and maybe 10 people dead already. The emergency crews are working around the clock, in very dangerous conditions.   Bush is supposed to visit tomorrow," he added.

"Oh, that makes me feel A LOT better," she said facetiously.   "Let's go.   Everything is okay, here."   She grabbed her veterinary kit and started to jump in the truck, but Buck caught her arm and held her back.

"Lucky, you can't go, it's too dangerous," he said, resisting her repeated attempts to wrest her arm free. Finally she gave him such a look of disgust and revulsion that he immediately let go.

"Look, I'm going," she announced, "and you can come along if you want."

Buck frowned his disapproval but got into the other side of the truck anyway. They sped off into the night and Buck could feel the steely vibes just pouring off of Lucky. She was not really mad at Buck, although she was dead certain she did not like the way he grabbed her. It was more that she was upset at everything, and Buck was the nearest something to experience the most of her consternation. They drove in silence, although Buck almost said something about the way she was pushing the truck, much like she had been pushing her horse the day before. The curves of Freedom Boulevard could hardly contain her energy, and she left not a small amount of rubber on the road behind them. He almost said something, but he knew she was headstrong and would only say something hurtful and would probably drive even more recklessly afterward, and so he clutched the dashboard and said nothing.

A certain electricity hung in the air as they sped into the setting sun along Highway 1. Everywhere there were strange signs of what had happened, burnt out buildings, debris heaps, and hanging smoke, but nothing prepared them for the scene that awaited them as they approached downtown. Lucky figured that the area might be closed off so she parked at the top of Mission Hill by Holy Cross Church and they walked down towards the town. They walked between the Mission and the Old Adobe and could feel the restless spirits dancing about. Lucky carried her veterinary kit on her back, more for comfort than thinking she might need it.

"Strange, this old place looks no different," Buck said about the Adobe, the oldest building in Santa Cruz that had of course survived many earthquakes already. Lucky said nothing and just kept pushing forward, coming to the stairs that descended down the hill to the Town Clock and the beginning of Pacific. As they came to the first landing on the staircase they had to stop for a minute and gasp. The scene before them was totally unfamiliar. It was not the tranquil and green Pacific Garden Mall that they had enjoyed so many times before. Instead it was a war zone. It looked as if indiscriminate artillery shelling had been going on, and down in front of them was the pile that had been the Santa Cruz Coffee Roasting Company. There were fire engines and police cars all about with lights flashing but no sirens. The most noise was coming from a group of civilians that were circled about the former Coffee House who were chanting "Hell no, we won't go!" to a group of police officers who seemed intent on making them do just that.

Buck and Lucky bounded down the last few stairs and joined the group on the outside. They were jostled about, and the first attempts to get any information were futile, and the shouting and pushing were getting so extreme that no one could be questioned effectively. Finally they found an old Japanese man named Fred that was a friend and who was standing on the outside. They pulled him under a tree on the edge of Pacific.

"Fred, what's going on?" Lucky asked him.

"Why the clash?" Buck added.

"Hey, guys. You way up here?" Fred called out loud. "I hear Watsonville is a mess, too." He was talking to them but he was also preoccupied, as everyone seemed to be. The chanting continued and a line of cops in riot gear stood between the crowd and the rescue team. The air had a rancid smell like someone had been burning old sneaker. There was a strange collective effect of an earthquake because it was felt by everyone yet everyone experienced it differently. In general it caused everyone to be hyper-aware and at the same time somewhat distracted. The overall impact is that everyone was concerned and a bit wild-eyed.

Lucky grabbed his face. "Fred, look at me. What is happening with Robin?"

He blinked and answered. "Oh, you don't know. Robin is trapped in that rubble somewhere and the rescuers won't let anybody help. People are getting intense."

"You can say that again," Buck emphasized. "What is everybody trying to do?"

"Everybody just wants to get in and dig," Fred told them, "but the authorities won't let them help." Buck just nodded but in a flash Lucky was gone and making her way to the front of the crowd. She got to the front and tried to squeeze through but the line seamlessly closed in front of her. She started to fume and steam gathered on the visor of the riot cop in front of her.

"Look, Mr. Robo-brain," she started, "I have a good friend in there who may need help and I have to get through..."

The line remained perfectly still. Some others in the crowd egged her on. "You go, sister."

"Look, you don't have to be a mindless drone, you know," she reasoned to the blank visage. "You can think for yourself, and act independently. So what if you lose your job, you might just gain back your soul." If the cop had blinked no one would have known. Buck finally made it to the front of the crowd and came up beside her.

"You have a choice," Lucky continued. "You don't have to be part of the machine."

"Look, Lucky..." Buck tried to intervene and took her by the arm.

"Don't touch me!" Lucky spat with such vehemence that Buck immediately pulled away. "Listen, Sir, I...I am a doctor, I might be needed in there." This seemed to have an effect on the officer. He raised a hand and motioned over a man behind him in a suit and a radio plug in his ear.

"Can I help you, Ma'am," said the officer, obviously some sort of superior.

"I'm a doctor, and I might be needed in there," she lied.

"Do you have clearance," he asked doubtfully.

"Yes, I do," she said matter of factly.

"Oh," the superior officer replied with a slight change of tone. "May I see it."

"Well," Lucky tried to think. "...it comes from a higher source than your bureaucracy."

The officer's expression became even harder. "Well, I'm afraid you're going to have to take it up with...Him." He pointed up.

"Uhgg! The arrogance!" Lucky turned around and started to push back through the crowd. She made her way back past the clock tower and up Mission Hill, not even looking back to see if Buck followed, but he did anyway. She got into the truck and reached over to unlock the door for him, a peace gesture of sorts. He got in but did not look her in the eye. She took off down Highway, grumbling to herself and Buck and Whoever else might be listening.

"Of all the pig-headed, ignoramous..." she went on in a continuous stream, "ridiculous male chauvinistic know-it-all things to do, stop everything as if to ensure that she will be dead, the bastards..."

Buck finally had to say something, "They're just trying to do their jobs..."

"Well, they should do them a little better!" she snapped back. "She may not have much time and they are just in there lollygagging spending more time in crowd control than moving mortar and bricks..."

"It's extremely dangerous work..." Buck tried.

"Yeah, dangerous for the victims..." Lucky went on. Buck did not even try to say any more. He just sat and looked out at the road and tried to cope within in his own way. Lucky kept calm now and just kept the dialog going in her head. Slowly it quieted and she could finally hear Buck's breathing. She had learned long ago that he rarely communicated his upset feelings but she could always tell by his breathing. It never became exactly a sigh, but it was a little too deep.

"Look, I'm sorry," she softened. "You know I am just worked up. I don't even know what to say or do."

Buck softened too, and his breathing became lighter. "I know...but...a doctor?"

"I know, I know, but I could have helped," she reasoned.

"I was afraid with the cops in a situation like that you could have gotten in real trouble," Buck figured.

"Oh, nobody's getting in trouble, but I am sorry I snapped at you," she smiled at him and it almost relieved the pain.

"I...I just think, you getting into with the cops would not have helped Robin right now."

"Oh, Robin..." Lucky sighed, and began to sob. Buck watched he cry as she drove, and part of him really wanted to reach out and comfort her, but he was not sure anymore. He was not sure if she wanted it, but he was sure he did not want to offer it not knowing. He sat there against his instincts, just watching. Lucky knew he was resisting his own instincts, and she felt like she had lost something, but she did not reach out. She had been comfortable comforting herself for a long time. Instead she just continued her ongoing speech out loud again.

"Some things are meant to be just a 'job,' you know," she maintained. "Some things, like rescues, are meant to be a spontaneous outpouring of community hope and heroism. Some things, like singing songs, playing sports, telling stories, have been taken away from most of us and have been assigned to some professionals while we are expected to sit on the sidelines and watch. Well, as soon as you do that than guess what? As soon as you delegate it to some pro who is supposed to be the best and so only he can do it, then you fail. You miss the point. You don't feel the heart, you don't build the body, you don't feed the soul...you don't save the girl." Lucky bit her lip and just kept driving. Buck kept his silence, but at least his breathing was calm.

They made it back to the ranch with barely a word. They discussed driving by Watsonville to see what had happened there, but decided against it. It was crazy anyway and besides it was getting too dark and they could go check things out tomorrow. They made a few brief references to ranch business and they drove onto the gravel road leading through the gates. Buck said a brief goodbye without looking at her and at some point his breathing had become deep again, but that could be anything really and Lucky could not bother herself with that now. She had some real bones to pick. She was finally becoming determined to face what had really gone on. Maybe that cop knew more that he realized when he said she should take it up with the Big Guy. At least, that is what she was determined to do.

She went into her house to check on her parents, and found them in the familiar positions they usually held at the old ranch, Dad sitting at the table staring at the floor and Ma fussing about the kitchen.

"Hey, folks, how you two doing?" She asked perfunctorily.

"F...fine...d...dear," her Dad struggled to get out. The adrenalin had worn off and now he seemed a bit worse for the wear.

"Lucky, there you are," Belle said. "I can't find anything in your kitchen! What's the news? Where's Buck?"

"Buck went home," she kind of snapped back at her mom, indicating that she did not want to talk about him right now. "Santa Cruz is a mess. A friend of mine might be trapped in the rubble."

"Oh, Dear, don't worry," Belle tried to console her. "I am sure she's all right."

"No, she's not all right," Lucky shot back. "Nothing is all right."

"Try not to take it so hard, Honey," her Mom persisted.

"I won't. I'm fine," Lucky lied, but Belle did not notice. Bud looked up, though. He had a sense Lucky would not say she was fine if she was. "Look, I'm okay, really. I'm going to visit a friend, tonight."

"At this hour? Who?" Belle was concerned as usual, and unusual things made her unusually concerned.

"Somebody you haven't met, I don't think," she said.

"Oh really?" Belle raised an eyebrow. "A man?"

"No, not a man, Mother," Lucky became a teen for a moment. "You don't have to worry, okay? Wait, this is my house, remember, I come and go sometimes you know." She gathered some things, a blanket, some water, and stood next to the door ready to go out.

"Lucky, be careful," Buck said, staring straight into her center. He had a way of coming out of his space like that and cutting Lucky right to the quick. She stopped and went over to hug him and kiss him on the head.

"Don't worry, Dad, I'll be careful, really," she said, finally with enough conviction to convince them both. "I might not be coming back tonight, so don't wait up."

"Oh, dear, don't you at least want something to eat first," Belle reached for an old standby. "It's getting late and you must be famished." With the intuition of a mother Belle had of course been exactly right. Lucky had not eaten all day, really, and she was feeling a bit light headed, but food was not what she wanted right now.

"No, thanks, Ma, really," she went over and kissed Belle on the cheek. "I'll have something later, okay. I really should be going. Good night, okay?" She said as she walked out the door.

"Good night, sweetheart, and God bless," she heard Belle say as she closed the door, and she heard Bud breathing in a way that reminded her of Buck. She brushed all that off and went off to the stables to get Tiding. He was at the front, as if waiting for her, and she silently got him ready, grabbed a lantern, and was out on the trail as the last distant rays of the sun danced on the air below the horizon. The stars seemed to be watching as she rode out into the moonless night, and she welcomed their company.

"Okay, I'm coming," she said out loud into space. "I don't know what you want with me and all this but I'm coming. And I do know what I want. I want some answers. I want to know what the hell is going on. What is going on with Robin? What the hell is this all about? What are you thinking? Why does this seem to be about what was happening yesterday? Answer me," she commanded nothing, or so it seemed. She rode on further into the night, until she came to a spot where she could tie up Tiding safely. She wrapped a lanyard tightly around a tree and tied it to his bridle, removing the bit from his mouth so he could feed on grasses comfortably. He just stood there looking at her.

"Don't you worry, too," she said. "I'm going to be fine. Don't worry about the Coyotes, either, they just make a lot of noise. And the cougars around here are all too fat on deer meat to bother you." Tiding did not seem to be worried. Lucky lit the lantern and proceed out into the woods. They still had that otherworldly feel. Things were so different that she lost her bearings at points, but soon she just kept going forward, realizing that it really did not matter where she was going. She clambered over broken stones and stumps, slipped a few times, and really began to feel lightheaded.

"Maybe I should have eaten something," she said. "So, are you going to show up, or do I have to hurt myself again?" she pushed through the brush with a bit of renewed vigor, and then twisted her ankle on a rock.

"Well, fuck it then," she gave up and collapsed in a heap. She set her lantern on a stone and wrapped the blanket around her, only to notice the footprint with the lotus petal markings on the rock above her. "Oh, there you are. So that's the way it goes, is it? Nothing can be easy, can it? But here we are. Okay. So what's up? I'm talking to you. Can you hear me? What's up?!" She was starting to get delirious. "Okay, listen, bastard, you put me through all that, so at least you owe me an explanation. You owe me, you really do, but

that's the way it is, isn't it? You push people, you hurt them,
you drag them out, and then you just leave them high and
dry? Well, why ME? Why? I don't get it, I just don't get it, all
the things, going on, crazy like, and all I'm doing, and no way,
no way for a girl to, you think there is something, and no..."
Slowly she drifted out completely, exhaustion covering her
more than the blanket that she had wound tightly about
herself. Silence descended, and the crickets came back as her
lantern slowly burned out. Cicadas and other shy voices in the
night joined in, for they knew something was afoot. There
was a flute-like voice gently out there floating with the other
sounds, and every other greeted it gladly. Lucky lay against
the stone and dozed peacefully, and a light blue lotus golden
glow settled beside her.

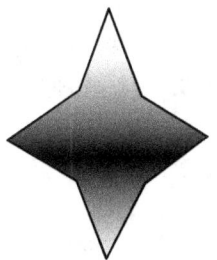

Temmo (8) Healed

Lucky instinctively cuddled close to the source of warmth beside her in the cool early morning hours, even though she did not know what it was. In those earliest dreams of the morning that few people ever remember she allowed herself to dive deeply into the close comfort of the presence beside her like she had never allowed herself to do with an ordinary man. She relished the scent, the touch, the warmth, and let it permeate her deeply.

A blue hand ringed with golden something touched her forehead, and she just noticed through her half closed eyes. Slowly she opened them fully, and all of her fury melted in the moment of bliss.

"Go...Govinda," she let herself finally say his name.

"Yes, it is I," He responded. He held her close like a heavenly shroud.

"You finally came," she sighed.

"I have always been here," He maintained.

"I...have been troubled," she confessed. She had been thinking of so many things to say to Him, but nothing seemed to come out like she had planned. She had a whole list of things to say, to confront Him about, to make him answer. Finally in His presence however, she found herself unable to speak of such things.   There was something beyond all that about Him that immediately enveloped her and made her mind think of other things.   It made her body tingle and do anything but just sit and ask accusatory questions.

"You've been wondering why," He led her to the point.

"Yes!" she released.   Her natural ability to let words flow finally came back.   "So much has happened since the other day, and I cannot understand why you would let it happen, but I don't want to press you with such questions and make you uncomfortable."

"I have been pressed with such questions for eons and have never been made uncomfortable.   Ask me what questions you like, but I might not give you answers you like."

"All right," Lucky began.   "Well, did you make that earthquake just for me?"

"What we experienced was just for us," He answered. "Other people experience what was just for them."

"Was death meant for Robin?" she continued.

"Death is meant for all people on this plane.   It was her time," He returned.

"Is she really gone now?" Lucky asked.

"Her body has been destroyed, but she is not gone. She is enjoying a heavenly reward right now," He replied.

"So she is in Heaven forever?" Lucky asked hopefully.

"She amassed a considerable amount of merit and will enjoy it fully in higher realms, but it will eventually be exhausted and she too will have to return," He answered.

"Why do you always give such short answers?" Lucky wondered.

"I like to be succinct," was his simple answer.

"Would you give me a longer answer if I asked for it?" she asked with a grin.

"Yes," He said with a grin.

"All right then, please tell me, in a somewhat longer form, why you are here, in this form, and what is the meaning of all that has happened since yesterday?"

"I have loved you for many lifetimes, and I have come to reclaim you. You were a gopi, and together we cared for the young calves in my kingdom long ago. We were lovers, yet we had to part, and that caused you much distress, yet I promised I would return to you to reveal a greater purpose for your soul. Yesterday was the beginning of your purpose for this lifetime, and my appearance came as a great seismic shock. I appear in every generation, in various forms, to be with my dear beloved ones, and the mundane physical world trembles with each of my transcendent steps."

"Who are you really?" Lucky inquired.

"I am Govinda, I am Jesus, I am Buddha, I am Yahweh, I am Allah, and All others, yet none of these are the totality of Who I Am. I am the Void of the nihilist, and Blind Chance to the materialist. I am the Universe that can be seen, and the Universe that cannot be seen, yet these are but a small mote in a single cell of Who I Am. The closest that words may come is that I am Love Personified."

"Why come to me now as Govinda?" Lucky continued, just wanting Him to keep talking.

"I come to everyone in the form that will best facilitate their highest potential. Though I am Everything, including Nothing, yet still I am a Personality, a Center of Perception that loves and thinks and feels. Although I love all Creation equally, still My Love is best experienced by those who love Me."

"Why choose me, now," Lucky persisted.

"No one need ask 'why me?' for the divine bliss of transcendence is a promise I have offered to everyone," He began. "However, each has chosen to experience my emanations differently, and so for each there is a special purpose."

"What is my special purpose, then?" Lucky asked directly.

"When we were lovers, you understood cows to be a very sacred animal. They are eminently peaceful spiritual animals, for they are an archetype, through the giving of milk, of the generosity of My emanations. We have often cared for My cows at My home, and you have asked to be of special service to them. Right here and now in this country there is a special need for cows and livestock to be better understood and cared for, and to this end you are admirably suited."

"I understand," she said, her mind and spirit relaxing into a grand expansiveness as only happens when one hears their life purpose spoken back to them. Now so many things made sense to her that had perplexed her for so long. She could feel that He was completely correct in what he said about her, and she allowed His words to fully sink in. The sun was slowly peaking over the ridge of the Santa Cruz Mountains, and below them the fog hugged the hills like a cotton candy blanket. The picturesque effect was that they were on their own heavenly islands in a white fiery foam sea.

"Tell me about your home," she asked dreamily.

"It is my home, but is not a planet like this Earth. It is in the Spiritual Sky, and is often called by such names as Krishnaloka, Heaven, Valhalla, and the like, for it is all things Paradise. Everything of beauty in any world is a small reflection of my home," He told her.

"I would love to see it some day," she wistfully hoped.

"It is here for us," He said, motioning his hand. Instantly a vista opened up before them that made the wonderful view they had been enjoying seem like a dark black and white picture. The plains that enfolded before her could only be described as a heaven for all creatures. Before her she could see cows grazing on iridescent grass, fed by streams of rainbow crystalline waters. The air was clear yet so fragrant that it was positively nutritious, and before she even knew what she was doing Lucky was running through the fields hand in hand with Govinda. They ran and played amongst the cows, who greeted them with joyous sounds and galloped along with them. They ran and danced and played for what seemed like days, yet the sun never set. Indeed there seemed to be no sun at all. Everything was self luminous, glowing with it own energy and potential, and nothing more so than Govinda himself.

"How is it that we are here for so long, yet I feel no hunger, no exhaustion?" Lucky asked him.

"We are outside of time and space as you know it, and this is your eternal home. However," He said with a slight note of gravity, "you must know that you have chosen something else for yourself right now, and you must return."

The realization hit Lucky hard, but she had known it all along. "Will I be able to return?"

"This is your eternal home," He told her, "Part of you is always here. Understand that great demigods have been striving for billions of years to come here like you have now, and they may strive for billions more yet. Coming here is not easy, just like pure love is not easy, but it is your destiny, as it is everyone else's. Yet others do not see this so clearly, and you chose long ago to help as many of them as you can."

"I...know," she accepted. "But, do I have to go now?"

"You may stay as long as you like," He allowed. "But, in a way, you have already left. Follow me, I have a gift for you." He took her down to a pond, and it was the most glorious patch of water she had ever seen. Out of it were growing tiny lotus flowers, but they glowed with a special iridescence. He picked one and gave it to her, and she realized that it glowed in such a way because it was made of solid opal. He reached under his shirt and pulled out a golden chain, affixed the opal lotus to it, and hung it about her neck.

"You must go back, because you have chosen already to go back, but some parts of this place stay with you always," He gave her.

"I understand that too," she nodded. "Only when I have finished my work will I allow myself to stay here forever." There was a very old part of herself that had finally emerged, and she knew that though this heaven was her birthright, she understood why she had chosen to forego it for so long. Understanding this, and knowing that part of her was always here, there was no reason to linger.

"There is a lot you understand," He read her mind. "But there is much you still have to learn. Everyone is moving in an infinite universe surrounded by infinite expressions of My love. When you truly understand that you will have accomplished much."

"But I love You so much, there is no way I could love anything else as much."

"You may think so, but I am everything, in everything." He tried to make a hint but she did not get it. "There are many paths that lead to the same place, but one may be the right one for you now."

Lucky resisted the implication. "I am yours, totally, now and forever, no matter what."

"I would never, could never, deny that," He allowed her the moment, "but you are meant to find Me in many ways."

"I look forward to each way, and long to know every side of You," Lucky said, almost hypnotically.

"And so you shall, sooner and later." He would not tell her the obvious, for there was nothing forceful in Him, though He was force itself. Everything was allowed to emanate at its normal pace.

Lucky breathed in the air of Krishnaloka, letting her soul embody its essence expansively. The streams and plants seemed to twinkle in her honor, and the cows began lowing in unison to create a song like she had never heard. "It's so beautiful," she proclaimed.

"Home is always beautiful," Govinda agreed. "Are you ready?"

"I am ready. I'm am so grateful, so much, for this, for You, and for everything," she sincerely thanked him.

"Thank you for enjoying this with Me," He said. "I have a special place in My heart for My cows and those who love them."

"I do love them so, and I will never forget, if I can help it," she promised. "How do I get back?"

"You are already there," He said. "Just close your eyes."

She obeyed Him, and immediately felt a change. Even without opening her eyes, she could feel it. She could feel pain, and hardness. She could smell dust, dung, and mold. She could hear flies, and an airplane somewhere overhead. She knew she was back, it was clear, and though she knew what she had seen was real, she could not help but fear that it had all been just a dream, some kind of vision. In that moment she realized that she had just experienced all of the typical aspects of a vision quest, from the fasting the day before to the night alone in the woods. Perhaps it had all been just a glorious, magical, sacred vision, and she was okay with that. Whatever it was, it was a gift.

Then she remembered, and she felt a soft coolness against her neck. Still with eyes closed, she reached to her chest and felt the form of a small hard lotus blossom.

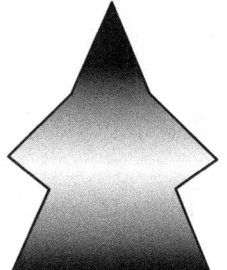

Nonna (9) Appeased

Belle could tell there was a change in Lucky, and she could not help but notice the new lotus necklace that she wore. She also could not help but notice, that despite all the dust and grime that covered Lucky, there was a glow about her that Belle could only interpret as the sort that happens to someone who has fallen in love.

"Good morning, Ma," Lucky said as she put her stuff away. Bud was off working on the ranch somewhere and Belle was frying up some eggs for breakfast. "That smells great. I'm famished," Lucky told her.

"I bet," Belle returned, a bit suspicious. "It looks like you had quite a night, last night."

"I did indeed," Lucky agreed as she grabbed a bite of eggs from the pan.

"Now, wait just a minute," Belle complained, a bit perturbed but happy to see her daughter looking more like herself again. Belle scraped out the eggs from the pan and put them on the table with a plate of toast, fruit, and potatoes fried with peppers and onions from their garden. "So who was it that you went to see last night?"

"Just a very good friend, Ma," Lucky assured her. She dove into her breakfast, finally fully appreciating the name of this first meal of the day.

"A new friend?" Belle fished, happily watching her daughter eat.

"An old friend...reacquainted," Lucky specified, motioning at her food just to distract her mom from the topic. She really did not know how to explain all that she had been going through to her Belle. She knew that Belle was spiritual in her own way, but Lucky felt that she was stuck in an old paradigm that would only be able to explain her experiences as something delusional or demonic. Even Lucky herself was not sure how to understand it all. She knew it was not demonic, but, somehow, maybe, delusional. There was a strange and almost frustrating aspect to all of her encounters with Govinda that walked the line between illusion and reality. There seemed to always be the nagging possibility that it was all a dream, but then there was something tangible to indicate otherwise, like the footprint or the opal lotus around her neck.

"It is so beautiful," said Belle referring to the lotus necklace, as if she were reading Lucky's mind. "Did your friend give it to you?"

"Yes, He did," Lucky confirmed more than she intended.

"Aha!" Belle exclaimed. "So it is a man. You said your friend wasn't a man."

"Oh, Ma! Okay, you got me," Lucky exasperated. "It's just that...it's not like that."

"I think it is like that," Belle figured. "I can tell by how you're glowing. Plus, you're out all night. What do you expect me to think?"

"Why do you always have to think?" Lucky asked. "Can't I just have a bit of private life?"

"Your whole life is private!" Belle professed. "Always out mysteriously by yourself, never letting anyone into your private spaces. Oh, I didn't mean for that to sound like that." They both laughed. "Is he a least a good man?" Belle smiled weakly.

"The very best, Ma, I promise," she smiled back.

"I just wonder what you are going to tell Buck," Belle sympathetically declared.

"Nothing!" Lucky unsympathetically declared.

"Nothing?" Belle wondered. "How can you tell him nothing?"

"Because it is none of his business! Uhggg! Can't you let it go?" Lucky was a bit sharp with that one.

Belle was definitely hurt and her eyes watered up. "Listen, a mother just always cares and can't let it go, something which I hope you will understand some day."

Lucky was frustrated with her mom's perspective but she did not want to hurt her any further. She just had no idea of how to explain what she was going through to her mom. Finally she hit on an idea that seemed obvious but that she had resisted. She decided to ask a clear question in her head.

"So, are You really always with me?" she thought as hard and clear as she could.

"I am always with you, as I said," came an instant and steady response from a flute-like voice in her head.

"Than what should I say to my mom to make her feel better?" Lucky asked in her head.

"Put your arm around her, tell her not to worry, that nothing that you are experiencing is contrary to Buck's feelings, and that sooner or later you will come around."

"But I don't know if I believe that!" Lucky said out loud.

"What's that, Dear?" Belle asked. "What don't you believe?"

"Oh, nothing, Ma," Lucky brushed her off.

"Are you sure you are feeling all right?" Belle asked, a definite note of concern returning to her voice with a little weight added by her returning hurt feelings.

"Just say it," said the voice in Lucky's head.

"Okay," Lucky said, and she stood up and put her arm around her mother. "Look, Ma, don't worry. Nothing I'm experiencing is contrary to Buck's feelings, and I'm sure I will come around sooner or later."

Belle melted in the warmth of Lucky's reassurance. "Oh, thank you dear. I know you are so special and that some day you will come around. You always turn out to be right, and I just have to learn to trust, I guess."

The immediacy and wisdom of her mother's response surprised her. She felt touched by her Mom's words. "Thank you, Ma. I love you so much," she said as they embraced more fully.

"I love you too, Dear," her mom said and they lingered in the embrace.

"I told your mom what to say, too," said the clear voice in Lucky's head.

"You did!" Lucky said out loud in her mother's ear, and they pulled apart.

"I did what?" Belle asked, rubbing her ear and casting a suspicious eye at Lucky. "What are you talking about? Are you sure you feel all right?"

"Oh, great," Lucky thought. "Now what should I say?"

"Say, as usual, you don't know how you feel, but you are certain everything will be all right," the voice instructed her.

"You know, Ma, as usual, I don't know how I feel," Lucky began, "But I am certain that everything will be all right."

Belle laughed and smiled. "Well, at least now you're finally being honest. Yes, I believe too that everything will be all right." She was comforted now enough that she could go back to her normal routine and she started cleaning up the kitchen. Lucky gratefully returned to her breakfast.

"Well, thanks for getting me out of that one," she thought. "Anything else I should tell my mom?"

"Don't you perhaps think you should thank her for the delicious breakfast? Food should always be eaten with full gratitude" the voice of Govinda answered her.

"Uh huh," Lucky mumbled while chewing.

"What's that, dear?" Belle asked.

"Ma, I just wanted to thank you for this breakfast. It is so delicious!" Lucky added through a full mouth, perhaps the only polite thing to say through a full mouth.

"Oh, bless you sweetheart," Belle positively bubbled. "I wonder sometimes if you all notice what I do around her."

"We notice more than we say, definitely," Lucky added, rather amazed at how just a few simple words could put her mom in such a better mood.

"Thanks for that," she thought in her head.

"Anytime," came the flute-like response.

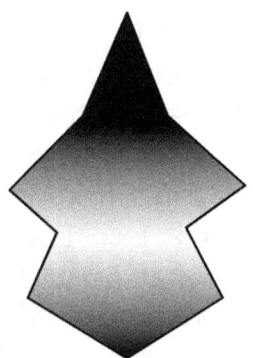

Adekka (10) Pleased

Buck brought up the reigns tight as he approached Watsonville. A huge cloud of smoke was about to engulf him, and he was not sure how his horse would react. He had taken to riding Luck everywhere he could since the earthquake. The roads were often blocked to cars, but he could always get through on horseback. It had been full time work ever since, what with the repairs to be made and his extra work of trying to help the ranch get back up to speed, but he had always found a little extra time and energy to go check things out and help in the community at large. Word had been circulating that a camp had formed at the fairgrounds of people that had been displaced by the earthquake, so Buck had decided to ride out and find out how they were doing. Times were hard, things were rough, but there was something larger going on, Buck was certain. People always thought that everyone would panic in an emergency, showing fear and suspicion and generally working from their lowest selves, but instead the opposite seemed to be the case. People seemed to bring out their best side. Sure, there had been a few reports of looting and some strange violent occurrences, but in general everyone was really rising to the occasion and helping out.

Even at the coffee house in Santa Cruz where Robyn was now confirmed dead, everyone merely was trying to help in some way. Buck now realized that most just needed some kind of guidance, some kind of real leadership. For some reason it did not seem to come from the normal channels, the politicians and the bureaucracies. Instead, they seemed to be more in a state of panic and frustration. The visits by the Governor and the President appeared to be more like photo opportunities than anything else. But the people themselves really poured out of the woodwork to try to make a difference.

Of course, a lot of the woodwork was shaking and crumbling which seemed to make everyone come out quite fast. As he slowly rode towards the cloud of smoke, it would swirl and dance, parting every once in a while to reveal a sprawling mass of fires and tents and people in the distance. He could hardly believe what he was seeing, and the smoke seemed to be blowing erratically, odd in the nearly windless day. Luck started to act up, anxious about something, and Buck started to feel strange too. Luck's footfalls seemed unusual, alternating soft and hard, like on some kind of drying mud. The smoke was all around them now, and seemed to thicken to where hardly anything could be seen. He brought Luck down to a slow walk, and this seemed to calm the horse down a bit. The smoke was from the fires, certainly, and mixed a bit with coastal fog, but he also detected a hint of sage and sweetgrass.

It may have been the odor, or it may have been something even more subtle, but Buck began to realize that there was something more than smoke swirling around him. A multicolored light twinkled and flickered up ahead, and he strained to see it more clearly.

"Who's there?" he asked, and as if on cue the smoke gracefully parted to reveal the glowing figure of a regal woman draped in gold and shining dark like some giant mysterious sunflower.

"Welcome, I am Queen Califia," she said, and her voice came out like a choir. Buck was stricken by the sight and brought Luck to a complete halt. He dismounted and fell in the dry grasses at the feet of Queen Califia. Her feet wore sandles of sea otter pelt with gold buckles. "Please arise, my son, for we are both servants of the same Divinity."

Buck rose slowly and beheld her in her fullness. "How can I help you...Your Majesty?" he asked.

"My people need you," she said and gestured through the smoke. Immediately a swirling tunnel opened like a portal and he could see faces of all shapes, colors, genders, and sizes. Each one wore a look of despair, concern, angst, or anxiety. They all seemed to be struggling with their own issues, trapped within their own issues. There were children crying, and elders with their heads down, and Buck was overwhelmed with a wave of compassion.

"I am here because I know you could see me, and I know you could understand my message. Know that upheaval is a part of my great land. It is a true paradise from end to end, yet it is a land of eternal transition. My people come from the world over, thinking they have found a golden end to the trail, but the trail does not end."

"I believe I understand," Buck said solemnly. "I will try to do your demands justice." He bowed, which seemed a bit awkward but he did not know what else to do. He looked more deeply at her, for she seemed to invite his gaze, and he saw deep parts of her being etched from the land. In the depths of her dark skin Buck could see mountains and valleys, green and golden hills, and he even thought he could make out the San Andreas Fault.

"I see you see within me," she said. "I was once a mere human, much like your friend White Buffalo Calf Woman, but now I am stretched across the landscape. Through love, admiration, and belief, I have risen to become the very essence of this land. Though I once ruled from an island off the coast down south, I now am ensconced in this entire land that bears my name." She spread her arms wide and they seem to let loose a bounty of images of the land, redwoods, canyons, deserts, everything stretching out to the distance. And then there were people, from all places of the world, streaming in. "All people of the world have always come to me, not just in your time. Countless ages have seen all peoples of the world, from all corners of the globe, come to me, by land, by seaon ships made of reeds and wood, in the air in strange craft. They have all come here, and found a corner of my body that they could call home. All the tongues of the world have been spoken here for longer than men can try to remember. And all have spoken of how they tremble when I shake. But I shake not to make them fear, but to make them think, and remember. Remember why they came." She shook her hands and Buck saw everything mixed up and tossed around, then disappear as she closed her hands and lowered her arms to her sides.

"I see..." he said feebly, because he could not think of much else.

"My son, you are and have chosen, so you carry a great burden. Work as you do and let my words be lightness in your feet and resilience in your hands. You cannot fail," she assured him.

"I will not fail," he assured her. She merely nodded and started to fade into the mists. He watched her go, watched her become the golden fog that encircled the hills and the light that broke through to show the way. Even though there was no wind, the smoke blew away revealing the path down to the fairgrounds below. It was still quite a ride, as he had to go around Pinto Lake and past the old Catholic church, but he and Luck were sprinting now. As they passed an old oak grove next to the lake he saw the golden form of Queen Califia disappear into a tree.

"I live in these trees, and anyone needs to see me they can find me here," she said, as her form became emblazoned in bark. He kept riding hard, past the old Catholic Church, but then he noticed a shape crumpled down next to the entrance to the cemetery. It was old Pete Capitanich, and he held his head in his hands. Buck rode up and came to a halt in front of Pete, who hardly looked up.

"Pete, what's up? You all right?" Buck asked him.

"Oh, Buck, it's you," he put his head back in his hands, and Buck now noticed that he was covered in ashes. "No, everything is not all right. I have lost everything, and I have come here to die with my family."

"What happened?" Buck was shocked.

"Everything! Gone! I am stricken like Lot. Now all I have is ashes to roll in. Fire after the earthquake. I tried to put out, but was too fast. Burnt stable with animals, house destroyed. All gone. Now I die. Join family."

"But Pete, you can rebuild. You have done it all before," Buck pointed out.

"No, now I am old. Too old to begin. Done. Finished. Now I die," and he turned his shoulder to look in the cemetery. "Mary is in there, you know. I should be with her. Should have joined her years ago. Foolish to start farm after she died. This is message." He slumped even further into his ash.

Buck was struck with sudden inspiration. "Look, Pete, I need you. Come with me!" Before the old man could protest he reached down and picked up his frail frame in one motion and had him on the back of the horse. Immediately he galloped down the road along the apple trees on the side, Pete hanging on for dear life.

As they neared the fairgrounds they were immediately thrust into a chaotic situation. A huge crowd had gathered around a Red Cross aid truck next to a food truck, and shouting and scrambling had broken out as a fire spread through the food supplies. Apparently a barrel that had been lit for cooking had spilled over next to some oil, and this had quickly spread to the truck. In the panic it had been hard to sort out who was who, so many bodies scrambling this way and that in the smoke. Buck and Pete jumped right into the fray and helped others put out the fire. When the smoke finally cleared it was apparent that many people had been trampled in the confusion, and much of the food intended for the hungry crowd had been destroyed. Both Buck and Pete hardly spoke a word as they flew from one task to the next. Buck was treating the injured, setting splints, putting on bandages, cleaning cuts. Pete was saving what food he could from the burnt truck, making a feast out of nothing like he had been taught by his Croatian forebears.

It was obvious to Buck that the Red Cross volunteers were overworked. They all looked tired and dirty to the point of being almost inhuman. At one point he had been working with someone so dirty it took him a moment to realize that he was working with Pico.

"Pico! I didn't even recognize you!" He said to his friend.

"It's true, Amigo," Pico agreed. "We are all not quite ourselves. So much to do."

Buck barely had time to agree before he was dragged into another issue, helping to set up more tents from the Red Cross. There were literally and figuratively fires to be put out everywhere, and one or two that needed to be lit. Buck met a few other leader types that he had not known before, including Ramiro Gonzalez, Tito Begovich, and Julia Caldwell, all from Watsonville. They were the natural leaders in the situation, and were soon acting together out of sheer intuition. After a time, late into the night, it actually began to calm down, most of the children with full bellies and safe in cots in tents, the adults still shuffling around trying to organize the bits of nothing they still had left. Buck, Pete, Ramiro, Tito, and Julia were huddled around a campfire, discussing plans.

"The authorities don't have the capacity to deal with all this," Julia was saying. "FEMA will take weeks to act, and even then who knows what they will be able to do."

"But we do have God with us," Ramiro said. "I thought all was lost tonight but we made it."

"Yeah," Tito agreed. "When that truck caught fire I thought we were all a goner. I was praying to Mother Mary for a miracle, then Buck and Pete ride in here like the friggin' cavalry." They all laughed.

"Just in time, that's for sure," Julia agreed. "But we need more cavalry still."

"And a few Indians, too, I think," Buck added. "We're all in this one, together," and he thought of Queen Califia with gratitude.

"We will take all the help we can get," Tito affirmed, and they all laughed.

"What else can we do?" Pete asked and they looked around the fairgrounds. Suddenly something dawned on Buck.

"You know, this is a showgrounds, what about some kind of benefit show?" he proposed.

"That's a great idea!" Julia exclaimed. "I'm surprised we did not think of it before. In fact, I have a friend up in Santa Cruz that can help us out. Any of you hear of M.C. Hager?" Blank stares, heads shaking.

"Maybe we can get some artists to volunteer," Buck said.

"I know Jorge Santana, and he might be able to get his brother Carlos," Ramiro said. "And Los Lobos has some family around here."

"It's worth a try, eh?" Buck said. They looked out over the fairgrounds again, fires here and there stretching out into the distance. There was too much need and pain to resist any potentially positive idea, and perhaps that is why they ignored more realistic lines of thought that may have derailed the idea.   Instead, they let their thoughts swirl with the smoke into the evening sky, dreaming as only the devastated can.

Pete came up to Buck and put his hand on his shoulder. "Where to next, my friend?" he asked.

"Back to the Lucky Star," Buck said. "There is plenty of work still to do there, and we could use your help. You are really needed," Buck stressed.

"Buck, it's okay," Pete assured him. "You have already saved me.   These hands can still feed people, still hold a wrench or a hammer. This old Pete, he is not done yet!" he said as he thumped his chest.

"Not by a long shot," Buck agreed. "You outworked men half your age!"

"Except for you, you worked like three men!" Pete exclaimed. "And for me, I thank you," he said more quietly but intently, with a watery eye.

"Oh, Pete, don't overestimate my contribution," Buck shrugged it off. "Although I sure feel tired like three men right now." He walked over to Luck who was tied to a post and brought him back over. He jumped on and then helped Pete on the back, and they rode back over to the rest of the emergency workers.

"All right, my new friends, we have to get going now," Buck said to the group. One by one, Tito, Julia, Pico, Ramiro, and the rest stood up and began to applaud.

Ramiro called out at the top of his lungs, "Amigos y amigas, Viva los Gringos Heroes!" A cheer spread around the whole camp, and Buck and Pete blushed in the dark.

"Well, until tomorrow, get some rest everybody," Buck said as he turned Luck on the road and rode off, really just wanting to get some rest. Pete hung on for dear life again, breathing the finally clear air like someone just escaped from drowning.

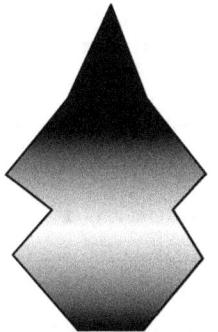

Amanna (11) Greased

"People are homeless and hungry and you're thinking of a rock concert?" Lucky said a bit strongly. Buck and Pete had ridden in late at night and had been telling Lucky about the scene at the fairgrounds. Belle and Bud had gone off to stay with a friend who had been hardly touched by the earthquake, thinking they might give Lucky and Buck time to be alone, become more intimate. But Lucky was tired, eminently pragmatic, and unmoved by the emotions that Buck and Pete had experienced with the group at the fairgrounds, so it was natural that she should be a bit more pessimistic. Buck and Pete, being tired and worked over themselves, did not take it all too kindly. Buck started to get worked up, and so Pete just excused himself to go tend to Luck who was outside.

"Listen, you don't have to shoot down an idea before considering it," Buck protested.

"Well, have you ever thought about more realistic possibilities like lobbying the government agencies for more aid or doing a collection around neighborhoods that weren't so hard hit?" Lucky shot back quickly.

Buck just let it sink in, and let go of any temptation to argue with her. Something in him was just too tired. Something in him had grown tired of trying to convince her of things. He had a feeling in his heart that he wanted to share, some kind of magic that was hard for him to express, and he was worn down from trying. He just turned around, put his hat back on, and walked out the door.

"Those are great ideas, I might just suggest them," he said as he closed the door behind him.

Lucky threw a towel at the door and grumbled. Then she ran up to it and opened it and said, "Buck, wait, it's just..." but it was too late. He and Pete had already disappeared into the darkness.

"Oh, I suppose that was all my fault," she said out loud to no one, she thought.

"If you suppose so," came a thought in her head.

"Oh now you show up!" she said out loud again, this time knowing she was speaking to her friend, Govinda.

"I have been here all along," Govinda responded.

"Well, why didn't you tell me something better to say?" she asked.

"You didn't ask," he answered matter-of-factly.

Lucky began to let it all out. She started throwing things around and cursing everything for a good minute or two before she finally calmed down. "What am I supposed to do? I love you, but I can't have you! I have Buck, but I don't know that I want Buck. I've got more work than any man with half the respect! Just as soon as things start to get a little better You shake everything up and it is worse than ever! I don't know that I can take it anymore!" Finally she just stopped and stood breathing in the middle of her kitchen.

"Are you done?" came the quiet voice in her head.

"No, I'm not done," Lucky revived her tirade. "All that I do, it is never enough. Never enough to get respect, never enough to get real answers, and now I'm going crazy having an argument with a voice in my head! It is all some slippery slope and I just keep sliding! How am I supposed to take all of this?" Gradually she slowed down and was just breathing heavily in the center of the room again.

"Are you done, now?" asked the small voice again.

She resisted for a minute and then gave in. "Yeah, I'm done."

"Good. Are you ready for an answer?" He asked her.

"Yes! Thank you! Anything! What? How do I know You're You and I'm not just experiencing some psychotic episode?" she threw her hands up in the air, and then caught herself, still a bit self-conscious about having an active conversation with a voice in her head.

"Do I sound crazy?" He asked.

"No," she said simply. "But how do I know you're not just a voice in my head?"

"Does it make a difference?" He asked.

"Yes," Lucky insisted. "I don't want to be crazy!"

"Okay," He answered, "because you asked, and because I love you so, I will tell you how to tell the difference. I am always here for you, but you are always free to walk away from Me. You can always deny Me, and turn away. Some psychotic neuroses could never be silenced so quickly."

"I never want to walk away from you," Lucky insisted. "I want to learn how to always be closer to You."

There is an old science of spirituality you are meant to learn, the science of Yoga. You are to meet a good friend of mine, Babaji. You have heard of Mt. Madonna?" He asked her.

"Yeah, the mountain and the city park oh, you mean that crazy ashram-retreat place up on the hill?" she wondered.

"That's the place. You must go," the inner voice confirmed. "He is a man there who will help you understand."

"But I told you I am not sure I believe in all this Indian religion stuff," Lucky said at loud.

"Reality does not require belief, although it helps" Govinda replied.

"Are you saying that a single cultural description of reality takes precedence over all others?" Lucky asked pointedly.

"No, not absolutely. It does for you right now," Govinda replied. "That is the point. Each story of God has something to offer someone, and right now there is much you can learn from the Hindu religion."

"But I told you, I am not sure that Hindu religion has what I need to learn right now," Lucky complained.

"You will learn of many faiths from many teachers. You do not know what you need to learn, because you have not learned it yet," Govinda reasoned with her.

"I need more than that," Lucky said. "I need some sort of visceral proof that what you are saying is real! I need something tactile, something hard and soft at the same time, I want something that will fill me, surround me, overtake me, and show me what God is, what God can be, something that can show me who you really are..."

"You have asked," Govinda said. "I know what you need, but you need to ask. What you ask for is here for you in this form." This time, somehow, the voice was not in her head, and the presence was not imaginary or intellectual. It was the flute. An odor came first, something like jasmine, or gardenia, or lotus. It was like some incense that could not be burned out. It came first, but it seemed to follow the flute like an echo, or did the echo follow the flute?

Lucky began to recognize when transcendence started to overtake her. It was something that was hard to describe, even to herself. It was time outside of time, it was place outside of place, it was something very different but all too familiar. It made her feel like waking life was a dream, some sort of prepackaged false reflection of something that was really real. All she knew is that when she sensed transcendence, He was inside of it. Whatever it was, He was with it, He emanated it, but nothing of it was separate from

Him. He was no man, but he was a person, a real person, infinite yet singular, a bundle of contradictions yet at the same time the answer to every paradox.

He was there, and He was the answer to all that she asked, the object for all of her yearnings. He came to her again, shining like the sky in a golden cup, beaming more beauty than she could have asked to behold. He was everything she had demanded, when she had demanded everything, and yet He was even more than she could have asked for. In each aspect He answered needs that she had never even identified. Questions she had not asked, hopes she had not dared to hope, dreams she did not dream of dreaming.

He went over to her, and took her hand, and she melted into him, forever his. He lifted her, and carried her to a room that was hers, but not hers. It was draped with delicate tapestries and jeweled strings and growing lotus vines. Her bed was her bed but not her bed. It was her bed but in some other fashion, some other form, infinitely more resplendent.

"In this form, I can be your lover," Govinda said. "In India they have held a conception of me as all things, God as Lover, God as Mother, Father, Friend, Child. It was because of what you longed for, the form that you wished for, that I have come to you this way." He told her, and she understood. She realized in that moment that there was so much about God that she did not know, so much that she still had to learn. And she realized now how much she loved this form, how much it moved her. He took her down to the bed, and He took her, He knew her, He loved her, like He loved her as a gopi so many ages before. He filled her, He gave her everything, and more. He was everything a man could be, He did everything a man could do. He showed her that nothing was dirty, nothing was unholy, when in the full consciousness of God. He took her all the way, and beyond, for there was nothing that was not part of the perfection that he was teaching her. He showed her what was meant in Tantra, what was taught in ancient secret mystery schools. He showed her things that were meant for her alone, and after a time that felt like forever, her showed her the climax of full blissful ecstasy, from crown to toe, blowing away all feelings of separateness in a peak thrust of unity. She was there, and she stayed, feeling Him, His home, His music, His strength, His fullness, floating like a feather in a sea of warm pleasure, so much joy and contentment that she lost herself. She lost time, she lost place, she lost consciousness.

When she awoke, she was in her bed, and it WAS her bed, although it was different. It still smelled like jasmine, or gardenia, or lotus, and the light streaming in through the window was like no light she had ever seen. Oh it was sunlight, but it was different, or maybe her eyes were different. She was different, that much she finally realized. Her life was now forever changed, she concluded. Nothing could ever be the same, no one in her life would ever be the same. She was so changed that surely everyone she met would be changed, because how could anything be the same?

"Hellooo?" came Belle's voice from the kitchen door. "You awake, dear? Ready for some breakfast?"

Lucky came wandering out of her room, rather oblivious of her appearance, which was as disheveled as her insides were blissful. She blithely wandered over to her mom and gave her a kiss and a hug.

"My don't you smell nice," Belle said. "Is that a new fragrance?"

"I'm not wearing any," she said with a smile, not connecting the dots. Belle froze for a minute and looked deeply at her daughter.

"You're wearing something," Belle concluded. "Something floral."

"Oh, that," Lucky realized what was going on. "It's just...a new soap."

"A new soap, eh?" Belle responded suspiciously. "Dare I say you didn't just come from the shower."

"Oh, maybe last night," Lucky reached. "You know, I like to take showers at night."

"Yes, and you are a terrible liar," Belle surmised. "And you are strangely dreamy. Did you have a visitor last night?"

"Oh, Ma, does it matter?" Lucky wondered.

"So, you did have a visitor last night!" Belle concluded. "Mothers can tell these things. And probably the same one that gave you the lotus necklace too, huh?"

"Oh, Mother, it really doesn't matter," Lucky maintained. "What's for breakfast?"

"Trying to change the subject, too," Belle guessed. "I'll wager too that you did more than sleep. He certainly skedaddled quick, didn't he?"

"Maybe he's still in the bedroom," Lucky changed her tactics, perhaps trying to make her Mom uncomfortable with the whole discussion. Belle would have none of it.

"Well, bring him out, then," she suggested. "I'm sure he's hungry, too."

Lucky shook her head. "It's not so simple. There's no one there."

"It never is simple these days any more, is it?" Belle complained. "Well, I would like to meet this new man in your life someday. He is a man, isn't he?"

"Yes! Of course," Lucky replied. "I mean, mostly..."

"Mostly? What's that supposed to mean?" Belle inquired.

"Look, Ma, forget it okay? You wouldn't understand," Lucky claimed.

"I might understand more than you think," Belle stated, a bit hurt.

"It's not that," Lucky tried to explain, "It's just that...look, when I know how to explain it, you'll be the first to hear about it all, okay."

"I guess that's about all I can ask," Belle resigned herself to breakfast. "Eggs and potatoes okay?"

"Sounds wonderful," Lucky said. "I'm famished."

"Well, coming right up. Your dad will be in soon," Belle said as she opened a window. "Well it does smell flowery in here. Wears fragrances, eh, is he a hippy type? A bit effeminate, maybe?"

"Mother, please!" Lucky exclaimed.

"Okay okay," Belle gave in. "I'll stop going on about it. But I do want to clear that fragrance before your Dad gets in. It seems to hang in the air. It is pretty."

"Yes, it is," Lucky agreed. "Well, you'll have it smelling like eggs and potatoes in no time."

"Yes, it will for sure," Belle agreed. "How are the ranch repairs coming along? Have you seen Buck lately?"

"Of course, I saw him yesterday," a bit too incredulously.

"What's wrong? Did something go wrong?" Belle detected.

"No, no, he just left, last night..." Lucky trailed off.

"What, he left last night what..." Belle dug. "He didn't have a run in with your new friend, did he?"

"No no, nothing like that," Lucky shook her head. "He just was a bit upset, that's all."

"Upset? What about?" Belle wondered.

"Oh, it was nothing," Lucky brushed it off. "We were both just...tired."

"Well, don't you upset that man," Belle scolded her. "He probably senses something with you and this new friend, and the ranch needs him right now."

"Don't worry, Mom, Buck won't go away," Lucky said, but somehow she wasn't so sure, for some reason.

They finished making the breakfast together in relative silence. Belle knew something definitely was going on. A mother's intuition could not be fooled very effectively. She knew Lucky was hiding something, but she did not want to press it. She knew that she would figure it out sooner or later. Lucky, for her part, did not like keeping anything from her mother, but how could she ever explain what happened the night before in terms that her mother would understand? She felt convinced that her mom would think it was some sort of demonic possession, or something. Belle's God most definitely did not come down and have sex with women, no matter how spiritual they might be. But she knew that the bloodhound side of Belle was on the trail, and would keep hunting down as many clues as she could. Lucky really had no idea what to do, and then she remembered the message about going to Mt. Madonna. Maybe that would help. It certainly could not hurt. The name seemed to have a significance, too. Perhaps in the figure of the Madonna there was an image of God that could bridge their different perspectives, immaculate conception aside.

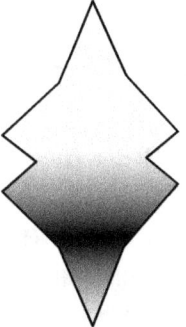

Agappa (12) Babajied

The road up Mt. Madonna was curvy and quite beautiful. Buck would probably think of a woman on these roads, Lucky thought. Thinking of Buck for the first time in a while made her heart quicken for a minute. She really did not want to hurt him, but she felt she could not give him what he really wanted, right now. There were so many thoughts about her night with Govinda that she felt he fulfilled her in every way. How could she ever explain that to some old Indian holyman? She had stopped by the Watsonville library to find out a little more about this strange man who lived on the top of this mountain in a yoga retreat, and what she found had quite startled her. Baba Hari Dass, or just Babaji as his followers called him as a sign of respect, had led an interesting life indeed.

Lucky had almost expected to read of some controversial figure, perhaps some sort of charlatan a la Maharishi Mahesh Yogi, the leader of the "Red People" who had taken over the town of Antelope Oregon. All she really knew of the Maharishi was the story of how he had disappointed the Beatles and had been the inspiration for some song, a poor fund of knowledge garnered second-hand from biased western media sources, certainly, but one that had been sufficient to color the perception of most Americans towards Indian yogis.

Baba Hari Dass, on the other hand, seemed to be so spiritually pure as to be above reproach, and Lucky could find no source that even hinted at a negative impression of him. He had been born near Almora India in 1923, and he had practiced yoga for his entire life, spending much of his early life living as a mendicant in the jungle. He had been practicing a vow of silence since 1952 and taught primarily by example and short messages scrawled on a tiny chalkboard, a rather unlikely practice for a charlatan, Lucky thought. He had become widely known in the western world through the book "Be Here Now," a simple tome that Lucky had nearly devoured in less than an hour, by a former Harvard professor who had become a devotee himself, Baba Ram Dass formerly Dr. Richard Alpert.

The teaching and relationship between Babaji and Ram Dass was so simple and pure that Lucky could find no error in it, no dogmatic fogginess or irrelevant discourse. Babaji had founded the Hanuman Fellowship in California in 1974 to spread Ashtanga (Eight-limbed) Yoga, and, perhaps most telling to Lucky, had broken significant gender barriers by mentoring his pregnant student Jeannine Parvati's prenatal Yoga, and supporting her desire to continue practicing throughout her pregnancy, considered taboo to some traditionally male-centered Yoga strictures. The result of this relationship was the seminal *Prenatal Yoga & Natural Childbirth*, a book that Lucky had seen many times on the shelves of her mother-friends. This last bit convinced Lucky that there might actually be something to this silent Yogi, but she really had no idea what to expect.

As she turned the last curve onto Mt. Madonna Road off of highway 152, Lucky anticipated some ramshackle buildings amidst weedy fields and some hippy commune type shelters. The simple gate stood open as her truck pulled onto the property, and Lucky was astonished by the carefully manicured gardens and immaculate statuaries, even gasping as she caught sight of the frozen figure of her Govinda amidst other forms of elephant-headed deities and lion fountains spouting streams of gushing water. There was certainly an elegance to the place that reminded her instantly of the land she had first visited with Govinda.

"It's like someone else has been there too and wants to replicate it here on Earth," Lucky thought to herself.

"Babaji is a regular visitor to my home," came the flute-like voice of Govinda in her head.

"You really care for this Man, don't you?" Lucky thought out loud.

"I love My devotees more than I love Myself," He affirmed.

Lucky parked her truck in the shade of a redwood grove, watching some students disembark from a bus near a large lotus pond. The pinkblue blossoms made her think of her Lover's skin. Everywhere there seemed to be hints of him, and other references she did not understand but felt must be appropriate, like elephants and monkey-headed gods.

There were so many buildings, all perfectly designed and built, that she did not know quite where to go. The books she read had said that Babaji was a master architect, so she should have guessed that the grounds would be spectacular, but they were surprising nonetheless. As she stood admiring the majestic temple grounds floating over the exquisite views of Monterey Bay, the distinct sounds of a flute carried over to her from one prominent building in the center of it all. Instinctively she followed it to its source.

As she removed her shoes in the anteroom of the large hall, she noticed two dogs lazily glancing her way from the front. "Even the dogs here are blissful," she thought as she distinctly saw one of their eyes twinkle. After removing her shoes, seemingly predicated by the shoe-filled shelves that lined the wall, she continued toward the source of the music. As she rounded the corner into a large room booming with the music she was struck with such an image that she thought that she was surely losing her mind.

Right there in the middle of a large group, she could clearly see her Govinda doing ceremonial battle with a tall man with multiple heads, all talking in unison. She rubbed her eyes and nearly fainted until she gradually realized she was watching a play of some kind with the most remarkable masks she had ever seen. All of the participants in what had gradually revealed itself to be a rehearsal where intensely focused on the proceedings that no one noticed her entrance, no one, that is, except a small figure in the corner who was staring right at her and absolutely beaming. She figured this must be Babaji, and he slightly nodded, as if in affirmation. A woman devotee standing nearby noticed the direction of his attention and came over to Lucky. The woman walked softly and gracefully and approached with hands pressed together in the prayerful symbol of greeting.

"I am Sita. May I help you?" she asked.

"I am Lucky Star. I would like to speak with Babaji," Lucky said.

"I am afraid that would be impossible, right now," Sita said. "We are in rehearsal for the Ramayana. You could make an appointment..." She was stopped by the Lucky's gaze which was transfixed by Babaji who was still staring at her with such blissful familiarity. Sita turned around and with a simple hand signal Babaji motioned for Lucky to come sit down near him. Sita bowed and motioned for Lucky to come on in and sit down. She rather timidly took the designated spot and followed Babaji's gaze back to the scene in front of them, which continued unabated. Babaji seemed utterly delighted with everything that was going on, and as he glanced about Lucky seemed to notice things for the first time. She saw exquisite costumes and masks all around, including one she recognized as the monkey-god from outside. She also noticed some technician types who were operating remote controls that must be the answer to the many-mouthed monster. Mostly she was transfixed by a young man with blue skin dressed in gold who symbolized her Lover, she thought.

Babaji noticed her attention and quickly scribbled on his tablet which he showed to her, "Almost lifelike, eh?"

"Yes, almost," she agreed, having just thought how no earthly actor could really capture the majesty of her Lover.

"Govinda?" she asked, pointing at the blue-skinned actor.

Babaji quickly wrote, "Rama—the same," and nodded.

Lucky was transfixed by the action in front of her, with its magical gods and mythical monsters all singing and backed up by heavenly sounding music. Time rather slipped away when suddenly she realized that Babaji had signaled some sort of break and most of the actors broke apart and started taking off masks and eating snacks and talking amongst themselves. Babaji scrawled another message as Sita came and sat down beside them.

"I wanted you to see our rehearsal of Ramayana," Lucky was able to read before Babaji effortlessly erased it with the graceful swipe of a small cloth.

"What brings you up to our ashram?" Sita asked her.

"A friend...told me to come," Lucky answered, not elaborating, and Babaji instantly responded with another message.

"Some friend," the simple white on black slate communicated for the Yogi.

"Yes, some friend, indeed," Lucky said, her defenses lowering. "A lot of questions and unusual experiences have led me here." The Indian Master's eyes glowed, and Lucky seemed to feel a presence in her mind that was similar to Govinda.

"Are you here?" Lucky said in her head.

"Yes," came two voices in harmony, and Babaji nodded.

"So, you know Govinda?" Lucky asked out loud.

"Govinda is one of the names of Krishna," Sita expounded. "An avatara of Lord Rama and Vishnu." Babaji just continued to beam.

"Well, I don't quite understand all of that, but I do know that an amazing being very much like that character, has been coming to me, and...uh...changing me," Lucky tried to explain.

"If you have seen a vision of Vishnu," Sita began, "you are very fortunate. Many holy people have meditated for years to have such a vision." Babaji shook his head but was still beaming.

"But that's just it," Lucky said. "I wasn't even really meditating. I was just mostly minding my own business, and he just...came to me."

Babaji was now writing out a rather long sentence, and Sita and Lucky waited with patience and excitement. He finally finished. "Perhaps many lifetimes of meditation."

"But I'm not even sure I believe in other lifetimes," Lucky protested.

Babaji wrote again.   Lucky was beginning to experience what was a common feeling of many devotees at the ashram, the delightful anticipation of those simple written words flowing from the hand of Babaji. Finally it came, "What other proof do you need?"

Lucky began to suspect that this small holyman was operating on a level wholly unlike any other she had met or encountered before.

"Can you read my mind?" she thought rather pointedly.

Lucky heard a very distinct voice, different than Govinda. "Only very loud thoughts that I am meant to hear."

"Oh so you can speak words in my head," Lucky said in her mind, "But I thought you're not supposed to talk."

The same mental voice responded, "I vowed not to speak, not not to think. Besides, it is hard to write on a chalkboard in your head. Perhaps it is all your imagination. Does it make a difference?"

"Yes," she said out loud. Lucky still was not sure if she was not just hearing voices, but she really began to think it might not matter. Babaji's everpresent smile and his simple responses were sufficient to calm Lucky's concerns about what he might find in her mind. She did not really have any big secrets, but everyone fears a bit what others might think of them if all of their thoughts were apparent. Somehow Babaji emanated such unconditional love that she no longer really worried about anything that might be in her mind, and slowly her tongue was loosed until she was telling the whole experience to both of them.

She went on and on, going into exquisite detail, speaking freely in such a way that only a saint with a vow of silence can elicit. Certainly he was not likely to spill many of her secrets on his little slate, and Lucky felt pretty certain that Babaji would not disclose much of any that she said. He merely sat with an air of pure compassion, only occasionally nodding and twinkling and beaming with love the whole time. Sita listened as well with rapt attention.

"...and He seemed to be pushing and pulling me at the same time, accelerating me for some purpose that only He understood," Lucky was spilling out. "He led me along paths I never knew existed, physical and spiritual. It was all so strange, and yet at the same time so familiar. I suppose it must be from some past life experience, because I was confronted with so many alien experiences yet I never resisted a thing. He seemed to know exactly what I needed, what I was thinking, what I was feeling. I just never expected to find God in this way, you know, as a lover. How can God be a lover?" She finally asked a question, and Babaji obligingly wrote an answer.

"You are a Gopi," his latest message read.

"A Gopi?" Lucky asked. Babaji glanced at Sita in some sort of non-verbal que.

"A Gopi is one of the milkmaids that were the lovers of Krishna," Sita explained. "Together they cared for his cows, and their physical love represented the highest form of Sacred Union. In our beliefs God can be experienced more than just as a Father, also as a Mother, Friend, Lover, even a child. Many believe that the highest form is as a lover."

"Now some more begins to make sense," Lucky understood. "It is about love, and also much about cows. He has said that I am to help the West heal our relationship with cows." At this Babaji seemed to sparkle and agree strongly. He quickly wrote a new message.

"At Home his main sacred task is to care for his beloved cows," he wrote.

"Yes, they are beautiful, and I know his love. Have you been there?" Lucky asked.

"Yes, in Samadhi, but not as his conjugal lover," someone seemed to say, and Babaji nodded and seemed to have said it as if he was tired of writing, or as if the emotion of the message was quicker than the hand. It seemed they could go on forever, but she thought that perhaps she was taking up too much time of the rehearsal. As if on cue, the actor who was playing Rama came up, blue paint and all, and humbly interrupted their conversation.

"Excuse me, Master," he addressed Babaji. "May we resume rehearsal?"

Babaji responded with a simple flourish of the hand that communicated so much, like go ahead, no need to ask, you should have been doing it already. The actor hurried back to the group which was spontaneously reforming around the action. Lucky thought about how much he did not look like her lover, now, so earthly, such a pale reflection.

"Why blue?" Lucky asked Babaji, who merely smiled and pointed to the sky. The actors resumed their elaborate dance and performance, and Lucky marveled at the spectacle of it all. It was so much energy, so much spirit, that it almost seemed garish, yet there was a purity to it all that excused all excesses. Lucky thought how this really was a reflection of the work of her Lover, how He did so much with so much flourish that it could so easily be seen to be overdone. Yet everything was done to the perfect extreme, provide the most fulfilling experience. As she sat through the rest of the rehearsal, she gradually lapse into complete wordless silence, overwhelmed by the complete spectrum of the scene. She felt like she had found a home, one that was not her true Home, but one that perhaps was the closest facsimile on Earth. She saw the commitment of all the people, the depth of devotion they all had for Babaji and his teachings.

All this went on, seemingly at his direction, yet he never said a thing. He hardly even gave directions on his tablet, yet somehow he really was directing it all. He seemed to suffuse throughout all of it, yet a part of none of it. Somehow he expanded through all of it, all the while just sitting in his little body at the side of the room. Lucky could not help but feel immense love for him. He looked at her and seemed to beam even more in response.

As the evening wrapped up Lucky just bathed in the immensity of it all. She still could hardly explain all she had been experiencing, but at least now she felt less alone in it all. Of course, it was hard to explain the glorious communion she had been going through as being alone, yet her upbringing had really never really prepared her for such events. And this of course brought to mind her mother, and she still did not feel any closer to knowing what to say to her. She suddenly felt the need to ask Babaji, who was still sitting silently by her side.

"What can I say to my family about all this?" she asked him.

He quickly wrote an answer, which was, "Family bigger than you think."

"Yes, I'm sure it is," Lucky mostly agreed. "But I'm talking about my actual mother and father."

Babaji quickly wrote out another response, "Me too." Lucky understood what he meant, that somehow they were big enough to understand all of this, on some level, but she still did not know how she could present it to them. Well, she sure knew how to talk to her mom, and she certainly had confronted her on many heavy issues in the past, but something in her almost did not want to. There was something pure and unique in her experience with Govinda and she kind of did not want to share it with her mom. Maybe she would understand it on some level, but Lucky felt she could not really understand it in the way she felt it. Well maybe her mom could not really understand it, especially the sexual elements, but Lucky knew she would continue to push relentless until she found out something. Lucky really was an open book to her mom, and she was comfortable with that, she just wasn't sure that her mom would be comfortable with all that she might discover about her daughter. And her father, well her father, although he would probably learn to accept what she had to say, was like many men his age in that he seemed to avoid all topics that dealt with sex or feminine issues, and he seemed so fragile that the shock of such a discussion might kill him.

Lucky looked to her side and Babaji was just staring at her with utter compassion. He wrote something again. "My father died at 56." When he noticed that she had read it, he added, "Very young." He wiped the slate clean and just left it blank, but continued to look at her in such a knowing way that she felt he really understood. Oh sure, a skeptic could describe a purely logical sequence of their meeting that could explain everything without psychic powers, but she somehow felt he just naturally and easily could read her mind. If he had a reaction to this last thought, he did not register it. He just looked at her, into her, beyond her, with her, something of her she could not say exactly. There was some aspect where he just looked, and whatever she was ready to see in herself is what he seemed to be looking at. In this sense he was some sort of eternal witness, never judging, just watching in some blissful detachment.

She allowed herself to just sit in his presence as the performers finished up, packed their things, payed their proper respects, some bowing silently, some thanking him verbally, and some crouching forward to touch his feet, and finally filing out through the door. Sita was some sort of manager for the whole affair, but as such she seemed a perfect extension of Babaji, effortlessly understanding even the most understated of his directions. She dealt with all the last rehearsal details, and then came up to the two of them, and suddenly the three of them were alone.

"Well, what do you think?" Sita asked Lucky, beaming love at her in the same familiar manner as Babaji.

"I am blown away, literally," Lucky responded. "I don't know quite what to think. It might take some time to absorb it all."

"Well, I hope you will come back to join us again," Sita said hopefully.

"Oh, my, certainly, that is the least I can say," Lucky affirmed. "I just don't understand it all really."

"Just part of being alive, I would say," Sita commented, and Babaji agreed.

"Thank you so much for everything," Lucky said. "I have to be going, but may I, perhaps, spend a private moment in the gardens?"

Babaji smiled and responded with a gesture that very clearly said, "My gardens are your gardens, please enjoy them." With that simple goodbye, Babaji said so much, and as she left the room and put her shoes back on, Lucky realized that not talking, in some ways, was an aid to communication. Sita was seeing her out the door, and the same dog was out front wagging her tail in approval.

"This is very rare, you understand," Sita pointed out. "And auspicious."

"I do understand," Lucky replied. "And I am very grateful. I feel like I have found a new part of my family."

"I believe you are a sister," Sita said. "Perhaps from many lifetimes." She added a wink and bowed with her open palms pressed together.

"Perhaps," Lucky said, and she also bowed with her hands together. "Thank you, Sister."

Sita just smiled and turned gracefully, but seemed to say "thank you as well." Everyone said so much without words around this place, Lucky thought. It is what must come from living and not talking. She thought she might give it a try, now and then. She walked around the building to go into the gardens, and was stunned by the beauty of the sunset over the Pacific Ocean. Reds, oranges, yellows, and violets mixed like rainbow sherbet, and Lucky thought that there were times when this world was so beautiful that she understood why Govinda created it.

"I am glad you like it," came the familiar flute like voice in her head.

"I love your friends and family," she said to Him.

"I am glad, because then you begin to truly understand," he whispered to her.

"Perhaps I do," she thought.

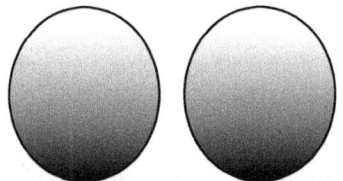

OnaOna (13) Entangled

Buck rode up to the ranch, tied Luck up by the trough, and paused for a moment before he went into the house. He had been dutifully doing his work about the ranch for several days without going in to say hello to the family. He was sure they had noticed, and he certainly did not want to seem rude. He just did not know what to say, and did not want to feel uncomfortable in front of everyone with so many unsaid emotions flying around. Finally, thought, he knew that something had to be said. At least to Lucky. Belle and Bud would probably understand, and probably even take his side, but he did not want it to go that way. What was the point of getting the approval of the mother and father if you could not get the approval of the daughter? In all, he had just had enough. Too many things had gone on for too long. He knew stuff was changing for Lucky, and though he still felt the same in so many ways about her, he was changing too. Gradually he steeled his determination and entered the house.

Lucky was alone in the kitchen, and this made him feel better. Even as he saw her, though, he began to wonder what he could even say to her. What could he say that he did not know already how she would respond? It had been coming for a long time, though, and something had to be said, if only so that she would know that something had been changing inside of him. Perhaps she understood that already, too, like they seemed to understand so much about each other. At least they used to. But, even if that had changed, was not that what he wanted to say anyway, and would she not have sensed it already, too. Perhaps, but only by saying something would he get it over with. He walked into the kitchen.

"Howdy, stranger," she said, with a resonance that she perhaps did not intend. "You've been scarce around here lately."

"I've been taking care of my jobs," he said defensively.

"That's not what I mean," Lucky defended herself. "I mean, you haven't come into the house lately."

"I know, that is part of what I have come in here to talk about," Buck said tentatively.

"Oh?" Lucky said, slightly suspicious but also anticipating what was coming. "Please, talk."

"Well," Buck cleared his throat. "Look, I know we've been going through a lot, we've gone through a lot, alone and together, I mean, not together, but, well, you know what I mean..."

"Do I?" Lucky asked.

"Well, I think you do," Buck believed. "I just had to speak with you, to tell you..." He paused.

"Yes, go ahead," she prodded.

"You see, I've hung around here for a long time," he began. "Kind of waiting..."

"Waiting for what?" Lucky kept asking short questions, trying to get him to just say it, whatever it was.

"Oh, you're not making this any easier," Buck complained.

"I'm not trying to make it hard," Lucky pointed out.

"I know, I know," Buck relaxed. "Look, it's been a long time that I've...been in love...with you, and I don't know if I can wait around any longer."

Lucky's countenance softened and she approached Buck and put her hand on his. "Look, Buck, that is very sweet. You are very dear to me. I could even say I love you, because I do, but something in me...isn't ready...or, just can't."

"I know, I've known it for a while, I guess," Buck said as he stared at the floor. "I just thought I'd wait for you to come around, maybe..."

"Buck, I never asked you to wait..." Lucky pointed out.

"Yes, I know that too, but we just seemed so right for each other," Buck reasoned.

"Yes, we do...did, but, Buck, I'm not right, it's just me, I don't know what's up," she figured. "You are such a special person, I know I would be stupid to lose you, I would, but I lost myself somewhere along the way. I...I just can't. I'm sorry."

"I understand. I knew it, already, really. I don't know why I'm wasting our time," Buck shook his head. "God, I feel like such an idiot!"

"No, Buck, please," Lucky reached out to him. "Don't take it like that. You are such a great guy, and you have been so much for me and my family. God knows my mother will fume at my turning you away. It is natural for you to want us to be together, and any normal intelligent woman would have snatched you up long ago. But it's me, it really is. I know that sounds like a cliché, but it really is me. I am really kind of screwed up. Something is not normal in me, and I don't know when or where it all started, but I have just got to work on me, right now."

"All right, I get it. I can accept that, finally," Buck guessed. "I...don't mean this to sound harsh, but...I don't know if I can stay here at the ranch."

Lucky gulped quietly. She had not really expected this, although she figured she should have. She really had come to rely on Buck to run the Ranch for the last couple of years, and had totally depended on him since the earthquake. Good hands were hard to find and keep, especially with her reputation and her stubborn ways. "That's...understandable," she said, a little shakily.

"Now I won't leave you in the lurch," Buck reassured her. "I'll help to build a new crew here, find the right replacements, Pico is ready to step up, and Ol' Pete sure could use something to do..."

"Oh, come on, Buck, neither of them are a lead of your quality," Lucky said with her manager side coming out.

"Well, thank you, perhaps, but don't underestimate those two, you know. They will do just fine," he said with a definite note of finality. In that moment both of them realized it was true. Buck was leaving and Pico and Pete would do just fine. It would certainly be different. Lucky would have to be hands-on again at the Ranch. She realized in a rush just how much she had come to depend of her special link with Buck to keep things moving along smoothly. She felt a bit queasy when she thought how she would have to shift things to make them work without Buck.

"Where will you go?" she asked, now herself looking at the floor.

"I don't know," Buck shook his head. "Somewhere. Anywhere. I think somewhere I can help people. I like doing that, lately."

"Oh, right, the benefit," Lucky looked up. "How is that going? Look, I'm really sorry I ever was negative about that. It really is a great idea."

"Thank you. It's going really well," Buck brightened. "We got this guy helping us up in Santa Cruz, and it looks like Bill Graham might be on board. You know, I started some of your ideas, too. I got a lot of community donations and we have a FEMA temporary office helping out down here now."

"Wow, that's really great, Buck," Lucky was sincere. "You know, you really do belong helping people. I'm sure you find a lot more appreciation out there than with me."

"That's for sure," Buck laughed, then cleared his throat. "I mean, I've always felt very welcome here and very much a part of the family, you know, except...well, you know. There are some really special people out there."

Lucky had some sort of premonition, and she felt a shiver. She really did not know what was out there, for her or for Buck. What was she doing, anyway, dumping this perfectly good man for what? For an avatar? For a manifestation of God on Earth? What did that mean? Maybe it was all just an illusion. Maybe she was going crazy, making one of the great mistakes of her life. She could not be sure, but she had to go on her feelings. She had to act on her intuition, as she always had, because it had always led her right. But how was it leading her now? She could not even say, for certain. It was all so maddening, and she just could not see how she could share all of it with another person right now.

"Buck, know this, you will always be precious to me, and you will always have a home here on this ranch, if you want it," she assured him.

"Just not the sort of home I want, eh?" he said sardonically.

"I'm sorry, I just can't give that to you. Don't pressure me," she kind of spit out.

Buck began his retreat to the door. "I'm sorry. No pressure, never has been. I've always worked for my keep here." He reached backwards for the kitchen door handle.

Lucky softened. "No, Buck, I'm sorry. You have been...are...irreplaceable. It's...just me, really."

Buck opened the door, understanding but still hurt. "I know, it's okay, I understand, really." He was halfway out the door. "Take care of yourself, Lucky. I have always loved you..."

"Oh, Buck," Lucky failed to hold back tears, now. "I have always loved you, too, really...just..."

"That's okay," he stopped her. "Let's just leave it at that. Goodbye Lucky." And he was gone.

Lucky let the door close, and then collapsed on the floor in tears. Why was she crying? She did not know. She did not understand any of it, she just cried and cried. Cried like a flood, cried like someone who had just been dumped, like she had been rejected herself, when she had let him go. Part of her wanted to get up and run after him, go tell him that she was wrong, that she really loved him and wanted to be with him forever, but she was stuck to the floor, paralyzed.

"WHY ARE YOU DOING THIS TO ME?!" she yelled at the top of her lungs.

"I do nothing," replied a faint voice in her head. He seemed to be growing fainter, and she feared abandonment.

"Why are you leaving? WHAT"S UP WITH YOU!?" she demanded.

"I never leave..." and the voice seemed to fade out altogether.

"UUUHHH!" she screamed, and then was interrupted by her mom coming through the door.

"Oh, Dear, oh dear," her mother embraced her. "Whatever is the matter?"

"Oh, mom!" Lucky let herself melt in sobs in her mother's arms.

"What happened? I just saw Buck leave, and he hardly said hello," Belle said, mystified.

"Oh, Ma, he's leaving!" Lucky informed her mother.

"What!?" Belle was shocked, and she pulled away from her daughter. "But how? Did he refuse you?"

"No, no," Lucky shook her head. "I refused him."

"But I don't understand," Belle started to get emotional herself. "If you rejected him, why are you crying?"

"Oh, Ma! Caused I'm messed up, get it?" she stated flatly. "I'm totally 'f'in screwed up."

Belle's demeanor stiffened. She was beyond being patient with her daughter. "Girl, if you know what's good for you, if you are this messed up over this, then go run after that man!"

"But, Ma! I don't know what's good for me!" Lucky was getting hysterical. "That's what I'm saying, don't you get it?"

Belle got calm but hard. "Yes, I do get it. But I think you don't. Why won't you just trust me? Go after him and claim your life."

"Mom! I'm not like you!" Lucky claimed. "I'm not the kind of woman made to just latch on to some ranch hand and serve him all my life, okay?"

Belle withdrew into herself and away from her daughter. "I see. Well, you really better just work on what kind of woman you are, then." Tears began to roll down Belle's cheeks as she quietly went back out the kitchen door.

Lucky burst into a new bout of crying. She cried until her tear ducts were empty. She lay on the floor, oblivious to the dust and the grime, oblivious to her matted hair. She just lay they there, unable to move.

"So, where are you now? Where is that love now, huh? That special, gold-plaited unconditional love? I need it now!" She stood up, and started to walk about the room. "Come on! You said you'd never leave me! Now I've wrecked my whole life, and for what? What are you? Where are you? Why are you leaving? WHY HAVE YOU LEFT ME!?"

She could hear nothing, only an echo, "Why have you left ME?"

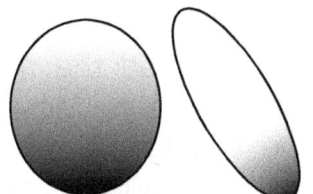

OnaDua (14) Organized

Buck was generally able to stay focused and keep his mind off Lucky, even when he was the ranch. There was always plenty to do, and Pico and Pete had not been easy students at learning the ranch business. It was not that they were not smart enough or good enough, but they just seemed to resist the whole thing. They seemed to feel that Buck and Lucky were just being stubborn, and that the whole thing was going to blow over, and they were going to just fall back into their old roles again. When it came to working with the new committee for the Earthquake Benefit, however, they were all in peak form, working like whirlwinds as if there was no limit to their energy. They all came together to a meeting in Watsonville at the High School, handling all the preliminary aspects of meeting preparations, from having enough tables and chairs to making sure the coffee was fresh and hot.

Julia had invited me to the meeting to bring along some level of professional show business acumen that was needed in the mostly amateur community organization event. Most of the gang were there, Julia, Buck, Tito, Pico, Ol' Pete, and a growing crowd of other members of the community. Everyone was sharing stories of where they had been during the quake. We had all been affected by the quake in a different way, depending upon where we were, yet united by a common sense of heightened purpose. I had been clinging for life on a beam at the Barn Theater at UCSC, only somewhat reassured by the realization that the thick redwood supports supporting the theater had already lasted through the 1906 earthquake.   I had the fortune of still having a house, minus electricity, and so felt a distinct drive to help those who had come through with less.   Many others had come through with similar stories, each having that particular minute or two seared into their memory.

"I was down by Tortilla Flats, by the beach," Julia was saying to the group that had assembled pre-meeting, "when I saw this long crack form down the street and come right between my legs."

"Must have been a male earthquake," Ol' Pete said, garnering a laugh from the mostly male but casual group. Julia was certainly a beautiful woman, and she had the poise and charitable heart that made all men putty in her hands.

Buck slapped Pete on the back of the head. "Hey, you dirty old man!"

"Well, I'm old, so why not be dirty?" he replied with a form of logic.

"Thanks for defending my honor, Buck," Julia said, a bit coyly, but with humor.

"My pleasure, ma'am," he said, giving Pete a scowl but then a wink when Julia turned away.

"M.C. here tells me that stagehands can be a bit crude," Julia said, pointing in my general direction.   "So I guess that's what we're inviting into our midst."

"Only when they are awake," I point out. "Which is a surprisingly small portion of the day." This also garnered a laugh. Stagehands were second only to Teamsters when it came to being acceptable targets of denigration.   We continued the banter for a few minutes as more people came in and joined the group, exchanging more personal stories and updates.

"So how is the latest book coming?" Julia asked me. "M.C. writes as well as works the stage," she told the rest of the group, which still informally chatting and moving about.

"Oh, it's coming along well," I said. "Plenty more inspirational material every day."

"Do you write about things that actually happen or make it up?" Tito asked me, handing me a cup of coffee.

"Thanks. Both, really," I answered. "I like to mix it up. It's all fiction really, but there is plenty of historical material and actual people mixed in to give it real flavor. I like to keep the readers guessing."

"What are you working on right now?" Julia asked.

"A book about the ghosts of Rock and Roll," I said. "Real stories, but I like to play with the narrative and tweak the perspective and all that. I usually put myself in as the narrator or character or something."

"Interesting," Julia said. "So can you be a God-like narrator and a character at the same time?"

"No, God is a different character altogether," I gave respect where it was due. "My narrator is more like a fool with inside information." That was meant to get a laugh, but it kind of went out into the field.

"How do you get time to do all that and produce shows?" Buck wanted to know.

"Well, it's surprising how much of the time backstage is downtime," I said. "And so I always keep a notebook handy, and instead of reading the paper or eating donuts I try to write another chapter." A good laugh, this time. I always resorted to self-deprecation in a tight spot. Stagehands were always good for that—comic relief.

Thankfully Julia changed the subject. It took the pressure off from always having to say something witty. "So Buck, thank you so much for all the fundraising. You have been really making so much possible for all of us, making us all look good."

"You look good all by yourself," Pete had to put in. Buck slapped him on the back of the head again. "What?! You saying it's not true?"

"Of course it's true but that doesn't mean you have to say it!" Buck maintained.

"Well, thank you both," Julia blushed, then gathered some papers in front of her to gain a moment. Buck and Pete seemed to be pulling off a good one together, reeling Julia in like a fish, but they were really just doing it spontaneously, having some fun. Julia did not really need much coaxing anyway. "You two are going to be a handful, I see."

Buck and Pete continued a little pantomime half in jest, Buck scolding Pete and Pete acting innocent and slightly perplexed. "Perhaps we should get down to business," Julia launched into it, Buck and Pete finishing their bit with a few light nudges and repeated shushes. "Now, M.C. here has helped us score a major victory. It seems Bill Graham has agreed to take on our benefit." There were a few impressed exclamations and exhortations amongst the group, as if that was the ultimate guarantor of success.

"How did you pull that one off?" Buck asked.

"Well, we just fit into his plans, actually," I said. "They are already planning a benefit in San Francisco and this will just go along with that one. I talked to him at Shoreline and it just seemed like a good fit."

"He's going to volunteer his time for our community?" Pete asked.

"Well, no I never said volunteer. He just agreed to promote it as another earthquake benefit," I informed them. "There are definitely going to be expenses, and not many professionals will do it for free, especially the stagehands. I'm willing to put in through my time, and we will try to get the artists to give what they can, but a benefit is still run like a professional show, just with the proceeds going to the cause." The reality kind of sank in, but it did not really seem to be a deal breaker for anyone.

"What artists are you considering?" Pico asked.

"Well, Bill thought, since it's Watsonville, Santana and Los Lobos would be appropriate," I leaked. The oohs and aahs seemed to say that there were no objections on that level.

"Well, that's wonderful," Julia said. "Are there any complications or issues?"

"Yes, aren't there always," I said. "Mainly, with the venue. Right now the fairgrounds are so tied up with disaster relief that they think there is no way they could host a concert of twenty thousand people or so."

"Surely they will be flexible," Buck said.

"Not necessarily," I told him. "Right now there are some massive issues with sanitation and security and whatnot, and since those are the same issues that we want to increase tenfold, they are not much into it."

"What kind of space do we need?" Tito asked. "Does it have to have lights and sound and everything?"

"No, we can bring all of that in," I said. "Really we just need a big field with parking."

"What about my burnt down farm?" Pete asked. "You can have that. Like some kind of Woodstock West."

"No offense, Pete," Buck protested. "But that's kind of out there, hard to get to you know. Don't we need something more centrally located?"

"Yes," Julia agreed. "Centrally located is good."

"What about here at the High School?" a voice said from the back of the crowd that seemed to get general nods of approval from the group.

"We'd have to get official approval from the school board," I said. "But it could definitely work, in the football field, maybe."

"Well, I'm the Principal," said the voice, moving forward. "Let me introduce myself. Carlos Reyes, Watsonville High Principal, and I'd give it my support. And I think we have a good portion of the school board here now, and I'm sure they'd give it their support." A small chorus of "ayes" around the room. "We'll officially vote on it next week, but I see no reason why we couldn't work it out. Especially with Santana!"

"Okay, then," I agreed. "Let's look into the high school." Everybody really seemed to like that idea, and the meeting seemed to carry on from that point with a momentum of its own. We zipped through normally sticky issues, like security and scheduling, with the Chief of Police already on board and a general sense of determination that just swept aside any possible issue with an air of inevitability. There was definitely a charged feeling going around, which had been the norm since the earthquake, but there was more going on here. Buck and Julia had definitely settled naturally into leadership roles, and I fully supported them in this regard. For my part, I knew there would be all sorts of logistical issues up to the day of that would take my attention and I needed to be able to let others step up and "take the reigns," so to speak. Buck and Julia were taking more than the reigns, getting a definite charge from their position and each other's presence. And everyone seemed to fully approve of the combination, even Pico and Pete, who had a few reservations remembering Lucky, but in the end they joyously joined the procession of approval, recognizing a good thing when they saw it.

Everyone basically zipped through the rest of the issues, probably glossing over some important things, but I was not about to poke holes into their plans. Reality might do that soon enough. Producing shows was a difficult business, and benefits were even harder. It seemed everyone wanted to produce a benefit for this or that favorite cause, wanted to get Bonnie Raitt or Jackson Browne, or both, to come out and play for free. Everyone figured that Bill Graham could just come in and spread pixie dust around and suddenly there would be money for everything. The reality was that such plans rarely played out. An old joke is that if you wanted to raise a million dollars for something you started with $2 million and threw a benefit. But, if there was enough momentum, enough community support, just the right connections, and God wanted it to happen, than you could make it work. Right at that point it seemed like we might meet all those conditions, so I just let it play out. Certainly the earthquake had changed people, brought out the best in everyone, and this time it just might work. At that point I just smiled and nodded and thought about all the things we would have to do. Finally we officially adjourned the meeting, and we turned into the usual after-meeting casual meeting. The final group was much like the beginning, and it was apparent that we were really the main cast of characters of all this. Principal Reyes, stayed with us, occasionally glancing at his watch to let us know that there was a time issue.

"But why can't we get volunteer stagehands?" Buck asked.

"Well, volunteers can do a lot of things," I let him know. "But Bill Graham Presents has an agreement with the stage local here, IATSE Local 611. Certainly we will need all the help we can get. No capable person willing to help will be turned away, but the basic professional stuff on stage will have to be done by the union."

"I never realized that putting on a show was so complicated," Tito said.

"Well, we're not talking about community theater," Julia pointed out. "We are talking about a concert for 20,000 people."

"That's right," Buck agreed. "And if we are going to do this at all we might as well do it right." I loved to see the approach they were taking together, basically backing up whatever I had to say. After all, I really was not trying to pull anything except putting on a great show. This is what it took to make it real, and by running with it Julia and Buck were showing that they might just have what it took to pull it off.

"But do you really think that we will get 20,000 people here?" Pete wondered.

"If we get Santana and Los Lobos," Pico said, "Every Latino and Latina from here to Salinas will show up, and that is just the beginning."

"He's right," Principal Reyes agreed. "Hell, we get nearly that many for a homecoming football game!" We all laughed.

"Not just Latinos, either," I pointed out. "As an earthquake benefit everyone from the whole county will be here."

"All right, then," Pete acquiesced. "I guess my farm really wasn't a good idea after all."

"Yeah, think of Woodstock," I said. "They predicted 100,000 and they got half a million."

"What!?" Principal Reyes exclaimed. "What have I gotten myself into?"

"Relax," I said. "THAT is not going to happen, but we might get around 20,000, which is a big estimate. Might not quite be that, but it should definitely be enough to make it worthwhile."

"Okay, well, looks like we got our work cut out for us," the Principal said and looked like he might get a little bit overwhelmed, or maybe he was just getting tired. "You know, it is getting late, so, like they say, you don't have to go home, but you really can't stay here."

"Yeah, yeah, we should get going," I said.

"Hey, why don't we go out for a drink, and discuss this some more," Julia proposed.

"That's a great idea!" Buck responded quickly.

"Uh, Boss, remember," Pete reminded him, "We got to put in that new feeder at the ranch tomorrow at 7am."

"Si, ohhh," Pico rubbed his temples.

"So what?" Buck retorted. "I'll sleep when I'm dead. This is real life, right now."

"At my age," Pete went into his old man comedy character, "If I don't sleep, I will be dead. Remember, we all came together."

"Hey, it's okay, I'll take you guys home," I offered with a little twinkle. "If they want to go out, let them go out."

"Oh, I see, abandoned for a beautiful woman again," Pete complained.

"But you have your dirty old man thoughts to keep you company," Buck said.

"All right, let's go then," Julia said excitedly. Something was definitely afoot.

"Okay, come on. Don't want to get in trouble with the Principal," I said and I started to herd everyone towards the door.

"Thank you, really, for everything," Principal Reyes said.

"No, thank YOU for being our host," Julia said.

"No problem," he said as he locked the door. "Let's just pull this off without any casualties, okay? Can we do that?"

"I think so," I assured him. We walked to our cars, and Buck and Julia had already joined at the hip and hardly even said goodbye to us. On the surface they were already engrossed with planning issues, but the rest of us could see that they were really engrossed with each other.

"Uh, Boss..." Pico was going to try to interrupt him with some mundane work issue.

"Don't bother," Pete said. "He's gone already."

"Right," I said. "Come on, Gents. Jump in the car." We got in and made our way back through the back roads past Freedom out towards Corralitos. Pico and Pete had pretty much taken up full time residence at the ranch and were settling into running the place. As we pulled up, something in the air seemed to imply that things were really changing, and they tried to cover their unease with questions about stagecraft and other things leading up to the benefit. I was more interested in Ranch issues, always wanting to write some kind of modern western book. They told me about Lucky and the Lucky Star brand, which I saw all over, of course, and after a pregnant pause they told me about Buck's relationship with it all. I now understood more of the subtext of the evening. In all, we became fast friends, and we understood that something like an earthquake really did change people, or, rather, it brought out who they really were all along. The three of us were as different as could be, age and culture wise, but we were united by something greater, the need and ability to serve. We felt ourselves, somehow, to be critical pieces of some larger puzzle, and that served to define us more than any previous labels. As they got out of the car and went their ways in the ranch, I felt some powerful pull of a sort of future nostalgia. The feeling kept with me as I made my way up Freedom Blvd. towards Santa Cruz. What was uniting us? What story was bringing us together in ways that were more important than the smaller stories we had been telling ourselves for our whole lives. Time would tell, perhaps.

I thought about Buck and Julia, and Buck and Lucky, and myself and anyone, and the whole drama of people and events. "Do you know what you're doing?" I wondered.

"Don't I always?" answered the voice in my head. "Do you know what you're doing?"

"Never," I thought emphatically. "I'm just waiting for instructions."

"You got them tonight," came the response.

"All right," I responded, and I drove through the night, trees passing like blurry ghosts in the ocean mist.

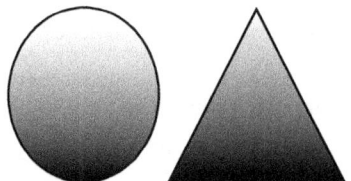

OnaAtrua (15) Dramatized

The many-headed demon Ravana, with multiple mouths moving in unison, strut his hour upon the stage, relishing his moment of near victory as he stole Sita, the wife of Rama. This central storyline was ancient allegory in India, Sita being the Sanskrit word for Wisdom, a goddess even still revered in the West as Sophia. Lucky began to understand more of this, and understand the role of her new friend Sita, and had come to be a volunteer for the touring production of Ramayana, now in final dress rehearsal at the Performing Arts Center at UCSC. As an official UC employee I was Technical Director for the production, the single paid position for the show, which was no simple feat as it entailed managing hordes of volunteers, mostly off-hour engineers and other science types, as they each contributed this or that remote controlled demon or flying monkey, and the dragon. The dragon was our particular great challenge, a life-size scenic piece filled with levers and gears and dismantled fire extinguishers that was a true monster.

The dragon came to me as a bundle of pieces that would be rigged to the flyrail, the counterweighted rope system on the side of the stage. This monumental project consumed all of my attention, while the volunteer engineers where absorbed with more prosaic tasks like figuring out the frequency cross talk that made Ravana's mouths move when Rama spoke, creating the humorous aspect of the appearance of the demon's extra heads mocking everything the blue man-god said.

There was an aspect where I knew the Story was having fun with us, but I had no idea how intricate it was going to be. There were seemingly endless layers within layers of allegory and message that all pointed to a common understanding of the nature of meaning. Babaji just sat in a seat in the audience, directing it all but not saying a word, not even writing much, letting it all suffice with the right people doing the right things, with merely a gesture or two now and then. He certainly was enjoying the whole thing, beaming continuously in his way. I could see that to him it was all a glorious graceful dance, and he had earned the position of just sitting and watching it all come together. To me it was an endless bunch of independent technical projects, improvised by small separate teams, some of which were even potentially dangerous, that all needed to be tweaked and woven into some sort of seamless whole, hopefully without any casualties. I did not, would not, confront Babaji with my own frustrations, because I already knew what he should say, or rather, think, "Perfect! That's why we hired you."

Lucky had become the personal assistant to Sita, who, as Babaji's personal assistant, pretty much seemed to do what he did, which was beam all the time, although in a more verbal way. Sita seemed to understand the particular challenges that I was facing, or at least said so, and Lucky and I were becoming friends. Babaji, in his seemingly effortless way of assigning the proper combinations and allowing things to unfold perfectly, had set up Lucky as the direct person in charge of me, handling directions and information and scheduling and such. He really seemed to be following a larger script than this particular show, however, because there was really nothing for Lucky to do in that regard, but she and I became friends through the whole process. Knowing her to be searching for knowledge, I took to justifying her position by flooding her with all the technical issues as they arose.

"Cross-talk is interference, when two radio-frequency controlled devices interfere with each other," I explained to her about the continuously active Ravana mouths.

"But didn't the engineers put them on different frequencies?" Lucky asked, seemingly truly interested in all this stuff. This may have been an esoteric concern, but for all I knew it could have led to the solutions of real problems. Babaji knew this all along, I am sure, or at least was wise enough to see the patterns and just go with them.

"Yes, but when those frequencies are close and are in a place with lots of steel and concrete that bends radio waves, like a theater, then they can interfere with each other," I explained.

"So what can they do?" she wondered.

"They are going to have to tweek freeks trial and error until they find two that don't cross," I lingoed. "Which is going to be a pain because all those circuits are now imbedded in plaster masks. Might be straight audio feedback, as the system is voice triggered. Right now I have much bigger problems."

"The dragon," Lucky intuited.

"Exactly. The dragon." I said with an air of severity. "The main issue is that no one can tell me exactly how much this stuff is going to weigh in the end, which I need to know so I can add the appropriate counterweights on the rail. I need to even figure out if this is enough for a rail to handle, but these engineers assure me it's fine." There was so much going on I had to run around all day and Lucky had to keep up.

During the specific scene two engineers pulled violently on two puppet lines, while two others ran the rail up and down, and others ran a two foot mouth and adapted fire extinguisher flaming breath, getting quite carried away, almost literally, in the excitement and spectacle of the moment. The effect was enormous, and every scenic and prop trick suddenly worked. I stopped the Dragon, however, to much protest, until I pointed out that the combined weight was pulling the metal up at the floor below the rail, threatening any moment to pull out of the ground and hurl weights into the air and the dragon to the ground.

Fortunately Lucky was there to see the whole thing, as was Sita, and Babaji knew everything, and under everyone's eye I quickly rallied certain volunteers and the university staff to fabricate in the shop a bumper that joined two rails together outside of the failing line, effectively doubling the capacity. The engineers were able to get as wild as they wanted to on the dragon after that, and the effect was a show stopper. Lucky knew everything that happened, and there was perfect challenge where every person had to perform to his or her highest, and during the next night the show came off perfectly, and stunningly so. The performers fleshed out their godlike characters, seeming to bring them to the room, and Lucky was transfixed by the story that she somehow understood to be about her lover. She was beginning to learn how a transcendent God could be many things, and yet always be One. The experience of Godness stretched through as many forms as she figured she could imagine.

I thought about Greek concepts of the Muses, or the Goddesses of art and performance. The presence of Divinity in story and human exchange became a key theme of our musings. I had learned through reading and from Babaji that the reality of the world around us is "maya" or "illusion." But Maya has another meaning as well, as "projection" or, in other words, a big show. Lila is the name of the Lord's Divine Play. All the people of the world were characters in the best script that could ever be written, and it was continually changing and being rewritten by each person, and being produced by God. So many, so many stories would be told simultaneously, each with equal profundity and eloquence, no matter who the players, all the time.

To think of Existence in such a metaphorical way soon loosed the fibrous roots that bound my mind's eye to more rationalistic imagery, and I began to have very vivid dreams where the Muses of Greek Antiquity would come to me to discuss my work. Nine goddesses, sensual yet aloof, describing the ways and means of the fine arts. I felt like I could hardly get any time off, even while asleep, but I did appreciate the Divine Presence. I understood the Muses to be a pure expression of Sacred Essence, not sexual, somehow, but definitely sensual, and in the deepest darkest moments of the fleeting shadowy recessions of the early morning halfsleep, they comforted me, sang me songs, and told me old stories that explained so much that I wish I could remember them.

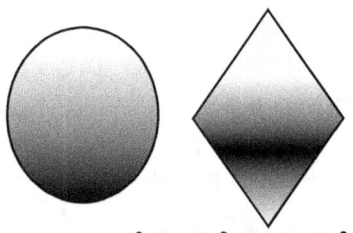

OnaKatero (16) Showered

There was no way that an earthquake benefit was going to go off easily, but that did not mean it was not going to go off well. There was too much energy around it all, too many expectations and too much excitement to not be something epic and historic. As soon as I realized it was actually going to happen I went into high gear and started bringing the best from all around to make it a real show. Against all odds we actually got Santana and Los Lobos to play, and Bill Graham was promoting, but even all that was hardly necessary because the earthquake had brought so much free publicity to the whole thing that we all knew it was going to be a sell out. To a lot of people, particularly Buck and Julia, that was the real challenge, the caveat that made it all worthwhile, so now they could relax. For me, it was when the real work began. It meant that it was not some pie-in-the-sky dream but was a concrete date that would have some concrete needs.

The first issue was that it was outside at a high school football field. Now some people, like Principal Reyes, thought that the football field was fairly well set up all ready for a large show, but they really had no idea. For example, in another meeting, the one where it got real, when I started to list off the things that we would need, like a stage, lighting, sound, fencing, etc., Principal Reyes said that would be no problem because they had all of that. I looked at him and laughed, as did Archie Romano from Bill Graham Presents who I had introduced to the group for the first time, and I explained that all that would probably be no problem because we would bring all that. Principal Reyes looked at us in disbelief as we listed the various companies that would be subcontracted, from sound to stage to lighting to generators to labor, and what each of those would cost.

"But how are we going to make any money for earthquake victims?" Principal Reyes asked.

"You have to understand," Archie was trying to explain to them, "You have to spend this money so that you CAN make money."

"Can we get any of these companies to donate their services?" Buck asked.

"They almost all have non-profit rates," I nodded. "And those would all apply in this case, which is why I have been pushing for our 501c3 non-profit status," I added, looking at Julia, who nodded.   She was sitting next to Buck, and it was obvious by their body language that they were becoming a couple. Everyone seemed to accept it in stride. "But no one is likely to donate their services." Every once in awhile I would go back to the Muses in my memory from the dream and try to squeeze out a little inspiration to keep me going.

"Look," Principal Reyes was still incredulous. "I have a brother-in-law who owns Watsonville Lighting. I'm sure he would be willing to donate his services. And we have a PA already, and our field has lighting."

"Is he serious?" Archie asked me.   "Watsonville Lighting, is that a real production house, or some lamp and appliance shop?".

"Basically," I nodded. "Home electrics." Archie threw up his hands and shook his head. "Look, Principal Reyes, all due respect, but we cannot use Watsonville lighting or your PA, and your field lights only maybe for house lights."

"Mercury halide lights?" Archie asked.

"Yeah, stadium lights, you know." I said.

"Walkout, at best," Archie concluded, meaning the lights would maybe be useful at the very end of the show.

"Listen," I think I know what's best on my field," the Principal insisted.

"He is serious, isn't he?" It was Archie's turn to be incredulous. "Look, when you decide to sign with BGP, for that couple of days, it's not your field anymore, got it? It's Bill Graham's."

"You look," Principal Reyes was getting a little upset. "If you don't like to play by my rules, you can't play on my field."

"DONE!" Archie exclaimed and immediately turned to me. "So the fairgrounds are out, eh? What about the Graham Hill Showgrounds you were talking about where we did the Doobies a few years ago? You got them as our backup, right, like we talked about?" With one swift sentence Archie had erased the rest of the room and was already advancing a totally different show. He was a very successful producer and he had learned to work this was out of necessity.

"You were looking into another venue without talking to us?" Julia asked me pointedly. Murmurs and grumbles rippled through the crowd.   I was definitely in a tight spot. I had made a career between negotiating between show business companies like Bill Graham Presents and non-profit organizationss, but it was never easy. There were certain things that production companies did that may have seemed rather crass and brazen to community groups, but they were merely survival tactics in a cut-throat business. BGP had already been running me around in circles in ways that my friends would not believe. We already secretly had booked the production companies and arranged for a back up venue, things that our activist group would have considered potentially improper, but the show as scheduled was two weeks away, and this was really just normal good show business practices. Nonetheless, all of this was almost impossible to explain to the mass of people that was there to serve the community, and they were all looking to me for an answer.

I really did not know what to say, and I considered momentarily just backing away from a situation that seemed too much like being between an unstoppable force and an immovable object.   Finally I just gave up really feeling the need to try, and I just retreated in my mind to my misty memory of the Muses from my dreams. Instantly I could see their faces again, whispering calm quiet secrets about just how to speak to people.   They seemed to just say that I, already, knew exactly what to say.

"I understand where you all are coming from," I began, "and that's while we're all taking this time here.   Please try to understand where Archie here, and everyone else we may deal with from now on, is coming from.   Santana and Los Lobos will not play if it is not BGP, and BGP does everything in a very specific fashion.   We all want the same thing and now we just have to make quick decisions.   Fish or cut bait, I believe, is an appropriate saying."

"They're bluffing," the Principal said to the group.   "I really doubt they could find another spot to do this at the last minute."

"Look, Mac..." Archie began.

"It's Carlos," the Principal corrected him.

"Yeah, Carlos," Archie continued, "Look, we will do this concert in a landfill if we have to rather that put up with this. Believe me, it's been done. Did you know Woodstock didn't even happen in Woodstock because of some last minute bullshit like this?"

"Really?" Buck asked.

"He's right," I agreed.   "Not only that, Woodstock would not have happened at all if Bill Graham hadn't come in in the last minute with his helicopters and saved the day."

"Really?" It was Julia's turn to ask. "Fascinating."

"Well," Buck said, "I think after all this we should just go with what M.C. says. He has been here all along and he has dealt with these types a lot apparently." He gestured at Archie. Everyone basically nodded, including Principal Reyes.

"Thank you," I said. "We basically have little choice but to go with what BGP says. There are a thousand different little reasons that Archie has for everything he says and we really don't have enough time to explain it all, that's why he might come off a little brusque."

"Why thank you," Archie said comically. "I would have said 'curt' or 'gruff,' but you are much more eloquent than I. We really all want the same thing, here. Are we back on target, then?"

"Isn't there any way we can save money," Julia asked. "You know, cut down production costs or something? Do we have to have big show lights?"

"If we have a show at night we have to have big show lights," Archie was emphatic.

"Well," Buck was thinking out loud, "could we have the show during the day?"

"I think so," I said, and I looked at Archie who shrugged his shoulders. We proceeded to go down the list of things that needed to get done, compromising where necessary, and we adjourned rather quickly, which to Archie and I meant a successful meeting. After all, to us, this was all about community spin. There really was not much anybody in the room needed to do but let the professionals do their thing, and as much as they realized this it would be much easier for everyone involved. There was a certain majesty around allowing people to do what they do best, but it was always hard to trust in such a way when something was so dear to the community. Everything became more and more extreme, inevitably, and this show ended up raining down on us, literally.

The day came quickly, without much room for error, and an army of stage production types descended on the small high school field. The sky had just opened with water, and it seemed only Noah would be working in a deluge like this. But my stagehand friends came out in force, Duke Charger and Yellowbeard amongst the riggers, Jake Kerringer and Johnny Robinson on sound, and a whole posse of plastic coated hands from all over to make it happen.

As soon as Principal Reyes and the rest of the community saw the rains coming down, something in them just figured it was off. We had to be at the field starting at 3am, and it had already been dumping like a monsoon all night. Principal Reyes stood in shock as the waves of stagehands and trucks rolled in despite the waves of rain, all the work doubled because of the necessary tarps, canopies, and plastics that had to be spread over everything, until he finally went home to be dry, seeing that it was all in good hands. Everyone did what they had to do, and the community volunteers, who had shrunk to a predictable core group with the deluge, were happy to see the army of stagehands doing their thing. For their part, the union hands barely missed a beat in the work, although you can bet they grumbled mightily nonstop.

Lucky had joined me with the production team, ultimately becoming a key volunteer with the group. At first she jumped back in, expecting to take a lead role beside Buck, and only then did she finally meet Julia. Naturally, they suddenly became intensely aware of each other, quickly being informed of the whole story behind each one with Buck from just about everybody in the community, and each woman seemed intent on out-performing the other in terms of volunteer effort. Buck and Julia were managing the volunteers in catering and security, and were out in the rain putting up fences in the distance, seeming to be having a great time when everyone else was pretty much miserable.

Lucky appeared to latch onto me as some sort of counter message to Buck and Julia, hanging around me with her hand on my shoulder or with her arm around me, kissing me on the cheek, and I suffered through it, actually not into what seemed to be a game, usually wanting to focus on other things, although I never pushed her away, of course. Somehow she seemed to be a human personification of the Muses, and I welcomed her presence. The stagehands loved giving me grief about my apparent position of privilege, particularly since I was able to stay in the main production tent most of the time with such a lovely assistant. Duke came in soaking wet at about 6 am, right after Lucky had gone to catering to get us some coffee.

"Yeah, it's your turn to be warm and dry," Duke the rigger was saying, shaking off water. "But Yellowbeard has to be a human sandbag, and a wet one at that." Duke was a handsome black man that did stand-ins and other show business on the side, or was he a stagehand on the side? He had been doing both for so long no one was sure.

"Hey, watch it, you're getting water on the plot!" I exclaimed. "What do you mean about Yellowbeard?"

"Sorry. He's up at the top of the steel holding the canopy in place so it doesn't fly away until we have it lashed down," he said, smearing the water on the plot with a wet towel. Johnny came in behind him, talking with Jake the whole time.

"Preachin' to the choir, mate," Johnny ran on in his Yorkshire drawl. "'E's in his ivory tent and 'e's no idea what's on out there...oops, 'ere 'e is." Johnny and Jake were two of my closest friends, and despite the fact that they were totally insane, they were excellent stage hands. Jake was a sharp edged loud conspiracy buff that had a remarkable likeness to Harrison Ford, and Johnny was a teabag expatriate that was always good for some British color to the scene.

"Do you know how much water is out there?" Jake demanded, dripping more water on the plans.

"I know how much water is in here," I said, grabbing the wet towel away from Duke and pulling out some dry paper towels.

"You've got the bloody Thames being dumped through a spigot out there," Johnny said. "This whole show might just float away."

"You're telling me," Duke said. "Me and Yellowbeard put all the tables in catering on top of palettes to get them above the water, and then the table next to us just started to float out the door!" Duke mimed the floating table. Stagehands had a way of amplifying just about any story for comic effect.

"Are you sure this show is going to go on?" Jake asked me. "Even Noah would be having second thoughts about now."

"The tickets say rain or shine," I answered. "And the news says it is supposed to clear up later today." I was no more sure than anyone, and I did not like the rain on a show day either, but it was my job to keep everyone moving ahead no matter what.

"Yeah, how much later?" Duke asked. "In time for load-out?"

"We're swimmin' out there and you're in your toasty dry hole sippin' cappuccino with your lovely assistant, none the wiser," Johnny tried to rib me.

"It's going to be wetter than a divorcee at a Chippendales show," Jake said. "What kind of audience are we going to have? People demanding their tickets back."

"Rain or shine," I repeated. "Besides, I've got twenty propane heaters on their way and Killer is going to fly Bill down in the helicopter. He can fly over to dry to field like he did at Shoreline. So do you guys have technical questions, or are you just in here to complain?"

"Oh, just complain, really," Jake said, and the others nodded in agreement.

"Yeah, we're practically done with the rig," Duke added. "We're just waiting for backline now."

Just then Lucky walked in with a couple of coffees, and the guys changed like night and day. They stood up straight, smoothed their hair, and looked downright cheerful. They seemed to be real gentlemen, but I knew the veneer would not hold for very long.

"Here is your cappuccino," Lucky said, handing me a cup. This was all it took, and the guys burst into a huge laugh. "What? What did I do?"

"No, it's not you, Lucky," I assured her. "It's just these nutball types I work with. Have you met the guys yet?" I asked her, and I made introductions all around.

"Please forgive our outburst, Ma'am," Johnny said, sounding suddenly like James Bond or some other sophisticated character not from Yorkshire. "You came in on cue as we were making jest of our compatriot here."

"Don't stop on my account," she said good-naturedly.

"I don't know how long they could stop on any account," I added.

"And you, what's that accent now?" Jake asked Johnny. "How do you really speak, anyway?"

"A bit like John Wayne, Pilgrim," Johnny said, suddenly shifting to West Texan.

"Well sail back to England," Duke said. "There's only one Duke around here."

"Eye, Cap'n," Johnny said in some nonspecific way familiar to everyone. Duke was the most senior to all of us, so he garnered a high level of respect, mostly because he was still willing to do anything to make a show happen even after all these years. He was the natural head of the crew under me, and he had been an inspiration to us all how he had pushed through the wind and rain all night. Everyone liked to complain but they were really working like a well oiled machine.

"When is Archie coming down?" Lucky asked.

"He supposed to come down at about 8 am with Bill," I said. "And Santana's guys should be here with the backline any minute."

"So, Killer is supposed to be flying in this stuff," Duke asked.

"Yeah, you know Bill and Killer, not much will keep them on the ground," I replied, talking about Mr. Graham and his Vietnam Veteran pilot. They were infamous in show business circles for keeping the show going, not the least of which was at Woodstock. After a heavy rain Killer had even been known to fly passes over Shoreline Amphitheater to dry the lawn, and I was counting on him for the same thing today. Just then a huge cloudburst came crashing down on the tent roof, making all of us jump.

"Oh, man," Duke said.

"That is insane!" Jake exclaimed. "And I should know. Are you SURE this show is going to go off? Even Killer won't be flying in this mess."

"The show IS going to go off," I assured them.

"All right, if you say so," Duke accepted. "Okay, boys, let's go stack those empties behind catering."

"And nick a bit o' joe simultaneous-like?" Johnny asked.

"What did he say?" Duke asked me. I often translated Johnny's English for the Americans.

"He said can you get coffee at the same time?" I interpreted.

"Oh, of course," Duke finally understood. "You know I believe in multi-tasking. Let's go. M.C. says this show, she's a goin'" They all filed out making noises like the three stooges.

Lucky and I were left alone and I let some of my guard down. It seemed impossible. It seemed like it could not be raining harder. We had to have some awesome level of faith to keep going. Of course, the stagehands were trained to keep going ahead until told it was all off, but then we all still had to load the stuff out, and sooner, so everyone pretty badly wanted to see the show happen at this point. It was my job, at this point, to determine if work should go on, however, and in most other circumstances I would have called it already. But I did have a source of confidence. The Divine Voice in my head had said it would be hard, but it did not say it would not happen. Somehow I sense the beautiful poetic sense of it all, and certainly the Muses seemed to be everywhere. Whether it was true or not, something in me believed that for something to be really good it had to be hard won. Later on I might grow past that axiom and learn to accept things more easily, but right now the Universe was more than happy to deliver things in the way that I expected.

Certain things were different than expected for Lucky, I could tell. I could see her watching Buck and Julia every once in a while. I think she was surprised at how little Buck seemed to notice her at all. He was certainly absorbed in Julia, but that was just the way he was. He might have noticed a certain change in Lucky, certainly he noticed that she had come out to help, but he could not register more, would not register more. Lucky may have felt a certain loss, but she drowned it in work, and the endless downpour helped. She was as efficient as ever, more than ever perhaps, and I was glad to have her, but there was a certain vacancy in her eyes, a definite distance. I could tell that we were bonding, like brother and sister, but that only helped me to see the distance that she was keeping between herself and everybody. There was a quality in a person that let you know that their soul was not exactly present, somewhat like I imagined a soldier on a battlefield might appear.

I suddenly felt a shiver, and I wondered for the first time if it was going to go off. Lucky seemed less of a Muse at that point, wet and distant. I felt that vacuousity familiar to those who have worked through the night, and the cappuccino could not fill the void. We both sensed the absence at the same time, apparently, because Lucky reached out and put her hand on mine, a simple gesture just to remind both of us that we were not alone. Somehow we could not summon that sweet voice within, and no dreamlike heavenly face appeared in our minds' eyes. We would have been disconsolate, depressed, desperate even, but we both knew that we just had to persist. That was the secret in times like this, just to persist, even in blindness, pushing through, even if in the wrong direction, just to keep momentum. As soon as we made the determination to go on, the outside world seemed to accept our decision. The rain was gone, had left sometime in the last few minutes with our doubts, and in the distance, echoing over the hills, we could hear the distinct sound of a helicopter.

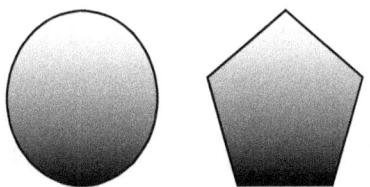

OnaPentero (17) Realized

Bill Graham seemed to carry his sunshine with him. All night we had thought we might never see the sun, and we were the sort apparently destined to toil away in damp dreary darkness to no real avail. But a man could embody a sort of Godliness in himself out of pure confidence. Surely Bill Graham was no saint, but there was a sureness in him that echoed a certain brashness that must have existed in God when he decided to create the physical universe with so many odds seemingly stacked against him.

He came out of the helicopter with a swagger and none of the crouching that others always did when exiting such a craft even when they knew the blades were well clear of their heads. When Archie climbed out behind him, he seemed the exact opposite, holding his had and running like he was on a battlefield. Inside the cockpit Killer through some switches and climbed out to inspect his baby.

"M.C.! Everything in order, I expect," Bill said as he walked up to me, past me really, and on to inspect the scene.

"As best as can be expected, Sir," I said, hoping it was not too much of a disaster scene. "Much of a storm on the way down?"

"A little damp, that's all," he said as he headed to the stage.

"A frickin' gale!" Archie said quietly following behind, his knuckles and face still pale from his wild ride. As we approached the stage, the transformation was remarkable.

The backline truck had arrived and Duke was directing the guys as they pushed it all onto the stage like some kind of ballet of boxes. The sun had come out, and a definite steam was rising off everything, not least of all the stagehands. Lucky came up, and Bill seemed to notice something other than his business for the first time.

"Why, hello," he said. "I don't think I have met you before. I would have remembered.

"This is Lucky Star, Bill," I said. "My assistant from the community for the show."

Bill eyed me with a combination of suspicion and respect. "Well, M.C., what else have you been hiding down here?"

"There really is an amazing group of volunteers down here, of all shapes and sizes," I said. "And they would all like an opportunity to meet you. They are quite thankful that you have taken on this show."

Bill's expression turned slightly more prosaic. "Well, I don't have a lot of time today, you know," he said. "We've got two other shows going on." He turned back to Lucky. "Ever take a ride in a helicopter?"

"No thanks," Lucky said, unimpressed with his star power. "I don't have a deathwish."

"Very well," Bill said, and immediately brushed past us towards the stage. "Hey Duke, you staying dry?" he called out.

"Hardly," Duke called back. "Let's just say I haven't drowned at least."

"All right, the least you can ask," Bill responded with a laugh. He was quite familiar with most of his crew, and like a king utterly assured of his power, he liked to dispense with formalities. We all walked around the site as Bill inspected the various aspects that interested him at any given time. The crew was pretty much on autopilot now that all of the gear and instruments had arrived. Things fell into place in such a way that made me wonder what sort of magic medicine Bill had that made things fall into place just by arriving. Why would the Muses favor one man so? Certainly he was smart and charismatic, but many people were that, and yet could not quite pull off what he did. Then I realized that it was a matter of timing and appropriate effort. The Muses needed someone like him, much like Babaji for the production of the Ramayana. It was not exactly what either man did or said, but rather what they represented. There needed to be a personified focal point. I had heard that a pack of dogs without an alpha male or female would constantly fight and grapple to determine who should take that position, but as soon as that was determined the rest of the dogs would fall into line obediently. It was a similar thing with stagehands or with community volunteer groups. Most of them knew what to do from years of experience, but would often just degrade into chaos unless there was a top dog around.

Bill strode around with Lucky and me finishing off the last issues. Killer was directed to make sweeps over the field to dry it off, and band members started to trickle in. This sort of management was Bill's forte, and before long everything was handled and we had a show ready to go. Principal Ramirez, Tito, Ol' Pete, and Pico had taken up nearly permanent positions next to catering as they realized that everything was pretty much done. Buck and Julia stayed busy the longest, instinctively knowing where something had to get done, or at least paying attention and wanting to keep busy. They would be putting up dressing rooms one minute, directing the portable toilet deliveries another, and gathering together the ushers for an orientation the next. Finally, however, even they could find nothing to do in that inevitable pre-show period when there was nothing to do but wait. Los Lobos and Santana arrived with typical flourish and quickly disappeared into the dressing rooms. A large crowd gathered outside, seemingly oblivious to the moisture. Roadies and local crew milled about and finally it seemed that the show was inevitable. I stood in mild shock, disbelieving that just a few short hours before I had doubted that this show could even happen. Now it was apparent that nothing could stop it. Somehow I felt a Divine hand in it all, because no person's single contribution, even Bill's, could explain it all. As if on cue, knowing that his work here was done, I heard the sound of Bill and Killer taking off in the helicopter from in back. I was in charge again, but it was rather anticlimactic. There was nothing to do, except perhaps reflect on it all, and perhaps that was exactly what I was meant to do.

Lucky and I stood watching the whole scene and eventually Buck and Julia made their way up to us.

"Good job, M.C." Buck said. "Looks like you did it."

"WE did it," I said, including all four of us with a gesture. "But we'll save the back patting until after load-out."

"Sure, sure," Buck agreed. "And you, Lucky, you seemed to have impressed Bill Graham." With this comment Julia seemed to move closer to Buck which seemed to make Lucky move closer to me.

"Really?" Lucky said nonchalantly. "Well, I'm not impressed. Big deal. All this money and what have we raised for the community? A couple tens of thousands, maybe?"

"Well, it's more than that," Julia spoke up. "There are a lot of community groups out there working with the people and organizing. This event means a lot to a lot of people."

"I guess so," Lucky allowed. "I see it has worked out well for you guys. I guess I'm just looking for something more."

"Aren't you always," Buck quipped.

"What's that supposed to mean?" Lucky asked pointedly.

"I don't know," Buck backed off. "I just meant, you know, you always seem to be reaching for more."

"Whatever," Lucky said.

"Hey, Buck, let's go see what's in catering," Julia said, pulling on his arm.

"Gladly," Buck agreed, and they turned and walked away arm in arm.   Lucky tried to hide something, but something was revealed at the same time. I could feel the irony, the cruel reality of a love spurned, but by whom? Lucky felt a definite longing, but for whom? The long tail of the impact of her decision was still passing, and might be for some time. Perhaps she was finally beginning to understand the scope of her choices, and she still agreed with them, but, like a child who had chosen chocolate over vanilla, she could not help but feel cheated in some way. I could sense her slipping away, running somewhere in her soul. Even in the midst of the craziness of the show backstage, we both seemed to be going somewhere else. The artists went onstage and did there part, but somehow it was all far away. The crowd went crazy, yelling with the release of their first abandon and carefree enjoyment after a major disaster, and we just went far away inside.

"I think I have to go somewhere," Lucky said to me at one point while Santana was onstage. "Black Magic Woman" was playing and a got an eerie sense of the power of this woman and the moment. I knew I was part of her story, but I was not with her. I liked her, but I did not have the same crush that I felt Buck still had for her. I was not so masochistic. There was too much going on in this woman, too much that might not be figured out for some time. I was fascinated in her as a story, but another part of me was careful to keep her at arm's length. It was like I could feel the presence of some older brother staring down at me, or some big boyfriend. Whatever the case, I was instinctively drawn to her as a brother, and she seemed to appreciate this.

"I think you're already gone," I said.

"You can tell? So, do you want to go with me?" she asked casually.

"Maybe, but I don't think I can," I said. "Whatever you're hunting you might have to find on your own."

"Perhaps," she said. "But I like your company."

"Well, I'll be with you in spirit," I compromised. "We both have a lot going on, if you know what I mean. I think there might be plans for us that go beyond what we know."

"Well, I'd like to think so," she said, "because I don't know anything right now."

"Then maybe you're just meant to go out and learn," I said. "You've made your money. The ranch can run without you, right?"

"Probably better without me now that I've screwed up with Buck," she said.

"So go on," I prodded her. "Go out and find your destiny! What else have you got to do that you haven't done already?" I had learned many years before not to try to stop someone who was leaving. It worked better to give them a little push.

"Yeah, you're right," she said with some kind of renewed energy. "What's keeping me around here? I might as well just take off and find whatever wherever anyhow!"

"That's right," I said. "Go for it!"

"Okay! Thanks, M.C." she said, with a kiss on my cheek. "You know, you're all right."

"Ah gee, shucks," I said, somewhat feigning embarrassment. That seemed to break the ice of the day for us. We were able to enjoy the momentous nature of the moment. A whole community had been pinned underneath the rubble of shocking events, kept on there toes by aftershocks of harsh realization. Now they were being given full license to let go and experience the relief of cares driven away by strong rhythms and screeching electric guitar. Everyone seemed to revel in a unique level of abandon, caught up as if drunk with something more than liquor. The magic of the day changed many lives, not just Lucky's and mine. Buck and Julia seemed fused in a resolute commitment to experience the full draft of intensity together, clinging psychicly together with a tinge of desperation. Every time Lucky saw this, she seemed to be driven further away out to her distant horizons. I let her go, and allowed myself the luxury of exhaustion as the show drew to a close. The rest of the crew seemed unified in doggedness as they gathered for the out. Certain members, like the riggers, had had a chance to go off to motel rooms to get a few hours sleep, but they seemed none the fresher for their breaks.

"I woke up laying on my bed," Duke said, "and I suddenly thought the room was leaking. Then I realized it was just me, that I was so wet that I was leaving a puddle underneath me." We were tired enough to laugh at anything, and so we all found this incredibly funny.

"I just curled up on a roadcase to rest my eyes," Jake said, "and I opened them up and it was four hours later."

"At least you geezers could go pass out," Johnny said. "As A2 I had to stay awake for the whole boring thing."

"Boring?" I asked. "Don't you like Santana?"

"Nah," Johnny waved away with his hand. "He's so wooden. A bloody wanker. If I'd a had 'alf my wits about me and a pick I'd a showed him some real guitar."

"I don't think he has much to worry about then," Jake ribbed him, and they both laughed.

"All right gang," I focused everyone's attention. "I know we're all tired, but we're not done yet. Let's pack up this gear and get these trucks loaded and out of here." Everybody snapped to like dedicated and devoted craftspeople and workers and began the task of dismantling the whole thing. Everyone oddly had a bounce to their steps, buoyed by the knowledge that we had accomplished the nearly impossible, and that we were actually almost done. There are strange reservoirs in the human spirit that reveal that energy is more than a bodily component, that capability in people is more than just a tank of gas that can run dry. The load-out seemed to reveal that there was always a little more to give when we had already been drained of more than everything. The road cases rolled up the ramps, the trusses came down, and the sky thickened again and it began to rain anew. It dumped copious drops, but it was different now. We had triumphed, and no mere precipitation could dampen our spirits. The rain came as an exclamation point, as one more reminder that we were working miracles out here. The sky unloaded on us because it could now, because there was a certain heightened heroism and magic in the fact that the rain encased the show like a pair of parentheses, yet we kept going.

Buck and Julia kept getting closer to the very end. Duke, Johnny, Ol' Pete, Tito, and Jake kept getting funnier. I kept getting more philosophical, and Lucky kept getting propelled off into the distance.

"Where is she going?" I asked in my head. As a writer I often addressed a Writer in my mind.

"She is looking for Me," came the answer, "And she will go to the ends of the Earth."

"And what will she find?" I wondered.

"Her way home," was the last that I heard. I watched the rain come down, seeming to coat the cast of crazies in a layer of tears, but no one seemed unhappy. They all just did what they did, quite well, and before any of us knew it, it was over. The trucks were gone, the trash was gone, and it was all part of history, just a memory. But we were glad we had been there, just to know, just to remember, and to resolve to make more.

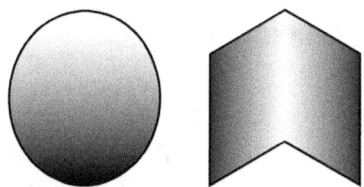

OnaExorto (18) Confronted

We left the show in our lives and seemed to speed off on different paths, chasing our own meaning in a sea of cognizance. Everyone knew that something momentous had happened, and everyone wanted to take that energy on to new things, yet nobody seemed to know where to go with it. I went on to the next show, and the others went back to the Ranch, but nothing was the same. Nothing had the same immediacy, the same charm of collective determination, that we had experienced after the earthquake. Slowly we were realizing that life does go on, that, even after a major life changing event, not so much had changed after all. I went back to Shoreline for a few more shows, another Bridge Benefit, and kept wondering what it was all about. Somehow I knew this story was not about me, I was just a bit player, a side story that ran the danger of distracting from the real issues at hand. I went into my hole, and made a conscious decision to let go.

I had felt something, I had participated in it, but like any author I had to let it become whatever it would become. I asked the Author in my head to give me answers, and He was forthcoming. He gave me stories, and I realized better the part I was to play. I let Lucky go off, for she was pushing of on some mythical journey, and the Author in my head let me know in no uncertain terms that that was THE story, that this was HER story. Buck was going off, too, but not alone. He and Julia moved on together, and it was THEIR story, and that I was merely being honored with the responsibility of telling it.

How to explain the swirl of feelings that even Lucky herself did not understand? At least she had the bravery to go with her convictions, living life as if the point was living, not some end state acquired or won. She certainly had fashioned a conviction of sorts at the concert. Watching Buck and Julia get close in front of everyone would have caused her pain if she were allowing herself to feel pain. Instead, she felt a growing determination to reconnect with her higher love. But He was so damn elusive, or so she thought. She knew it was some kind of dance, some game that would ultimately turn out to be child's play, but, like a kid on the playground the feelings were very vivid in her heart.

I called her up to connect before she left, for I could sense she was leaving. She had that air about her like the ancient mariner too long on land, and she wore her dissatisfaction like an albatross around her neck. I rode down to the ranch and found her trying drill some information into Ol' Pete and Pico out by the water plant. Some years earlier Lucky had installed a state-of-the-art water treatment and reclamation plant, to provide for drinking water for the cows during dry spells. I had been told by Belle that they were up here so I found my way up the hill and saw the three of them cleaning the equipment, elbows deep in muck, attended by a lone cow that seemed to be supervising.

"I know it sucks," Lucky was saying as she was slinging slimy gray matter into a row of buckets, "literally and figuratively. But if you regularly clean the silt traps you get up to three times the life on the filters."

"I jes never heard o filtering water for cows," Ol' Pete kind of grumbled. "This is people water."

Pico kept his mouth shut but seemed to humph his agreement.

"Well, people drink milk," Lucky retorted. "And where do you think they get the moisture for the milk? From the air? I'm sorry guys, but you have to do this exactly like I say, or how can I ever feel it's safe to leave?"

"Don't worry, I'm old enough to do what I'm told," Pete rasped, "but I'm older enough to grumble about it at the same time."

Pico kept his mouth shut but seemed to humph his agreement, and the two doubled their muck clearing efforts to prove their point. They were so intently focused on the task in fact that no one seemed to notice me standing right there. No one, that is, except the cow, who ambled up to me with what seemed like a smile and gave me a solid nudge, causing me to stumble and laugh.

"Lindy, what's the...oh, M.C., it's you. I didn't see you come up."

"You guys were so busy, don't let me interrupt you." I said, patting the cow. "So this is Gimpy."

"Hey, who told you that?" Lucky shot out defensively. "Who told you that? You been talking to Buck?"

"Buck? No, Buck is tight lipped about everything," I said. "It's everyone else that likes to talk about you and Buck." Pico redoubled his efforts and Ol' Pete began to whistle as he worked, both looking far too innocent to be believed.

"Who else have you been talking to about me?" Lucky playfully demanded.

"Just your mom and dad, you know," I admitted.

"Oh, I get it," Lucky nodded. "You're writing a book about all this, aren't you?"

"No, not right now," I confessed. "Maybe in a few years, though." Some stories took years to mature, so I was in the habit of following some even if I did not know exactly where they were going. This story seemed to be splitting off in all sorts of directions.

"Well, this story is about to skip town, and you rejected an offer to come along," Lucky announced. Pico and Ol' Pete settled down to a quiet steady rhythm, better to overhear the conversation now that they no longer were in the hot seat.

"Oh, come on, Lucky," I said. "You know this is a journey you have to make by yourself, because you're looking for something that is uniquely for you, right?"

"I guess so, but I do get lonely," she said quietly.

"Trailblazers often do, but then they're looking for a different sort of company than the settlers they pass along the way," I offered, intending the slight pun on "settlers."

"Yes, well put," she said. "So what will you do, stay here with your work?"

"Well, sort of. That's what I came here to talk about. I'm leaving myself, in a way," I informed her.

"Really? You're leaving Santa Cruz? And you won't come with me?" she asked.

"No, I'm staying here, I'm just, well, leaving the story," I explained.

"I don't understand, explain more," she requested. "You are a part of this story."

"All stories sort of intersect, don't they?" I reflected. "I'm still going to follow the story, I'm just going to write myself out of it. I might return to it, years from now, who knows? But right now I need to let you go off and experience it. I get too lost in philosophical detours and run the risk of derailing the entire train of thought."

"You're also pretty heavy on pun-like metaphors," she commented.

"I guess I'll have to lighten up on that too then," I punned. "Look, I can't stop, that's why I have to leave the story, but, please, I came to ask you, use me, use my friendship as a muse. Write me, anything you want, everything you can think of. Write me as much as you can. Think of me as your trusted confidant in all your adventures."

"Why, thank you, M.C. It does feel nice to have someone to confide in," she allowed.

"Well, it's a small part but I aim to do it well," I boasted. "It is the least I could do."

"No, you could do much less, trust me," she maintained. "In fact, if you're serious, let's take a walk and talk in private for a moment, if you don't mind."

"I don't mind at all," I beamed.

"Hey, maybe we mind," Ol' Pete protested. Pico seemed to humph in agreement.

"Sorry, Pete, no more grist for that mill," Lucky said. "You guys will have to make up your own stories from now on."

"Ahh, but yours are much more exciting," Pete protested. Pico seemed to humph in agreement. Pete turned on him. "Can't you say something more than that? Speak up for yourself!" Pico seemed to humph in disagreement. "You can't ever make management level if you don't speak up."

"Maybe, maybe not," Pico supposed. "I just wait til there's something worth saying."

"He's got you there, Pete," Lucky claimed. "Who knows, someday you may have to manage the ranch."

"Thank you, Senora," Pico said. "I pay very close attention to you."

"She's not talking about that," Pete said.

"What do...Oh!" Pico exclaimed, realizing the double meaning of what he said. The rest of us burst out laughing. "See! That is why I keep my mouth shut!"

"No, no, Pico, don't worry about it," Lucky assured him. "I appreciate the attention, don't listen to these guys."

"What did I say?" I asked.

"You laughed," she accused.

"You laughed too," I defended.

"Yes, but you laughed at Pico," she contended.

"Well who were you laughing at?" I was curious.

"Myself," she suggested.

"You were laughing at yourself?" I doubted.

"Yes, because I was momentarily flattered by the attention," she claimed.

"Only momentarily?" I countered.

"Yes, only momentarily," she insisted. "Pico believes me."

"Do you believe her, Pico?" I interrogated him.

"Si, Senor," he let out.

"Why?" I wondered.

"Because, she's the boss," Pico concluded, and we all laughed.

"All right, guys," she segued. "Stay focused. You're doing good work. M.C. and I are going for a walk."

"Okay, okay, get to work, we know," Ol' Pete groaned. "Well, Pico, it looks like its back to my stories, like that one where the rat chewed the corn off my toe. Remember that one?" Pico groaned his acknowledgment. "Funny thing is..."

"It cured it..." Pico finished for him.

"That's right, it cured it," Pete did not lose a beat. "I'd tried cuttin' it off myself many times but to no avail, but this time..." He faded into the distance as we walked up the bluff away from the water tanks. The pipes and filters were tucked in a little quarry left over from the lime kiln days, and were soon invisible behind a wall of buckeye and bay laurel. The effervescent scent mixed with the spring air and created an intoxicating brew, which we quaffed in great long breaths. We had meant to talk, but we were so mesmerized by the busy beauty of the foraging bees and birds that we just walked along in silence. But who knows what is silence? Perhaps more can be said in a few moments of non-talk than in entire speeches of distraction. People seem to know this, and the best conversations are started with this quiet understanding, but almost everyone gets dissatisfied with this and is compelled to speak.

"M.C., am I crazy?" Lucky asked.

"Sure," I responded casually.

"What do you mean, I'm crazy?" she took aback.

"I don't know. What did you mean?" I retorted.

"Well, am I crazy to leave all this?" she specified. "All this bounty, all this blessing?"

"Oh that. Sure you're crazy, but isn't that the point?" I posited.

"How so?" she considered.

"Some people always choose the comfortable over the unknown, some people always choose the unknown over the comfortable." I reasoned. "To each, the other type seems crazy. What is sane to you might seem crazy to others."

"But what if what I'm looking for isn't out there?" she agonized. "What if I come back and everything is the same?"

"Impossible," I declared.

"Why?" she pondered.

"Because you will have changed," I knew.

"Perhaps, but what if other people have changed, too?" she continued.

"That is inevitable," I acknowledged. "It is one thing you just have to accept, except that in my general experience people usually change for the better."

"Except when they die," she excepted.

"Especially when they die," I included.

"How can you say that?" she asked.

"Are you still afraid of death after all you've been through?" I inquired.

"Shouldn't I be?" she supposed.

"Isn't living more scary?" I suggested.

"Why are we talking in questions?" she wondered.

"How else can you talk about death?" I pondered. With that, there seemed to be no more questions, or statements to make for that matter. We walked along, enjoying the day. We eventually came to a promontory were we could see a major portion of the ranch, stretching over the hills towards the sea. It seemed to glow with some special fecundity, as if there were greater forces of fertility which were at work here. Lucky sighed and I felt I could sense what she was thinking. It was a grand place, mythic and wondrous, yet she was leaving it behind. She had brought the place back from the brink of disaster, and now she was leaving it, like a sparrow with a mended wing, disappearing into the sky.

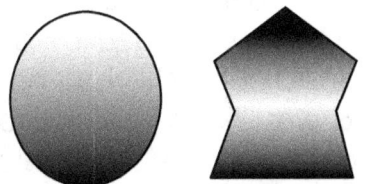

OnaFammo (19) Launched

Lucky began writing right away. Volumes of letters detailed every aspect of her journey, like some encyclopedia therapeutica. I had originally intended to let the material speak for itself, merely inserting the letters for the central portion of the story, but this immediately revealed the irony behind the fact that life, in most cases, could use a good editor. Undoubtedly the lives of the great men and women of history were on average filled with mostly mundane events, bodily processes and the like, and perhaps the element that signaled heroism was only a matter of small percentages. Perhaps Leonardo Da Vinci was only 20% more creative than the average Vincian, but that was enough to capture the name forever. Perhaps Joan of Arc only heard voices 15% more often than Bernadette of Arc, yet no one remembers Bernadette (and she gave Joan some good religious tips). Often the sense of clear purpose and undying courage is written by later chroniclers in safe study dens who have a romanticized ideal of their subjects. This had the unfortunate effect of discouraging future heroes and heroines, fearing that their human side separated them from their idyllic mythic champions.

Those ancient chroniclers where not trying to dehumanize their subjects, however, nor did they necessarily exaggerate the heroic feats. They did, however, perform the necessary task of editing the stories, cutting out the mass of droll everyday material and making connections that may not have been apparent before. Lucky certainly made heroic choices, but she too was dogged by a tragic flaw, similar to Hamlet's indecision, though she had no trouble taking action. Instead, her mind was like a race car on sand, burning up a lot of fuel going round the same old track. Her wheels sprayed all the grains of thought onto the letters, providing plenty of material but in dire need of a detailed wash and wax. I might have driven my metaphors into the rail with alarming regularity, but she would cast up metaphors in great flocks and shoot at them with a shotgun of eclectic verse and prose.

11/27/89 Okay, M.C., you asked for it. You told me to write freely, so here goes. You want to know what the story is? The story is about Gods' loves, all of the Gods, they're all Love, Every God's Love, Every God's a gift of Love, Every God's Love is a gift to everyone, Everything is a Gift of God's Love. Love is All, All is God, God is Love. Love God, love All.

Was Lucky crazy? Possibly. Was Lucky inspired? Probably. Was there a line between the two? Hazy. Anyone who dared to look beyond the norms and styles of the times had to be a little crazy, but a lot of crazy was not inspiration. Just enough crazy was genius, too much crazy was just crazy. What made this a good story is that Lucky always skirted that line, pushing into every unexplored pathway that wandered in the proximity. What kind of story was it? A mystery. Love was a mystery for Lucky, and she pursued it like some romance gumshoe. A love story too. A mystery love story. So who died? Who didn't? That was not the mystery. The mystery was, who got it before they died, and how did they get it. No one makes it out alive, but who makes it live is about who makes it about love.

I had the habit of listening to some rather authoritative voice that occasionally spoke within me, but it was more of a mentor-like voice, generally loving but always reserved, that I figured everyone had more or less as well.   In my more reductionist and rationalistic periods I would refer to the voice merely as my higher self, or my conscience.   In my more meditative moments I occasionally experienced the voice as a direct link to something that appeared to be cosmic consciousness.   I never experienced anything like Lucky did, loving God like some dripping palpitative passion.   I finally accepted that God was actually giving each of us what we wanted, what we were comfortable with, what we could assimilate.   Part of the love was that we always seemed to get more of what we needed than what we asked for.   Lucky would ask for something and hardly know what she was asking, and she always seemed to get it and a little bit more.

Before she left, Lucky had visited Babaji and asked for some references, as she had figured India was a great place to look first.   She had interpreted the recent events as indicative that God had left, yet she thought there had to be a point to the subcontinental flavor of her visions, so maybe He went to India.   Best to have a friend refer you to some leads when going to a foreign land, so Lucky thought.   The morning weather was not auspicious as she went up to Mt. Madonna in the last few days before she left.   The dense fog blew in hazy gusts, obscuring the gardens and the statues, blending into rain every other bank of clouds that ploughed through.   Babaji was sitting alone in Samadhi in the main hall, seemingly oblivious to the lashes of wind and water that struck the window spasmodically behind him.

Lucky approached him with utterly no recognition, and she wondered what he could sense in this state.   She figured he could still hear, and probably was well aware of her presence, but chose to stay far away.   His manner reminded her of her Lover, and she almost resented something in the aloofness, but it had no weight.   She sat there, waiting for an answer, or some sort of acknowledgement, yet none came.   She knew that there was a point he was making, and she probably needed to hear it, but it annoyed her a little nonetheless. She probably should have just sat down and joined him in meditation, but instead she decided to stand defiantly right in front of him.

11-27-89. Ha! I thought, If he wants to sit there all day, I can stand here all day. Only after at least an hour of standing, ankle bones grinding into my heals, did I finally start to think about things, which was his intention, I know, but I still resisted. Why is it always in his time? Why must we always be taught things with parables and mysteries? I was going, and was just about to leave when Sita came in, nervously observing something in my posture.

Lucky was one her way out, but she had to pass the gate keeper first. It was Sita who broke the silence.

"Is there anything I can help you with, Lucky?" she asked.

"I came to ask Babaji if he can introduce me to advanced teachers in India that can help me find what I'm looking for," Lucky managed to respond.

"I can introduce you to advanced teachers but they may not help you find what you are looking for," a voice came into her head.

"Can you help me find what I am looking for?" Lucky asked aloud.

"I have already pointed the way, but you were looking at my finger," came the voice again, just as Babaji stirred for the time, lifting a finger that gradually pulled his hand behind his back, grabbing his slate, his eyes still closed and him still seemingly in the bliss of Samadhi. His hand seemed to work automatically as he scrawled something and handed it to Sita.

"It is the address of an Ashram in Calcutta with which we are affiliated," Sita informed her. I will go and get you all the information necessary, and I will inform them that you are coming." She set the slate down next to Babaji and hurried out of the room. Lucky still stood watching Babaji, half in defiance and half in awe and obeisance. "Can I at least have your blessing?" she thought, as clearly and loudly as she could.

Babaji opened his eyes for the first time, and they burned with the fire of an eternal sun. Lucky lost herself momentarily in an instant of pure illumination. But she got suspicious, and guarded, and the connection severed, and Lucky regretted even that moment's doubt. Babaji lowered his eyes and picked up the slate. He quickly wrote out a sentence and handed it to Lucky.

"The path to what you seek lies within," the message read.

"Oh, I know it is, I know that's the lesson, but there is something else going on, really," Lucky let out in a flurry. The artificial reserve gone, she lost all inhibition and poured out her thoughts to Babaji. A lesser man may have been overwhelmed by the barrage, but Babaji seemed to keep his stance in Samadhi the whole time. "I know he is in my heart, our hearts, everyone's heart, He's a Spirit, He is everywhere, but he came to me in a physical body. He came to me and split the earth. There is something going on here, and the answer is out there," she finished, pointing out over the ocean.

Babaji wrote another note, "There is no out there."

"Well I looked around and there seems to be not much in here," Lucky said, touching her chest. Babaji just waved his head side to side which seemed to signal neither yes nor no. "Or, rather," Lucky continued, "I know that path to Him, I think I knew it...in a past life. But now I am alive for something else."

Babaji wrote again, "Lila is often hard to distinguish from Maya."

"What does that mean?" Lucky asked when she read it, but Babaji merely closed his eyes again and returned fully into Samadhi.

"Ask about it in Calcutta," a voice said to her, and she felt Babaji had left, as if he had flown off astrally to India to begin planning her reception. Lucky felt closure, and she made her way out to parking lot. Sita ran out to her can with a folder of information, wished her luck, and this was the last any of us in California would see her for 10 years, at least in person.

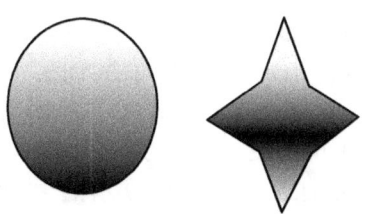

OnaTemmo (20) Recovered

Lucky sent me a flood of letters that lasted over the first year. She visited one amazing place after another, and met truly astounding people, yet none of which seemed to be what she was looking for. If she were looking for a quest, perhaps she found one, taking her question around India.

12-16-89 I did not wait to find out what Babaji's last statement might mean, that "Lila was often hard to distinguish from Maya." I went by the University Library before I left and got a couple books on it. It seems that "Lila" means "the Lord's play", like a play or a dance, or music, specifically played by my Beloved. This I understood. It turns out "Maya" means matter as illusion, or the unreality of the physical world, and this was supposed to be a bad thing. This I did not understand, except maybe as a paradox, because nothing was not my Beloved, and nothing of Him was bad.

Lucky had run into the age old theological problem of evil, trying to reconcile a transcendental Lord with the harsh conditions of physical reality. She also continued to reach out and help animals, especially cows. At first she was charmed by the Indian custom of allowing cattle to roam free, and thought she had found the answer to compassionate bovine agriculture. Over time, however, she witnesses how poverty in general led to poor conditions for animals. People who lived in poor conditions usually kept their livestock in poor conditions. Conversely, as conditions improved for animals, so did they improve for their people.   After a typhoon in Bangladesh she witnessed first hand how animals suffered even more than humans in such a calamity. Livestock was not rescued after a natural disaster, and at best it was shot out of its misery for meat by international aid workers.   She began the first stages of a non-profit foundation to rescue animals in disaster situations, which she named H.E.L.P, or Humane Emergency Logistics Program.   Eventually she had her own answer for why God allows evils in the world, for, as she would say, "Because he wants us to get off our asses and do something about it."

The headquarters of H.E.L.P. were in Benares, but soon offices had sprung up all over Asia. Although the primary mission of the foundation was to aid animals in emergency situations, the growing board and membership decided that humane animal husbandry was a continuing emergency situation. Lucky grew the project like so much else in her life, trying to set it up to be self-sufficient so she could go off and do her own thing. For the most part, H.E.L.P was a smooth operation, quietly growing worldwide, with generous cash infusions from Lucky Star Organics, of course. Only when disaster struck, like the large quake in Istanbul where they successfully rescued 200 Arabian horses and over 2000 goats, did Lucky take front and center and command her organization.   Organic Goat and Cow dairies were built in disaster areas to provide food for the local population while simultaneously teaching them organic farming.

As her quest was fundamentally a spiritual quest, Lucky also continuously trained in various disciplines. First she had been initiated in Raja Yoga in Benares, and she decided her life path was through Karma Yoga, which she interpreted as the path of spiritual work in the physical world. Her devotion was very pure, and her discipline strong, but still she could not find her Love. Every where she traveled she sought out the holy places and the holy people to pay homage and give respect, believing them all to be another form in honor of her Beloved. In turn she was received with honor wherever she went. Because she always asked to meet the animals first, everyone's trust seemed to follow their animals' acceptance of her.

10-10-90   I am beginning to understand how much my Beloved adores diversity.   Diversity of forms, diversity of opinions, diversity of species. Everything unique, everything unusual, everything it's own. His own, part of Him. I feel this so clearly now that people and animals seem to feel it in me too.

Of course the entire continent of Asia was too small for Lucky, and she began H.E.L.P. chapters in Africa and South America. She kept up correspondence for over a year, then sent one last letter. She did not say anything specific, but she hinted that she was tired of all the endless work and was thinking of disappearing into a monastery somewhere.

1-15-91   The rainy season, again. It brings out the bear in me. I want to crawl up in a hole and sleep. I can't do anymore, too much to be done, always more to be done. He who desires worthwhile work will find no shortage. I need to go within again.   All this Lila, all this Maya. Is there a difference? Why does He evade me? And yet, I had a dream where He came to me and said, "Raddha, Raddha, why do you fly away from me?" And he chased me through dense jungle, and I understood why I was fleeing, but I can't remember now. Maybe I couldn't handle His perfection. Was I too little, or was He too much for me? I always wanted to take in all of Him, but He never ended, and I felt overwhelmed, and so I fled.   Also, I fled, because, secretly, I hoped He would chase me.

That was pretty much the last we heard of Lucky for awhile, at least until she started showing up on television, in newspapers, in music videos with rockstars she was supposedly dating, but no one saw her personally. Lucky was everywhere, and she was always linked with the growing Lucky Star Organic Brand, but she was never seen in person. Everything worked automatically, and Lucky had become a darling of the media. To people back home in Corralitos, Lucky had become almost completely a legend. Rumor had it around Freedom that Lucky was running everything from some cave in the Himalayas with the help of some tech wiz's from Bangalore. Whatever the case, she was the local kid done good, and every one came to love her unconditionally as a favored daughter, an old friend, or a fond reminisce, and everyone talked about her as if she were their own. Except, oddly, rarely was she mentioned in the rebuilt old house of the Lucky Star Ranch, and never at all in the home of Buck and Julia.

Ol' Pete and Pico had done a good job of taking over the Lucky Star Ranch operations, and resigned themselves to the fact that Lucky and Buck might never be back. For the most part they exactly replicated everything they had ever seen Lucky do, and their memory was pretty good, and they trained many hands in organic farming, but they never changed much really. Lucky's style built on disruptive and revolutionary change had somehow become institutionalized as a boutique brand. Bud had at first jumped back into ranch work after Lucky had left. He had a new sense of vision behind the organic husbandry, and the effect on his own physiology was such that he seemed to have a near full recovery from his stroke symptoms. He rode horseback with Pico and Pete, like the old days, and they restored several hundred acres of conventional farmland. Bud would fade in and out in his various conversations, and Pete would often carry him along, metaphorically. They would ride the hills and Bud would ride the years, each turn a story, each mound a memory.

Belle disappeared in the kitchen. She hid behind endless roast chickens and casseroles, soups, pies and salads. She had cable TV installed for a small set in the kitchen so she could watch cooking shows all the time, adapting the latest heart-healthy recipes to their tastes, and explaining it all to Bud in endless monologues. Secretly she started making extra plates and leaving them out on the back porch for the angels, sometimes, or St. Michael, or Elijah, and Pico would come to gladly play the role. Belle thought that Bud really remembered nothing anymore, and that he did not really even know all that she was saying, but that the attention and stimulation would be good for him. In fact he watched her very closely, and noticed everything in detail. One eye would peak out through the silver hanging remnants of his hair, following Belle like a pitted ball baring. He noticed just about every new thing she did, but he just did not mention anything.

Buck and Julia had a huge wedding in Nisene Marks State Park under a waterfall. They had an idyllic honeymoon in Maui and then settled down in Aptos at the end of Freedom Boulevard. They were only short drive from Freedom, but for them it felt worlds away. Buck started management of Shamrock Farms, the largest organic dairy in the world. In fact, it was a series of dairies all along the West Coast, and Buck was spending most of his time traveling from one to the other. He saw more farms in more various conditions all claiming to be organic that he had to standardize. The main offices were embarking on a growth campaign spurred by venture capital from Palo Alto, so they had been buying up dairies across the land. Buck was making good commissions but his benefits were still poorly defined. Julia had been producing a series of environmental events and festivals, and was feeling a strong desire for children, with an instinctive hint of anxiety she could not explain.

On June 7, 1997, June Claire Smith was born in Sutter Maternity Center as Comet Hyatuke hung in the air like a phosphorescent smudge across the sky. Julia knew she was a miracle, and relaxed into an acceptance of something. Buck knew that June was a great love of his life, allowing him to give himself more freely to someone than he ever had. June grew fast and healthy, like a summer vine, and Julia and Buck held her close. He told her endless stories of his work, and his youth, but he never mentioned Lucky. She was like a ghost amidst the golden hills.

Just about everyone in the tri-county area talked about Lucky Star and saw her on newsstands and billboards, but they never saw her personally, and she never saw them. June Claire saw Lucky's picture all the time, even though they never bought Lucky Star milk, and Buck quickly put away any paper that had her picture, and turned the channel if she came on the TV. June saw this and was drawn to that image even more, sensing more beyond what was known from the others around her. Julia gave her everything, and she expanded like a like a morning glory climbing over last years dead growth.

"Hey Junebug, what you staring at?" Buck asked June playfully as he came into the livingroom one day. Two year old June was transfixed on the TV set, even though the volume was down, and Buck noticed that Lucky Starr was on the news delivering an address. He quickly went over and turned it off, causing June to begin crying, then screaming. He hurried over and tried to comfort her, but it was too late, Julia was already running in from the garden.

"What happened?" Julia asked as she rushed June into her arms.

"I just turned off the TV," Buck said defensively. "I was going to pick her up and bring her outside."

"Then just pick her up and bring her outside, sweetie," Julia said in a consoling voice, either to Buck or June or both, as she walked out to the garden. "If you don't like what she's watching on TV you could just change it."

"I just don't think she should be watching like that," Buck said as he headed out to the garden behind them.

"You're right," Julia said, mostly convinced. She did not waste the luxury of over-deliberation. "There is so much for all of us out here." Julia came out in a song that she had been working on out about the leaves and the flowers, and June immediately lost her earlier concern and was joyfully singing along. Buck's heart blended into a wave of warmth as he saw them sit in a shaft of light next to falling petals. He joined them on the turf and encircled them both in the strong but gentle safety of his arms. They knew then, something they could not say. They knew that this was something very good, and that they should appreciate it for all they could. An old guardian watched over them, spreading some halo-caste shield, giving them those precious moments that they held in a transcendental sweetness, some older icon than the Madonna and Christ, a Golden Child and her parents circled in sacred warmth.

Half a world away Lucky was still connected to them, although she may not have understood how. Lucky felt like she was still at home even when she was India. She thought of things back home and felt like she was there, and she began to see Him everywhere too, back home and abroad, everywhere, nowhere not Home, because nowhere was without Him. But somehow she was without Him. She could not go home, she went all over, everywhere, but home. Everywhere she was needed, everywhere she went, but home. But back home, she was all over, she was everywhere, on everyone's lips, except in those two households, and even there she was on everyone's minds, even though she was no where to be found.

So Buck expanded, Julia rejoiced, June thrived, Belle baked, Bud watched, Ol' Pete persisted, Pico endured, and Lucky never did come home. Nothing could bring her home, it seemed, because she was already home. She had expanded so fast and so far in her consciousness that she could begin to sense all of her family and friends as part of a large web, a large interconnected tapestry that rose through all threads. But back home, home was still home, and things happen, ancient and certain, forgone and unavoidable. Ancient rites of life, from before the dawn of time, echoed in our conceptions of God as Father and Grandfather, Earth as Mother and Goddess, things set by deeper drives than instinct, that can and will, like a salmon to a stream, draw all things home.

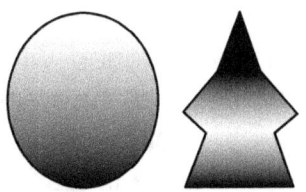

OnaNonno (21) Led

It was a cold night in early 2001 and Buck was already up putting June back to sleep when the call came through. Julia was asleep, something that for her was rare these days. She had gone back to work recently after June's birth, and she just never seemed to be able to get enough rest. Buck was trying his best to keep the chattering June out of earshot of the slumbering mom, so he had gone up to a upper room where they could quietly watch through a clear skylight the moon break through the clouds. The night was cold and crisp, clear as a mountain stream, and the moon cast a long shadow.

The phone was down in the living room so Buck really could not hear it at all, and mistook it in June's cooing. Julia ignored the call for as long as she could, figuring they would leave a message, and they could all hear it, but they never left a message. Instead, they would hang up, and call again. Finally, Julia had had enough, and she came flying past Buck and a calmer June in the dark who had eventually heard the ringing too. Julia realized that such persistence could not bode well at such an hour. Julia and Buck had developed a level of intuitional acuity, especially since the birth of June, that rivaled any the two of them had felt their entire lives. They lived in a heightened sense of appreciation as if they suspected that such days could not last. In such appreciation they reached a plateau of eternity, the long expanse of now given to those who honor the gifts of the present. Julia answered the phone and listened with persistent focus, then handed the phone to Buck as he handed June to her in one fluid motion that made the baby chortle pleasantly.

"It's Pico, he says Belle is lost," she said as she handed him the handset.

"What?" he asked, hearing but not understanding, as he began to listen to the voice on the other side. "Pico, Pico, slow down! My Spanish isn't that good. Retardo! Wait, slowly, en Anglais. That's right. She did? When?" He covered the mouth piece and spoke to Julia. "He says she just disappeared, like she wandered away. He thinks he sees a single set of tracks heading out from the back door..." They paused for a half moment in thought.

"Tell him to get Pete," Julia interjected.

"Where's Ol' Pete?" Buck said simultaneously. He listened and turned to Julia. "He says he's at his own farm and won't answer the phone, says he takes out his hearing aid at night."

"Buck, you've got to go," Julia realized.

"I'm coming right over, Pico," he agreed. "Get Luck ready, I'm gonna need her, and some another steed and two night kits, you and I will go out. All right." He hung up the phone and immediately sprang into action, grabbing a shirt off of a chair, hanging up the phone, and rushing upstairs.

"What's a night kit?" Julia asked him.

"Blanket, flashlight, first aid, flares, gun, rope..." Buck rattled off.

"Gun? Why a gun?" Julia challenged him.

"It's just a tool, just in case," he justified. "You never know what's out there, cougars, snakes, you know..."

"Well please be careful!" Julia begged him as she followed him up the stairs. "I'll pray for you, for your protection...and for Belle."

"That's great, and go ahead and call the sheriff too, please," Buck said frankly. "I'll take all the Divine help I can

get. You just take June upstairs and get some rest, okay?"
He took her in his arms and tried to comfort her. She could
feel his strength, and she felt a vibration, a quickening, and
she knew he was beginning to pulse on another plane. She
felt a Sacred Presence around him, and she knew it was good,
so she smiled and kissed him, letting him feel her reassurance.

Buck understood the gesture, and he was grateful for
her tender demeanor. He pulled the rest of his clothes and
shoes together with renewed vigor. As he kissed his wife and
daughter, his chest swelled with the heart of the heroic father,
and he pulled his hat off the rack and headed off into the
night. As he got into his truck for the fifteen minute drive, he
noticed his clock read 12:12, and he shivered, more in
anticipation than fear. He noticed the night swirled with the
hinting essences of misty mystery, the half moon flickering
through clouds to cast sparkles in the dew that hung on the
Spanish moss. Buck could feel the ghosts out tonight, Ohlone
natives, Spanish, early Americans, mingled on some
purgatorial plane. They seemed to gather in expectation, like
some answer lay nearby to their turmoil.

Buck pulled up his collar and turned on the radio, KPIG
107.5, and on was local favorites Creedance Clearwater
Revival singing "Midnight Special." The lines of Freedom Blvd.
faded in and out in the mist, and wall of gray surrounded
Buck's truck sporadically, causing him to slow occasionally.
He was trying to make as good a time as possible, sensing
that Belle's life was at stake and he was critical to her survival.
His senses were humming, and multiple impressions seemed
to be coming at him from somewhere, but he had to focus on
the driving. Things were blurring, wavy gray lines causing a
perceptible ripple in his view. It had only been ten minutes,
and he could not even tell which part of the road he was on in
the fog. He had to slow to a crawl for a moment, the Tule fog
hugging the ground like congealed cream, and he weaved in
and out of somewhere. He had only been out twelve minutes,

the clock read 12:24, so he was shocked when Pico came out of the gloom waving his arms.

"You missed the turn in the fog, Senor. Los Espiritus. They are out tonight." He said and he crossed himself, like many men grown spiritual in the face of the unknown. His eyes were wide and his face pale, and Buck could tell that Pico was halfway out of himself with fear.

"Impossible!" Buck yelled through the gust of wind that was blowing the fog in large sound dampening billows. "I just left. We must be lost."

"Si! Impossible!" Pico screamed back. "Si! We are lost! Belle is lost." A bolt of lightning cracked the sky and the rumble proceeded only moments later, rolling over the hills like a rockslide of sound. "Senor, follow me!" Pico shouted as he bolted back the road towards Buck's place. Buck reluctantly put the truck in reverse and followed Pico's damp white shirt which was the only thing visible in the gloom. Occasionally bolts of lightning would flash the landscape, splashing their vision with shadowy streaks. As they passed under the Lucky Star Ranch sign, Buck had to begrudgingly admit that they had arrived, but everything seemed twisted and out of place, nothing missing or moved, just in a different space. Buck felt the hair rise on the back of his neck as another bolt of lightning came down nearby, crashing simultaneously with the thunder.

"Pico!" Buck shouted as he brought the truck to a halt in front of the house. "Did you get the supplies?" He noticed someone rummaging around in the house. "Who is that in the house?"

"The supplies are on the horses in the stable ready to go. That is Bud in the house, and he is a bit loco." Pico answered both questions.

"Loco?" Buck wondered.

"Si, loco, Senor. He sometimes knows she is gone, and wants to get her, but does not understand," Pico tried to answer. "You must convince him to stay here."

"I see," Buck realized. "Well, get your poncho on and bring the horses out. I'll go in and talk to him. Buck rushed through the gathering storm, buttoning up his coat and pulling down his hat as he entered the old ranch house. It seemed a strange parody of itself when he briefly remembered the old times he spent here. Now, the soul was gone, but the structure hung on. Bud was rushing about the kitchen, fumbling and mumbling.

"Dern batteries! Why keep 'em if they're dead. I told you they got a place you can take 'em..." Bud went on. He persisted with a sort of extended momentum, but there was nothing at the root, nothing to sustain it all.

"Bud! I've come to find Belle!" Buck announced.

"Oh, Buck, there you are," Bud wove him into his stride. He was gathering odd bits of gear, like a thermometer, a clothespin, and a piece of string, and putting on layers of clothes haphazardly. "Find Belle? She went into town to get batteries. I told her not to keep dead ones. We need them for the flashlights for the search."

"Pico has lights with the horses," Buck informed him.

"Don't listen to him! He's crazy! El Loco, you know," Bud said, circling his finger around his ear. "He thinks Belle is out wandering in the storm, I told him he's crazy, she's out at the store, getting batteries for the search, lights all dead, you know. Crazy night, drives some men crazy."

"Bud!" Buck said, taking him by the shoulders, making Bud freeze for a moment. "The search for who?"

Bud's face froze in horror, realization, and an attempt to communicate through a frayed line. "Buck, Belle is gone! She is lost, out there...no lights." Bud started to writhe in Buck's hands and panic pervaded his demeanor, but he held something together. He trembled with a barely contained regularity.   Suddenly he became deadly still and lookeld sharply into Buck's eyes.   What he said next sent a chill down Buck. "And Buck, be warned, she's not right in the head."

Buck wondered for a moment, and realized he had missed it for months now. Belle had Alheimer's. "Bud!" Buck was trying to sound forceful, reassuring and trustworthy all at once. "You have to stay here! Wait for the sheriff. Tell him where we went! We are going to follow her tracks, okay? You have to stay here!"   Bud tried to nod, but he was trembling so much his head just went all over the place, making no particular commitment. Buck led him upstairs, into the bedroom, and set him on the bed. "Bud, wait here for the sheriff, okay?   We are going to go out and find her."

Bud stared blankly towards the floor, shaking lightly, and then he suddenly jumped up and shouted "Belle! Belle! Come out, damn it! I need you! I need...I need...HUH!...SHE needs...she needs me! She needs me!" He started to run and Buck caught him forcefully and put him back on the bed.

"She needs you to wait here for the sheriff! Got it, Bud?" He was practically yelling at him now, hoping to get the point across. Bud recoiled like a chastised child, curling up and nodding agreement. "Okay, so wait here, I will be back with her soon, I promise. Wait here, Bud!"   Buck slowly backed out the door, pointing an accusatory finger at Bud, trying to pin him to the bed with intent. Bud remained docile, relaxed in his acceptance, and Buck finally turned and went down the stairs. He did not see, nor did he even suspect, the subtle move with which Bud silently followed him through the shadows all the way out the front door.

"All right, let's go Pico," Buck said as he came up to the stable.

"Okay. Where is the old man?" Pico asked.

"He is in his room, waiting for the sheriff," Buck claimed.

"Waiting quietly?   I don't believe it."   Pico was incredulous.

"He's there, I tell you." Buck insisted.   "Let's get going while there are any tracks left.   You said there were some tracks out the kitchen door?"

"Si Senor," Pico led him around the house.   "It has not yet rained, so we are good.   Over here by the porch."   They both stooped down and brought a bright light to the ground. They changed the angle, and advanced a little, checking back as they went along.

"She went north, towards the canyon, of course!   The roughest spot on the ranch," Buck exclaimed.   "I'll tell Bud to tell the sheriff we went to the north forty."

"Buck, you don't understand," Pico reached out to him plaintively.   "Senor Bud is in no shape to tell anything, he is loco, and I am worried.   I take care of him every day for years now.   I know him.   Only I can tell what he is going to do. Why have we not heard him rustling about?'

"He is up in his room, I tell you," Buck kept on insisting.

"I am sorry, I do not think so," Pico protested, and ran upstairs.   He then ran all over the house and then came outside again.   The wind picked up with another lightening strike, and the first moisture started to fall from the sky.   Pico stopped at the top of the porch.   "Buck, the entire house is empty."

"What?"   Buck was still disbelieving.   "BUD! BUD! Oh shit! He's gone! Look for tracks."   They both scrambled around the house, checking the various exits.

"Over here, Buck!" Pico called out from the front.   Buck ran around and joined him.   "Look here, another set of tracks right behind yours, Bud's leather boot soles, look."   He outlined the smaller fainter prints that trailed behind Buck's own.

"I'll be damned," Buck said.   "You were right my friend, that wiley old dude slipped out right behind me.   Look at those strides, he was running. South towards the slough, too. Damned opposite direction as Belle. Pico, get the horses, let's go. We have to split. You have to go chase down Bud before he hurts himself while I go after Belle. Can you handle him?"

"Si, si. He calls me loco, but he knows me, and he will trust me," Pico reassured him. "I will get him, and you, be swift, find Senora Belle." They went over to the stables to get the horses, and as they opened the door Luck and Tiding stood ready to go in the shadows. They seemed to understand the situation, and came out expectantly. Pico grabbed Tiding, knowing who Buck would choose, and mounted the gelding, turning quickly to the south. "Adios, Amigo, go with God."

"I will, my friend, you too" Buck said warmly in a brief moment of silence, then a thunderclap sent both horses galloping in opposite directions, riders holding on as much as directing their mounts. Immediately they were in different realms, charging past dark amorphous obstacles in the night, their small lights almost more blinding in the fog rather than revealing. Buck felt the familiar presence, and he remembered his search for Lindy, and he wondered for a moment if Belle would be in his secret canyon. He stopped every so often to make sure he could still see Belle's tracks, and fortunately, as the earth was soft, they stood out clearly. He noticed that the tracks led away from the stream that wound down from the canyon, and he felt relieved for not having to track her through that rocky terrain. However, her tracks wove their way up towards the summit, and he felt a shiver when he thought about an old woman trying to make it along the summit with the weather the way it was.

Gradually, as he approached the ridge, he became uneasy as the earthen trail became mostly stone. He stopped for a moment at a last heel print, certain that this was likely the last one he would find. He knew the next step in chasing anything, and that was to think like his prey, in this case,

Belle. But how could a tracker get into the mind of someone who was losing it? Still, Buck had to try. He noticed that she had, for the most part, followed the old trail up to the summit. He knew that typically, when they went to the summit rocks they would follow a familiar arc across the stone face, but he could not quite remember it and he couldn't quite see it either.

"Hey, Luck, my best girl," be whispered into the mare's ear as he slowly dismounted the animal. "I'm afraid I'm going to have to leave you here." She snorted something of a disapproval, but she knew she had no choice. Buck tied her to a nearby manzanita trunk, and stared hard at a broken twig. He braced himself against the wind that pinned his coat against him like damp linen. Luck hoofed the earth and snorted more loudly. Bucks light seemed to dim as he set out across the dome of the rocks, or perhaps the background had become more lit. Buck's eyes shifted focus back and forth trying to hold the scene until he finally gave in and allowed a deeper vision to guide him. Luck snorted again, and Buck set out across the stone. He envisioned an expanse before him, with some glowing source in the distance, and that source was Belle. He did not really think that she glowed, but he did not know how else to picture it, and he somehow had to find her in this gloom. Somehow he advanced quickly over the living rock and scree, coming at last to a spot where his memory seemed to fail him, or he had failed the trail, or the hill had failed the trail, because suddenly the ground disappeared. Buck hit his bottom hard as he returned to earth, and he barely managed to skin-rippingly grab a manzanita bush to bring himself to a halt.

After mentally checking his body and deciding for the most part that his skeletal structure was undamaged, he also had a heart-rending supposition about Belle that she might have experienced something similar. His light had slid further down the hill and burst out with a flash. He looked down through the black and thought he could see. There was no moon, and no stars, but everything glowed, and glowed most strongly right out in front of him. He could tell that the slope in front of him was precipitous, basically an active slide, and that it traversed down into the canyons area of the ranch. He had another moment of recognition when he realized that he was probably coming down on his old secret nook in the mountain. He remembered how steep were the walls, and how sharp the rocks. He still slid steadily down the mountain, maintaining his equilibrium by focusing on an undulating glow that emanated somewhere down below his feet. The pitch gradually increased and Buck found himself fairly shooting down the chute, barely slowing himself down with fingers like claws in the dirt.

As he plummeted the last several yards pretty much straight down, he realized that he should make a move to keep from hitting Belle at the bottom, and he seemed to see a group of glowing figures below him at the last moment as he sprung with his feet, pushing against the wall and sailing headfirst into the darkness. He landed thankfully on a sandy stretch with only a minimum of sharp gravel to grind in the reality of his position. Once again he did a mental review of the state of his bones and found them relatively intact, if bruised a bit. He lay with his face in the sand, noticing a fiery glow illuminating the grains, and he remembered the last time he was laying here. The light was the same, if yet deeper, more saturated, somehow more sad. He knew Belle was here, and he knew She was here, even before he turned around and got to his knees. When he did, he had to rub his eyes, not because they were filled with sand, although they were, but because he could hardly absorb what was in front of him. The light was pouring out of Mother Mary, her hair wrapped around a beaten and battered Belle, embracing her with what appeared to be arms and body made of millions of tiny women, somehow all mothers, all colors and races, like some huge mosaic, each moving as one with compassion and concern. As he looked closer he realized that the Mother was holding something blazing that was holding Belle, and as Buck's eyes tried to adjust he though he saw the Christ before it finally faded into the mist, and he saw her body lying there alone.

Belle was bloody and virtually unrecognizable except for her red stained gray hair and her light blue floursack dress, now tattered and muddy. But Belle's bulging face, looking almost like something from a butcher shop, was yet serene, shining with an inner beatific vision, and her eyes did not see Buck pick her up and carry her back to the horse, and she smiled through broken lips, and tears of joy ran in rivulets through the red.

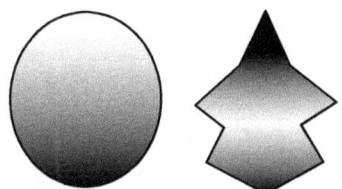

OnaDekka (22) Rescued

The strain of Buck's eyes matched that of his back as he rode into the red flashing lights surrounding the ranch house in the fog, carrying Belle in his arms and letting Luck lead the way. The lightning and the rain came in sheets, hitting in sudden jolts that Buck might have thought unusual at another time. He did not think much this night, for thought was a luxury for those left with energy, but he still felt. He felt things he would never remember for long, for he did not want to remember them, but these feelings changed him, and he was okay with that. Feeling came in waves, pain punctuated with deep anguish dimmed only perhaps by an approaching wisdom earned through years of persistence. Buck knew how to keep going. He knew he did not always know where he was going, but he allowed himself enough humility to make continuous minor course corrections and sooner or later get along pretty well, or so he figured.

As he carried Belle towards the waiting ambulance, he could not think of many of these things, but he did not waste energy blocking the feelings, so he felt an imbalance. His heart wondered why this would happen, where was everybody that should have taken care of Belle. She had taken care of people her whole life, and no one was around for her in what might be her last moments. What happens to people? He felt and knew the absence, sure he had to acknowledge a Divine Hand that was everywhere, had guided him to Belle and sheltered her until he got to her, so he knew about That, but the people were not there, no names came to his mind, but there should be people there, for a lady like Belle who had done so much for so many over the years. Then he realized that he was people, and he felt a little better.

As Buck handed Belle over to the medics, he saw two men riding a single horse over the south ridge along the road, flashed out of the shadows now and again by the bolts of lighting, emerging as out of a felt painting into the lights and commotion of the ranch house. No one else saw the other riders until Buck ran over through the mist, knocking through some officers to get to the two men. He took Bud down into his arms, and Buck marveled again how light the old man had become. He had a gash on his head that was bleeding lightly, his whole body was smeared with mud, and he was mumbling continuously somewhat coherently, loud enough in some King Lear cackle for everyone to here in the storm.

"Ah there you are Buck I was trying to tell Pico here that Belle has gone to the store, and I was going to find her, to get her, but he forcefully brought me back, just picked me up and brought me back..." Bud went on.

"Bud," Buck almost yelled, "Belle is here, Belle is here."

Bud stopped himself for a minute as Buck carried him to the ambulance. "What? She is?" he asked. "Well then I told him she was all right, just take me up to the kitchen with her, we'll be all right."

"Bud, she's not all right," Buck tried to explain. "She's here but she's not all right, and you're not all right."

"Waddya mean, I'm not all right? I'm fine!" Bud insisted, and tried to straighten up in Buck's arms.

"You're not fine," Buck insisted. "You have a gash on your head, and Belle is hurt, too."

"A gash?" Bud felt at his head and looked at his hand. "You're right, I'm bleeding. Must have been that Pico, he must have hit me."

"I did not," said Pico, who was right behind them.

"You must have hit me," Bud insisted.

"I picked you up out of a ditch," Pico informed them. "How do you think you got all that mud all over you?"

"Well you must have pushed me into the ditch," Bud claimed.

Buck tried to calm things down as they came up to the medics. "Now, Bud, no one pushed anyone, you two had accidents tonight, and these people are going to give you some help." The medics were prepping Belle to go into the ambulance. "Belle is here, and she is going first."

Bud looked down at his wife on the stretcher, and slowly he began to shake his head. "No, no...that's not Belle. That is nothing like Belle. Belle is in the kitchen. I have to go..." He began to struggle in Buck's arms. "Let me go! Let me go! Damn Pico, I said she's all right, let me go..." Buck could not resist, and he let go, let Bud go into the medics, let his feelings go without a thought. He felt the absence still, but he did not want to be the only one anymore, he wanted to be absent too, he had to be absent too, he felt he was already absent, absent in the old man's yells with Pico in his place, so he faded further, or maybe it all faded altogether, but soon it was in the distance, flashing lights rushing off to some distant destination, until they were all gone. There had been police interviews, and descriptions, but everyone faded away, and soon Buck was alone, getting into his truck for the drive home.

"Well at least the rain is letting up," he actually said aloud as he started up Freedom Blvd. He knew every turn, and some inner angel kept the truck on the road as Buck's consciousness wanted to slip away. Still he made it back, and did not think, could not think, but feel again, as he saw his wife Julia come to him with their daughter in her arms. What he felt, he could not tell her, but she could know, did know, and he knew she knew, because she had been there too, with his heart. The three met at the door in the kitchen, a single embrace, holding the love and warmth of home and return.

They knew too much, and did not dwell, but held deeply, knowing that they had earned the warmth and reassurance of each other's presence when so many outside were cold and alone. The pale light signaled some end to the night, but the storm held sway in its dying echoes of fury spent, the misty window shadows of the trees outside quivering, damp and bent and beaten, bowing to a new endurance. Buck held his family deep in his embrace, and remembered that spark that seemed to be the Heart of All Compassion that had held Belle that night. June and Julia felt the tremor of sheltering affection, and hummed their warmth in return.

Julia broke the non-words. "You found her, and she was hurt, now at the hospital..." she surmised.

Buck nodded. "And Bud. Hurt not so bad, but...not so good, either."

"But you saved them," Julia pushed on. "And you saw something."

"Many things," Buck agreed. "Did you see too?"

Julia tried to see what she saw. "I saw...you seeing things, right?"

"Yes," was all Buck could say anymore, really. He struck out in thought on various descriptions of what he had seen, but none of them really made sense, so he just guided them up the stairs and into bed and hoped they understood. For the most part they did.

June cooed with that instinctive satisfaction of the dream state caressed by the presence of one who had been away and in danger, in this case her dad. He lay her softly in her bed and caressed her forehead. He thought in his heart that he could never describe the feeling when he looked onto the happy sleeping face of June. He brought the blankets up close around her shoulders and placed a stuffed horsey that was her favorite under the covers with her. June's arms wrapped around the toy animal of their own accord and she felt one more tiny addition of comfort and bliss in her distant dream land.   Buck went back in the room and discovered Julia had been stifling a coughing fit.

"You don't need to stifle it," Buck said, concerned. "It's not good for you."

"It's not good to cough endlessly till me throat is sore, either," she worked out. "And it is no good to wake up June and make her worry more than she already does."

"She is sound asleep in blissland," Buck said in reassurance. "You just worry about yourself."

"I'm tired of worrying, about you, June, medical bills..." She went on.

"Don't worry about any of that, it will work out, you'll see..." Buck really believed it, because he had to, and it lacked no conviction, still there was something missing. Julia did not notice anything missing, however, and took her husband in her arms, accepting his warmth and his strength into her. Sweet release, and they went off their separate ways together in dreamland.

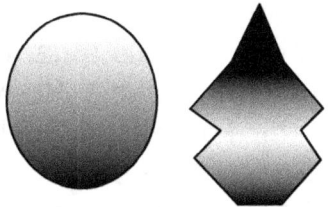

OnaAmanna (23) Remembered

Nothing else was stirring as Buck got up and dressed without waking anyone as if going to work, not daring to disturb the rare peaceful slumber that momentarily pervaded their house. He dressed warmly, for he could tell by the color of the first light that the world outside would still be overcast and wet. He silently cursed the few loose boards in the stairs that he had not yet fixed as he made his way through the gloom to the kitchen where he passed on his usual coffee making. His mouth and spine missed the familiar java warmth as he considered making a pot but he doggedly pushed through to the truck. His fingers slipped on the door handle and his hand protested with a familiar pain. Buck knew that he was tired enough to have that crusted feeling in all his senses, but pain came through loud and clear.

The road out to Highway 1 retained the fingers and tendrils of fog that had characterized the night before. Buck could not suppress a shudder. He knew he had witnessed something mystical, something magical, when he had rescued Belle, but there was no way to think about it, or so he figured. The repression remained as a ripple that occasionally passed through his stoic demeanor like a tremor through a sandcastle. He probably would have broken down, given in, given up, long ago, if he could. Instead he guessed he would just die one day mid-stride, taken out by some colossal blow, or pushed to internal hemorrhaging. This somehow seemed appropriate to him, and somehow seemed an appropriate thing to be thinking about at this time, to him. His mortality comforted him like a warm blanket. He was never the type to want to live forever, he knew that would prove tedious and painful. Something somewhere deep within him remembered that, in passing on, there was rest and peace.

Those who choose to accept their own death, however it comes, live with a certain invincibility. Buck was beginning to feel fine pushing into realms of new extremes because he knew it would inevitably end the same. He felt there was some greater peril hidden in inaction, some shameful neglect to use the time wisely, that drove him along now, down Highway 1. He felt he should not have to be taking care of this, and he could not help but think of Lucky, and where the hell she had been for years. He had let her go, certainly, but he still felt like family, and it was not right that Belle and Bud were going through all this and had hardly any knowledge of the whereabouts of their own daughter. They probably had no knowledge about most anybody around them anymore. To see Bud's reaction to Pico had sent a chill down his back. This man he had known all his life, more than his own father, and he had seen him as the embodiment of all that was good and true and honorable, the sort of things that were so rare that a young boy who cared had to search out. Bud had always been all of these things, a rare western gemstone persisting in the swirling dust of unfinished modern manhood.

Bud's mother had died two years before, and Belle had also been like a mother to him over the years, feeding him and giving warmly as long as he could remember. He was actually happy to be able to help her, now, if he could. He told himself that he should not be doing this, that Lucky should be here, but he could not let himself admit that he missed her. He missed something, some sense of knowing, a certainty, a familiarity, and he thought Belle missed it too, and somehow that is why she went wandering the night before. Bits of branches and greenery lay scattered about the road, and he would occasionally have to swerve around the bigger pieces. One had the vague shape of a human lying down and Buck pictured the crumpled shape of Belle from the night before and winced.

He was ahead of the morning commute traffic so he made it to the hospital quickly. As he checked in at the front desk he had trouble at first getting to see Bud and Belle, as he was not official kin. A call to the sheriff eventually cleared that up and he learned their current condition. Belle was in intensive care and was still listed as critical. Bud was listed as stable but catatonic with sporadic dementia. His room was nearer so Buck went to see him first.

Buck cautiously peered from the door and saw Bud sitting up in bed against some pillows. He had a new bandage on his head and he stared at a television hanging from the ceiling that was turned off. Buck slowly walked in but his presence did not seem to register to Bud. His eyes stared fixedly at nothing, or something that Buck just could not see. Buck placed his body directly in Bud's gaze, and he actually seemed to register something. Perhaps an eyebrow raised slightly, but Bud still looked ahead and stayed where he was. He did manage to speak in half a breath.

"Buck," was all that came out.

"They said you were catatonic," Buck informed him.

"They...don...no..." Bud was able.

"Belle is..." Buck began.

"Dead...I killed her..." He suddenly turned towards Buck completely, water filled the black holes of his eyes, and his mouth fell open in horror. The image rent Buck deep in his soul, his lifelong image of masculine strength reduced to this strange weeping wraith.

"No...No sir...not dead," Buck stammered. "She is critical but alive. I am going to check on her now."

"She has moved on!" Bud said with crisp clarity. "And I sent her there, by being so cold. A buttercup of pure love like

Belle needs real affection, not this stumbling...st..st...stiff..."
He quickly lost clarity and composure as he faded back into
his interior space. "I killed her! Drove her into the ground!
And Pico too! He hit me! And Luck..." He stopped himself.

"No sir," Buck pleaded with him. "No one's fault. Belle
loves us all, and she is still alive...Please, sir."

"Okay...It's okay," Bud said lifting his hand. "She's gone
on, even if her body hangs on. I am almost there most of the
time too." He pointed up. "The Real Old Man up there still
has something for me down here. Probably too mean still, got
to work some of it off. Belle is done. She was so pure that
she was done long ago, she still held on for us, you know. I'll
joining her soon."

"Sir, you are not dying!" Buck insisted.

"Wake up, boy! We're all dying!" Bud laid out. "But
no, you are right, I am not dead now, and may not be for
awhile yet. That's what I'm saying, but...Belle is done."

"Well, I am going to check on her, because I don't think
so. I think she is still alive. I'll see what I can do." Buck
started to turn and go out the door.

"Buck!" Bud stopped him with the strength of his
voice. "There is one thing you can do..."

"Anything," Buck offered.

"Promise," Bud said.

"Promise what?" Buck asked.

"No, promise first..." Bud insisted.

"What? That's ridic..." Buck started.

"PROMISE!"

"Okay! I promise! What?"

"Promise not to come after me..."

"But, Bud, I can't..."

"You promised! So help me God, and you know He
will, you cannot come after me!" Bud flared with a fire, and
Buck knew not to argue with his elders.

"Y...Yes, sir," was all that Buck could say. "I need to check on Belle." He quickly whisked out the door. He could hardly stand the pressure of it all anymore. Watching Bud this way, having this required of him, was too much for him to handle anymore. As he headed up to the critical care unit, he found himself speaking out loud, and he only vaguely realized that he was talking to Lucky.

"You heard him...he said Belle was driven there by Luck...then he stopped himself. Did he mean the horse? No. He couldn't say it, that his Lucky Star had shot past the horizon...No one left for them. Nope. Save all the damn animals in the world, but leave kin to die alone...What is that? Who deserves that? Will I get that too? Will you all leave? Will June break my heart, too?" By the time he made it to Belle's room, his eyes were completely filled with tears. The pooling moisture created kaleidoscopic lenses to break and scatter the light coming from the room, and Buck could hardly see. As he looked through the mist into the room, he thought he could see the Virgin Mary again, her heart open and blazing, holding a bundle next to Belle. They both cuddled the shining infant, and Buck though he could make out thousands of tiny prismatic angels, singing to them.

Buck wiped his eyes with his sleeve, and the scene settled into a more mundane aspect. The Virgin Mary became a nurse checking Belle's vital signs, and the angels were the various lights on all the equipment about the room. Buck still seemed to hear music echoing in the distance, but he figured that must be something funny in the ventilation. Belle's face was till swollen beyond recognition, and bandages covered most of her visage.

"Can I help you with something?" the nurse asked beatifically.

"I'm...I'm here to see Belle," Buck told her.

"Are you family?"

"Yes," he said simply. He was too tired to try to explain otherwise.

"Are you...Buck?" the nurse asked, and she flared with a bit of the Holy Mother intensity and vibration, or so it seemed to Buck.

"Yes, how did you know?" he wondered.

"She mentioned you," the nurse revealed. "Every once in awhile she comes out and she starts talking. Not to me, particularly, just out loud, kind of like sleep talking. She mentions Bud, and I know there was a Bud checked in with her last night. And she mentioned someone named Lucky, although that seemed to be a girl, and she mentioned Jesus, and I'm pretty sure you're not Him, and she mentioned someone named Buck, so I guessed..."

"Yeah, good guess, I...guess..."

"Let me leave you alone," the nurse said as she gathered her things.

"No, that's not necessary, really," Buck protested.

"No, I must," she insisted. "I have to continue my rounds." She looked back at Belle. "You know, you can talk to her. She might be able to here you. I think she would be glad to know you were here."

"Yes, I think she would be glad to know I was here."

"Just press that button if you need anything," and she was gone.

Buck walked up to the bed and stared down at the battered woman that had been so much of a mother to him. He put his hand to her cheek and it was warm which seemed good to him. He shuffled a bit on his feet and fiddled with the zipper on his jacket.

"Hi Belle, uh...that was quite a ride we had last night, eh? We saw some crazy things, didn't we? I know you must have been seeing something, or you would not have gone out on a night like that. Don't worry, I don't blame you. I would go to the ends of the world for you. No bother really. You have lot's of people here to support you, that love you. I love you.   I have always loved you, just like I have always loved...uh, Bud is here. He is okay.   He is worried for you. I'd like to tell him that you're doing better. He says...uh...he blames himself, a bit, but I don't let him think...he thinks...um...he thinks more clearly, right now, it seems, mostly.   You would like to see him...he would like to see you...and, well..." he finally had to stop. He had no more in him. He might have cried, but he had no more in him.

"Buck..." The voice seemed to float from everywhere, and it took a moment for him to even hear it. "Buck...thank you..." He finally realized that it was coming out of the mass of bandages.

"Belle! Belle, don't talk! You should conserve your strength." He put his hand on her arm and she turned towards him.

"Buck...It's not like that. Energy is for reaching out, while you're here. You're here. Thank you. I know how much you have done, how much you have gone through."

"No, no, Belle, it's nothing. It is YOU that have gone through a lot." He tried to turn it around. "You have to rest so you can get your strength back."

"No, no, Buck, that's not what it's about. It's okay. Jesus is with me, and he has told me a lot. He has told me a lot about you, and about Lucky, and Bud...I understand so much better now..." She started to beam underneath the bandages. "It is all so beautiful...so beautiful...He has shown me many things...many things are going to happen...and a GRANDSON...oh my...can't you see, Buck?" Her countenance changed slightly. "Buck? Is it dark in here?"

"You have bandages over your eyes," he told her.

"Oh, yes, I can feel something..." she acknowledged. "But I can still see...everything is a strange color, like a milky rainbow...and I can see through things, like there you are...and Jesus is there next to you...and Mary...and, the walls, the walls are like tissue...and look, there's Lucky! I knew Lucky would come! That's really why I did it, you know. I'm sorry it was so hard for you. I know it was hard for you, but it will be wonderful, really, you and Lucky, and a Grandson!"

"Look, Belle, I'm sorry, but...uh...it is not quite like that...um...Lucky couldn't make it, she's not here...we're not together..."

"What's that, Dear?"

"I said, we're not together, me and Lucky..."

"No, quiet Buck, I'm talking to Jesus. He says...what? Oh, he says you won't be able to understand. He says not to try to convince you, that he told me so I would not worry anymore."

"That's right," Buck agreed. "You needn't worry any more."

"Oh, Buck, it's all so beautiful! I finally understand it all with Lucky, and why she could not see how she loved you..."

"Please, Belle..."

"She might understand, Lord. You could talk to her. Yeah, me too. He says He's tried to talk to her."

"Yeah, I bet He has," Buck nodded. "Belle, Lucky is an independent woman, you know, and she has chosen her own path. I don't know why, but it has led far away, and she hasn't come back."

"Yes, she has," Belle contradicted him. "She is here. She knows, she went off, but she couldn't leave completely, really, Buck, with you, too. She'll tell you. I'll ask her."

"Lucky is not here, Belle, I'm telling you..."

"I am here," Lucky said from the doorway. Buck gasped and almost lost his footing. She had just stepped into the doorway, unnoticed except by Belle, of course.

"See, I told you. Lucky! I knew you would come!"

"OH Mom!" Lucky ran to her bedside. "Poor dear! I came as soon as I could."

"Really?" Buck could not hold back. "Ten years is as soon as you could?"

Lucky was unfazed. "As soon as I could after I heard. I thought maybe she had..."

"Oh, I see, a funeral will bring you home. I wondered."

"Buck, I'm sorry," and she truly was. "I know you have gone through a lot..."

"Do you? Do you have any idea how...no, uh...I'm sorry. I have been going through a lot."

"It's okay, kids, can't you see?" Belle asked. "Oh, Jesus says you can't understand. I see...well...listen then, don't worry, it's all more beautiful than you realize."

"Yeah, Ma, we're here, we're listening...we love you so much, and I am so sorry..."

"No dear, don't worry. Look, I understand now. Jesus told me. He said He was the one you had fallen in love with. Was it really the lord you had fallen in love with?"

"Well, yes, I guess so..."

"No problem, dear, to love the Lord is to love everyone. You can still love the Lord and love Buck, too."

"It's different, though, Mom..."

"I don't think so. Jesus has been right about everything, and he even said I am to have a grandson!"

"Mom, I'm not going to have a child, I'm sorry."

"That's what you think, now..."

"No, Mom, I know this, okay?"

Buck grabbed Lucky's arm and pulled her over to the side. They were both surprised by the feel of it, and it immediately thrust them into an old familiarity. He spoke softly to her, but Belle still heard everything.

"Look, maybe we should just humor her. She keeps slipping in and out of clarity. She gets some crazy ideas. I think we shouldn't argue with her."

"I can't lie to her," Lucky protested.

"You can't argue with me, and you can't lie to me," Belle interjected. "I see things so clearly now. Lucky, I am so sorry for doubting you. I see so much about what you are doing now."

"Mother, you have been everything for me. I am sorry...I...wasn't everything you needed of me..."

"But you were more, much more, I see that now."

"Uh, look," Buck fidgeted. "I think I should go now, okay?"

"You can stay," Lucky said.

"Uh, no, I have to go. Belle, I'm sorry, I have to get going, but I will come back soon to see you."

"No Buck," Belle shook her head. "I have to be going, too, only I won't be coming back anytime soon. It is so beautiful. But, Bud, take care of Bud, Buck. He needs some help. Listen to him, do what he says."

"I can take care of Dad, Mom," Lucky claimed.

"Buck knows what I mean. Listen to Bud, Buck."

"What is she talking about?"

"Well, I...I don't know. Just keep a good eye on Bud."

"I...will," Lucky looked at him suspiciously.

"I...I really have to go. Belle, I love you."

"Oh, Buck, take heart, you are more loved than you realize," Belle revealed.

"Yeah, well, goodbye..." With that, he left. He just could not handle it all anymore. They were left alone, and somehow the atmosphere was quickened, as if the business at hand could now progress quickly.

"The Lord is here, you know," Belle said. "He says hello."

"Really?" Lucky said nonchalantly. "Hello back, then."

"He says He loves you. He has always loved you. He says He loved you back during the earthquake."

"Oh?" Lucky was being slowly disarmed of her psychological defenses. "I'm not sure I believe all that."

"He says that fortunately existence does not require belief."

"Ask..." Lucky began but halted when she realized how her mom had echoed her Beloved's words from so long ago. "Ask Him...why He left me?"

"He says He never left you. You left Him," Belle maintained. "Yes, I can see that."

"But I went all over the world looking for Him!" Lucky complained.

"He says He was here all along."

"Then ask Him to appear to me now," Lucky suggested.

"But He is right next to you!" Belle pointed out. "Why can't she see you? It's okay, you can. You don't need to worry about me."

"What's He saying?" Lucky asked.

"He says He is not here for you right now. He says He's here for me, but I don't need Him. She needs You. He says you will come around later. I believe that." Belle calmed down to a quiet peacefulness. "And Bud, go to Bud, okay, Lucky, he's the one who needs you."

"What does...Jesus say?" Lucky wondered.

"He says...what? He says...He has to take me now. Really, now? Oh, it's so beautiful! I'm sorry, Lucky, but I want to go. Is that all right? He says I have to go. He says He loves you always. Tell Bud I love him always. OH! So beautiful."

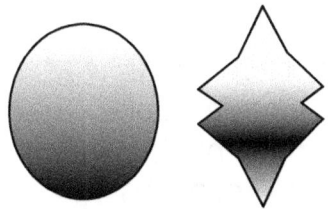

OnaAgappa (24) Relieved

"Hello?" Buck answered. June squeaked excitedly in Buck's arms as he answered the phone. It was a Sunday night and he had been enjoying time at home with his family for the first time in a long time. He did not expect the voice on the other side to belong to Lucky.

"Hi Buck, it's me," she said, somehow confident he would recognize her voice.

"Uh, hey..." Buck hesitated. "Um, I'm sorry I didn't make it to the funeral, today. I tried, but, you know, I didn't really, uh..."

"No, no, Buck, don't worry about that. Everyone knows how much you have done," she assured him. "That's not why I'm calling."

"Oh really, why are you calling?" he asked casually. June kept grabbing at the phone and cooing and gurgling, inserting a newly learned English word here and there, trying to get her daddy's attention.

"I was just calling because..." Lucky's voice trailed off as June finally grabbed the phone and threw it on the floor. Buck felt some sort of emotion welling up that ultimately expressed itself as frustration. He picked up the phone and tried to bob and dance with June in order to distract her.

"What was that?" Lucky asked in response to the crash.

"That was just June," Buck said. "Now what were you saying?"

"June?"

"Yes, June, my daughter."

Hearing her name June responded with more vocalizations. "Daddy humhun bluvdee bib."

"A daughter! My goodness! I'm sorry, Buck, I didn't know."

"Yeah, you missed a lot."

"How old is she?"

"She's three."

"I'm free!" June exclaimed, holding three fingers in the air.

"That's wonderful, Buck," Lucky said. "Congratulations."

"Thank you," Buck replied curtly. "Now, what was this you wanted to talk about?"

"I'd like to meet with you and talk in person," she proposed.

"Why? What is it? Why can't we talk about it now." Buck pressed.

"Well, it is rather big and complex to talk about over the phone."

"If it is all that fired important that you would call me after all this time then you call tell me what it is now."

"Uh, okay..." Lucky paused trying to find the right words. "Um, Buck...look, I need you."

"Ha!" Buck cut her off.

"HA!" June echoed her father.

"No, not like that, I mean..." Lucky struggled to regain her footing. "Uh, let me try again. I have a substantial business proposition for you."

"Yeah, I gathered. What is it already?"

"Uh..." This was not easy for Lucky. "I would like you to come run the Lucky Star Ranch."

"No," Buck responded quickly. "Anything else?"

"I'm willing to pay you twice what you make with Shamrock."

"Not enough," Buck replied. "Anything else I can help you with."

"Buck, I'm in a bind. I have to get back to H.E.L.P. and I need someone to take over. With Ol' Pete gone, and dad a job in himself."

"What about Pico?"

"He's gone."

"What?"

"He disappeared. I think the thing with Dad was too much for him."

"Damn! It was the way Bud was accusing him, I bet. He had no buffer. You should have been here, you could have taken care of your dad and kept Pico around."

"Buck, I am sorry I have been gone, okay? I have to do what I have to do."

"You don't have to do anything, you just do what you want to do."

"I don't want to argue about it, I just..."

"I don't want to talk at all," Buck said. "Any other business proposals?"

"Listen, I will pay you three times your salary at Shamrock."

"It's not about the money?"

"What's it about then? Is it personal?"

"Well, no," Buck lied. "It's just, I have doubts about your absentee management style. I think the Ranch is neglected with all of your other projects."

"You mean you would want me around to micro-manage?"

"No, not exactly..." Buck pondered. "A ranch just has to be a top priority for the owners to manage it well."

"I would let you manage it however you like," Lucky was desperate. "Look, I'll even give you half-ownership."

"Half-ownership?   My, you are desperate.   Half-ownership for a ranch manager? That is not good business."

"This is a special offer to you. I wouldn't offer it to anyone else."

"You trying to buy off your conscience?"   Buck suggested.

"Not at all," Lucky was emphatic. "I just know there is not a better choice in the world for this position. This is not easy for me. I am doing this because of my love of the Ranch."

"Your love of the RANCH," Buck stressed. "Well, when you leave things you love they don't always respond in the way you expect."

"Yes, I know, I have learned that in many ways, believe me."

"I believe you." Buck allowed. Julia entered the room and took June from his arms, and then waited while Buck talked on the phone.

"Is there anything I can say for you to consider this position?" Lucky asked.

"No," Buck stated firmly.

"All right. Then I won't waste any more of your time," Lucky decided.

"Thank you. Good-bye." And he hung up.

"What was that about?" Julia asked.

"Just a business proposal," Buck tried to dismiss the topic. "Hey, want to go out to dinner tonight?"

"I'd love to go out to dinner, but don't change the subject. What kind of proposal?"

"To manage a ranch. It's beneath me."

"Which ranch?" Julia pressed. She was beginning to suspect, but her reaction was turning out to be different then Buck suspected.

He hesitated. "...the Lucky Star."

"Of course. With all the changes. When is the funeral?"

"Today."

"Today? And you didn't go?"

"No. I...I didn't feel up to it."

"Oh...okay" Julia paused while she considered things. "So, that was Lucky on the phone, was it?"

"Yes."

Julia paused only a moment. "What did she offer you?"

"Three times Shamrock."

"Oh Lord! Three times your Shamrock salary?"

"Yes. And half the Ranch."

"Half of the Lucky Star Ranch?! And you didn't take it?"

"No, I don't want it."

Julia started to get worked up. "Honey, do I have to remind you that we have some unique responsibilities and expenses coming up."

"No, of course not. I just...I can do this myself. I don't need Lucky Star's help."

"It sounds like she needs your help. Has Shamrock responded to your requests about coverage?"

"Uh...yes, well," Buck swallowed. "They say they can't change our coverage because of the group plan they have enrolled in, and some other this and that..."

"So why not consider the offer from Lucky, especially if you can make demands, maybe get some real coverage."

"I thought about it..." Buck said. He softened suddenly and took up his wife and daughter in his arms. "Julia, I want it to be about us, now. I want to focus on you and June, take care of you. I am tired of that Ranch and all of its needs."

"You are hardly home, now. Traveling all over the state for Shamrock," Julia softened too, and spoke quietly in his ear. "Buck, I know there are a lot of feelings there, and feelings for Lucky, and I'm okay with that. You knew them long before you knew me. All I have to ask you is, do your feelings for Lucky get in the way for your feelings for me?"

"Not at all," Buck was certain. "You are my life, my everything, you and June. Nothing...in life...can come between us."

"Then what is the problem?" she looked deeply in his eyes.

"I...I don't want you to be hurt, or jealous, or anything. I don't want you to think for a moment that there is any other object of my love but you two."

"That is very sweet. I don't want you to be hurt, either. Would working there be painful for you?"

"No, not at all. I'm a grown man, I can handle it. I'm worried about you."

"I'm a grown woman, too. Please no more worrying about me than necessary. And, I have to say, with what she is offering, if me and June are your only concerns, then don't you think you could get over your hurt and take this?"

"My word, you are right again," Buck realized. "I see how I have been selfish. I was trying to make a point, or something. I was trying to let Lucky flounder in her own choices."

"And prove what?"

"Next to nothing, except maybe how stupid I can be," Buck smiled.

"So, what are you going to do?"

"I...I will call her back and...and maybe negotiate some more."

"Now, don't do this if you really don't want to. I am not pressuring you."

"No, I know. Really, I want to do it. Are you kidding, that much money for riding around a ranch? Being able to see you two several times a day? Of course I want it, but I have to set it all straight. Make it just right."

"Okay, then. Are you going to call her?"

"Yeah, uh...I don't have her number," he fumbled.

"Hit redial."

"Oh yeah."

Julia picked up June and headed towards the kitchen. "I'll get out of your hair...give you some privacy." She was gone before he could protest. He squinted at the keypad, thought for a moment, and hit the button.

"Hello?" Lucky knew who it was but she held her breath back.

"Hi, Lucky, it's Buck," he was informal again.

"Hi, Buck." They both were talking like it was about the weather or sports.

"I've decided to negotiate with you, if you are still open."

She had to squelch an excited squeek. He did not notice. "I am. What do you need?"

"Well, to start, three times my salary at Shamrock," he began.

"Okay," she was a business woman. "What, exactly, is your salary at Shamrock?"

"One hundred twenty..."

"Thousand?"

"Yes."

Lucky swallowed hard. "And?"

"And half the ranch?"

Lucky's throat closed. "I will have to talk to my father."

"I understand. It's not for me, not in my name."

"Whose?"

"June Claire Smith. In a trust."

"Oh, okay, sure. I mean, I'll talk to dad, but you know, that shouldn't be a deal breaker, right? If I agree to it?"

"No, not if I can get some kind of agreement with her in it. Because I want you to know, it's not for me. I don't want the Lucky Star, not like this. I just want you to know I'm not trying to take the ranch from you."

"I know that, Buck, I do. I'm surprised I could get you to come back at all."

"To the ranch? Well, of course, I love the ranch."

"Then we have a deal?"

"Not yet. There is something else. The most important thing." Buck paused.

"What is it?"

"I need you to guarantee 100% medical for me and my family, with all copays and no limits, including any extraneous therapies or additional treatments." Buck finally caught his breath. He had been rehearsing the entire list.

"My goodness, Buck, of course, but...why? Are you okay?"

"Yes, yes, I'm fine. It's...not for me."

"For who, then? June?"

"No, not June. It's...Julia."

"Julia? What's wrong with Julia?"

"Julia has advanced breast cancer."

"My God!" Lucky gasped. "I'm so sorry. I didn't know."

"I realize you did not know. Now do you understand better?"

"Uh...yes, yes, of course. Full medical, everything. How is it? Has it been in remission?"

"It was but recently it has returned and a spot has appeared on her lung."

"Oh dear, Buck, anything, anything I can do..."

"I tried to make it clear..."

"Oh, right, of course. Then, do we have a deal?"

"I believe so." With that, Buck hung up, and Lucky let the receiver slowly fall as she stared into the distance.

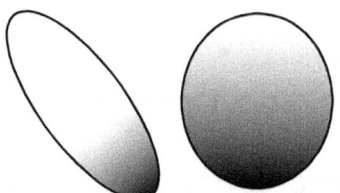

DuaOna (25) Restored

As Buck, Lucky, and Bud rode up to the ranch house it almost seemed like old times. Of course, they all felt the difference, but they also felt something new that they welcomed. It was a sort of ease, almost a comfort, as if they really did not worry about anything anymore. Gone was any feeling of loss or desperation. They just rode and enjoyed it.

They came up to the front tree, and for the first time in a long time there was a child in the tire swing. June twirled and spun with sheer delight as Julia spun her round as round. It was hard to tell which girl was having more fun and they cavorted in the shade.   Julia had taken to the life of the ranch quite naturally, and now nicely filled the simple blue country dress with white frills. June had a matching outfit that Julia had found at the Goodwill, and the two seemed to be immersed in some nostalgic oil painting, almost enough to make Buck forget. Almost.

Bud had insisted that they move into the ranch house with him. Everyone seemed comfortable with that, even though Lucky's more modern house would most certainly stand empty just down the hill. Lucky still stayed there when she was in town, of course, and had set up the apartment above the garage as an American West Coast office for her various enterprises. Interns from the University had made it into a center of sorts for various alternative agriculture practices, attracting the back-to-the-earth types that Bud liked to call "hippy throw-backs." All seemed to agree that the old ranch house was the more family-friendly environment for the time being.

Nobody seemed as comfortable and at home as June and Julia, which was either strange or to be expected because they were the ones that everyone was worried about. But they both grew into it all very well. June had appeared to grow seven inches just in the ten months that they had been there. She seemed to expand into the surroundings in a way that reminded Bud of Lucky many years before. Certainly June caught some bossy bug, some virus that made young girls take control of the world around them. As the others rode up she stopped the game with her mother quite abruptly.

"Playtime over," she announced authoritatively, which made her mom smile. Julia smiled so much more often and easily lately, and this is what Buck zeroed in on as the horses came to a halt. In one quick move, impossible for Julia to check, June slipped out of the tire swing and ran up to the horses.

"Whoa!" Buck yelled at both the horses and his daughter as she latched on to his leg and shimmied up to his back before the horse had even stopped.

"Like a dern squirrel, you see that?" Bud exclaimed. Julia finally made it over to the horse as well.

Lucky nodded and laughed. She had immediately taken to the young girl as June did to her. Lucky now fully understood and agreed with Buck's choice to bequeath half of the Lucky Star to the little firebrand.

"Go go go!" June shouted, kicking her small but gangly legs in a fury.

"Hey hey, there, little trailblazer," Buck calmed her.

"You said we going riding t'day. Go!" June commanded. Luck seemed to respond directly to her and started to turn.

"Woah, there, girl, we're not going anywhere just yet," Buck said again to both Luck and his daughter. Luck seemed to listen but not June.

"No! You said we go!" June tried to grab the reins out of her father's hands, and Buck seemed to enjoy it only a little less then all the others, who were fully in stitches. In one single move Buck grabbed June around the waist and dismounted his horse, standing in front of his wife with his daughter in his arms and a smile that matched Julia's. June was the only one not smiling. Lucky was laughing and delighted. Was she jealous of the beautiful young family? Maybe, in some far off place inside her, but mostly she was just immensely relieved that the Lucky Star Ranch seemed to have a new lease on the future.

"No, not down, up on the horse!" June fairly writhed like a cat up to her father's shoulders, and crouched and quieted as if stalking something nearby.

"You better do as her majesty requests," Julia laughed as she took her daughter's place in Buck's arms. As if for greater stability June stood on Buck's shoulders and conformed her body to the back of his head.

"I was promised a picnic with you, first," Buck stood his ground, loving the look on Julia's face as she melted into his chest. "We were going to have lunch and go riding later."

"NO! Not hungry. Ride now!" June shouted and leapt from his shoulders straight to behind Lucky on her horse, like a mountain lion hitting its prey. "Come on, Lucky, let's go!" The mare started to take off but Lucky brought her easily back around, June holding tightly to her waist and kicking her legs. "No, away, let's go..."

"Hey, June," Buck lost his humor as he rubbed his shoulders. "You can't just ride off like that. Lucky has better things to do."

"Oh, really?" Lucky said as she turned the horse around yet again. "Well, why don't you two just go have your picnic? We're going riding." She picked up her reigns and pushed off.

"Yay!" June or Lucky or both cried as they rode off into the green hills. Spring lay like a cool blanket over the coastal bluffs, dripping life across the Ranch as was expected of the favorite season around those parts.

"Hey, let them go," Julia held Buck as he resisted the urge to mount Luck again and take off after them.

"Do you think they'll be all right?" Buck asked.

"Better than all right, I'm sure," Julia said.

"Well, good, then," Buck relaxed, and felt his heart melt into his wife's. "Where are we off to?"

"The creek up in the canyon," Julia immediately suggested.

Buck started to hesitate but let go in the warmth of Julia's embrace. "How could I say no? You are positively glowing!"

"I know, but I can't get my hopes up," Julia said, obviously hopeful.

"The doctor said there was no sign of remission," Buck quoted officiously. "You're definitely getting your strength back and you look great."

Julia laughed. "No, not about that, it's that I might..." she started to blush. "I just can't get our hopes up..." She buried her head in his body.

"But what are you talking about? You just might..." a look dawned on Buck's face like the spring equinox morning sun. "You don't mean...you might be...pregnant?"

She nodded in his chest.

"Woo-hoo!" Buck shouted, throwing his hat up in the air. He grabbed Julia and started to twirl her around, making her squeal with delight. Abruptly he stopped as if fearful he might be hurting her.

"Oh, honey, it's okay...I'm not some china doll," she protested, wanting to continue being whisked off her feet.

"Okay, then," he allowed, and he spun her around more gently, the delight still full within each of them.

"How far along?" he ventured to ask as they came to a stop.

"Not far. A couple months," she figured.

"What did the doctor say?"

"Well, nothing yet."

"What?! You haven't told him? Why not?"

She hedged. "I just didn't want to get our hopes up until I was more sure." It was more that she did not want to get her hopes dashed.

"Are you sure you are strong enough?" he asked, his demeanor becoming much more concerned and cautious.

"Very sure," she assured him. She looked deep into his eyes. "Buck, I know I can do this. I know I am meant to do this."

Buck paused for a moment, lost in the thought of loss, believing that all gifts must have a cost. Julia took charge, blasting from deep within a hidden reservoir, surging now with great health, bursting life in such a way as to dispel doubts in even the most cautious of celebrants. She jumped up in his arms and kissed him deeply, filling him with such ecstasy that he could not help but pick her up and spin her around once again, only this time with a precise gentle touch that is the hallmark of the greatest strength. She thrilled to the release, able to let go of everything ponderous and troublesome, lifted literally and figuratively in an ancient dance of eternal continuance.

In the distance Bud carefully put the horses away. What he did he used to do unconsciously, his hands knowing horses on their own, able to loop leather and hemp and rings of steel as if the harnesses and saddles themselves just moved to where they needed to go, but now he had to think of every step. *This strap loosens here. That pad stacks there.* He used to think of many things while he worked. Now he just thought of one thing, besides the myriad steps he had to hold in his mind to make everyone forget he might not be able to do things anymore.

"You thought you could get away like that," Bud said aloud. Was it to the reins in his hands as they fell off the horse's head, or maybe the horse? *This bridle goes there.* He did not even notice very quickly that he was done, the horses in their stalls. He did not brush them like he used to. He knew they needed it, but he knew he could get away with not doing it. He used to be meticulous to a T, but now he just did enough to get by, the least he could get away with and not be noticed.

"I might just get away with it," he said. Was it to the stables? He was thinking of Lucky, because he knew that she would notice, that she would brush the horses and clean their hooves later, and that she would likely know that he had skipped those steps even though he had said for years that a good hand never skipped those steps. But he also knew that she would just think that he was relaxing in his old age, mellowing with time. In fact, he felt the same as ever, and never would have left the horses like that if he did not know someone would care for them, it was just that he needed all his strength now for each step pushing through the pain.

"I might just get away with it," he said. Was it to the gate?

June and Lucky had gotten away with something. They rode in wild abandon, whooping and hollering as they rolled over the hills and canyons of their extensive ranch. June was in heaven, soaking up each aspect like a sponge. Lucky was thrilled to share the land in a way the she had only ever explored it herself. She wove the common sense lore of her father with the creative sense of her own childhood experiences and her advanced alternative education.

"You can't let the cows eat this moss, it gives them gas," Lucky said as she stopped near a giant gnarled coast live oak that dripped with pale green overgrowth. June laughed at the reference to cow flatulence. "A major source of greenhouse gasses could be eliminated if people knew how to properly feed their livestock. You've got to break it off this high, above a cow's stretchy neck. And look, you can break a twig with an acorn and make a doll." She deftly tore a branch with an acorn, stripped it down to two twigs for arms and two twigs for legs and the acorn for the head. She carefully draped it with the light green moss, creating a beautiful feminine shape as if the moss were long hair hiding breasts and hips and even feet. June squealed in delight as she accepted the talisman, knowing somehow she had been shown a great magic from the land.

They bounded through places Lucky had not seen in many years, and some she had only seen once. They passed a familiar depression in a stone and June made a command.

"Stop here!" she said, mostly to the horse who instantly obeyed her.

"Why here?" Lucky asked.

"Because my 'maginary friend likes it here."

"You have an imaginary friend?"

"That's what mama calls him. She says he's not real, but he's real. He's says momma is going to die."

Lucky gasped despite herself. "Your Mom is not going to die."

"Yes, she is. But it's okay. She's not going to disappear, silly," June said, as if chastising her for denying the inevitable. "He says everyone dies, but they don't disappear, they just change."

"What else does he say?" Lucky asked, still only casually interested.

"He says momma is going to have another baby."

"Oh really? Hmmm..."

"Yeah, a boy. I said I want a sister, but he says it is a boy, and it is good."

"Any other secrets that he has told you?"

"Yes, Sky says you know him."

"Sky?"

"Yes, I call him that, because of his color."

Lucky gasped again despite herself. "His color?"

"Yes, blue like the sky. You know!"

Lucky tightened her lips and now engaged June with complete attention. "What else did he tell you?"

"He said you love him, and he loves you."

A third gasp escaped from Lucky, but this one was softer and warmer. "He has a strange way of showing it. Does he say why he left?"

"He says you left him trying to find him."

"That makes a lot of sense," Lucky said sarcastically. "Any other gems of wisdom?"

"He says you are meant to be married to Daddy."

"What?! That's terrible. You don't have to worry about that, your daddy is with your mommy."

"I'm not worried about that, silly! Mommy is going to die, remember?"

"He might just be wrong, you know," Lucky maintained.

"He is never wrong."

"Oh, well, it's all silly," Lucky tried to brush it all off. Suddenly she found herself in the unusual situation of being overwhelmed by topics that a four-year-old had no trouble accepting. "Let's go back to the house." She prodded their horse and he took off immediately for home, instinctively knowing the feel of that prod and the direction intended. Lucky's mind raced with the latest revelations. She had not anticipated any of this. She kind of knew that He was seldom, if ever, wrong, but she resented what she felt was being tossed aside like that. She felt angry as if she were being pawned off on some lesser lover to make up for her Lover's growing disinterest. She knew it made no sense, but she felt a growing resentment inside of her, and she did not know how to dispel it. She wanted to push her horse hard in an old familiar way, but she reined in her impulses.

Her senses remained heightened as she returned to the stables with June and began to put her horse away. She noticed every detail of what her father had done, or rather, not done, as he had put the horses away. She finished each of his tasks with a growing sense of antagonism, annoyed at what seemed an extended male plot to abandon her with extra work. In all it was an hour of work and grumbling, and June was not nearly having as much fun as before.

As they closed up the stables, Julia and Buck ambled back into the yard, blissful in a way that only annoyed Lucky all the more. June was merely relieved to be back with her parents, having fulfilled her desire to ride the ranch and glad to leave Lucky who was beginning to tire her.

"Mommy, Daddy!" She ran up and jumped in their arms with as much gusto as she had left them a few hours earlier.

"Hi sweetie!" Julia said. "How are you?"

"GOOD! How are YOU?" She kissed her dad on the cheek.

"Good," Julia replied, her eyes glowing. "Listen, Honey, we have some very special news we want to share with you, but we don't want you to worry."

"It it about Brother?" June preempted innocently.

"What?" Julia was taken aback.

"But, you don't have a brother, June," Lucky tried to correct her.

"No, the one Mommy is going to have for me," she corrected them.

"Well, oh my..." Julia faltered. "Well, in fact, the news is that I am pregnant, but we don't know if it is going to be a boy or a girl."

"Sky say's it's going to be a boy. I said I wanted a sister, but Sky say's it's good."

"Sky?" Buck wondered.

"Sky is her imaginary friend," Julia informed him.

"How come you didn't tell me about this before?" Buck rather grimly demanded, somehow concerned though still firmly in bliss from the day's news. Lucky appeared to busy herself with a broken latch on the gate as she listened carefully to their conversation.

"Oh come now honey, it isn't important," Julia tried to console Buck.

"Not important? Our daughter is seeing things that aren't real and it is not important?"

"He IS real," June insisted. "He told me about Brother before you knew."

"Listen, June," Buck reasoned. "We can't get our hopes up about whether it is a boy or a girl. There is also still a possibility that the baby may not survive."

"He will survive, and he will be a boy," June still insisted.

"There, there, dear, you may be right," Julia said in hushed tones as she brushed June's hair with her hand.
"I am right," June continued. "Sky said there is always a boy to replace the man, and now that grandpa's gone..."

Lucky suddenly dropped her pretense of fixing the gate and joined the conversation. "Grandpa gone? Buck, have you seen my father?"

"Bud? Yeah, he put away the horses and went into the house, I thought," Buck vaguely recalled.

"No, he didn't," She realized. "He did something else." She quickly ran back to the stables and started walking intently looking at the ground, following a track to the ranch house. She looked up and then quickly disappeared inside.

"Is there something wrong?" Julia asked, June seeming almost like an infant again in her arms.

"I think Lucky fears Bud is gone, and...oh no..." Buck stopped.

"What is it?" Julia pressed.

"Grandpa gone," June said.

"Just something Bud said in the hospital...now I am beginning to understand..." Buck paused pensively. He knew, he had an idea, and he remembered his promise.

"Did he tell you he was going to leave?"

"Not exactly. He just made me promise not to come after him." Buck bit his lower lip.

Lucky came rushing out the door. "Buck, he took his pack, his canteen and sleeping roll."

"Yeah, figures..." was all Buck could manage in response.

"Look, towards the road," Lucky turned as if to run into the distance. "Dammit, he probably hitched a ride. I'm going to make some calls." She ran into the house again.

Buck wandered back to Julia and June. "What are you going to do?" Julia asked him.

"I don't know," Buck replied, shaking his head. "I made a promise..."

"I know, but Buck, it's Bud," Julia reminded him, for whatever it was worth.

"He made me promise, and I think I know why," he reasoned.

"Why? Why would someone want to disappear, not letting love ones know?"

"He knows we know. Why? Because he is already gone, Julia. He has gone on. He has nothing left, here, and he wants dignity, at least."

"Dignity? How? Dying in some ditch? And nothing left? Look at all this here, this is all his."

"No, he passed it on, already. He is done, Julia, I'm telling you, he has decided."

"What have you decided?"

"I...don't know..."

Lucky came bursting out of the door, a bundle under her arm. "Buck, get the horses in the trailer and hitch up. I am sure he went south. He wants me to think he went north, but I am sure he went south. I have called the sheriff's department and have some contacts out there with their eyes out. Now you..." She stopped, suddenly realizing that Buck was not moving. "What's up with you."

"Um, Lucky, I can't go with you," Buck squeezed out.

"What are you talking about?" Lucky quizzed him.

"Bud...made me promise...not to come after him."

"What?! When?"

"At the hospital."

"Way back then? And you didn't tell me?"

"Bud made me promise..."

Lucky yelled in the air and grabbed Buck by the collar. Julia and June stood clear in shock. Lucky shook him firmly, though he barely moved. "He made you promise not to come after him, not not to tell me! Right? Am I right?"

"Y...yes," he admitted.

"UUHH! Typical!" Lucky said as she let go of him. She started to storm away. "Well, you both think you have me fooled, don't you. Stupid men! What the hell? You won't get it, though. I will find Pa, with help or without." She disappeared, trailing now a swirl of dust that flickered in the light, outlining the chaos that had now attached to Lucky.

"What are you going to do?" Julia asked him again.

"I made a promise, I can't go after him..." He barely got it out when Lucky came whizzing past, brushing him aside. She went into the house again.

"I made a PROMISE..." Buck stressed.

"But Buck..." Julia almost pleaded.

"I can't go after him..." he said emphatically as Lucky came out the door again with a bundle in her arms and rushed over to the garage.

"Then..." June said, raising her head in her mother's arms. "Then, go after her." She pointed at Lucky getting the trailer ready.

"Yes, Buck, go after her," Julia said without hesitation. Buck looked into his wife's eyes and wanted to say something. There was definitely something there that should have been said, but it would not come. Buck could not explain what was tearing his heart, how he could love so much, how he could lose so much.

"I...I love you," he told Julia and June as he gave them a quick hug. He ran off to help Lucky with the trailer.

"What are you doing?" Lucky asked him.

"I'm helping," he said as he plugged in the signal wires.

"I thought you made a promise..."

"I never promised I would not help," he figured, and he cranked up the hitch. Lucky was actually moved to the point where she stopped for a second, losing her stoic exterior. For a moment it almost all slipped away, all her composure, all her control. She almost wanted to melt, the way she would when her dad would yell at her as a child. She wanted someone else to be strong. But it was only a moment.

"All right, you can help. But I'm still angry with you. You should have told me, you asshole," she let out.

"I know," he agreed. "Now I know a lot. It finally makes sense. I just didn't see it coming."

"I guess, although he pretty much told you straight out."

"Yes, well, I can be slow sometimes, you know," he tried to excuse himself.

"Yeah, that's right. I forgot about that part of you," she picked on him. He had forgotten about the part of her that would poke his open wounds.

"Shall we go?" he asked, not waiting for an answer before getting into the truck to back it into the trailer.

They quickly and quietly got the horses into the trailer, jumped in the cab, and were gone in a shimmering cloud of chaotic dust.

June and Julia made their way back into the ranch house under a sky that was beginning to turn crimson. She pulled the shawl close about her and June and went into the house. She marveled at how calm June was. She was at home, downright peaceful. Julia could feel it too. The house was different, now. It was a different shade, maybe, maybe no. It was different lighting somehow. Maybe not. Was there a smell? No, just the green onions in the kitchen. But it was completely different, somehow warmer. Something in the house embraced them, comforting them, letting them know that everything was just fine.

Then she knew it. Julia knew it like she knew June was right about the son in her belly. Now the house was different. Now the house was home.

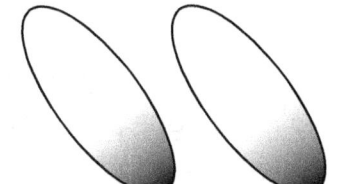

DuaDua (26) Retrieved

The truck rolled onto Freedom Boulevard and the horses complained in the back. It was if they were not in support of the whole enterprise. There seemed to be something hurried about it all, something against the grain. No one really wanted to be doing this, least of all Lucky, but she could not understand why her father would not understand that she would have to come after him. No, he knew she would come after, but he had been more concerned about Buck. It was that he seemed to think Lucky would not find him, but Buck would. This incensed Lucky all the more, and gave her pursuit the heat that arose around it all.

"So you think he went south, not north?" Buck wondered.

"Yes, south," Lucky said as she turned left away from the setting sun.

"But his favorite places were north. Nicene Marks, Henry Cowell, Big Basin, he loved those parks."

"Don't try to mislead me! Yes he loved those parks, was truly at home there, even said he would like to die there. He remembered saying that too me. You see, just what he wants me to think! He thinks I would get lost for days in those parks, never finding him. Well, he was going to a park, trying to disappear, but he went south."

"I don't know..." Buck vacillated.

Lucky turned at him fiercely. "Well I do! Keep your mouth shut, you and your promise!"

Buck was glad to let go of it. He kind of sensed the change in her. She was becoming softer again, knowing that he was trying to do right by her father. He smiled to himself.

Like he was courting her again, trying to impress her father by doing the right thing. He thought about Bud going south, and he thought of parks in that directions.

"The Pinnacles," he said, realizing.

"Pinnacles National Monument, exactly," Lucky agreed. The sun was almost down and they realized where they were headed in the dark. The Pinnacles were a picturesque stereotypical example of harsh western landscape. They burst out of the central valley of California like a strange crystalline range. Half of the unusual formation was still 400 miles south near Santa Barbara but the more significant peaks were just behind the prison town of Soledad, having ridden the Pacific tectonic plate north in the millions of years since their formation. Some day the caves and crags would plunge into the ocean near San Francisco Bay, but now they stood a strange lonely vigil out on the edge of the valley, thrusting into the burgundy sky like the old broken teeth of some giant dinosaur.

Bud had always loved the wilderness, and anyone who had ever gone hiking or camping with him, which Buck and Lucky both had many times, knew that a different side came out in Bud in the wild. Buck drove slowly down the road. He wanted to help, always wanted to help, but he knew help came in many forms. He pushed the truck a little going by Rocks Road, but other than that he drove like a granny on Sunday.

Lucky pretended not to notice. Right now she was still so angry with him that to let any of it out at all would release a torrent, so she kept herself behind a screen of disinterested incredulity.

"You going to take back roads the whole way?" she finally had to ask.

"Well, with the horses, you know..."

"Oh right, the horses...but it's late, no traffic to worry about. Oh, whatever." Lucky amazed at how much had changed between them. At one time Buck would have immediately noticed even a slight change in her mood, a tiny shift in her outlook. Now he seemed to notice almost nothing other than what she showed on the surface. Or was he hiding it too? It occurred to her that she could not read him anymore either. Well, whatever then, she thought, she might as well come out and say it.

"Look, Buck, I'm not mad that you made a promise to my father, or that you intend to keep it. I am mad because you did not tell me that he was thinking of taking off. Can you understand that?"

"Yes," he nodded.

"Can I ask you why you didn't tell me?" she asked with extraordinarily graceful calm.

"Yes," he nodded.

"Okay...Why didn't you tell me?"

"I forgot."

"You FORGOT?!" Gone was her calm. "My dad gives you some cryptic command to not come after him, and you FORGOT?"

"Well, it didn't make sense until today. Everything was so hard in the hospital, and everything had been so good lately at the ranch, I just didn't put it all together until today."

She stared at him with her mouth nearly agape. "My God, you're telling the truth.'

"Yeah, basically."

"Here I thought maybe it was some ancient male covenant or something, turns out it's just good old stupidity."

"Well, hey..." Buck vaguely tried to defend.

"Did you even think of it again after the first day?"

"I thought about it a couple of times," he admitted. "I should have said something, really, I even thought about telling you, but everything was going so well with Bud I just wondered if I remembered it all correctly."

"Oh, well, you remember it correctly now, you think?"

"Yeah, now I get it. I should have realized he would try to chase after Belle, someway, somehow. And I would have thought he'd gone up north, you know, Big Basin or Castle Rock."

"Yes, exactly, which is why he was wrong to tell you not to come after him, because you'd go the wrong way, and we wouldn't have known at all that he was planning to leave all along until you let out that he had told you not to come after him, in clear considered intent. That also told me that he was planning to evade me, clear and simple, so he would go south."

"And you are sure you would go to the Pinnacles?" Buck asked, although he knew she was right.

"It's the only place that's big enough and close enough," Lucky surmised. "He wants to disappear into the wilderness, I'm figuring, and he knows we'd be after him, or at least I'd be, and so it would have to be somewhere big and close."

"And you're sure we should go after him?" Buck cautiously asked.

"Yes, yes, Buck, he's my father," Lucky argued her case. "He cared for me, then I cared for him, and he can't just disappear."

"Kind of ironic for you to say that, don't you think?" Buck ventured.

"What do you mean by that?"

"I mean, you disappeared...left people that cared for you."

"Buck, that is QUITE different," she insisted. "I went off to find myself, not die off in the desert, okay? You could have looked me up, anytime. It seemed when I left you were quite happy staying here. Aren't you over all that, yet?"

"I guess not," Buck realized. "It's been hard to be happy staying here, too. Nothing's been quite the same. Everything's been falling apart since you left, slowly but surely. Julia helped to heal my heart, but... Things had been so good lately I thought something different was possible, but...I'm sorry."

"I know, I know," Lucky softened. "Look, I'm sorry, too. I am mad at my dad and I am taking it out on you. I know I can find him, I just have to focus. We are still connected, you know, like the way you and I used to be."

"Used to be?"

"Yes, used to be, as far as I can tell. That's life, right? I can still feel my dad out there, he's down in the Pinnacles. He feels me coming, too, and he is doubling his efforts."

"I could believe that," Buck gave.

"So are you going to ride with me to get him?"

He paused. "I'm sorry...I can't do that."

She did not pause. "Whatever. I can do this myself, no problem."

"Well, I'll tell you what I can do..." he offered.

"Oh, please, do tell me what you CAN do," she said, perhaps a bit too sarcastically, she thought, but he did not notice.

"Well, if you do not come back after 10 minutes, I can come out after YOU."

"Buck, there is NO WAY I will be back in 10 minu...oh, I get it, I think I get it. Just remember, I am going to ride hard."

"I can ride hard, too."

"Sure, but ten minutes behind, by the time you catch up, probably whatever is going to happen will have happened."

"Perhaps that is best," Buck figured. "At least, if anyone is hurt, I can help."

"Okay, I get it. Well, then, I accept whatever assistance you are willing to give."

They drove the rest of the way past Salinas in relative silence. Something had reconnected in them and they were satisfied to just let it be. They had an understanding, and Buck would be able to help and not break his promise. His new sense of something being settled gave him more lead in his foot, and Buck pulled out onto Highway 101 and started making good time towards the Pinnacles.

"Hey, what about the horses?" Lucky asked.

"Oh, there's no traffic, they'll be okay," Buck newly deduced.

"Yeah, okay, well, we're almost there. We'll be going in after dark. The Rangers might stop us or impound the vehicles."

"I know. I figured I'd drop you guys off on a dirt road off the southwest corner of the park, and then hide the truck, and come back to where I dropped you off. That should put me at least ten minutes behind."

"That should be perfect," she relaxed a bit.

"Hopefully perfect will be enough."

"I think it should. I'm sure he is just starting up the hill now, on foot. He probably feels me coming, but on horseback I can make up all that time."

"I hope so. I still have a bad feeling about this," Buck confessed.

"Well get over it," Lucky said. "You're going to need all your feeling out there in the rocks."

Buck did not answer, but just stared into the distance. The sun was now just a red whispy memory in the sky, and they had now turned onto the country road that led the final way. The dark desert bushes zipped by on the side of the road, and Buck could not help but feel they were leaving familiar territory. He had that feeling that made his hair stand on end, that gave him 'chicken-skin.' Something in him was beginning to think it was possible to leave the earth without traveling through space. It was another one of those times where reality seemed to be bending, and the little wisps of cloud that now passed as they climbed in elevation swirled around the seams.

"Right there," Lucky called out and pointed. "Stop right there. That's the spot."

The truck came to an abrupt halt and the dust clouds mixed with the mist and gave a particular smell. Lucky got out and threw the beam of her flashlight on to the ground. She walked along the turn out and scanned the earth.

"Look, here! Prints! Some car stopped, and one person got out of the passenger side." Buck was now by her side examining the tracks. "And look, cowboy boots."

"Could be anybody. Could be some tourist," Buck tried to reason, but he started to get Lucky's horse out of the trailer.

"Buck, some car dropped off some guy here within the last couple hours. He had cowboy boots on, and they never came back to pick him up."

"You're right," Buck had to agree. They finished getting her horse ready to go, and she was immediately on his back. "Go get him," Buck said as he smacked the horse's behind. Lucky took off into the hills as Buck got back into the truck to hide it in some nearby wash or fire road.

As Lucky raced through the rocky foothills, she could tell this was going to be a different ride than she had ever had. First off, the dust in the air and the complete lack of a moon made visibility almost nil. Even her particularly powerful flashlight seemed to barely coat the blackness. The horse was more timid than usual, but still barreled ahead entirely in the false belief that Lucky new where she was going. Like anyone driven by some great passion, she had a general idea of where she was headed, but she had no idea where she was going.

The white dust of the trail blended perfectly with the random stone outcroppings that where becoming a more dominant part of the landscape. As Lucky rode up into the surreal environment her horse trod carefully.   Lucky fairly leaned all the way to the ground as she studied for lack of tracks. That was how she had to do it, because she knew her father, and knew how he would try to obliterate his trace with small shuffles and skips. He probably carried a small branch with a wisp of needles that he used to sweep any obvious marks, his own but also the marks of others, and that is what Lucky had to look for, the absence of tracks.

She could do it, more on instinct than anything else, following some intuitional track, all the while leaving rather obvious and unnecessary marks for Buck to follow behind her. They cut deep into the southwestern side of the Pinnacles, and then the absence of tracks stopped. All over, in every available nook, there were tracks of every animal, but mostly coyotes, plus piles of scat containing all kinds of bits and pieces of animal and plant, predominantly the pits of Indian plum that grew abundantly in the park. Every passable area had not been crossed by a human in years, in each direction. Lucky had lost track of her father.

She got off her horse, and it became clear to her. He had known she would come on horseback, so he would take the first opportunity to go where a horse could not. She tied up her ride carefully and patted it on the neck. She looked around the rough terrain and could see nothing that looked like a man passed, but somehow she sensed him, perhaps she smelled him. Whatever the case, she started up a scree field that went up a side of one of the peaks, and she knew she was right behind him. As if to make it even harder for her, or somehow more dramatic, the weather condensed into a thunderhead, the wind picking up with approaching flashes of lightning coloring the landscape a flickering electric blue.

The terrain became positively vertical as Lucky pushed ever upward. Intermittent flashes lit the stone, and she could momentarily see her father climbing about sixty feet above her. He seemed to be making unbelievable speed. Lucky could not understand how he seemed to progress further up the steep rock than she could. She was nearly at her limit, or so she thought, when the rain started coming down. Rain came in sheets in a torrent rare for the Pinnacles. Hand holds dissolved in her fists, and her eyes became flooded and bleary, fingers numb and fumbling. Each time a flash would light up her father, he seemed to hold on to the blue glow for a little longer. Pretty soon she could see him between flashes, bounding up the slope not like an old man, but like some kind of mountain goat. In the pace she recognized He whom she had chased for so long, His blue skin glowing and muscles strong, but nonetheless her father. Her father's face, his countenance, but a God's aura, a God's pace. She pushed, she pulled, but she could not keep up, could never keep up.

She was not sure at which moment she lost her grip, for she was looking up, not knowing how he did it so far up there. And just as she was watching Him near the top, she saw him peel backward, and grow off of the cliff. He was nearly in free fall, but He never left the cliff. He expanded into a huge blue version of Himself, all the way to the ground, and extended out a hand to catch her as she fell. She had not even realized she had fallen when she saw a huge hand cupped beneath her, and she found herself in the hand of a huge blue version of her father.

"How...why...I mean...why?" she asked, sitting in the giant palm.

"You were falling, I had to save you," he answered matter-of-factly.

"No, I mean, what are you? I mean, a big blue version of my father, really? What's that all about? Why won't you explain things?" She stopped to breathe. He changed into Himself, glowing like her lover of old, shining like the sky clad in sunlight. She sat cross-legged on the ground before him.

"Ask anything you like," with a gentleness that spoke of eons of patient explanations.

"Give me my father back," she insisted.

"I cannot do that," he said.

"You cannot, or you will not?" she pressed.

"I will not, because he does not wish it. I cannot force someone back who does not want to go."

"Then what can you do?"

"I can answer your questions.'

"Where is my father?"

"He is with Belle, and happy," he informed her. This stopped her, satisfied something in her, and she knew she could not pursue those questions anymore. She decided to change tactics, for she could not let Him go, would not let Him go without pressing something out of Him.

"Who are You, really?"

"I am who I am. I am the Alpha and Omega. I am the All, everything is in Me, and yet I am No Thing, Nothing, Not a Thing, yet nothing is Not Me."

"Words! Crazy words!"

"You asked a question in words, and thus I answered."

"No, show me," she insisted. "Show me your true self."

"Do you understand what you ask of Me?"

"Yes, yes! Show me! No blue space men, no giant fathers, You! All of you!" she pressed.

"All right. Then, behold, with mystic vision that I grant you, a sight the greatest seers and saints tremble to see."

He began to grow again, pushing apart the clouds, splitting into many versions, filling the sky. The stars circled His head like a crown, or His heads rather, for suddenly he was some opulent holographic fractal, faceted with an infinite number of Selves like a mirrored jewel, each face different. His eyes were blazing with the fire of pure fire, expanding forever. She saw Govinda, there, in the middle, but also He had the face of Jesus, and Buddha, and a hundred hundred other Gods, a chain of Faces extending forever, and hands forever, hands forever working, doing, and mouths. And

Goddesses, it seemed He was also a She, more beautiful again and again than the next. There was Mary, and women from apparently all over the world, a giant black woman, too, all blending together. And lovers of her Lover, and wives, thousands of wives, all being perfectly served by their Husband, all so strange a beautiful they made Lucky gasp. How was it possible? What was He, or She, Who had Lucky been loving for all these years? There seemed to be no boundaries between aspects of Himself, or Herself, locked together, bouncing back and forth, like interwoven snowflakes falling through a rainbow. Extending into everything, people, animals, unknown species bowing in worship.

There were alien faces, too, strange and unusual, almost nonsensical. And there were terrible faces there, also, demons spitting fire, monsters eating flesh, devouring whole cities, whole planets consumed. And Beyond, some gaping chasm, a void, a vast ocean of nothing, with a vine snaking out of the Void, and a flower, like a lotus, carrying out all Creation. She saw legions of saints and angels, singing praises. She saw great men, greater than the angels, and she saw them see her, saw them see this Vision of hers, and saw them fall to their knees in supplication.

She saw even greater numbers of souls, almost numberless, struggling in blindness, fighting their petty wars, unaware of the grand scene of which they were a part. And they were all swirling back deep into the dark void, a hole, a mouth that was somehow Govinda, her old friend, her lover, but she could not take Him in, now, this way. She was overwhelmed, and she cried out, losing consciousness.

She dreamt, and in her dream, her Love shrank, became tiny, and He entered into everything, like an atom or particle. She saw him with many hands, working with pure grace, also holding a flower, and another a scepter, and some ball, another a flute. His hands moved everything, but seemed to touch nothing. It was a dance that never ended, and it was beautiful to Lucky, but perplexing. She tried still to understand her Love, but this form was still too intricate for her to encompass. With great mercy shining in His eyes, He transformed into the familiar form of her two armed Lover, dressed in gold like the sunshine. He picked her up and put her on a horse. He gently mounted behind her and they rode out, and she faded in and out of consciousness. She felt safe, at home finally in his arms. She felt the love fill her in a way she had not in many years. It was dark, but the lightning still occasionally split the sky. In the brief light she saw His face flickering into Buck's. They were the same, in some way that she had never seen before, but she knew it was in her mind. As she slowly became fully conscious she realized that Buck had her on his horse. He led her horse behind, and he held her firmly in his arms. She wondered about her father.

"Buck...dad..." she managed.

"He's gone, Lucky. Let him go."

"But...what did you see?"

"It was dark and wet, but, damnedest thing..."

"What?"

"Well, he climbed high, and jumped off, right into a lighting bolt. Vaporized, I tell you. The thunderclap knocked me off the horse, and you off the wall. I have got to get you to the hospital. I don't know if there are internal injuries."

"No, I'm okay, He saved me," she said.

"He saved you?"

"Yes, He saved me. A big blue hand came out of the sky and caught me. I am okay, I'm telling you."

"Lucky, I have to get you to the hospital, okay? I don't know what you saw, but I saw you fall a long way."

"No, it's okay. I will go to the hospital, but I'm just telling you that I am okay."

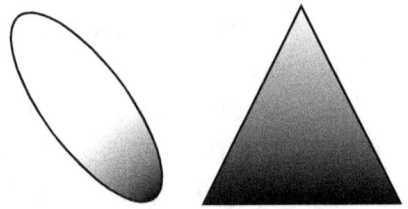

DuaAtrua (27) Retreated

Lucky had to go again. She had to go. She really had no idea what kept her searching, what drove her to all parts of the world. Part of it was compassion for the animals. She knew there was much to be done for those who had no voice of their own. Part of it was compassion for herself. She would not admit it to herself, but she felt strong stirrings as she saw Julia growing fuller with Buck's baby every day. Some part of Julia's spirit expanded, too, spreading out into the ranch house and the land. June seemed to follow her mother's energy out into every nook and cranny of the Ranch, and Lucky felt different. She felt like there was not much left for her here anymore.

Of course, everyone knew that things were the way they were meant to be, for the most part, and true love coursed through them all as they went about the business of an organic dairy farm, but Lucky did feel uncomfortable, sometimes. She felt like the big black hen in the chicken coop, Bruja. She was a mighty bird, bigger than all the other reds, but she was not in charge. Scarlet, a particularly fine red, was the alpha bird, and Bruja was always on the outskirts, always trying to escape, always running away, even though she could dominate the smaller reds. Lucky felt that maybe she should vacate the coop and let Julia roost and nest in peace.

Something had changed with the passing of her father, too. Beyond the adjustment that everyone has to go through upon losing a parent, Lucky had to deal with losing both parents in a short period of time, plus, she felt, the loss of something else. Her Vision stayed with her, parts of it, at least, and the images haunted her. Something in her was awed, as much in love as ever, but that love was different. The images of all the lovers of her Lover made something in her rebel. She loved Him as much as ever, but it could not be the same.   She longed for something else, for some other part of him. She remembered the black Void, the whole hole, the mouth, and she longed to sink into it.

She left one day, quietly. She had set everything in order.   She had thought about visiting Babaji up on Mt. Madonna, but she did not want to see the statues. She gave Babaji a mental farewell, which was really more than she gave everyone else. She wanted to just leave, of course, and she did, hopping a plane and starting a whirlwind tour of her offices abroad and the homes of some old friends. She did have an eventual destination in mind, of sorts, but she allowed herself to wander through almost every place she had ever been.   Everywhere she went she tried to take care of old business.   She tied up any loose ends, putting systems and people in order. Everyone loved to see her, but they soon got the impression that she was preparing for a long, if not permanent, absence.   Everywhere it seemed so much the same that she almost was following a script.   First she would greet old friends, then she would get down to business, then they would gradually realize that she was getting ready to go, and people would gradually accept. Sometimes there was a party, but often the ones who loved her the most would not even show up.

After about a year she found herself in India again. She visited some of the old sites, helped treat sick animals, helped train new veterinarians, but she was always on the move. She had an inspiration that stayed in the back of her head that was connected to the vision she had back at the

Pinnacles and something she had heard while in India before. Every inspiring spiritual student heard about the holy men reported to live in the remote fastness of the deep Himalayas. Legions of seekers from the West had come to the mountains of Northern India trying to find the rumored "Great White Brotherhood" otherwise known as Shangri-La or Shambala. It was some conspiracy of conscious men, great minds that had found refuge deep in the mountains, possibly masking themselves with psychic powers.   Stories still circulated regarding great crystal cities, hidden from the eyes of normal men, perhaps existing in some bridge dimension between worlds, perhaps just a clutch of meditating monks cloistered in some cave. For generations, mystics from the west had come on great treks trying to find these holy men.

Something deep in Lucky had many times wanted to go on such a trek, but it seemed too stereotypical for her, and she always had some pressing reason with the animals to keep on working.   She understood the concept of Karma Yoga, that she was advancing on her spiritual path with work on the physical plane, but she was getting too good at it.   It was more and more obvious that her work could get done without her. She had set up things so well that she almost worked herself out of a job. From the Ranch in California to her veterinary school in Ranchi, India, she was wanted everywhere but needed nowhere.

After another year in India she could no longer pretend she was needed.   She continued her promotional work, but even her image seemed to work without her.   A major campaign in Europe had just hit stride, and they had years of clips and stills that her marketing people had only begun to tap. A documentary film 5 years in the making was coming out, and she had written a book about animal communications that was now nearing the top of the New York Times bestseller list. She flew around for awhile promoting the book, but eventually she felt as saturated as most of her markets.   One day she saw a parody skit of one of her commercials on Saturday Night Live, featuring a ditzy woman saving animals in a disaster zone while humans were dying nearby, and she became completely disillusioned with the public world.   It seemed as if she was being pushed out of human interaction wherever she went.   Soon it was the easiest decision in the world to follow her old romantic idea of adventure and disappear deep into the highest mountain range in the world.   She did no longer care what anybody thought, or how she appeared to the world.   People would always say some of the worst things, so she no longer even thought about listening.

Lucky thought it was almost melodramatic that it seemed to always come back to mountain climbing.   To literal almost, she felt, but as vivid as she could expect.   She loved the hill country, as always, so fertile, and started walking to Katmandu, starting in Ranchi, and she brought no staff, no pack, no bedroom, just sandles and a brown sari and scarf. She was going to the Mountain, she felt she knew what that meant.   There was an echo from her Vision with its gaping black Void, or was it a Womb?   Something large, dark, and vast, perfectly symbolized by the Mountain.   Her students, young and old animal lovers, came out to cheer, bringing in their arms various animals that had just recently become well enough to come out in the sunshine and fresh air, grateful faces squinting in the brilliance of the day.

They walked her out of Ranchi in an ecstatic procession, mostly very young and very old, animal and human alike, walking and singing alongside Lucky as she headed into the hills.   The air was soft and warm, moist and alive, thick with a vital ether that filled Lucky's lungs.   She new what was ahead of her, though.   She was determined, and there were always obstacles to order when she set her mind on something.   She had come to expect them, and perhaps that was part of the problem, but she knew they were coming.

But now, just as she expected, she could enjoy the most beautiful parades, a magic family strolling towards a deeper health.

Gradually her friends started to thin out. What had been a throng of hundreds became a dozen diehards, including a three-legged dog, a monkey that had lost a hand, a goat with broken horns, a wingless chicken, and a few children. They stopped in the evening near a stream, and a couple of the children pulled out some bundles of rice and vegetables, and a few simple bowls and cups. Some of the other children started gathering local edibles from the stream and nuts and berries from the woods, and the small group had a veritable feast, the food multiplying like a vegetarian loaves and fishes. A boy started a small fire, and some others made a small lean-to out of fallen branches and banana leaves, bound with braided fibers. Lucky sat in the middle, facing the fire, and thanked her benefactors. The sun sank into the Western sky as they settled into a comfortable lump of human and animal, the monkey and dog having become fast friends.

Lucky had a small girl as a friend at the Ranchi school, Sahani, who was an orphan that had lived at the school for some time. She looked tiny, but she spoke English well, and she could have been almost a teenager. She reminded Lucky of June, a girl way ahead of her years in wisdom, and she had an almost nonstop commentary going on as she sat in Lucky's arms next to the dog and monkey in front of the fire.

"The dog could not help it because he had to go somewhere but his master would not always let him out and he would go on the floor inside and his master would get so angry and start to kick and stomp, until one day he kicked him out of his house with two broken legs, one we could fix but one we had to cut off and nobody really wants to adopt such a dog..."

"What happened to the monkey?" Lucky had learned that she could only make Sahani pause for a little with a question.

"He got his hand caught in a monkey trap, the metal kind with teeth and a spring, and he came right up to the animal clinic with his hand in a trap. He had worked the chain free, but his hand was destroyed, but he had sores too, but we took care of those, and that was about three years ago and he has been with us since..."

"Sahani?"

"Yes?"

"Thank you for the information, but perhaps now is the time for silence," she tried to hint.

"Oh, I like silence," Sahani said. "I like to listen. There is always a sound, you know? A sound deeper than the next, a sound behind the silence..."

"Sahani?"

"Yes?"

"Shhhh..."

"Do you want me to be silent?"

"Please."

Sahani smiled, and without a pause settled into a deep comfortable quietude. They watched the red dance of the flames and the setting sun splash over the faces huddled together in the little shelter. The faces were small, but the eyes were big, and they twinkled with wonder and gratitude. Lucky hoped they knew they would have to go back to Ranchi, figured they knew, that this was just some special send off camping trip, just a single night out for everyone but her. She would have to send them home the next day, perhaps, but tonight they could just huddle in the warmth and enjoy the closeness. They stayed all night in a light trance of blissful transcendence, resting in the deepest sense, unthreatened and undisturbed.

The next morning the camp cleaned itself up right away, and the group did not seem to be breaking up. The dozen children and animals just milled about, getting ready to walk some more. More food was found and shared, and all remnants were cleaned up with the help of the dog and the Lucky was about to send them all home but she did not have the heart. She almost was about to say that they would have no one to take care of them without her when she realized that they were actually taking care of her, and that would have been an empty threat. The kids would respond to responsibility, she knew, and they would take the group home if she stressed how people would be worried back at the school. She would have to use that tact when she decided to force them to turn around.

For the time being, however, she could not resist the camaraderie. Most of the kids spoke only Hindi, and Lucky regretted having not learned, but Sahani was always there to translate things for her. As they passed local villagers and farmers they were recognized as a sacred procession, and they were given garlands of flowers and offerings of rice and cool water. All was shared by the small troupe as they made their way up the hills that grew ever steeper.

Sahani asked a lot of questions of Lucky as they walked along, fascinated with all tales of Buck and the Lucky Starr Ranch, which seemed like tales of Hollywood celebrities to her. She pressed for more when Lucky hinted of her Lover, Over time even the youngest began to realize what a trek actually meant, the many, many steps, the hot dusty road, even the monkey tried to hitch a ride on the dog whenever he could.

The maturing sacrifice led to a more introspective mood for most of the group, and even Sahani eased her constant reportage. They were not unhappy, though, and they felt prepared with cheerful demeanors for each increasing degree of the slope before them. But they proceed in silence. The sun was high overhead, and the children began to naturally walk ahead looking at the ground in front of them. Lucky looked around at the increasingly beautiful countryside, and the children all walking along staring straight down, and took it as a sign that the time was nearing to send them home. The final straw came when one of the young boys who had been tossing a stick in the air lost control of it and tripped a girl, causing her to scrape her knee and begin crying. All the kids started running about calling out, and Sahani was speaking quickly in Hindi trying to get the girl to quiet down. Lucky decided it was time to lay down the law. As soon as the girl had quieted down a bit, Lucky called Sahani to her side.

"You need to tell the kids it is time to go back," she informed her.

"You are going back to Ranchi?" Sahani asked.

"No, not me, you all," Lucky said. "All of you."

Sahani was shocked, like she had been shot. "Us? Leave? Why? Who will take care of you?"

"I will be fine. I need to take this journey on my own. You all will have to go back. You need to tell them."

"But..." Sahani's lip was quivering.

"You have to tell them," Lucky was firm.

Sahani turned to the group and spoke, slowly and haltingly, making exasperated gestures towards Lucky and the road back home. The other children started shaking their heads, and had tears well up in their eyes. They were not afraid of being alone, but torn up by the sudden revelation that they might have to leave the pilgrimage. Apparently they had all figured that they were in it for the duration, and Lucky watched their faces fall in despair as they realized they were being sent home.

Lucky agreed to let them set up one more camp and leave in the morning. The hands worked more slowly that evening, each bit more heavy and laden with the heavy hearts of the workers. The kids had lost some inspiration, and seemed to almost feel betrayed, like Lucky was just another adult, when she had seemed to be a free soul casting off all worldly concerns. They gathered by the fires, but their eyes were not as large, nor did they glow, but they did each have two small liquid crescents at the bottom, threatening to grow in a torrent of tears at any moment.

They huddled and cried off and on all night. As if on cue or drawn by the hurt feelings, strange large animals came by in the night, giving a sinister air to the camp that it had never had. Although Lucky did become slightly more concerned about the safety of the kids, the night threats merely hardened her resolve that the children had to go back to Ranchi. In the darkest hour of the night, when some stirring thing seemed to come to close to the camp, Lucky got up and started to build up the fire. She stirred the coals and added some more fuel, making a show of it as if trying to educate the kids how to deal with potential predators at night.

As the morning sun peaked over the Eastern horizon, it was obvious that they were all awake. A few of them started to clean up, and spoke in hushed tones to each other. Sahani seemed utterly deflated, somewhat resigned to her return to the school and normal life.

"Look, they need you back there, and they will be worried, right now," Lucky justified her position.

"I know, we must go..." Sahani sighed.

"I will be back soon," she tried to reassure her, but her voice quavered a bit.

Sahani shook her head. "No, you don't come back quickly."

"Uh, yes, you got me there...but, I need to do this. I'm not needed back there right now. I need to find myself, by myself."

"You will find yourself by yourself soon enough," Sahani reasoned.

"Make sure the kids will be safe," Lucky directed her.

"We will be 'safe,'" Sahani said it like "safe" meant "practically dead."

"Thank you for everything, Sahani, really, I love you very much."

Sahani softened at this, losing all pretense of being angry or anxious. Her heart was pure devotion to Lucky, and she understood why they were being sent home. She would do her best to follow Lucky's instructions.

"I love you, too," she said, embracing Lucky around the waist. The rest of the kids came to embrace her too, and they stood as a mass for one last time, feeling the warmth and the love. Their hearts turned and they all laughed and cried for joy, remembering the magic, and realizing that with the memories came the magic, and it would stay with them forever. They were still sad to be leaving Lucky, but they regained their inner glow. They led the animals a short ways away, and turned to watch Lucky.

Lucky paused for a minute, lost in the view of the unlikely pilgrims, and smiled, but she quickly composed herself, and turned around to head away, lest she give the kids the idea she might change her mind. She advanced about twenty yards and then turned around to look back at the kids, who stood unmoved in their previous spot. Lucky gave an exaggerated aggressive move, and the kids jumped a little and then started back down the road, feet shuffling as they led the animals back home.

Only Sahani stood and watched Lucky, not moving until Lucky had passed out of sight.

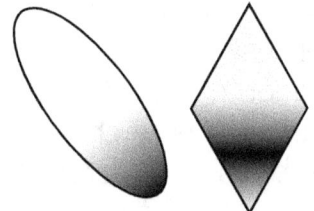

DuaKatero (28) Pitted

The ground became harder, the air hotter, the hill steeper for Lucky now that the kids had gone.   She occasionally looked back, but she resisted any urge to go back to the kids.   Parts of the road, now going through canyon country, became more ominous, and she almost convinced herself through fear for the safety of the kids to go back and escort the kids back home.   But she decided against it, knowing that the kids would be okay, and that there would be some other feeling of duty that would challenge her to stay, and there could always be some reason to stay, unless she just let it all go and let herself go away. She cried, too, after leaving the kids, suddenly not feeling like the only adult anymore.   She cried over what she lost, over what kids lost, over loss in general.   She cried until she was empty, and she continued up in the sun with crisp lips.

She continued the internal part of the journey, the part that was the real reason that she had needed to leave the children behind. Each step took her higher, and deeper, and her body was starting to respond to the stress by releasing endorphins into her bloodstream. She could feel the closeness of spirit about her, she could feel something that must have always been there but she just had not noticed. There was an iridescence over all things, especially living things, and a passing dragonfly made Lucky positively jump in amazement.

It glowed like some prismatic eye of God, and she immediately remembered her Vision.

She wondered about the personal nature of it. Something in her was now chasing the impersonal part of it. Something had been too personal in her vision, too many lovers, too many sinners, too much. She wanted some clean and simple Truth, like the giant Void that swallowed all in her Vision. Somehow that was very comforting to her, and she had heard similar things about Buddhism. Someone had told her that Buddhists have no God, but that they worship Oblivion. Somehow that sounded very attractive to her now. She also knew that the original Buddha, Siddhartha Gautama Buddha, had been born in India but had traveled north. Somewhere in the mountains she would leave the land of Hindu gods and enter the land of Tibetan Buddhism. That is where she was headed, determined to find a Tibetan Buddist Master. She focused her mind on this intention, and continued up the road.

Clouds had begun to form in the sky, and Lucky could feel the moisture in the air. Streams had become more common as she proceeded, and seemed to carry more water. She still passed the occasional local, but they treated her differently, now. They were more distant, cautious, less inclined to offer food or assistance. The wind picked up, and she began to descend into a more rural area. Mountain streams were channeled into carefully tended rice paddies, and the setting sun lit the valley like a golden bowl. Lucky figured that she was getting nearer to Katmandu. The weather boded rather ominously, brooding over the valley like an angered mother bear.

The rain came sudden and hard, and brought with it a sudden drop in temperature. Lucky looked around as the light disappeared and witnessed a rather inhospitable looking environment, tilled fields and not a tree in sight. As the wind whipped up she thought she could hear crying in the storm.

She huddled in a ditch near a larger bush, and curled into a ball. She was covered with water, and the sky opened up with lighting and thunder.

"So, is this enough of a dramatic scene for you to make an appearance. This seems like your style," Lucky said as she huddled in the storm. Her mind easily dislocated from her body, and she floated in a sea of warmth. She could see herself, outside herself. Saw herself curled in a ball. In the bush she saw movement next to her body, and the whole bush seemed to heave. She saw a glint of scale, and soon realize that the bush fairly burst with an occupant, which was the largest cobra that Lucky had ever seen. It shined a metallic blue whenever lightning struck, and Lucky watched it raise over her body. It spread its hood, giant like a palm frond, and covered her body like an umbrella. She floated there, watching it, and then came back into her body.

"NO!" she yelled, quickly rolling over to the side, almost as if she feared the snake as a cobra, which she still kind of did. It reared back, still spreading its hood, but now as a sign of grand resplendence.

"I don't need you now," she yelled out. "That is not what I am looking for."

The snake transformed into the gloriously beautiful form of her Lover, and she felt her heart gush with desire and anguish intermingled.

"What ARE you looking for?" He asked.

"Something beyond You, beyond the personal, something great and true and impersonal, like a spiritual sky."

"The greatest and truest spiritual sky is within me. Those who seek the impersonal spiritual sky eventually make their way to Me, after many, many ages."

"But why? Why a personal God? Is this crazy? Am I crazy? How can this be?"

"It is the Way of Love, the Way of Devotion. Love is personal, and it is the grandest thing that lies behind everything else."

"But why so many lovers? Why unrequited love? Why complications? Why not a pure a beautiful empty bliss? Why not, with all this work, just true and simple rest."

"And so it shall be," He said as he raised in size and became translucent like a cloud. "Then, to your work, and to your rest," He proclaimed, and disappeared into the storm.

Lucky was definitely back in her body, and she shivered as the wind blew ever harder. In the distance, with the wind, she heard a definite crying, a strong bleating, piercing through the storm.

"Always a storm, a storm and mountain," Lucky said to the wind. "And an animal in need." She got to her knees and listened.   Water had enveloped her now.   She lost the boundary between water and flesh, she waded and swam through the air, pushing towards the sound.   The lightning flashed, giving an almost comfortable old friend of a blue light over everything, streaking her eyes with just enough information to find her way, stumbling through the fields.

The sound hardly had recognizable form, but Lucky could feel the emotion in it.   An element of desperation coupled with fear drove the sound, and Lucky thought she identified the voice of a young calf.   As she made her way through the splattered darkness, she felt a pull in her gut. Something moved inside her, and it seemed to be connected to the sound. It gave her direction, and she was pulled by her insides up a slight rise and then down into a gully.

The darkness at the bottom of the gulch moved and thrashed with a new wetness. Water splashed and grunted, matching Lucky's increasingly disturbed intestines, and the bleating was somewhere nearby in the foreground.   Lucky groped her way forward, finding a path down amongst the many unfamiliar objects that passed under her fingers and toes. She actually began to wonder about the sudden lack of lightning when a bolt finally etched the sky and gave a sudden flash picture of her new surroundings. In the frozen retinal image she could make out the scene. A large mother cow had fallen into a swollen stream and was struggling with a broken leg, while her calf stood nearby, panicking. Lucky could detect a spot where a dike had given way, plunging the mother into the water, and her calf must have been trying to make its way to her.

She quickly bounded down the muddy slope towards the cow. She could sense the large animals stress, and could tell that the cow was nearly drowning after repeated attempts to stand on a broken front leg. In the waist deep water Lucky got in close and put her body against the cow, pushing up on the shoulder of the broken right front leg. The cow somehow understood, and thrashed anew trying to stand. Lucky discovered that hidden source of fortitude that blesses those in situations of great duress, and managed to serve as a fourth leg of the animal, and together, in the dark, they walked over to the shore. The cow collapsed on the bank where it was safe for the time being, and her calf came over and started licking her face. Lucky first lay against the cow, rubbing and making soothing sounds.

When both mother and calf had calmed down somewhat, Lucky began rooting about the environment looking for materials. First she found a couple hard flat rocks, and upon striking them together produced a decent sharp edge. In a bamboo thicket at the edge of the stream she proceeded to chop and strip various pieces, knowing at times that she was damaging her own hands in the process, but proceeding along with little pain. Her fingers could feel little in the cold and wet, but she was driven with her blood and heart pumping adrenalin and endorphins into her system. Soon she had a pile of splints and long strips of bark.

The cow was still relatively calm, laying on its side and breathing heavily. The calf had curled up against its mother's back, no longer bleating but still wildly looking about. Lucky brought her improvised medical materials and kneeled in the mud next to the injured mother.   Lying with her head downhill, Lucky stuck her foot firmly in the cow's armpit and grabbed the hoof below the break. With one firm heave she pulled the leg into place, hoping she had set it right as the cow moaned and kicked. Lucky stayed away from the cow's back feet but held on firmly to the bottom one. When the cow had settled down, she gingerly felt the area of the break, discovering that the bone had wedged sideways, twisting the hoof inwards. With a great sigh she wedged herself down below the cow again, gripping the leg as she began to pull, using her weight and leverage to pull the leg into place.

Out of the darkness a hoof hit Lucky in the head, knocking her back. The stars she saw may have been a break in the storm, had the rain not been sleeting harder than ever. She shook it off, happy to feel with her fingers in the dark that it must have been mostly a glancing blow. Another streak of lighting lit the diorama in her head, with the splint materials lying off to the side of the calf and cow with what now seemed like four straight legs. Lucky found some forgotten genetic knowledge and starting setting a leg without western medical supplies. She remembered finger traps that she had woven back on the ranch with cattails leaves, and she realized in her minds eye that she could add bamboo ribs for rigity.

Somehow her hands knew what to do in the dark, cold and battered as they were. It seemed that, as soon as Lucky could do no more without seeing, another bolt would streak the scene, giving her a photo-image to go by. She saw the cow's leg, and how to wrap it all around like a basket, stiffened with ribs. Within a half hour it was done, and Lucky could not believe it would work, but knew it would.

No sooner had she thought she was safe when she realized that the water was still raising steadily. Where the calf and mother had been lying on dry land was now under half a foot of silty fluid. She examined the slope and found a deep eroded gash going up the side that she quickly attacked and dug at until she had a fairly evenly graded channel going up to the top of the dike. She got the calf first into and up the muddy gash without too much struggle. The calf seemed at first reluctant to leave its mother until the cow kind of thrashed in its direction as if to chase it off. Lucky braided some of the bark strips and tied them around the calf's neck, half leading half pushing it up to the top of the dike, which seemed relatively safe for the moment.

The difficulty of moving even the much smaller calf made Lucky realize just how daunting would be the task with the mother cow. She tied the calf to a small tree, for she sensed it would come right back down in the gully after her if it could. She knew that she would need more rope of sorts so she stripped some more bamboo and wove a triple braid. It bristled and crackled but it was strong and Lucky made a great loop which she hung around her shoulders and put below the leg of the cow. She grabbed hold of one of the cow's horns and pulled on the loop with all her might, trying to leverage the cow over at the same time. The cow took the cue an heaved with her, coming to her feet in a mighty shift. Lucky pressed herself against the left shoulder and held fast, the loop tight around her shoulders. Tiptoe by tiptoe she edged the cow towards the cleft in the bank. The cow hopped and addled right on up, but Lucky barely had enough room to squeeze up with her. The muddy gash had become its own drainage, filling like a bloody fissure.

As she heaved in the last few feet, the whole scene seemed to collapse from some nightmare as the hill eroded and liquefied beneath them. With a few final mighty kicks of her hind legs, the cow ejected out of the gash onto the dike next to calf, the only solid footing she had managed to find being Lucky's crumpling body.

Lucky never saw the cow make it to the top with her calf, even though it was lit by another electric blue strike. She did not feel the small hands that suddenly appeared and took hold of her. She did not hear the squeal of the monkey or smell the wet dog that, she could have guessed, even in the dark, had only three legs. She would not remember how they examined with astonishment, the splint on the cow's leg, and how they took some more bamboo and made a stretcher. She could never recall how they strapped her to it and carried her off into the night, leading the cow and calf as the latest members of their ragtag crew. The lightning strobed stills through the night, capturing a stop-motion memory for the hills of this unlikely nighttime procession.

The children neither paused nor tired. They imagined that legions of ancestors had joined them, holding them up with some ancient power of intent. They knew, all of them, the way to go, not because they had ever been there, but because a light seemed to lead the way. The light might have been the small party itself, the way it enveloped them, but it hung forward like a carrot on a stick, bringing them at last to Katmandu. Lucky never saw the eyes and the amazed smiles that greeted them from those locals blessed with the opportunity to awaken at such a time. They knew that spirit was afoot, that a Great Presence was passing nearby. Their prayers floated like flowers strewn in the path of the eclectic pilgrimage.

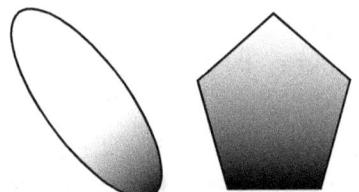

DuaPentero (29) Arrested

The sunlight was sharp but the air was soft and sweet and Lucky came to in what would be her first memories after that night in the storm. To her it was as if the dark and rain were turned off at once, and the dank smell of mud dissolved into a spicy floral fragrance. She had hardly opened a single eye when she heard a gasp to her right followed by eager footsteps fading away with the echo of a delighted cry.

"She is awake," Sahani called down a hallway. "I told you she would wake up today!"

It seemed like only a moment, but by the feeling in her body and the smell of the bandages that held her in various places, Lucky realized that she had been here for some time. She could not really turn her head to see the source of the voices that streamed into the room. Hushed voices still murmured with anticipation as a hand gently grabbed Lucky's wrist to check her pulse.

"Lucky, Lucky, you're awake, right?" Sahani managed to call out before she was shushed.

"Uhn...huh...ooooh," Lucky moaned.

"Miss Star, are you awake?" came an older female voice that sounded rich with wisdom.

"Uh...yes," Lucky managed through bandages that covered her chin around her head.

"Oh, that is splendid!" the elder female voice said in an accent that revealed traditional knowledge blended with a "proper" English education. She chased everyone else out of them room so they could talk in private. Two nurses, on male and female, checked her vitals, replaced her bandages, and ran some other tests on her. "I am Dr. Janeer Prakrti. You are in the Katmandu medical clinic. You have many injuries and have been in a coma. Do you know how you came to be here?"

Lucky cleared her throat. "I left a couple days ago on a pilgrimage and ended up helping a cow in a ditch during the storm the other night. I must have been hit pretty hard when the dike collapsed. How did I get here?"

The doctor hesitated. "Miss Star, please do not be alarmed...Please, leave us alone." The doctor chased out the attendants who had finished most of their examinations anyway.

"Why? What's wrong with me?" Lucky demanded.

"It's not that. You were severely injured but your body is healing quite well. It is just this...you were brought to this clinic by an odd group of children and animals..."

"The kids!" Lucky gasped. "Somebody needs to call the school in Ranchi and tell them they are okay."

"The school has already been notified," the doctor began. "Miss Star, the kids brought you in almost two months ago."

Lucky was stunned. "But, what must have happened...?"

"Much has happened. There has been much activity here. Many visitors. Many doctors from around the world. A man named Buck Smith was here."

"Buck was here?" Lucky's heart tried to jump for a moment, though she really would not let it just yet.

"Yes. He claimed next of kin, which was supported by some lawyers from your company, and there had been some disagreement as to whether you should be left here. It was determined that you were too unstable to travel, and you are to be flown out as soon as you are able."

"Flown out? What are you talking about?"

"You are to be moved to a hospital in Hawaii as soon as you can travel," the doctor informed her.

"Moved? When I just got here? I don't think so," Lucky pronounced.

"I am to inform them when you awake. Mr. Smith was to come then to escort you to Hawaii. We are quite proud of our facilities and the care we have given you, but I am forced to agree with the consensus that you should travel when you feel strong enough."

Lucky changed tactics slightly. "Well, of course, but I don't feel strong enough just yet. Just do me one favor and wait til you tell everyone, okay?"

"I can wait until tomorrow and we know more about the stability of your condition."

"That is fine, thank you. Tell me, can I visit briefly with my friends?"

"Briefly, if you feel up to it," the doctor looked concerned. "Shall I send them in?"

"Just one," Lucky specified. "The girl, Sahani."

"Ah, yes," Dr. Prakrti nodded. "She is fond of you."

"And strong headed," Lucky said. "Dangerous, like I was."

"I   beg   your   pardon?"

"Too wild," Lucky supposed. "Too daring."

"Perhaps. She and her friends were daring enough to rescue you."

"Perhaps. Perhaps I didn't want to be rescued by them."

"Suicidal thoughts are common with post-traumatic coma patients..." the doctor suggested.

"I didn't say I didn't wan't to be rescued, I said I didn't want to be rescued by them."

"All of these issues should best be covered with a therapist who will be visiting at some time early tomorrow."

"No, I'm sorry, Doctor," Lucky retracted. "I am just being dramatic. I am very much thankful that the kids rescued me, and I am quite grateful for the work you have done."

"Not at all, Madame," the doctor bowed her head slightly. "I am entirely at your disposal. I am aware of your work and I respect you greatly. I volunteer at a nearby monastery that is an animal rescue and rehabilitation center. The cow you splinted is there with her calf, a monkey, a dog, and a chicken. They have all made it their home and have even become mascots, of sorts. The monks are quite interested in the splint you created that night." The doctor paused and caught her breath. "I was also present that first night when they brought you in. It was such a pageant, the children and the animals, I was quite touched by it."

"Thank you, yes, I guess it was special," Lucky considered. "Sometimes I don't really understand things except in retrospect."

"That is natural, is it not?" the doctor put forward. "Fortunately, our bodies and other parts of our lives seem able to piece themselves together, even when we are not aware of it ourselves."

"Huh, that is very interesting, Doctor. I do really want to thank Sahani. Can you send her in? I will be ready for a full examination tomorrow."

"Well, I will come in later tonight to check on you, and the nurses will likely come in time to time. Word is likely getting out already, and it might be most wise to contact necessary parties tonight."

"Do what you think is necessary," Lucky acquiesced. "Please send Sahani in, if you would."

"But of course," the doctor smiled. "I am so happy you are well."

"Me too, Doctor. Thank you again."

The Doctor nodded and backed out the door. Lucky could hear a lot of shuffling and bustling outside the door. The examination room was clean and relatively new, but was made of rather cheap and flimsy materials, and most of the sounds made their way right through. She could hear what sounded like several languages, and even some animals at points. She could here the children, too, and could hear their disappointment when the doctor told them only Sahani could go in. She thought she could even hear some haughty command Sahani made to some of her friends, taking full advantage of the situation. Shortly she came bursting through the door.

"Lucky!" Sahani exclaimed as she jumped on the bed.

"Don't you 'Lucky' me!" Lucky said. "You are in trouble, girl."

"But why?" Sahani pretended to not remember what she had promised to Lucky.

"You know what you did, you little sneak."

"But we saved you," Sahani pleaded.

"That is beside the point, but thank you, I am appreciative of that," Lucky admitted. "I told you not to come with me."

"You said we could not come with you, so we went on our own journey, just near you."

"I told you to go back to Ranchi," Lucky specified.

"We did, but we came back," Sahani updated her.

"So you're going to fight me on the details, eh? Well, it makes no difference, now, but do try to do exactly what I say."

"I did do exactly what you said," Sahani reasoned.

"Well, I mean, do exactly what I mean, not exactly what I say."

"I don't know what you mean, a lot of the time," Sahani confessed.

"Well, you got me there," Lucky sighed.

"I like to get you," Sahani smiled.

"Well, thank you for everything you have done," Lucky smiled back at her. "I have another very important thing for you to help me with."

"Anything," Sahani offered, excited at the opportunity.

"I need to get out of here," Lucky said. "I need to escape before anyone gets here."

"But Buck is coming for you!"

"Buck? What do you know about Buck?"

"I know about Buck, and the Ranch, and..."

"Okay, stop there," Lucky cut in. I don't need to know about the ranch right now, all right? I should have figured that you and Buck would have been close as cousins."

"Of course," she nodded.   "He loves you.   He remembers fondly the days when..."

"Yes, yes, enough of that," Lucky stopped her. "Listen, if you are going to be any part of this, you have to promise me not to tell Buck what has happened. You must pretend you are surprised by my disappearance."

Tears welled up in Sahani's eyes. "Why must I always have to deal with you going away."

"It's part of life, Sahani. I have to go. I have to disappear somewhere away from everyone. I don't know exactly why, I have to go, but I promise I will come back. I will come back to you first, that is, if you keep your promise not to tell Buck or anyone else."

"I promise," Sahani said.

"Good. Now this is what I want to do..."

"Do you?"

"Do I what?"

"Do you promise?"

"Do I promise what?"

"Do you promise to come back to me first?"

"Oh, yes, Sahani, I promise to come back to you first, after I have found...whatever. I promise that I will return here, whenever I have found whatever."

"I accept!" Sahani smiled, now wholeheartedly enlisted in Lucky's plan. "What must I do."

"Okay, I need a few things. First, I need a full monks' robe, like the cold weather type, and some of the covered sandals like they wear. And then I need you to make some scene, some ruckus, right at sunset. Do you understand?"

"I think so. If I am to get you those things, and create a scene as you say, then I must get going and hurry."

"Yes, that is right. Do you think you can do it!"

"Yes, I think, better than anyone could," she said, more wondering than arrogant.

"Thank you, Sahani. This means very much to me."

"Thank YOU, Lucky. This means very much to me." Sahani quickly exited out the door, and Lucky could hear excited whispers and an abrupt settling as the little crowd went off.

Lucky simply breathed in and out for a moment. She wanted to think about her predicament but she knew that thinking really would not get her anywhere. She thought for a moment about Buck, about him chasing after her.

"How typical," she said, mostly to herself. "Chasing after me like I need it, cause I don't want it." The only solace she found was in planning all the little details of her escape. She would have to work on the nursing staff, to keep them from raising the alarm too early. Most of all, she knew, she would have to elude Buck. She might have to elude local authorities too, she figured, but she knew that none would likely track her, nor know her tendencies, like Buck.

She had learned a few things from her father's death. One thing was to do the unexpected, as much as was possible. Though she liked the idea of walking, or even horseback riding, on a spiritual quest, that would be expected of her.   So, she would ride as a passenger, hitch-hiking, something that Buck knew she hated to do. He may guess it, likely, but not until she had put at least a thousand miles between, or so she figured. She also figured that it was known that she did not like costumes, did not like to hide or disguise herself, and therefore, this time, she would go as a monk on pilgrimage. She chuckled to herself at the fact that it was not too far from the truth. She trusted that Sahani could get the disguise somehow, and she could handle any consequences.

She occasionally thought about where she was going. Buck would quickly guess that she was headed into the mountains, but at least these were the highest mountains in the world, the most remote range, and so she had a chance. She struggled to get up to a sitting position, wary not to be seen by one of the nurses. She winced as she realized the depth of the wound in her ribs. She gingerly fingered all the sore areas of her body, particularly her head, estimated for herself the extent of all her injuries. She was definitely battered, enough so that no one could ever really suspect that she would be planning an escape. Others would have said she should not even stand up, and here she was planning to hitch a ride hundreds of miles into the mountains.

Even the mental journey was long and hard on Lucky in her current condition, and she let herself sink back down onto the hospital bed. Within little time she slept, and it was the peaceful sleep like she had in the coma, except there were dreams coming back in, fading into view. She had the vision of a rider on horseback, fading into the distance, melting into the setting sun. She remembered considering trying to keep up, but figuring she could not, so she just let herself wander, walking along into the sunset.

She awoke to a small tapping on the door, and it quietly began to swing open. The angle of the sun through the window told her it was significantly later in the day, and she saw Sahani come in carrying an enormous bundle on her back. The little girl put the big pack down in the middle of the room and immediately got to work unbundling the package.

Lucky winced as she sat up. She could feel how much her body needed the rest, but it felt a little like too much rest, too. Her body had been in complete suspension for almost two months. Lucky decided she needed to break it in again with some strenuous activity, and she knew she would get it.

"This is the robe, and the sandles, and I brought you a bedroll, too, and a little sack with a begging bowl. It will make you look more authentic. And look," Sahani said, pulling out a long tan silk scarf. "This you can wrap around your hair, making you look almost bald."

Lucky came over and started to sort through the pieces. She quickly hid them in the hospital bedding.

"Thank you, Sahani. Next I need you tell the nurse that I am very tired and would like my examination now, before sunset. Do you have an idea for the distracting scene."

Sahani smiled in a frighteningly large way "Oh, yes, I think so, right at sundown."

"I won't have time to see it, or even know if you are doing it," Lucky said. "I will have to be on may way and trust you will succeed."

"You will succeed. You are Lucky," Sahani reassured her.

"That may be, but you will have to be lucky, too. And skillfull."

"Do you not think I am both of those things?"

"Yes, of course, and more. That is why I asked you to help me. I am eternally grateful."

"No need. I am honored to help." She walked to the door, and then paused. "Do not worry, Lucky. We will both succeed." She smiled, and turned to go.

"I know we will."

Sahani nodded and started out the door.

"Sahani..."

She stopped expectantly. "Yes?"

"Don't forget to tell the nurse to come in now."

"I will tell them." She started to leave again.

"And Sahani?"

She stopped again. "Yes?"

"I love you."

She smiled again. "I love you too." She briskly turned and headed out of the hospital. Lucky tried to imagine all the preparations that Sahani must be making, but her head hurt. She tried to think of anything, but she faded out again. There was that rider in the distance again. The nurses broke in on her reverie, and it was not hard to convince them that she was tired, confused and nauseous. It seemed to please them, somehow, as if it was what they expected. Lucky knew they would never suspect she was about to jump out the window. She very exhaustively talked about the doctor visits the next day, the examinations and such, and told them very emphatically to let her rest tonight, and not to disturb her under any circumstances.

The nurses were very supportive and fell right into their roles. They arranged for the evening meal to be skipped, and even put a "do not disturb" sign on her door. She was amazed that her plan seemed to be progressing almost too easily. Lucky lay back and tried to think of the upcoming days, but her mind could only draw a blank. Slowly she drifted back again into dreamland. She saw the lone rider ahead in the distance again, only this time he was closer. He turned, and she could see the blue lotus shine of His face. He looked almost sad, or forlorn, but there was still an everpresent peace and understanding aspect to His demeanor. He did not seem to be moving, but she did not seem to be moving either. She looked down at her feet, and they were stuck in mud at the side of a rice paddy. She could struggle, she could grapple with the stalks, but she was afraid she would stain her dress, which was shining white in the darkness.

The glow of her dress extended into the air around her, and a mist was all about them. Slowly the rider was enveloped, and finally he appeared to fade out altogether. Lucky looked down at her feet again, and they were on solid ground, but she did not move. Instead, the mists moved about her, and solidified into a puffy intermittent material. Each blob slowly coalesced with a sound, the distinct bleating of sheep. Each puffball was pure white, forming into a sheep, but the sheep glowed deep red as they all walked into the setting sun.

Lucky startled herself awake with a hidden memory reflex and sat up painfully. The last red rays of the sun streamed through the windows and bathed everything in a certain anticipation. As she pulled out the monk's robes she could distinctly hear sheep in the distance. At first she thought she was still dreaming, but the sound was too distinct, and coming closer.

She looked out the window and considered her escape. She was on the second floor but there was a rather sturdy looking drain pipe next to the window. She was so emaciated after the coma that she could not weigh much, but her hands were very weak as well. She settled on some modified pillowcases to protect her hands and allow her to slide down as safely as possible. The animal sounds were coming closer, and in the distance she could see a raising cloud of dust. She looked in amazement as the dancing dust cloud approached and pulsed in the red sunlight. She could definitely see sheep in numbers in the approaching cloud, and even an elephant behind the herd, but it was not until she saw the monkey on top of the elephant and the three-legged dog running around that she realized that this all must have something to do with Sahani's distraction.

She quickly burst into action, finishing her disguise and preparing to climb out the window. She heard shouts outside the door and almost thought her plan was about to be busted. When she heard animal noises, too, amidst the shouts, she realized what was going on. She protected her hands, opened the window, and climbed out.

She did not look back as she headed out to the main highway. She could feel the dust and the activity, and hear the chaos, and she just wore it all like a shroud. She made it through town rather quickly, stumbled out to the road, and, as if on cue, a large produce truck rolled to a halt. The driver waved to the back and she climbed in. As they rumbled up the road, Katmandu faded into a fog of dust and memories, laced with the sounds of animals and children.

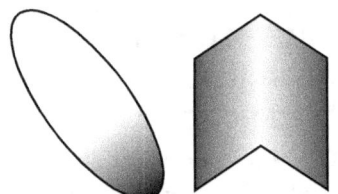

DuaExorto (30) Holed

The truck rambled on through the night and Lucky never did see exactly who was driving her, nor what was his entire load. It was apparently a lot everything, metal, wood, woven throughout with hempline, forming what seemed a spider nest on wheels. She worked her way in and found some bags filled with soft something with just enough space for her to lie down and somewhat cushion herself against the bumps and shocks of the steadily increasing incline.

Once she had wedged herself in she could not sleep, but she could think. Buck did come to her mind, with a certain smug satisfaction, for she was certain she had evaded him now, even if he had guessed her destination. She thought of her father, too, and how he had taught her well. A moment flashed where she remembered the hurt she felt when her father had run off to die, and she considered that Buck might feel some similar hurt. But, no, she decided, Buck had family left, but her father had been the last family she had. She could leave now, because she was the last. Let Buck have the ranch for his growing brood. She had a deep calling, knowing it like she had ever known anything, she had something, somewhere, waiting for her.

The night blurred into an endless bump, Lucky at least thankful that the miles might have been much harder on her still battered frame. She could tell by the dropping temperature and the rising angle of the truck that they were steadily increasing in elevation. She tried to find a way to rest by wrapping her arms in some dangling ropes, but the road would quickly take a turn that would send her jolting one way or the other. She reached that plateau point where it seemed it might never end. It did not take her long to realize that she was going far enough to be well beyond where Buck or anyone else would likely find her, even beyond where she might be able to find her way back. She gradually accepted the loss of location as a necessary part of the vision quest process, but she could not shake the feeling that maybe she was finally going too far. It may have caused her to momentarily consider giving up the entire enterprise and returning to Katmandu, but, like a fool who persists in his folly, she was too deeply committed to turn back now.

Most of the night was a dark smudge, invisible blows and unseen foes, Lucky fending for herself on each hairpin turn. Over time forms started to take shape and Lucky realized that dawn must be approaching. Just as she thought she caught a glimpse of a rising sun through slats in the truck, the whole enterprise came to a shuddering halt. Three quick but authoritative thumps on the front wall signaled that the stop had something to do with her, so she crawled out the back into thin cold air.

As soon as she stepped out she realized that she really did not previously have an accurate picture in her mind of the Himalayas. She had been on many mountains before, had even climbed Halfdome in Yosemite, but somehow she had imagined a more pastoral flavor to her imaginings of these mountains, yaks lazily munching sparse grass fed on glacier water in a cozy valley. Instead what she found was a vertical world. In places which at home were pocket wildernesses encapsulated in state and national parks, here they were bigger and were habitat for people as well as animals. Roads and trails traversed nearly impossible ledges and small huts were hidden in numerous cracks and nooks.

One larger path led up a crevice and led to a rock building that seemed to grow out of the projecting rock promontory. Fluttering flags followed the last few feet to the entrance where a procession of monks clad in clothes like her own were starting down the path.

Lucky took a few steps to glance at the driver and saw him throw the truck into gear and take off up the hill. She realized that he must have figured this was where she was headed, and she might as well not go against expectations. She was also glad that she was not in the back of the truck anymore, now that she got a good look at the terrain through which they had been driving.

The procession of monks was getting nearer, nimbly traversing a narrow path. Lucky saw that the path led them straight to her, and for a moment thought of diving off the road, out of sight, until she actually looked off the road and noticed it was pretty much vertical in opposite directions on each side. The monks walked in outward silence, all wearing the same simple ochre hooded garb, heads bowed, perhaps chanting inwardly, feet seeing the path on their own in their own way.

It was now painfully obvious that she would indeed have to stand directly in front of the line of monks, and none of them seemed to even look ahead and notice her. She began to prepare a speech, using gestures maybe, that might communicate something of her situation, when the group of monks actually altered their pace, coming to the road and splitting into two groups, left and right, stopping and tilting in unison in a decorous slight bow. The eldest amongst them, now at the center closest to the trail to the monastery, bowed a little further and brought an open hand slowly towards the path.

Lucky, her mind already trying to think in gesture, saw this immediately as her chance to skip the whole ordeal. She accepted the invitation with a bow of her own, trying to mimic their mannerisms in every way. She took to the front of the line in a procession back to the monastery, and tried to seem as graceful as they on the small ledge of a traverse. At least she did not trip, fall, and die, she figured. She did not even begin to think about whom they thought she was or who they had actually come out to welcome. There had to be some other monk supposedly about to arrive from somewhere, and Lucky was not keen to be stuck in a case of mistaken identity. She figured there had to be some back door to the place, leading up some hidden back path farther into the mountains.

Whatever her eventual escape route, certainly the best strategy at that point was to keep fitting in as long as she fit in. At the landing in front of the large wooden doors she stopped to the side and stood bowing as the other monks passed on by. Most of them disappeared somewhere beyond the door and as lucky followed the eldest in she found the two of them alone walking up a narrow staircase. Passageways split off to the left and right and there were innumerable places for the monks to have hidden quickly, but Lucky could not shake the feeling that they had just disappeared.

The elder acted normally, as much as Lucky could detect normalcy amongst these monks, and led her into a through a stone maze to a room near the back that appeared to be readied for a visitor. There was a simple cot, a desk, a chair, and a chamber pot, fresh linens and a lit candle. Nothing else. There was a window high up one wall, seemingly for light only. She was planning to leave the room untouched except for the chamber pot, but tried to give the air of settling in. The elder bowed and left backwards facing down while closing the door. Gratefully she did not hear him lock it, although the door was normally equipped with a keyed deadbolt on the outside and a knob lock. She quietly turned the lock on her side, and settled in for just a moment to take care of the private needs of an American woman masquerading as a Tibetan monk.

When she was finished and ready to go again, she carefully listened to the door as she undid the lock. Hearing nothing, she cautiously opened the door a crack. She heard nothing at all. That was good and bad. She was counting on the way to be clear, but had hoped that there might be some sound, some chanting or work noises, to cover her exit. Instead the place was dead silent. And slight noise she would make would echo down the halls. Oh well, she thought, any typical American teenager learned how to sneak out quietly, even on loose wood floors, and the stone floors of the monastery made that easier.

She made her way out into the hall and moved along towards the end she figured was the back. The place seemed to be lit mostly with some oil lamps placed periodically along the walls. She avoided one hall that seemed to lead back to a kitchen area, which was empty but would likely see activity sooner or later. There really was no one about, and she gained more confidence as she could see a source of natural light up ahead. She was still cautious as she stepped out into the crisp mountain air, but she preceded quickly ahead even before her eyes had adjusted fully to the outdoor mountain light. That was probably why she did not see the black Tibetan Mastiff that was blocking the path until she was almost upon it, that and the fact it seemed to know to stand in the shadow of a rock overhang that both hid it and made it look much larger.

Not that it really needed to seem larger that it was. It was already the largest dog that Lucky had ever seen. Its height alone was impressive but its thick coat gave it the apparent mass of a good size human. Since it was on a slight rise, she was pretty much staring straight in the eye when she realized what was going on.

"Oh my!" she exclaimed, but the dog did not react much and just stood staring at her.

"Uh, good-doggie," she said timidly. "Although I guess that doesn't mean anything to you. Uh, oh, body language, gesture, simple sounds, that's right." She held her hand low, palms low, and made soothing humming sounds. The dog still did not seem to react. She took this as somewhat of a good sign and started to move to the side to go around the animal on its left.

For the first time it reacted and moved just enough to keep her from passing. She slowly tried going the other way to its right, but the dog moved just enough to keep her from going that way. Still it seemed to have no other reaction. She almost wanted to try an quick left-right dodge like in football, but decided against it rather quickly.

"Man, even the guard dogs around here are monks," she said as she found herself back in her starting position. She decided to stand quietly for a moment, see if the animal changed at all, but it did not. She scanned the surroundings, and traced several significant cracks up the granite wall to her right. She saw the dog glance up to the same spot, and for the first time she sensed a reaction.

"Aha, so you know now I know your weak spot," she said, and immediately stepped to the left, getting the dog to follow her as before. Instead, with as much agility as she could muster, she faked left and broke right, sprinting up towards the cracks. She expected the dog to try to follow her, and even thought he might catch her, but by the time she was several dog lengths up the rock wall in the tiny cracks and she dared to look around, the dog was already bounding up the trail out of site.

"Oh great," Lucky said to herself, he probably knows where to catch me at the top." She aimed towards the more vertical section. "Well, he has speed, but I have agility." Lucky had done plenty of mountain climbing in her time, but usually with real gear, harnesses, and ropes. She was also still feeling the effects of her long sleep, and her muscles were trembling with the effort.

Fortunately the climbing was not too difficult, just enough to be impossible for a dog or other animal, it seemed. And there were definite traces of a path. Regular foot and handholds, worn smooth. Lucky ascertained that others had wanted to pass the dogs, but to where she was not yet sure.

After she had gone perhaps a hundred feet, the way seemed to part. To the left it seemed to flatten out at some point, whereas to the right it went straight up. As if on cue, a large furry black head peeked over the rock up the left path.

"Right path it is," Lucky said, as she clambered up the more vertical choice. Still there were clear worn areas, as if many hands and feet had made the same choice before. The dog just watched her climb by, still not making a sound, but immovable in his intent. Her muscles were protesting, not having overextended themselves like this in some time, but they were used to so many years of obeisance that they would never give in completely. Lucky just kept pushing, figuring all these worn handhelds had to lead somewhere fairly soon, hoping that it was not just a massive mastiff landing.

The way continued on up, and Lucky tried not to look down, but it just happened every so often. She did not suffer from vertigo, but a glance told her that to slip at this point was certain death. The handholds became more scarce, being replaced at points by what were, at best, smooth depressions. Lucky had faith that she was still following an old worn path, and she knew there had to be a way up, for there was no way back down. She discovered that she could place her sweaty palms fully in the depressions and create a suction cup effect, giving her an effective hold. She started to feel that maybe the monastic black dog was not such a big threat after all.

Most of the way she had been able to see a fairly good distance up the cliff, but she came to a point where a stone bulge pushed into the sky right above her. It looked like an impossible obstacle, and was worn smooth. She knew she had no choice so she pressed her entire body against the rock and started to inch upward. She could feel with her fingers that the bulge flattened on the top, and there was even a finger hold or two, but she would have to pull herself up blind.

She pulled and kicked, and rather quickly came over the hump onto a ledge. She ended face down, arms behind her, legs dangling in thin air, her nose about 10 inches from a set of black furry paws. She slowly looked up, and the dog was sitting on the path that snaked left and right, down the back one way and up to a cave of sorts the other. He was quite planted and wore the same stoic impression he had before, but seemed to be blocking her way down rather than up.

"You're up to something, aren't you," Lucky said to the animal. He did not move, but something in his eye twinkled. He was utterly at home on the rocky ledge, and he was utterly at ease and in control.

"No reason to attack, not now, at least, eh fella?" Lucky stood up like it was the most natural thing in the world and brushed herself off, and repressed an urge to pat the dog on the head. Instead she bowed slightly with her head the way the monks had and headed into the cave. The dog held his position.

Her eyes could not adjust easily, but her ears could tell that it was a sizable cavity in the mountain. Her nose could tell her that it had occupants, at least sporadically. The foot of the cave was well worn, and she followed what of it she could see. Her eyes slowly settled in, and she saw that she was not alone. The smooth silvery path of wear led within, towards a rise in the floor in the back which came to a natural peak, upon which sat a monk of considerable presence.

He was dead still in lotus position, eyes half-open, or perhaps half-closed. He seemed ageless and ancient at the same time, and Lucky wondered at one point if he were even alive. His face held some sort of expression, but Lucky could not identify it. Though there was little sign of life, there was a significant cover of dust over most of the cave, save the shining path in and the rise, and since the man was equally dust free, she surmised he must be a living man in meditative trance. There was another slight rise in front of the man about ten feet, and this was the most worn spot of all. Lucky noticed that the shining path led there and stopped so she decided that she might as well do the same. She tried to sit in a full lotus position, but her bones were not in the mood, so she settled for the half-lotus position. Surprisingly, the slight stone mound was comfortable in this way and she naturally settled into a patient contemplation.

Lucky had never been the meditative type. She did not doubt that it worked, that something was accomplished by such activity, but she just felt that she did not really need to do it herself. Maybe she was cocky, maybe deluded, or maybe she just did not have time, but she had never done much of it before.

Sitting here seemed natural, however. The silence in the space held it own position, maintaining an effortless presence. Lucky relaxed, breathed, and paused. Thoughts went this way, then that way. There was something blue, but it covered everything, like some great spiritual sky. She stopped trying to classify it. She stopped grasping at anything, tired of seeing it all slip between her fingers.

There was a moment of nothing, no reflections anymore, no suppositions, no conclusions, nothing. No, not nothing. Something. A ghost of something, but more real than phantasm, somehow. A moment of being, pure being, and something else. Something she had been looking for. Release. Beyond release. There was a moment of real something between the other shadow somethings. Everything, everything in her mind, and it was all on her mind, slipped away, melted like a sugar crystal in the rain.

"Welcome." It seemed as if the mountain spoke. So clear, so deep, but not loud. The monk did not seem to stir, yet something had changed in his disposition. Perhaps his brow was lifted a tad, or the corners of his mouth, but he seemed happy and welcoming, like an old friend. Now she could hear the sound of his breath. She would swear that it had not been there before. He had more color in his face, and more warmth settled into the room.

Lucky lightly cleared her throat. "I..uh...I may not be who you think I am..."

He simply spoke again, hardly moving. "Are you not Lucky Star of Lucky Star Ranch?"

Lucky was more surprised than she should have been. She gulped hard. "Uh, yes," Lucky admitted. "You speak excellent English."

"Thank you," he said. "Cal, class of '67."

"Berkeley grad?"

"That's right. I am Dogzchen Rinpoche. We have been excited for your visit, particularly Rufus. He anticipated that you would immediately take the mystics path to me here. It is the hardest path, but the most direct. Straight up, is it not? I have not taken it in years."

"Rufus?" she asked.

"My closest companion, the dog," he said, motioning towards the cave entrance. "He is one of your biggest fans."

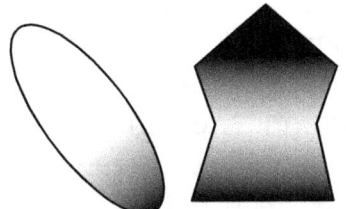

DuaFammo (31) Pursued

When Lucky had finally realized that no other monk was expected in her place, she made herself more at home in her room. Over a period of weeks she was a temporary resident of the monastery, more a guest of honor than a monk on retreat. She kept the typical monk's robe and footwear, but she no longer tried to hide her head. The monks never acted any differently, for what she could tell. They accepted her presence, but she was not expected to know anything or do much in regards to the needs of the monastery. Instead, Rinpoche gave her most of her instructions, which seemed to be mostly meditating, listening, eating, and sleeping, in that order. Rinpoche would occasionally say nothing, orAlthough he spoke excellent English, he was apparently the only one, or the only one permitted to speak to her.

From the monks' perspective this was the event of the year, and they were acting like giddy school girls at a rock concert, which only meant a slight mischievous smile might appear on their lips momentarily as they passed. To them it was like the Beatles had come to town.

It had been a long dry season and the weeks were unusually warm. Most days Rinpoche would be waiting for Lucky up in the cave, but sometimes he would take her to some other special area of the monastery. Rufus would pretty much follow her any time she came out of the main building.

Lucky came to realize more about why they knew her when they took her around back one day to the refuse area. She had come to understand that nowhere is as pure as it might seem at first. Romantic western representations of majestic stone castles on mountain tops rarely included details about the septic systems. Such details were omitted purposefully, for the hidden reality was seldom pretty. This refuse area was surprisingly clean and organized, however, and included a significant composting program with a large and varied garden.

Limited space necessitated that everything was carefully organized and tightly packed. There was a sophisticated effort for sorting and recycling garbage. One section was reserved for trash that had been jettisoned by expeditions climbing Mt. Everest. Rinpoche explained how they had lobbied some wealthy mountaineer groups and had obtained a small grant to remove such refuse, which climbers had been leaving behind for years.

Rinpoche led her through the aisles of garbage until she saw her face, smashed and stacked a thousand times. The writing was Hindi but the image was definitely western. Her own face, hair blowing in the wind held back by a cowboy hat. Lucky did not oversee the packaging of all the subsidiaries that they had included in their global family over the years. In fact, she did not much keep track of anything the company did any more.

"We are very grateful for your milk, and your cheese. We take your donations and make them into necessary supplies for our mountain schools." Apparently this packaging process was part of a communications gap. The monastery had won a grant as part of their international programs of food charity. The monastery had requested larger amounts in bulk, for they had to portion out the milk in doses smaller that the single pints popular in America. The Indian headquarters only gave out palettes of the pint-size variety. Here at the monastery, a single monk emptied out individual pints into the larger tin bottles that the monastery traditionally used to distribute milk.

"Yours is our favorite milk, and this is why," Rinpoche said, pointing to a package where it read, 'Ingredients: Milk and compassion."

"Padmasambhava is our patron, the Buddha of Compassion, who brought enlightenment to the Himalayas."

"I thought the Buddha was Siddhartha Gautama?" Lucky asked.

"Yes, he was. A prince born in India. There are many Buddhas, stretching back to the Primordial Buddha, and all are one."

"How is that possible?" Lucky asked earnestly.

"All have reached and maintained a state that we call Rigpa. Absolute Mind through cessation of mind. This is a state where distinctions are inimical," Rinpoche spoke of such things as if Lucky should already understand them.

"That just doesn't make sense," Lucky said, shaking her head.

"The Western mind loves to apply exacting standards of logic to all traditions but its own," the Rinpoche countered.

"You got me there," Lucky acknowledged. "Well, I am sorry about all the packaging." Lucky shrugged. "I promise to do something about it."

"Oh," Rinpoche smiled. "Do you wish to help Thogyal fold the containers before they are shipped back?"

"No, no," Lucky shook her head. "I meant, I can do something about getting you milk sent in bulk."

Rinpoche's smile faded. "Lucky, no need to make promises you will not keep."

"But I can make that happen," she insisted.

"Perhaps, your intentions are good, but you will not do it," Rinpoche said.

"But..." Lucky was about to argue with him but she realized that he was probably right. "Okay, okay, I'll fold cartons." She sat down and started to fold.

"Good," Rinpoche said. "I thought you might find that rewarding." Rinpoche went about his business, but Rufus stayed next to Lucky, casually watching her work. She felt a warmth in her spot, a certain presence. That must be Thogyal, she thought. The mound of folded cartons was already tremendous, and there was something about the ground that suggested many such loads. There was an area where a few empty cans and milk stains indicated most of the fresh milk was emptied into cans there. A pile of empty cartons stood in between, a thousand Lucky Stars, emptied and piled in a haphazard heap.

"My God, what a mess," Lucky said out loud, and the words seemed to hang in the mountain air. Some kind of lesson was painfully apparent by the whole absurdity of the scene. Lucky was usually so meticulous about her image and her personal environment, and now it had become quite clear that her karma extended out well beyond what thought was her own little world. This must have been the whole reason that Rinpoche had brought her to this area.

Lucky got into a meditative trance as her hands got the hang of the job by themselves. There is a certain freedom in menial work that allows the mind to flow freely in realms of its own while the body automatically takes care of the task on its own. Lucky thought of other similar tasks of her childhood, like milking the cows or brushing the horses. She realized that she missed such work as she had transformed into a strictly management world. Recently she had not even done much work at all in the professional world, for she had set up things to run on their own. Now she realized that, on their own, things might develop into something in her name that she did not know all about.

She had been folding for almost an hour when a stack of cartons with legs came walking up the path. When the stack was almost upon her, a face appeared from behind to peek around. With a gasp all of the cartons fell to the ground, along with Thogyall who was now on his knees, murmuring some kind of prayer.

"No, no, get up," Lucky said as she helped him to his feet. "It is I who should grovel in front of you." Thogyall was arguing with her in a gentle way and fumbling with the cartons on the ground. Lucky bent over so fast to help that they bumped heads, and they both laughed. There really was not enough space in Thogyall's work area for two people, so Lucky gracefully moved around him back to the path. She took his hand, kissed it, and said thank you, looking him directly in the eyes.

Lucky might not have known it but Thogyall was getting choked up and unable to speak. He merely just kept bowing in the small particular way that the monks had, and there were tears in his eyes. Lucky thanked him again and slowly made her way back up the trail. She had almost wanted to keep folding cartons, but there was an aspect of the task that was hopeless and unfinishable. Lucky had the inescapable feeling that there was nothing to do, that nothing could be done, that nothing should be done because it might very well be the wrong thing. Hundreds of people under her banner, all trying to do the right thing, had come up with this ridiculous situation of her face spread on milk cartons in a dirty stack in the Himalayas. Where else had her face found itself?

She was walking up the trail towards the cave, Rufus at her side rather than blocking her way, when she saw the steep Mystic path going up the cliff. She had not climbed that path since the first time, ever since she had made fast friends with Rufus, but now she wanted to try it again. Maybe there was something more to it that just a way to avoid the dog. She made for the cliff and immediately Rufus bounded ahead.

Her hands felt the old spots as she made her way up, and they felt like old friends. Stories were told in those worn spots, volumes of feelings and aspirations clung in each crack, histories held in a slight smoothness. She made her way more easily this time, her muscles tight and energy high from all the healthy mountain living she had been doing recently. As she gently swam up the mountain, she sensed something else there, a new awareness. There was a sense that there was something deep about living metaphors, when people had come as far as had those who had made this pilgrimage before. There was a reason that it all came to climbing, because the climbing became easier. It was the simplest way to overcome obstacles, climb over them. It created a new space for compassion, because life was not merely an endless stream of difficulties with no solutions. The attempt to overcome was the whole point, it was all that was necessary. People changed when they made an attempt, whether it ended in failure or not. And that change in character was the reason for it all, not some distant summit. And maybe failure led to a greater change in character, so maybe failure ultimately led to greater success. Except, of course, when failure led to death. But, with all the recent talk of reincarnation, maybe not even then.

She realized all of the sudden that she had reached the top and Rufus was sitting there as usual. Perhaps that was a part of it, too. The more one climbed the less one noticed the strain. The thoughts suspended the muscles, over time, and they climbed on their own, undirected. She looked at the dog, who raised an eyebrow slightly with the attention.

"You know more than you're sayin', don't you?" she asked him, not expecting an answer, but was surprised when he blinked and looked down. Lucky saw it was communicating great affection and compassion, as much as such a guard dog could show.   She wondered momentarily at the significant display of emotion from the normally stoic animal, and walked into the cave with a sense of portent.

"Are you ready?" Rinpoche's voice echoed out of the darkness.   Lucky's feet knew the way and she found her accustomed spot and sat in half-lotus.

"I am," Lucky responded immediately, trying to at least sound confident.

"Do you know for what you are ready?"   Rinpoche asked again.

"Uh...not really," Lucky admitted.

"Good," Rinpoche stated.   "No one knows what it coming when they face the Infinite, but they can feel in their heart if they are ready."

"That's pretty much me exactly," Lucky pointed out.

"All right, then.   What I am going to give you we call the Phowa," Rinpoche said matter-of-factly.   "Under the guidance of the Blessed One, I will charge your being with Divine Light, which will acquaint you with the View."

"The View?"   Lucky looked around at the black walls. There was a great view from the outside ledge, but there was nothing but a distant white hole from her vantage point.

"The View is the closest translation to the word that we use to describe the proper perspective on the material world," he explained.   "In the rite of Phowa a master uses his accumulated merit to charge the energy of the student, allowing her to rise quickly to the View.   It is similar to what you made have heard called Darshan in India."

"A spiritual jolt?" Lucky surmised.

"Very much so.   It is very helpful to one who is ready, but it can be overwhelming to one who is not."

"And do you think I am ready?" Lucky asked.

"A good question.   I think you will not be overwhelmed, but you are perhaps a bit too eager.   I am not sure how you will handle what you may find there."

"What might I find there?"

"Yourself."

"That is what I have been looking for."

"And running from."

"What?"

"You cannot be looking for yourself unless you have left yourself. And it is hard to leave oneself. You have to keep running."

"Well I am sitting still now."

"And thus you are about to catch up with yourself."

"Ooo, that kind of makes me want to get up and go," Lucky protested.

"Exactly. You see, that is why you must face the pursuer and the pursued, and realize they are the same."

"All right, then," Lucky shook her head. "Let's go."

Rinpoche lowered his lids slightly, and began to chant, "Om mani padme hum." His tone was deep and clear, and he seemed to breathe in a circular way, so that the chanting never stopped. Lucky had heard the chant and others in her stay at the monastery, and she understood that it had to do with compassion and dedicating the spiritual merit garnered in the practice to all other sentient beings in creation. This was natural for Lucky, a part of her makeup, and she allowed herself to float in the compassion for all life. She pictured momentarily many of the animals she had loved and cared for over the years, and she had no trouble igniting her compassionate heart.

As she drifted in bliss, she became aware that the cave began to sparkle around her, just barely perceptibly. Rinpoche must have sensed her heightened awareness, for he started to chant with a more crisp intonation. Lucky could see as well as hear the change. The sparkles that had appeared around the cave were concentrated on the forehead and heart of the master. All at once, the sparkles intensified into a fire circling his entire body, pointed in front. The blue-green cool flames gathered in intensity and flashed out, hitting Lucky in the chest and head.

Lucky burned a bright blue, and the entire cave melted into blazing light. When Lucky had settled herself, her inner eye adjusted itself to the luminosity, and she saw that the cave was still there, but it was made not of cold hard stone, but of a shining matrix, jewels of light strung together in a net. Somehow she could see it in its entirety, a tunnel stretching deep behind, and the mountain face dropping out below. She could see the monastery, and its walls were like ephemeral tissue, glowing with some internal potency. Everything was transparent, but perfectly clear. People were transparent, too, but they glowed in a more dense way in certain parts of their light body. A great red globe near the heart, a brighter bluish light on the top of the head, and various bright spots hung like a chain of jewels in between.

She saw Thogyall working at his pile of milk cartons, and a brighter fire burned in a line through his whole body. Suddenly remembering Rinpoche, she returned in an instant to the cave, and witnessed the master as a blinding column of iridescent rays. It was a source, or a channel to a source, of blazing compassion and wisdom. Bathed in the light of knowledge, Lucky learned many things for the first time. The first was that she could see everything from all sides, almost inside out. The other was that she could move her consciousness around the world just by the power of thought. She held certain places in her head, the ranch for example, and she flew there instantly through a shower of golden threads. She could see the same glowing human shapes moving around, and even saw Buck on a horse stop suddenly in the meadow above the ranch house. The beauty of his image blazed in light on top of Luck the horse, similarly blazing, would have taken Lucky's breath away had her light body been breathing. He looked around, almost as if he could sense her, and Lucky could see blue light flaring most brightly around his head just as he seemed to look directly at her.

The blue light looked familiar, and Lucky was not ready for something about it, and her consciousness withdrew like a banana slug that touched something hot. She expanded back out through California, discovering that she could alter her scale as well. She allowed herself to grow, and saw the lights of millions of people concentrated in various parts of the land. She also noticed that the lights changed with various states. Some had small lights, some were bigger, and a few burned with bright violent reds and browns, whereas some tended towards the blue.

It occurred to Lucky that the colors must correspond to emotional states, for she could see a few that seemed to be in confrontation were showing the most dark muddy red, when others in meditation were more violet and blue. What was apparent next was that most people tended towards the blue. Contrary to her expectations, fostered mostly by the media, the vast masses of humanity were incredibly peaceful, interacting with warm intentions and loving relations. There was constant sharing of food and time, cooperation on a massive scale. Only in a few relatively isolated places was there the conflict that so often dominated the evening news. Everywhere she could see special souls intermingling in peaceful and loving ways, and she had a sudden flush of great sympathy. The feeling flowed between them with a periwinkle twinkle and wove itself outwards towards the stars, which hinted they were made of the stuff.

She felt a great turquoise Presence there, behind It All and she knew it was her Lover. She knew that all pathways led to Him, for they were coming forth from Him. He was the Source of Everything, but he was Outside It All. He was Outside Space and Time. There were only two directions, towards Him, and away from Him, yet both looped around. He was Unchanging, yet Endlessly Diverse and Dynamic. She floated through Him all, yet resisted being drawn to the Center. She knew Him, she loved Him, but she was not ready for Him, not Yet. He bloomed forth consciousness and light to all of existence, yet some could choose to find a shadow, and the shadows ran as deep as one could ever wish in any dark night of the soul, etched in sharp relief by the Brilliance of the Source. Lucky was choosing to explore the nearly infinite spectrum of colored layers in between light and shadow, and she drifted back into the relatively gray lands of mountainous Tibet.

Rinpoche was gone, his absence made evident by a certain crispness to the echo of a dripping fissure in the background. The air was sharper, bearing a different seasonal message on wisps of chilled fragrance. The light was different, too, spilling from the entrance hole with diffuse softness, piling up on the entry like snow on a window sill

As Lucky soon realized, the light was indeed snow, as a thick blanket covered the floor to about five feet from the entrance. Lucky shivered as she worked out her muscles for the first time in she knew not how long. There was a bundle of clothes and a thick robe in the corner, which, Lucky thankfully acknowledged, Rinpoche must have left with the consideration that she might come out in such a situation. She put on the additional layers and set out to survey the situation.

Looking out the mouth of the cavern, Lucky saw immediately that, to her dismay, for her to leave the ledge at this point would mean likely death. All the footings and ledges were completely sheathed in a wall of white. Any attempt to push out into the nondescript vertical terrain would inevitably lead to her final snow trip in a great slide down the mountain. She thought of making her way deeper in the cave, perhaps finding a way through the interior in some tunnel, and she remembered a flash of her meditation when she could see through solid rock like photonic gossamer and saw that the cave did indeed continue deep down into the mountain towards the monastery, but it was quite clear to her that her physical senses alone would not guide her so well through the darkness.

She was almost about to try going into trance again as perhaps she could go deep again and just wait it out, when she heard a single deep bark in the distance. It bounced off the mountain vasts and disappeared in the crevasses. She began to wonder if she had imagined it when a second bark came echoing across the frozen landscape. Then a third. And a fourth. The sound had come closer each time until it was literally shaking the snow bank, and the echoes crescendoed with a black furry nose sticking through the white wall.

"Rufus!" Lucky squawked in recognition. She had apparently not used her voice in some time. She carefully cleared her throat. "You came for me."

The dog burst through the last bits of snow and ice into the middle of the cave. As he shook the ice from his big black mane he practically pranced back and forth with excitement. Lucky had never seen him so animated, actually wagging his tail, though he still maintained a dignified bearing at all times. He carefully walked out to the new tunnel through the snow on the ledge, tamping his feet as if to emphasize for Lucky the delicate footing of the traverse. She gleefully pushed through behind the dog until they had emerged at the top of the long trail. She descended the remaining distance in sheer bliss, wrapped with a new awareness of the permeation of light within matter which seemed so obvious now in the shining flush of snow in the sun.

The monastery seemed deserted, and cold. Rufus led Lucky deep into one of the inner chambers where she found Rinpoche sitting in a chair next to a fireplace. She was not surprised when she discovered that she had been in trance for 4 months, but she was shocked nonetheless. The awareness was so tender that she could not go back to meditation in the cave for months, despite the fact that it was buried in snow anyway. Instead she read and studied deeply under the Rinpoche in the monastery Library, which she had not even realized existed before. Apparently most of the monks had gone down into lower monasteries with the cold, but a skeleton crew remained to keep things going.

Lucky learned that many things were possible in meditation, and that great powers could be acquired, but that these powers where more often seen to be obstacles rather than benefits for they distracted many ardent seekers from the ultimate Goal of life. Yet, as one progressed in spiritual practice, miracles could become an every day fact of life, but all focus had to remain on the Most High, however each person could conceive of It All, because that provided the way for grace to enter into each person's life.

Lucky saw how she had been resisting the highest knowledge of her Lover, at times, but she was finally beginning to understand how He was everywhere, in everything, and that as she recognized Him, so would he reveal Himself. Each moment was a dance between the God outside and the God within, both learning of Each Other and Themselves simultaneously. It was an ancient relationship thick with potent and inherent significance, establishing an undeniable meaning to even the smallest life. Every spark of existence was a crystal reflection of a greater brilliance emanating from a plane beyond.

Encased in icy rock in a Himalayan mountain fortress, Lucky discovered the warmth of the universe. She found how everything, even the greatest hurt, was ultimately a gift, for the alternative was nothing at all. She understood that evil was simply absence, the shadow of soul. All was a tapestry woven thick, dripping with riotous colors and scandalous patterns, mapping out an artistic maze of pure creativity, unleashing visual tales of outlandish heroism and brazen bravery. At stake was feeling, and awareness. Each spark of life chose its path along a windy universe, and every encounter, though merely a shadow play on an ephemeral screen, led to true feelings and critical knowledge of each other. The spirit grew and expanded with this sympathy, this embodiment of compassion. The self was not lost in spiritual homogeneity upon realization of higher states, but instead blossomed into a unique sacred expression of the infinite.

Lucky was so engrossed in her intellectual explorations that she hardly felt the need to explore this meditatively until well after the snows had melted. Rufus had been her calm companion for the entire time, and he remained almost entirely indoors as Lucky pursued her various inquiries. His noted absence one day persisted almost until dusk one day until she finally ventured out back to the cave trail head, and she found him sitting stoically staring right up towards the cave.

"It probably is time for me to go back, isn't it?" she said, wondering to herself if she meant the cave or somewhere beyond. "You always know the right time, don't you?" She accepted his counsel and prepared herself to go up to the cave. She casually ambled up the long way, this time, not in a hurry exactly to get wherever she was going. When she finally got to the top there was a distinct lack of formality to her entrance into the cave and her sitting in front of Rinpoche.

"Are you ready?"

"Yes."

"Do you know what you are ready for?"

"No."

"Good."

He chanted as if he had already been chanting all along, like it was breathing, and Lucky lost no time in wondering what might be coming. She saw and recognized that pure blue light, piercing the veil and playing on her awareness like shadows on the cave wall.

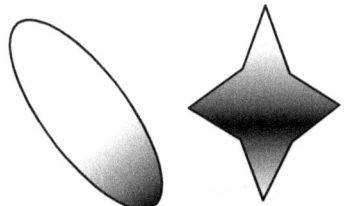

DuaTemmo (32) Van Winkled

Lucky saw the crystalline structure all around her, but she really did not pause to focus on any particular point of it. This time she had a very definite goal in mind. She no longer felt the need to hide or run away. She decided she wanted to head directly towards the abode of her Lover. She knew it was all metaphor, but that there was some place that some had called Heaven, some had called Valhalla or Nirvana or Samadi. She knew it was out there, that He lived there, and that she was going to find it.

She cast herself far out into the stars, plunging deep into the interstellar void looking for that gateway to beyond. She saw it behind everything, but no clear passageway appeared anywhere. It seemed just out of reach, like the end of a rainbow. Wherever she chased it out across the universe, it remained right in front of her out of reach. She ranged across the galaxy, over to other galaxies, and sensed many wonderful things, but never the door way into her Lover's land.

It was hard to say when she finally noticed the presence right beside her. She had given up racing about and was sitting quietly in utter lack of intention, and He suddenly seemed to have always been there.

"Where are you?"

"Beside you."

"No, I mean, where do you live?"

"In a place that is beyond what you can understand as anywhere."

"But can I visit?"

"Anytime."

"But where is the gateway?"

"Within."

"What?"

"You have been searching across material existence for the passage to My land. It is not there. It lies within yourself, for that was my first gift."

Lucky did not hesitate when she finally grasped what He was saying. She turned her mind's eye around, and gazed deeply into she that gazed in return, as in a deep still pool. In that consciousness itself she saw the door, as simple as a step to the left, hidden within folds of her own understanding. She enfolded in blissfull awareness and slowly slipped behind all of the projections that she had hitherto considered to be the real world. In slipping behind herself, she found the direct link to Him that was her Self, and she took herself by the hand to be led into His kingdom.

It stretched like a vast tableau, far more dramatic and vivid than she even remembered from her previous visit. Everything glowed from within, but it was also significantly more substantial than anything in the mundane physical world. It was like a child being given a rose after years of having seen only black and white photographs. Lucky understood how the entire physical universe was really just an echoed, and shallow, colorless reflection of this grander dimension. It finally made sense to her how everything was made in His image, how humans where made in his image, but just an image, a reflection, a recollection. This place, His home, was beyond place. It was not the tip of the pyramid, or its base, but was the mountain from which the pyramid had been chipped. But, having given the stone for the pyramid, the mountain remained undiminished, merely gaining the distinction of having birthed a pyramid.

There were great temples in his land that seemed to have grown out of the sacred soil. The plants and trees grew with fractal like complexity into shapes of geometric grace. Everything was completely organic and autonomous, yet living from some inner compulsion that brought out automatic diversity with sublime symmetry. Nothing was exactly the same, yet everything bespoke of a similar inspiration, something of deep common compassion. She found it all to be drenched in Him, everything enmeshed in a delightful web of Himness.

"Welcome Home," He said, putting an arm around her.

"I want to stay," she said, attempting to preempt some premature ejection from Eden.

"You can, but you won't."

"But I say I will."

"What you say is supposition, what I say is fact. Some day you will choose to stay here with Me, but now you have chosen to find Me elsewhere."

"I looked for you everywhere, but I could not find you anywhere."

"Blame not the View for the dimness of the eyes."

"The problem is with my eyes?"

"The physical eyes see physical things. You have a greater single eye that sees from within."

"I see, I mean, I think I see," Lucky ventured.

"Yes, you do see, things that many saints have longed for years to see. You have seen, but you have not always recognized what you were seeing."

"But I see You everywhere," Lucky insisted.

"The point is not to just see Me everywhere, but to see Me everyone."

"In everyone?" she wondered.

"As everyone."

"But there are some nasty folks out there."

"Am I?"

"Not You, them, those others."

"None are but am I."

"That makes no sense."

"No sense but I am."

"But if You are You, than why am I?"

He paused so that His answer would land. "Love."

"Yes," she said simply, and accepted. There was nothing else to say, nothing else to ask. There was no more yearning in her, no more demands. It all just came to her like a tame tabby cat into her warm lap on a cold day. Everything she had chased around the universe, came up to her and sat in lap, just as she had finally stopped chasing.

She stopped thinking, stopped talking, it was already way above all that. People had thought that telepathy was something like radio, thoughts projecting through the ether, but it was really just a knowing. It was reaching within to that place where everything was always connected and knowing that the answer to all questions was already there.

She let herself be there, immersed in the precious momentous place of Now. She was here, His home, always here. She felt it, remembered it, and knew she was always here, wherever she went, she was still always here. Everywhere was a dream, and she was here, dreaming it, and it was dreamt because such a grand place had to foster grand dreams. The Earth was one such grand dream. It was a fantastic scheme, a bold proposition, a sublime elocution, for it was indeed a great story. It was told with the transcendental wit and humor of her Lover, perpetually restaged to the delight of a returning audience.

She saw the cows down by the stream, strolling in dreamy bliss. The herd knew something in its form about the deeper meaning of life, like a school of fish. Each member was an independent entity, free to act on its own, but when it keyed in to the greater awareness of unity held within the group, it could act in tandem to accomplish things impossible for an individual. It could move and sense and know things together, experiencing a larger sense of self by belonging to the larger set.

They walked and danced amongst the herd singing and dancing. He played his precious flute, and she allowed herself to sing. When she heard her own voice here singing, she almost turned around to look for someone else, for she had not heard herself for some time. Sure she would sing to herself often enough back on the Earth, but here her voice had a different timbre and an etheric quality that surpassed anything she had heard before. She had always wanted to sing like that, somewhere deep inside, and had maybe dared to dream of accompanying a flute player like her Lover, the Stealer-of-Hearts, but she had never really known how it could be possible.

It was so natural and easy to be here with Him, so familiar, that she wondered why she would have ever chosen before to leave. It was so comfortable and true that she began to suspect that she may have been expelled from paradise.

"Why do I recall having been cast out of here?" she asked him at one point when they had momentarily taken a break from the music.

"When all is one, to become two is to be cast out."

"But I am like Eve, did I sin and get cast out of the garden?"

"The only sin is to leave the garden, and the only punishment is to be outside of it, unable to see the path home."

"But why would we leave the garden?"

"For the joy of returning."

"Do you always have such a curt and direct answer?"

"No."

"Okay." And that was enough. She had never been so quick to accept answers, but never had she been given such acceptable answers.

They spent the rest of the day walking hand-in-hand. In Lucky's mind it certainly could have been forever. The days were different, for there really was no sun, so to speak. Everything was illuminated by some intrinsic glow, but there were still cycles. As the very air cuddled her close, Lucky could tell that evening was settling. There was no sunset, nothing to set, but there was a change in the intensity of vibration that signaled the end of the day. It was like that moment when all the birds start to sing after the sun has passed below some distant hill and the mists would emerge from the dark woods. Dusk, the time alone, more than how it came about, was an absolute. It was a perfect magic, illustrating a basic truth, so it must have had its origin there in Perfection itself.

Everything was living, even the stones, and everything would react to the things around it. The rocks tended to look like those around them, exhibiting another herd effect, but could change color or texture en masse if some mood or emotion passed over them. The trees visibly moved and swayed, reaching towards Lucky as she passed. Certain branches hung low, like weeping willows, plump with fruit that would reach towards her. As they neared Lucky's grasp, the fruit would change to whatever she imagined, from plum to guava to luscious ripe persimmon, and in one mischievous moment she imagined a hot dog and a cell phone, and upon seeing close facsimiles settled her mind on a pomegranate and walked towards her Lover.

"So, Govinda, is that your name?" she asked him.

"That is one of My infinite names."

"Which one should I use?"

"The One which makes you think of Me most clearly."

"Than I will call you One. Tell me, My One, what is this all made of?" she asked, grabbing a desire fruit and making it change repeatedly in her hand.

"Consciousness."

"And what are you made of?" she said, touching His face.

"Consciousness."

She paused for a moment, with her hand against His cheek, daring to caress Him. "Why can't I have You as my lover, all the time?"

"To find Me in a lover, you must find Me as a lover. Right now you are living the life of a cold monk."

A shiver suddenly came over Lucky, and a cloud passed over the sacred valley. There was nothing over head, but the colors of everything turned to more earthen tones with shades of gray, just as if some cloud had passed.

"What do you mean?" Lucky reacted defensively. "I have a very full life. I am president of a company, a well-known organic dairy farmer..."

For the first time ever He interrupted her. "None of those things are you. I am not talking about what you have done, I am talking about what you are doing to your body right now."

Lucky touched her chest. "I am here, what have I done."

"This is your eternal light body. I refer to your body of flesh and blood."

"Oh, yes..." Lucky struggled to remember her body, sitting in some cave in Tibet. Why did it seem so far away? It was all like a dream, but she saw new parts of the dream. She had treated her body rather rough and cold, like a monk. She had pushed it hard, like her colts, giving it little free room for pleasure. She saw her own consciousness of herself unwind, loosening old mental knots that had been her only real binds. Thinking of her body, she saw it deep in the cave, and for the first time in her life, she had compassion for her own self, or rather, for her body.

"I...I have to go," she said apologetically.

"Come," he said, walking towards the desire tree.

"No, I have to go back," she protested.

"I know. Come." He took her hand and led her towards a fruit. "Where is it you would like to go?"

"The cave," she said and saw simultaneously, as it formed at the end of a long tendril. Her love drew her in, and it drew her Love with her.   But he changed as he traveled.

"And I will come with you, for I have business there," He said, as He changed into a Buddhist monk.

"What is Your name?" she asked.

"Padmasambhava. I have to go help an old friend." With those words they flew as light to the old cave, but as they approached time and space seemed to stretch out, as if something beyond both was passing through. Lucky felt that they were somehow not moving anymore at all, even though clouds were passing by them at blinding speed, they never seemed to get closer to the cave.   Soon she detected movement in the center, two dots proceeding upward with great speed.   As they came closer they resolved into the figures of Rinpoche and Rufus, flying up side by side.

"Oh no! What does this mean?" Lucky cried.

"Fear not, for this is a moment of great joy and celebration. Even the blades of grass in the field tremble in anticipation of a soul realized," He tried to console her. Suddenly Rinpoche and Rufus were right in front of them.

"Oh, bliss of greatest joy!" Rinpoche exclaimed. Rufus was wagging his tail. "How could my joy be more multiplied? My greatest love and my dearest lost student."

"The greatest joy is ours, Dear Rinpoche, for you to have lived as you have. As a father is more delighted by the feats of his sons that his own, you have made me more happy and pleased than I could have asked to have been."

"Oh, Master, you make my heart burst with joy!" Rinpoche exclaimed.

"So, before you two explode with love," Lucky butted in. "Just what exactly do you mean by 'dearest lost student.'"

"I am sorry, Dear Lucky," Rinpoche bowed slightly. "I looked for you, but I could not find you. You were lost in the ethereal realms. I could tell you were okay, because your body did not age or decay, and you still breathed, only rarely. I just could not find you. You went somewhere I could not go."

"How...long...was I gone?" Lucky asked tentatively.

"Ten years," Rinpoche replied. "Much has changed since you left."

"I am sure. Tell me, what has happened..."

He interrupted her for the second time only. "It is time. Our brother is not to be concerned with such things. All things as you need to know will be available to you. Right now is a magic time, a time so important that it transcends all else in place and mind. It is the time when a soul becomes an Enlightened One, a Buddha, when Heaven and Earth bow to each other and touch, all things heralding the sacred bond of Life and Spirit."

Lucky realized that this was what was causing the effect of the bending space and time, that she was witnessing the Buddhahood of Rinpoche occurring right in front of her. He was blending with the infinite light, becoming his own hue within it, Rufus blending together with him. There was sound as well, chanting and laughing, Rufus was barking. The clouds were coming at them from all ways, as if they were traveling in all directions. At the very center were her teacher and her One, space and time bending in towards them. She felt herself start to spiral outward, and knew she was leaving.

They waved goodbye, and Lucky could feel the love, and she could feel the joy, although she could feel some profound loss as well. They were in a giant whirlpool now, like a hurricane, or a galaxy, and she was being pushed out towards the edge. In One sudden blinding flash of iridescent light and cacophonous sounds of chanting and laughter, they were gone. Or she was gone.

She was flying over the Earth. She could feel pain below her. She thought she was passing over Japan when she felt extreme distress, and she witnessed great waves of pain and fear emanate from the land. There seemed to be some great energy out of balance, as she sensed something in the water and the air. The ground trembled repeatedly, perturbing the subtle psychological airs with fresh spurts of terror.

Lucky continued into the mountains on the mainland, and was soon coming back into her cave and her body. It was nearly empty of everything, and as she came into her body she felt excruciating pain. She slammed into her body, really, and used her greatest effort to roll over and lay her body out. She could feel the stone, and feel the air. It was warm. In that way things had worked out for her, at least. When she finally could lift herself and get a glimpse of the air outside, through the cave mouth she saw a jet high above laying down a thick contrail, and she knew things were different.

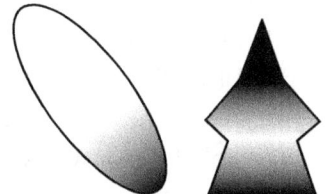

DuaNonno (33) Delivered

Lucky brushed herself off. She had first thought her skin was a strange color until she realized she was covered with almost half an inch of dust. The master's spot was empty, and also covered with dust. Next to her there was a new worn and clean spot, as if others had sat there to meditate. Lucky stopped at the mouth to the cave, for there was a simple prayer stone that read "Rufus," and she knew. They were gone, Rufus and Rinpoche, and that might be only the beginning of what had changed. The trail down seemed lonely, though no less trodden.

The monastery had kept her room seemingly the way it had been, and had welcomed her with great fanfare. Thogyal had become the new Rinpoche, and the place had thrived. That, at least, boded well, Lucky thought. Things had changed. No more cartons, at least. She could see a small area of refillable stainless steel containers. New prayer flags fluttered about, joining years of others fading in the wind. The place was still and always welcoming, but it did not feel homey to Lucky anymore. Her master was gone, Rufus was gone, and she was gone, really, had been gone for some time.

She was beginning to feel that way about a lot of the world upon coming that. Everything was familiar, but nothing felt like home. She knew deep within that she had been at home with her One, but now she also knew that He was everywhere, so she could be at home with Him anywhere. She was ready to return. She felt closure. She no longer felt a desperate drive to plunge forward seeking destiny.   She guessed that destiny would find her if she was where she was meant to be. Now she would just walk back, walk back home, this time, to the ranch. She had work to do, things that she had put on the back burner for too long.

No one really spoke English at the monastery anymore, and the loneliness did not take long to drive her away. It took her a few days to build up strength, but she was soon ready for the road. The other monks bid her farewell, and Thogyall had a tear in his eye as he led her out to the road. They stood on the road for awhile until a truck rolled up that looked remarkably like the one that brought her, except the driver had to be a younger man because he looked no older. He acted the same, just bringing the truck to a halt and waiting for her to get on.   Lucky looked no older, either, from what she could tell, but she no longer hid her womanhood. She accepted who she was, and was not afraid who saw it, or what she looked like. She had learned much about the life force and how many masters had learned to suspend aging by remaining in trance, but she figured it was a dead end anyway since the body was merely in suspension until consciousness returned. Better to just live in the body as it was until it was time to move on.

The driver had a hard life, no doubt, but he did not seem to have trouble living it. He made his cues perfectly, but never seemed to rush or stress anything. Lucky had a new perspective. Live was for the living, the body was for living. There was no sense in putting it on a shelf or in cold storage. Might as well take all life had to give until there was nothing left to receive. She might as well jump in with both feet.

As she climbed into the back of the truck she turned to say goodbye to Thogyall, and he pressed his hands together and bowed slightly. She did the same, and the trucks brakes were released with a screech as the truck began to slowly roll downhill. She took one last glimpse at the monastery and crawled in to find her spot. The junk in this load was packed quite differently and Lucky had to lay down under some crates, but she did find a relatively safe spot. The ride was as bumpy as before, but she had developed a few tools in meditation, and she was able to put herself in trance for the whole trip.

When they came to a sudden halt Lucky thought it had to be another brief pause. Many times on the road they had stopped for some business, and after a minute or two they would start off again. This time they sat. Finally after some time there was a sharp pounding on the back of the truck, and Lucky figured it was time to dismount.

As she got out of the truck, she expected to see some rural scene, but instead she was right in the heart of Katmandu. There was a crowd gathered around a black car which looked ultra-futuristic to Lucky. She was about to make her way around and try to disappear into a crowd when the door opened and out stepped a beautiful Indian woman. She had on business clothes, and Lucky noticed that the door of the car said "H.E.L.P." The woman seemed utterly possessed and in control, and she was smiling broadly as she approached.

"Welcome home," she said, holding out her hand. "You have not changed."

"Uh, thank you," Lucky managed. "I'm sorry. Have we met?"

"Yes, and you have kept your appointment," she said, waiting for some sign of recognition from Lucky. "I am Sahani, from Ranchi."

Lucky stood gaping for an instant before breaking into tears and laughter and hugging Sahani. They immediately warmed to each other, like two sisters long separated, and the crowd soaked in the blessings that surrounded them.

"How did you know I was coming? Did a little blue bird tell you?" Lucky asked as they made their way to the car.

"Thogyall texted me," she said, opening the door.

"Oh, he sent you some kind of message?" Lucky asked. "And H.E.L.P. let you use a car?"

"Lucky, a lot has changed since you were in meditation. I am President of H.E.L.P. now," she said authoritatively as the car spun down the street and out to the edge of town.

"Oh, my, well, congratulations! How did that happen?"

"I kept working with H.E.L.P. from the day you left. They sent me to college seven years ago, and I kept working ever since then. We had two interim President's who quit after a while. It was said the stress too much. I believe it. Four months ago, after two others had rejected the job, I volunteered, and was accepted by the board."

"Well, I'm glad they were farsighted enough to accept you."

"They weren't really, at first. They said that it would be too much for me, that I might buckle under the pressure. There has been much going on for the last several years, Lucky. Many natural disasters. A tsunami struck off Indonesia and killed a quarter of a million people. Hurricane Katrina destroyed New Orleans..."

"New Orleans, destroyed?" Lucky asked.

"Nearly. Levees broke and the Ninth District was completely under water. A massive quake in Haiti killed almost as many as the Indonesian tsunami. We engaged in massive animal rescue operations in each case. Our work is more accepted now. We have increased our budget tenfold. India is now a great economic power, and we have developed our capabilities admirably."

"That is fantastic," Lucky said. "I am very proud of you. Tell me, has something happened in Japan?"

"Yes, you knew about that?" Sahani wondered. "One of the largest earthquakes and tsunamis in history."

"And some technology or energy problem?"

"Yes, major problems at several nuclear power plants. We had teams in parts of rural Japan helping after the tsunami that have had to be evacuated."

"My, a lot has been going on," Lucky said, and then quietly watched the scenery going by."

"Lucky?" Sahani asked.

"Yes?"

"Do you ever wonder what has been happening back at the ranch?"

"Of course I do."

"Would you like to know?"

"Yes, of course! How is Buck?"

"Buck is quite well. He has taken Lucky Star Organics to new heights. You now handle a whole range of organic products, from cookies to salad dressing. He is revolutionizing the market."

"My that is exciting. Good for him! And what about Julia and June? How are they."

"Lucky, Julia has been dead for ten years. She died in childbirth." She paused to let the realization sink in. Sahani instinctively new that there was some information that might hit a little harder than other.

"Oh God," Lucky gasped. "I forgot, the baby! Did it...?" She stopped herself.

"Survive? Yes, a boy. They named him Buddy."

"Buddy?" Tears were thick already in her eyes. "After Dad? Of course. All that time, and I never knew. I am surprised Buck didn't come after me."

"He did. He was the one who found you."

"What?"

"Yes, he found you, in the cave, about seven years ago."

"Really? Why didn't he rouse me?"

"I don't know, perhaps he tried. He said you appeared to be alive. The monks assured him it was so, so that is what he reported to the rest of us."

"I...I never knew..." was all Lucky could manage at this point.

"I know," was all Sahani needed to say. They rode in silence for a bit longer and then soon resumed their banter. It was surprising to Lucky just how in tune they seemed to be. They discussed much more about what had happened, and Lucky felt like Sahani had done with H.E.L.P. just what she would have done in each situation, and Buck had done the same with Lucky Star Organics.

"I am very grateful to have had you to help in my stead," Lucky told Sahani.

"We have been happy to have you as a role model."

"I don't feel like much of a role model," Lucky said as she shook her head. "I feel like I abandoned everyone."

"Some may have felt it. Some have even said it at board meetings. But there was an image of you that prevailed. Some ideal that kept the rest of us going. And personally I knew that you would be back. Many thought you were lost, but I knew that you knew where you were, and so, sooner or later, you would find your way back."

"Thank you for the faith. It probably helped a great deal," Lucky admitted. She then began to tell Sahani the entire tale, omitting nothing that she could remember, and Sahani listened to every detail with rapt attention. By the time the tale came back to the cave they had already arrived in Benares.

There was a welcoming party for them at the office. Flowers and notes overflowed the entry way into the board room. News got around pretty quickly these days, Lucky figured. She made the rounds of the assembled guests. They had set out a buffet in the courtyard, and musicians were playing near a mixed bar. The jagged juxtaposition of this world and the one of the monastery was not lost in irony for Lucky, for she now felt greater sympathy for each of these various people going their ways trying to do their best for the world. For a long time she almost could be accused of being more sympathetic towards animals than humans, even though she bristled at such suggestions and pointed out that care for the planet meant care for all species, including humans. More than ever she was becoming aware of the magnitude of the connections between all living things. Everything was important, and anything could be critical, so she paid extra attention to people and their needs, now.

She was committed now to staying on to put H.E.L.P. in order, but she soon discovered that everything was very much in order. Very sophisticated management groups had taken the work of the organization to the next level, and most activities were handled by specially trained regional teams. More than anything, she was needed for her moral support. The story she brought with her, and her new energy, was like nectar to a hive of bees. They all sought her out, asking for her input or suggestions where almost none were needed, and Lucky listened intently and politely and offered cogent and meaningful responses. She found within herself a new capacity, one that she did not fight or struggle against. She could help just by listening, by showing interest, and bestowing intelligent praise. It was like a balm, or a salve, but one for the spirit.

Sahani was obviously delighted by the developments. She acted simultaneously as President and as personal assistant to Lucky, even though that was not part of her job description. She felt a personal responsibility to both the organization and the individual of Lucky herself, and she took care of both almost effortlessly.

The rest did demand some effort from Lucky. She rediscovered that one day of public relations can be more tiring than years in a monastery. At one point she had to give a brief description to the crowd of her years in the mountains. She dreaded trying to describe it all. She kept it quite brief, and even implied that she had merely been living as a monk the whole time and not in a trance of suspended animation, although everyone had heard the stories by that time. They accepted the variation in the story as a necessity and followed her every word, for she soon began to tell of her vision. She spoke of the View, and how everyone glowed with such potential peace and magic. Her audience was in the palm of her hand by that point, and they burst into a loud applause.

Lucky thanked them and then slowly made her way towards the door. Sahani came after her after giving the band the cue to start playing.

"Is it time to go?" Sahani asked.

"I need to go...uh...you can stay. You have work to do," Lucky reasoned.

"Our work here is done," Sahani said definitively. "Let's go." They quietly edged towards the door. Everyone knew what was happening, so they pretended that they did not notice when the ladies slipped out and into a taxi.

They stayed in a hotel room for only a few hours, to pack and wash up, and they booked a flight that night to San Francisco. Sahani effortlessly knew exactly what Lucky was going to want to do. She even knew when Lucky was in a talkative mood or when she just wanted to keep quiet. There were some times when Lucky seemed to want to listen, and she would ask questions about the business or about Buck's visit. Sahani was as happy as ever to be asked to talk about her favorite subjects so they were really relaxing into each other's company quite well.

The flight back to San Francisco was long and included a layover in Hong Kong. Lucky found out thankfully that she was not such a celebrity outside of the inner circles of her organizations, and she was able to travel anonymously. Sahani was by her side pretty much all the time, and she was surprised at how natural it felt, since Lucky had always considered herself a loner, pretty much. Now she was very glad to be traveling unrecognized except for one friend.

"Have you ever been to California?" Lucky asked Sahani at one point in the trip over the Pacific.

"I went to UC Santa Cruz," Sahani informed her.

"Really? I missed so much," she responded.

"And much missed you," Sahani said tenderly.

"Sahani, thank you so much for all that you have done. I am sorry that I let you down," she apologized.

"You have never let me down," Sahani reassured her. "On the contrary, you have met every single one of my expectations."

"I don't know. I just feel remiss about something, or someone, like I have let somebody down."

"Buck probably," Sahani said casually.

"What? He's always got along just fine."

"How do you know?"

"Uh, well it just seemed, I mean, I supposed..."

"Mmm-hmm," was all Sahani said finally.

Maybe she was feeling some remorse about Buck, but she just would not let herself admit it. She knew Buck well enough that he would not want remorse, but he might want...something. What could it be?

"Appreciation," Lucky said out loud.

"What was that?" Sahani asked.

"Appreciation," Lucky repeated. "At the very least he deserves appreciation. I should show him I appreciate all he has done."

"I am sure he would appreciate that," Sahani said in all honesty.

"Yes, he would," Lucky agreed. "Should we make an appointment with him tomorrow? I would like to see him."

"You will see him sooner than that," she predicted. "He is going to pick you up at the airport."

"Really," Lucky gulped. A lump landed in her throat. "Just me."

"Yes," Sahani said. "I have some friends in Silicon Valley that are going to pick me up. I am going to stay there for a few days and give you some time alone at the ranch."

"I don't need time alone," Lucky told her.

"I mean, alone with Buck and the family," she clarified.

"I don't need time alone with..." and she stopped herself. She probably did need to spend some time with them all, quality time, but she did not think that Sahani was a distraction from all that.

"Sahani, really, you are always welcome," Lucky stressed.

"I know, my friend, but I would like to take my leave to visit my friends."

"Of course, Sahani, anything." They both secretly thought that they had found the sister each had always wanted. Lucky thought about love, and thought about Buck. There certainly was a deep reservoir of feelings there that she had been holding back. She was tired of holding back, and tired of running away.

As they got closer to SFO, Lucky found herself becoming both nervous and excited about Buck picking her up. She had years of defenses and layers which were falling away. Why had she ever left like that? Why hadn't she come back sooner? What hadn't she known that Julia had died while birthing a son named after her father? These questions were what she imagined Buck would say. Of course he would be made, or distant, or whatever. But when she first saw him, and he came up with open arms and a warm look on his face, her heart melted.

Just as she was about to jump into his arms, he said "Sahi!" and gave Sahani a long deep hug. He then turned and offered Lucky a handshake.

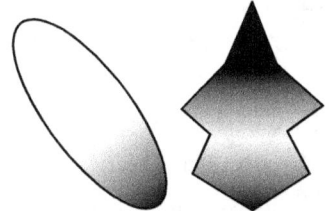

DuaAdekka (34) Returned

Lucky only feared for a moment that there was something romantic between Buck and Sahani. Turns out, Sahani had even lived at the ranch while attending UCSC, and so she had spent more time with Buck over the years than she had with Lucky. It was very natural that they had been excited to see each other. And Lucky did not doubt that their relationship was totally platonic, but she had a new possessive feeling around Buck that she had never quite experienced before.

They met Sahani's party at the baggage claim, and Buck seemed to know them well, too, and they treated Lucky with respectful deference, but they were not familiar to her. She was going to have to get used to a wide range of reactions to her return, she understood. She did feel that Buck's reaction had been a bit cold, but she had been giving him reasons to be cold for some time. She decided to meet his energy with polite warmth, and they proceeding peacefully out to the parking lot where he had left the familiar old truck.

"Wow, the same old truck," Lucky said as they threw the luggage in the back. "It's good to see some things haven't changed."

"A lot of things haven't changed, except me, maybe," he said, running a hand through his hair and patting his belly.

"You have changed?" Lucky asked as they settled into the car and began the drive down the coast.

"I mean, I have definitely gotten older, you know," he said fingering the side of his head with one hand as he drove with the other.

"You mean that little bit of gray, there? You think that make's you look old?" she cackled.

"Well, a bit, I think," he said.

"That's nothing. You look terrific. You still have a full head of hair. That gray just adds distinction."

"Well thanks, but I do have this belly," he said, touching above his belt. There was a slight bulge.

"You call that a belly? I almost have that and I have been fasting for years. You look as hard as ever."

"Maybe, but I have gotten older. You look exactly the same, like you haven't aged at all."

"I don't know. Maybe not my body, but my spirit has aged, Buck," she confessed.

"Oh, yeah?" he asked. "You always seemed pretty old in the spirit category."

"Maybe too old. I was so serious about everything. Buck, I really am sorry. I appreciate all you have been and done over the years

"Apology accepted," he said cautiously. "Forgive me if I am a bit reserved. You understand, don't you?"

"I do," she said. They traveled the rest of the way down through San Jose, except for occasional updates on historical occurrences from Buck.

"You know the Giants won the World Series last year?"

"No way! And I missed it! And I missed everything."

"You missed a lot. You know June has a welcome prepared that will be more like what you may have hoped from me."

"Oh, June! And Buddy! Buck, I am so sorry I wasn't there for you when Julia died."

"It's okay. That seems like so many years ago, now. I found ways to get over it."

"It seems like just yesterday to me. I am beginning to realize the monumental size of your accomplishment while I was gone. You never got together with anyone else?"

"Not for long. No body ever fit right. Plus I had plenty to do raising two kids."

"All by yourself?"

"Oh I had plenty of help. Professional help."

"Oh really? What kind of 'professional' help?" Lucky asked with a lilt in her voice.

"What, like you mean, psychological or sexual? No, I probably could have used those, but never took the opportunity. No, I mean nannies and kitchen and cleaning help. A necessary luxury in my situation, believe me."

"Oh, I believe it. I don't see how you did it even with all that help."

"You would be surprised what you could do when you have to," Buck demurred.

"That's true. That much I understand."

"It's really been a joy with June and Buddy. June teaches me and Buddy, and they learned so much from Sahi. They will be sad that she isn't with us."

"Yeah, what's this 'Sahi' thing?"

Buck laughed, "Oh yeah, that was 'cause when she first came that's how Buddy would say her name. It just kind of stuck."

"I see," Lucky said, almost feigning indifference.

"I don't get why she didn't come tonight. We're all set for her and she knows it. She's with good people, but they're not *family*."

"Oh right. Well, I think she might think we should have some time together. I expect she'll be along on Monday or so."

"Why would we need time alone from her? Hell," Buck occasionally swore. "She knows I could use the help with all this, and the kids will likely try to trek to Santa Clara if they find out she didn't come down."

"Headstrong, are they?" Lucky smiled.

"You bet," Buck laughed. "A lot like we were. Only they're better, Lucky. They got something. This next generation has got some things going on for them, real special."

Lucky looked at him deeply for the first time in years. She saw the new lines on the face, how they crinkled when he smile. He saw the love and joy in his eyes when he thought of his children, how he had let himself love them fully and completely, as he had always wanted to. Lucky began to get a true understanding of all that she had missed.

"Uh...as for...being alone," Buck cleared his throat. "So we weren't sure where you wanted to stay, you know, the new house is a pretty busy office, now. And there are some new buildings, solar studios, and a lot of different people, you know, and space, but you might feel more comfortable up at the old house, and well, June really wants you to bunk with her in your old room on top. Sahi stayed in your room before, because June was in the second room on top, but Buddy is there now, and we made the old den into a new apartment too, and a new bathroom." Buck finished with a flourish, as if he was completing a list of necessary things he had to tell her.

"Well, if it's all right with you, I think I might like to stay in the new apartment..." Lucky was starting to get a little more worried about the curves on Highway 17 and all the traffic. This was even a bit more unnerving than riding on a Himalayan junk truck.

"That's what I said!" Buck interjected excitedly. "June said you'd want your old room, Buddy thought you'd kick me out of your folk's room, and I said you'd probably really like the new apartment."

"Please keep your eyes on the road! I'm sorry, Buck, thank you, but, you know, that is your house now. I left. I understand this. I am your honored guest, now."

"Lucky, you are a part of that land, and that house, as long as you are alive. I'm just...like...a caretaker, you know? You are always welcome, because you are always already there."

Lucky let herself sit in the comfort of the welcome. She also became a little more comfortable with the road. They were coming down the last stretch and they could see the lights of Santa Cruz and Monterey lying like a large sickle on its side. Lucky did feel like she was being welcomed home. Perhaps that was the entire hope of people who left, that someday they might be welcomed back with love and gratitude, or, at least, some sort of acceptance.

Lucky thought it might be a good time to broach another subject. "So...you made it by the cave I heard."

"Yes I made it to the cave," Buck admitted. "I had to find out if you were alive..." He paused as if he had more to say but did not know how to say it.

"That is amazing that you zeroed in on my cave," she said. "I thought I had made it far enough to evade you."

Buck laughed. "Ha! I don't know about zeroing in. We had visited 42 temples and monasteries throughout India, Nepal, and Bhutan before finding the one with the cave. We were beginning to fear you had gone into China."

"We? Who was with you?"

"The kids, and Sahi," he said.

"You took them all over Asia with you?"

"Not every time. We'd go over every summer, for about ten days usually. The kids were on a houseboat in Kashmir with Sahi the last time when I found you. Rinpoche gave it away, by a slight pause, but he did not tell me anything.

"Rinpoche wouldn't give me away," Lucky insisted.

"Oh not on purpose," Buck acknowledged. "Unconsciously. I had asked the same question of hundreds of yogis, swamis, and monks, and almost all of them gave me a reaction like I was crazy or deluded to think such a thing. Rinpoche just paused thoughtfully, and waited a moment to say 'There is no such person in this monastery.' It seemed too specific an answer, probably truthful and misleading at the same time, so I guessed you might be nearby. I circled around back and was almost stopped by the biggest damn dog I have ever seen..."

"That was Rufus," Lucky said with a smile of recognition.

"Oh yeah? Well it seemed like there was no way he'd let me pass, so there must be something beyond. I knew your way with animals, so I thought it might be you. I climbed straight up the wall, and I thought the dog had me at the top for sure, but in the end he just let me go into the cave."

"He just wanted you to take the Initiate's Path, that's all," she informed him.

"Okay, maybe so...but I walked in, and it seemed totally empty, but I could tell people had been using it. That's when I saw your body."

"You didn't rouse me," was almost both a question and a statement.

"No...uh...how do I describe this?" he paused. "I came to make sure you were alive, not drag you back against your will. It...it didn't seem right to try to bring you out of it. I...I don't understand all of this stuff. It made no sense to me. You were there, but you weren't there, I know it doesn't make sense. I touched you, and you were cold, but still soft...supple like, you know? It kind of gave me the creeps, I'm sorry. I went back down to Rinpoche and confronted him, and he assured me that you were alive and that you were in that state by choice. There didn't seem like there was anything else to do. I came back, told everyone you were in self-imposed isolation, and left it at that."

"Oh, Buck, I had no idea," she put her hand on his knee. "I am sorry I put you to so much time and effort."

"Oh, that's okay. I don't regret any of it. I came to know some incredible people and made some unforgettable memories with the kids. Do you know how far out that monastery is?"

"No, I traveled there and back for about 16 hours each time in a dark truck."

"Well, that truck is the only vehicle that comes out that way twice a month. He peddles various wares between Tibet and Nepal. That monastery is the absolute least visited by western travelers. I don't know how you found them."

"I really just found myself there. I was following a strange call..."

"Mm-hmm," Buck managed. His words hung suspended. He really had no idea how to respond to that. He tried. "So, what did you see?"

"I don't know how to describe it. I can more easily say what I learned."

"What did you learn?" he asked tentatively.

She paused to try to let no words tell the story that words could not, but a pause is a mortal creation, set as an image of passing clouds or running water, as born as set to die each instant. The ancient mystic's dilemma, to explain an elephant in the dark to blind men. She chose to try, at least, to give words their due, and make a respectable attempt to tell Buck what she had learned and what she had seen.

"I learned a lot about...myself," she began, "...and my habits with things, and people, and life..." She was not sure where to take it. She breathed slowly. "I was trained and aided to see the View, which is a wide perspective of everything...I would have to say...my impression of what was happening was that my spirit left my body, and I could see all of life, all living things, as blending balls of light. I learned this is a reflection, a dream world, worlds within worlds. I saw that there are greater worlds, glorious realms above this one, but that this one is much more beautiful than people imagine."

"That is spectacular," he offered. "Did you resolve anything?"

"Yes. I resolved to live life more fully, and appreciate everyone and everything in it."

Even in the racing truck, the air hung still and heavy. "That...is very valuable wisdom. Maybe priceless, or maybe just expensive."

"Yes," she allowed. "I have much to repay."

Buck smiled. "No. Your account is clear." Lucky laughed. "Lucky, the whole universe conspires to make things happen for you like we all owe you a big bundle!" They laughed together for the first time in memory.

They pulled off the highway in silence, this time because they really could not think of anything that needed to be said. They thought of some things they might want to talk about, but they let them go, for now, understanding intuitively that they may need the peaceful silence together more than any words.

They pulled onto Freedom Blvd like they had a thousand times before. The encroaching fog at the heat boundary of the ocean air swirled around them like it had a thousand times before. But something had definitely changed. Lucky allowed herself to fall asleep against the window for a few moments, and Bud slowed down to a crawl lest a bump make her hit her head. He looked at her with mixed feelings, as usual, but they were definitely different feelings now. He still wanted her, as much as always, but she scared him too. He kept remembering that image of her, cold and frozen in meditation. He respected the miracle of it all, but it was almost too sacred for him. He had developed a love for his kids that superseded all else, and that made him feel protective.

Lucky awoke as they drove over the drainage bump under the Lucky Star Ranch sign. The fruit trees along the driveway swayed a welcome down and the remnants of the early blossoms provided a veritable tickertape parade as they drove to the front of the house. She was fully awake now. She could feel the charge. There was something happening here. It smelled the same when she opened the door in front of the house. She stopped for a moment to soak it all in, and Buck came around with her suitcases. He set them down dramatically in front of her, and held his arms out.

"Welcome home," he said truthfully and warmly. She threw herself into his arms and stayed there. The hug should not have felt so good. Neither of them expected it to feel that good. Neither of them were prepared for it to feel so good. They held it, they held each other, a transcendental moment, flashes of the truest simple care and concern, and the wind picked up appreciative gusts.

There was a squeal from inside and it seemed to be Buck's cue. He pulled back from Lucky, still holding her, but with a slight formal air.

"I can't believe I'm saying this, but..." he smiled. "I need to go slowly."

"Let's go slowly," she agreed and nodded as they hooked fingers and then let their hands fall down at their sides. Another squeal and a hoot came from the house, and Buck picked up the luggage. The door slammed open and out rushed a 5'8" blur with black hair that practically collided with Lucky. She grasped her like glue, and they squealed and laughed together. June shouted with glee and picked Lucky up in the air and spun her about. Buddy flew out the door and off the porch with Zipper, their yellow lab.

"Bet my dad didn't do that!" June shouted as she put Lucky down. "He should have. My you are as light as a quail feather!"

"I'll be filling out now that I'm back at the ranch," Lucky laughed.

"Yeah, we need some high grade organic cream, Doctor, stat!" June cried as they hugged and laughed some more. Buck started up the porch with the luggage and Lucky spun around towards Buddy and Zipper, who both leapt at her midsection.

"What incredible special new people at the ranch you two are!" Lucky exclaimed as they let her out of the embrace.

"Silly, YOU'RE the new one at the ranch," Buddy said, and he and Zipper ran up the steps after Buck. June took Lucky by the arm and headed in.

"She wants the apartment, just like I said, you guys," Buck called back.

"Really?" June stopped agape. "Okay, well, Sahi can stay with me...wait."

"She's supposed to be in your room, Dad," Buddy said as he ran in the house.

"Wait a minute!" June commanded, bringing them all to a halt except for Buddy and Zipper running far ahead. "Where...is...Sahi?" she articulated.

"She had to stay up in Santa Clara with some friends..."

"What?! What *friends*? She doesn't have any *friends* in Santa Clara, company people sure. This is family here. She can't get away with this!"

Buck turned around directly to face her. "Now, June, she is going to come down here on her own time, okay? You are not to do anything, got it?"

"Oh, sure, Daddy, whatever you say," she said with perhaps a bit too much sugar. They filed into their beds with surprising speed and settled in for a long overdue warm night's rest.

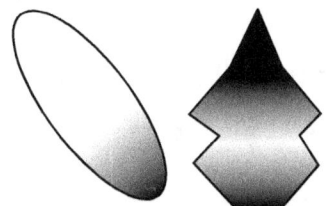

DuaAmanna (35) Grounded

Buck might have suspected that it was unusually quiet that morning as he opened the blinds out onto the meadow and his truck parked next to the corral, but he was not in a suspicious mood. He had almost expected June and Buddy to steal his truck, so he hid his keys and put a club on the steering wheel lest they try to hotwire it, which Buck would not hold it past them to be able to do. But the truck was there, just as he left it, dew glowing golden on the windshield with the new sun. There was just such a delicious feeling everywhere that Buck decided to go to the kitchen and fix an early breakfast.

He was a little bit suspicious as he started the eggs and potatoes frying in the kitchen and no one was there to bother him. He expected Lucky to sleep in late, but he figured that June would be up first thing bothering him about calling for Sahi. He would have thought it was suspiciously quiet, but there was just a trace of the faintest rustling, the barest traces of whispered ripplings, tumbling down the beams of the house from somewhere up above. Instinctively, Buck threw some extra eggs and potatoes into the frying pans. The coffee aroma hitched a ride in the ventilation and did its work on the remaining sleepers, and soon steps and creeks could be heard all over upstairs.

Buddy was first down. He started with an awful big yawn. "Hi Dad," he said with his mouth still wide.

"Are you hungry, pal? Or are you too tired to eat? Tough night?"

Buddy perked up. "No, no. The food smells great."

"Thank you. Pull up a plate. Where is your sister?"

"They're upstairs."

"Who is upstairs?"

"They are. June and uh...Lucky."

"June and uh...Lucky? Why the stammer?"

"Uh...uh...I forgot her name..."

"You live your whole life on the Lucky Star Ranch and you forgot her name?"

"Just for a minute!" Buddy protested, then turned to yell up the stairs. "June! JUNE! Dad wants to talk to you!"

Buck heard some fumbling upstairs, and door open and what sounded like it was being relocked, and feet coming down the steps. June broke into the room like a fresh mountain breeze. Lucky came down behind her.

"Wait is it, Daddy?" she lofted into the kitchen as the family took position in this most popular of rooms.

"What's wrong?" Lucky asked as she came down the stairs.

"Nothing," June said, a bit too quickly.

"Yes, it's something," Buck said. "Morning, Lucky, have some coffee. June, Buddy, have a seat." Buck turned the eggs and potatoes down low, and leaned against the sink with his arms folded.

The kids sat down dutifully, looking terribly innocent. The shuffled, cleared their throats, and looked up with puppy dog eyes.

"Uh huh, yeah," Buck said curtly. "So June, tell me, don't you want to call Santa Clara to see if Sahi is coming down?"

"Uh, we already talked to her," June came back with quickly. "She will be down later today."

"That's strange, I didn't hear the phone ring," Buck mused. "Did you, Buddy?"

"Uh, no..." Buddy's throat caught. "We...we called her cell phone."

"That's also strange, because she told me she was going to turn her cell phone off today." He reached for the house phone. "Maybe I should call her..."

"No!" June cried. "I mean, no need. She said she would be coming later, but her phone would be off, so not to bother."

"So you guys just happened to get a hold of her early in the morning for the brief window she had her phone on."

"It was early all right," Buddy said under his breath.

"What was that?" Buck asked.

"I said, it is still early, what's for breakfast?"

"Don't change the subject. The sooner you two tell me what's up the sooner you eat. June, what were all those vocal rumblings I was hearing from your room all morning?"

"I was practicing the new song. The one we are going to play for Lucky when Buddy does his Trick Show. Lucky, you're going to love it. Buddy rides backwards and jumps through a hoop."

"Really?" Lucky said, acting impressed.

Buck interjected. "I said no changing the subject. So you were singing? That's what I heard? But you have quite a set of pipes, belting it out. I have never heard you sing softly, really..."

"Well, I didn't want to wake you up..."

"Seventeen years of waking me up with all sorts of vocalizations, and now suddenly you're worried about me?"

"Well, you and Lucky and..."

"This isn't working. I am going to try a different tact. June, go get Sahi and bring her down for breakfast."

"But, she...but..." June tried to say something.

"What were you going to do? Treat a guest rudely all morning, and then try to pretend that she arrived on her own later?"

"We...no...we can't...well..." Now was June's turn stammer.

"Nevermind, then. Buddy?"

"Yeah, Dad?"

"Go get Sahi and bring her to breakfast."

"Okay," he nodded as he stood to run up the stairs.

"Buddy!"

"What? June, he knows!" And Buddy ran up the stairs. June stared at the table in front of her.

"So. How? I thought you might take the truck, but it hasn't moved."

June mumbled something about a van.

"What?"

"We took the van," June said more clearly.

"What van?"

"The old white van from down at the office."

"Really? That thing hasn't been running for about two years!"

"We fixed it. We got it running about two months ago, and we kept it a secret until we might need it."

"How did you fix it?"

"Buddy got a transmission from the parts yard," she said, just as he came down with Sahi trailing behind.

"Good morning, Sahi!" Buck said. "Sorry for the midnight kidnapping."

"No problem," Sahani smiled. "I suspected they might try something. When I realized they had Pradip's phone number I figured it was better to go along with them."

"Well, it's good to have you here, as always," Buck bowed, and then turned to the kids. "But these two, I have only begun with these two. Now, some straight answers if you want anymore free days before adulthood. Buddy, you fixed the car two months ago?"

"Yeah," he admitted. "Mr. Anderson traded an old Ford Econoline transmission for a bunch of eggs, and it took about three weeks for me and him to sneak enough time to get it done."

"Hence the sudden plague of greasy fingernails. How did you drag Mr. Anderson into all this?"

"I told him it was a surprise for your birthday," Buddy confessed.

"It was a surprise, all right. How about the steering? The shaft was loose."

"We didn't check it. It seemed okay..."

"Uh-huh, SEEMED okay. And, it's unregistered. June, you drove an unregistered vehicle."

"We took the back roads," June pointed out.

"Oh, that makes me feel so much better. You two driving a dubiously working unregistered van 150 miles in the middle of the night, but at least you took back roads."

"But, Dad, we got Sahi back safely," Buddy pleaded. "She was gonna miss our show." Then, with a sense of intrigue, "She may have been in danger."

"She was in danger, all right. The minute you guys picked her up."

"You know, it was really my fault," Sahani broke in. "I knew all it would seem strange to June and Buddy. I should have come straight here."

"Yes, it was strange, I still don't know what was scheming in that mind of yours," Buck granted. "But, that does not excuse my kids going on some nighttime raid and then lying to me about it."

"I'm sorry, Dad," Buddy offered.

"Yeah, we're sorry," June sounded honestly remorseful.

"All right, I'm not going to continue to dramatize it all. Both of you, you're grounded. June, no driving of any vehicle for two weeks. And Buddy, no riding for the same time.

"Oh no! No! What about the show?" Buddy was beginning to panic.

"Calm down, don't worry. After the show, no riding for two weeks.

"Aw..." he said simply, a lot calmer at least.

"Dad, I was supposed to drive the interns to the music festival in Santa Cruz on Saturday."

"Nope. I know you both have things that you have planned, but those are the consequences."

"But you're letting Buddy ride in the show, can't you make an exception?" June was laying out as much pressure as she dared next to these powerful women. Normally she would have been willing to yell and scream almost as loud as Buddy.

"You guys prepared a show for Lucky and Sahi today. I'm not going to say you can't do it," Buck reasoned. "But you going with your friends to a music festival is different."

"It's for the intern program at the office! They're counting on me to drive them there!" She insisted.

"I will drive them there," Buck countered. "You can't do something like last night and think you can just keep doing what you always do."

"Oh! Maybe I don't want to do the show today now either."

"No fair! You promised!" Buddy protested.

"You would really refuse to do the show, after all that practice, Lucky and Sahi here for the first time in years..."

"No, I guess not. The show must go on."

"Yay!" Buddy yelled. Zipper started barking on the front porch and jumping at the door. "Coming Zipper! Dad, I am going to go out and practice."

"Hold on, breakfast first." Buck started pulling out plates and silverware, piling plate after plate with good organic homegrown food.   He put on a playful concierge personality to switch the mood.   "Ladies, please forgive that uncharacteristically crude and brutish beginning to your stay here at the Lucky Star Ranch.   As you may have heard, the warm sun and cool coastal breezes combine to create a lush and peaceful landscape which we hope you will enjoy."   Lucky and Sahi laughed and they joined in the task of getting the breakfast laid out.   Orange juice, fresh cut fruit, eggs, potatoes, toast, and homemade Loganberry jam finished the spread and they all sat down and gave thanks.

"We have much to be grateful for, Lord.   Thanks for bringing family back together safe.   May we keep doing all right in your eyes.   Amen."

"Amen" echoed around the table and was followed by clanging glasses and dishes as the family dug into the large farm breakfast spread.   Lucky had forgotten the sheer immensity of the American breakfast.   For a long time, even before her fast in suspended animation, she had eaten mostly lentils or rice for the beginning of each day.   Even though she was now the titular head of one of the largest fine dairy and agriculture conglomerates in the world, she herself subsisted on almost entirely vegan faire.

The rich smells were a feast in themselves.   Buck had known that both Lucky and Sahi were vegetarians, for the most part, and he had made a bounteous meal free of meat, but with plenty of animal richness.   Eggs, milk, and cheese from the ranch filled the table alongside fruit from the orchards and vegetables from the garden.   The ladies saw his deliberate attempt to welcome them into the home as if it were their own, which was how it should be.   Everyone enjoyed the thick layers of life that piled on with a detached urgency, replacing old mores with new miles.   They talked of the intervening years, the events of the world, and the events of the universe.   Lucky felt that she could hardly begin to fathom the direction things had taken.

"I am under a bit of stress lately," Sahi was saying, carefully buttering another pancake, "because I have been forced to shift our companies IT infrastructure over to the cloud."

"I have no idea what that means," Lucky said plainly, her mouth full of eggs, "but it sounds awful."

"Not really," Sahi shrugged. "It will save us a lot of operating costs, and we are registering with a carbon-free server center with Google..." She paused with Lucky's stare, which was not at all blank. Instead, as she sipped coffee or ate potatoes, Lucky's stare radiated an admixture of equal parts disinterest and perplexity, not a personal reflection on the recipient, in this case Sahi, but just enough disconcerting as to cause Sahi to take a momentary breath before returning to her pancake.

"I think you lost her," Buck suggested.

Lucky immediately snapped to, realizing the potential of misinterpretation. "Not at all," she responded. "Sahani has me forever," and she kissed her on the cheek.

"Oh is that how it is?" Buck let slip out.

Lucky frowned. "I don't know what you're thinking, but, for what she had done, Sahani has my undying allegiance for as long as I am conscious of it, from my spirit, not my body," she corrected him, using her full name as if to stress the antiquity of their relationship. Lucky went back to her breakfast and Sahi bowed her head in respect.

"I'm sorry," Buck offered. "I think I can understand that."

Lucky smiled. "Yes, I suppose you could."

They continued the rest of the breakfast in sweet silence. And it truly did break a fast for all of them, placing tiny trembling smiles on the edge of their lips. Even the kids forgot about their previous woes and just languidly absorbed the thick and rich atmosphere. Buddy never seemed to slow down, always getting up for more butter or milk or juice and always pantomiming his latest tricks, as if he were practicing them all continuously in his head.

"I can do a double flip," Buddy announced.

"How can you do a double flip?" Lucky challenged.

"I don't want you to do a double-flip," Buck warned him.

"What's a double-flip?" Sahi asked.

"I can jump from the saddle and somersault twice and land in the saddle," Buddy announced.

"Impossible!" Sahi claimed.

"Exactly," Buck agreed.

"No! I can do it," Buddy protested.

"How can you do it, Buddy?" Lucky asked him.

"I get the horse up to a full gallop, and I stand in the saddle. I wedge my foot on horn, then just as I pull the reins a little bit I leap off the horn and do a double backward flip."

"Double backward flip!" Sahi exclaimed.

"Backward flips are easier on horseback than forward flips."

"They sound impossible," Sahi reasoned.

"They are impossible," Buck repeated.

"They are NOT impossible," Buddy insisted.

"They're not IMPOSSIBLE," Lucky argued.

"Look, you have plenty of tricks to do for the show," Buck countered. "That one is too dangerous."

"But Dad," Buddy was getting desperate. "That is the highlight of the show!"

"I don't like that trick," Buck continued. "No one else is able to do it."

"That's why it's the highlight!" Buddy countered.

"Yeah, Buck, it's the highlight," Lucky joined in on Buddy's behalf. "You have to let go a little, not try to shelter everyone. People have to run free and experience life."

This hit a bit of something in Buck, and he just froze inside. "Well...whatever."

"Can I do it?" Buddy asked.

"I...guess," Buck wavered. "If you are very careful..."

"Woo-hoo!" Buddy yelled as he jumped up from the table and ran outside.

"Be careful!" Buck called out after him.

"My you have become quite the mother hen," Lucky said.

"Yeah, well, I had to be," Buck replied in a tone that left nothing uncertain."

"Oh, I'm sorry," Lucky remembered. "It must have been tremendously hard when Julia died."

"It was difficult," was Buck's understatement.

"Do you want to talk about it?" Lucky asked.

"Uh..." Buck looked around.

Sahi jumped at the opportunity. "Look, why don't both of you take a walk?" she suggested. "I'll clean all this up, and you two go check out your ranch."

"Sahi, I can do this," Lucky offered.

"Yeah, let us help," Buck weakly suggested.

"No, go take a walk," Sahi insisted. "You know, you two have been officially stripped of all but figurehead power. Don't make me get official on your ass!" she put out with mock severity. Buck and Lucky laughed as she pushed them out the door. They did not bother to resist and easily slid into the sunny springtime morning outside. Both of them could remember endless days like this, and they drank in the deep reveries and the sights, sounds, and smells of their home surrounded them.

"I have someone to show you," Buck said as he took her out towards the corals. "You know, since you've been gone, we've pretty much overtaken a lot of our competition, and bought a lot of them out. The Lucky Star has become just kind of a show dairy, educational you know. The kids have been doing a lot, and we take old dairy mommas that hang on. We're kind of an old cow's home," he revealed.

"How sweet!," Lucky intoned. "And appropriate." She started to lean towards him, but stopped. She was afraid of what to say. She was feeling things for Buck now, in ways that she had never let herself before, but she was still clumsy with speaking gently sometimes, and she never really let Buck know that her feelings were any different. He just went along with things, figuring everything would come out all right but suspicious of things in a way he had not been before. In many more other ways, things were hauntingly familiar, recalling many moments past but conjuring up new possibilities as the realities of the moment mixed with the wisdom of greater years.

"There's someone who would like to see you." Buck allowed something there, letting her know that he might have learned a lot, learned to see a cow as a person as she had often challenged him. She knew it was a cow, and she guessed who it might be, but she was still surprised when she saw the face ringed with brown and white.

"Lindy!" she exclaimed as she wrapped her arms around her old friend. The other cows came around and pushed into her, like some ancient bovine ceremony of return, and she felt their welcome. Buck edged his way out to the plaza, giving Lucky the time with her herd. Some binds could be stretched almost forever, yet remain unbroken. The strands of being that Lucky had woven from her very first breaths on the ranch served to tie her in a colorful web of the deepest feeling. She knew what it meant to belong, but now she could feel the truth of it in her place in the world beyond.

Buck's intuition led him a long the coral to the center of the plaza. June and Buddy had set up a relatively elaborate bandstand and obstacle course. A web of ropes held up three hoops about 7 feet off the ground and twenty feet apart. Buddy was off somewhere getting the horse ready and June was testing out a small PA with a microphone and music player.

"Hey June, I want you to tell Buddy he is not gonna do three hoops today," Buck called over to her.

"I will Daddy!" came shrieking over the speakers and made June drop the mic with an echoing thud. "Sorry," she said, much less amplified, and she picked up the mic.

Lucky came out behind Buck and surveyed the scene with a smile on her face. "Thank you so much, Buck. It is all very touching. You have done a beautiful job, here at the ranch. I fear I have been neglectful."

"Only you can know that," Buck looked down. "We have had a lot to be grateful for, a lot to you and this Ranch."

"Well, I feel like I see everything in a different light since I have been gone. Things are so different, even the things that haven't changed..." She was cut off by the sound of Shania Twain suddenly bursting too loud from the speakers and June screaming until she had found the volume control.

"Where's the music coming from?" Lucky asked. The tune settled into a mellow karaoke version of "Still the One."

"Oh, June has her iPod hooked up. It's part of her show," Buck informed her.

"What's an iPod?" Lucky asked offhandedly.

Buck laughed. "You were gone a long time, weren't you."

Lucky was about to come up with a playful retort when they were interrupted by the announcement of the approach of the main event. Sahani came out of the kitchen to catch the show.

"Ladies and Gentleman," June announced over the PA. "May I introduce, from Freedom, California, the boy wonder rider, Buddy and his horse buddy Bud!" June mimicked the sound of a crowd into the mic and Buck and Lucky joined in as Buddy came riding into the plaza, standing in the saddle with sequined chaps, flowing bandana and a ten gallon hat. He galloped in glory around the ring and slowed as he approached the hoops.

"WOAH!" Buck called out in a way that left no room to wonder who was in charge, and Buddy and his horse Bud came to a slow halt.

"What?" Buddy cried in protest.

"No three hoops today, I told you, not until you are really solid with two," he was firm.

"Ah, Dad, come on..."

"NO three hoops, period."

"Okay, two hoops then," and he was off around the plaza to gain running momentum. June turned up the music and sang the words to the song.

"And the wonder rider will attempt, to risk of life and limb, two hoops..." June announced during the guitar solo.

"Don't jinx him," Buck yelled out.

Buddy came around the plaza and gained speed approaching the first hoop. In a quick maneuver that was so unique to Buddy that few could even see what he was doing, he pushed of the horn of the saddle while simultaneously reining in the horse just a bit, pushing himself backwards and upside down through the first hoop. He landed with such effortless grace and immediately repeated the move with such ease as to quite all doubts. The small group burst out into applause aided by June's imitation crowd noise. Buddy came riding around with obvious pride and showmanship. There was something magical in his riding, something pure and angelic. Buck could not be blamed for bending a bit.

"Ta – da," Buddy shouted. "And now, for three!" The crowd went wild.

"No, I said not three," Buck insisted.

"You said not til I was solid that was solid," Buddy reasoned. He turned to Lucky for some help. She could not be blamed for being swept up in the moment. "Wasn't it solid?"

"It WAS solid," Lucky agreed.

"See, it WAS solid!" Buddy said. "Come on, Dad!" He looked pleadingly at Lucky.

"Yeah, come on, Dad!" Lucky said.

"I said no, it's not safe," Buck was not as firm anymore.'

"What's safe?" Lucky asked. "Come on, Buck! You can't hold back those you love all the time, you got to allow them some freedom." She meant it as a casual remark, something that might make a son get his way with his dad, but it hit a little deeper with Buck. It made him collapse inside, for reasons he could never say. Whatever, he said it.

"Okay, whatever, go ahead," he said.

"Yay!" Buddy shouted. He immediately got Bud up to a gallop and rounded the plaza.

"Now, the wonder rider will attempt three hoops, at risk..." June censored herself. "to his dignity." That was the one thing he never risked.

Bud came around the corner at the proper speed. Perhaps the first two came too easy. No one could see what exactly was different with the third. He went through the hoop and seemed to have it down. Maybe his foot slipped. Maybe the reins were too loose in his hands. Somehow Buddy missed to the left on the landing, just a bit off, and he came down to the ground on his back and neck.

The snap would be gruesomely etched on the memories of all present for some time. The sound was not unclear. It signaled great change. The rest of the day passed in the stunning clarity of a memory beyond time. What is remembered, the day or the memory of the day, played endlessly for the mind just for the faraway possibility of a different ending? But it was always the same. Buddy was taken by an ambulance to Dominican Hospital, handled marvelously well by the paramedics, nurses and doctors, but it had been fairly clear from the very beginning that Buddy would probably never walk again.

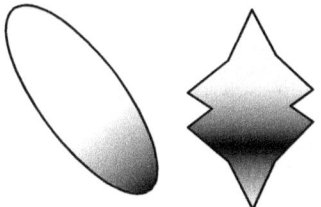

DuaAgappa (36) Embedded

Lucky's official celebration officially became something else with Buddy's injury, of course. It was shocking, but it was intensely bonding, as well. Buck and Lucky blamed themselves, as did June, but none of them ever held anything but sympathy for each other. There was a new tenderness, that particular sort of decency born of tragedy. Buddy stayed in the hospital for almost four months, and everyone would visit him as a family. At first he was shattered emotionally and spent days upon days crying. Nothing seemed to console him, his young life having been based on the advanced use of his legs. When Buck, Lucky, June and Sahani came by, however, he would brighten up, and showed amazing regenerative capabilities. But he never walked. He tried, he did all the exercises and more, but his legs just began a retreat that never really let up. The nurses and therapists loved him. He had a singular energy that captivated everyone and was not dependent on his legs.

The days stretched on, and it became clearer that they were going to have to deal with a changed life down at the ranch. The old house would need massive renovations to be wheelchair accessible, and it was finally decided that Buddy would move back into the apartment. They were afraid that Buddy might not like the idea, and instead he relished in the idea, at least until he heard that Lucky was thinking of moving back into the new house.

"She's supposed to be in your room!" he cried one day alone with his dad.

"I can't make her move in with me," Buck hemmed and hawed.

"Well, you could make a move on her," Buddy suggested.

"Buddy!" Buck scolded him for being so bold.

"Well, you could," Buddy pointed out. "You've been waiting for so long you forgot how to do anything but wait."

"Again...Buddy!" he scolded him again.

"I'm just saying," Buddy kept on. "You know how the mama cat acts funny every once in a while? That's how Lucky is around you..."

"Okay, that's enough!" Buck was blushing but Buddy did not notice.

"What? What's wrong with that?" Buddy really did not know what he had said.

"Well...nothing, nothing," Buck tried to change the subject. "Look, we're all here for you. We'll all be here, okay? We got some great ideas for the apartment."

"I want bars, monkeybars and ropes..." Buddy went with the change of subject. "And before all that, I want you to take all the pictures of mom in your room and put them up in my room."

"What? Why?"

"Well, June said...I mean, I want all the pictures of mom in my room...for comfort."

"I don't see why..."

"Dad, I want it, I want it..." He pushed too quickly into his crying pitch, revealing a bit of the muse in it, but absolute sincerity was not a prerequisite for sympathy with Buddy at this point.

"No problem," Buck responded tenderly, willing to agree to pretty much anything at this point. He came back day after day to try to raise Buddy's spirits, and it was an improvement to have him even ask for anything. Everyone was dealing with things in their own way. They all prayed regularly, and the divine wrapped around them in a gentle and forgiving way. They settled into a pattern that they had never known, really, a sort of regularity that, although laced with the sadness of Buddy's accident, provided a sense of comfort and home that none of them had experienced before.

Buck and Lucky took things slowly, inching into something once unlikely that now seemed inevitable. They were playful and flirtatious with each other, and everyone tried to edge them together in whatever way possible, but it was still not obvious where to go next.

One day when they were looking over some drawings in the kitchen they passed a critical threshold. They touched, first hands and then hips, and they allowed themselves to keep touching. Lucky had been trying to relocate down to the new house, but it had been taken over lately by the various organizations. Exciting things were going on, but there was not a lot of free space for a woman who was used to her solitude.

"I mean, I support everything they are doing," Lucky was saying.

"Yeah, I support it, too, but I don't see how you could live there. It's busy all the time."

"It's some really cool stuff, sure, but those kids are wild, you know?" Lucky shook her head.

"I remember when we were the wild kids," Buck laughed.

Lucky laughed too. "True, but these kids are some kind of collectively wild, as a group. I don't think we were quite so constantly obsessed with loud music."

"Are you kidding? Do you remember when I got sent to the office in fourth grade for blasting Fleetwood Mac over the class record-player?"

"That was different. That was Rock and Roll."

"Oh, I see," Buck smiled. "Hey, speaking of which, weren't you hooked up with Mick Fleetwood for awhile, years ago?"

"It was Lindsay Buckingham, actually. He was a rebound off of John Mayer. Quite an age difference between those two."

"Well, I can't compete with all that star power," Buck shrugged.

She pulled him around spontaneously, putting her arms around his neck. "Oh you can do more than compete, darlin', you can win."

"Oh really?" he said, more an acknowledgment than a question. He straightened up, threatening to lift Lucky off the floor if she held. She did not let go. He stood up further, lifting her a full foot off the ground. She held tight, looking deep into his eyes. His hard muscular arms grabbed her thighs gently below the buttocks and held her in a sitting position around his waste, her arms still entwined around his neck.

It was a moment of pure delightful suspension. Lucky melted into his massive chest, her nipples growing hard against his thin flannel shirt. Some great flood was loosed at that moment, an expansive flow of previously restrained emotion came bursting through.

They kissed, and it was like water in the desert. The kiss dripped with sweet life and filled their hearts with something cool and warm at the same time. Their minds both did a quick mental calculation and simultaneously came to the realization that they were both completely alone, would be nearly all day, and it had probably been planned that way. They also simultaneously decided it did not make a difference, and they started ripping off clothes in wild abandon.

He kissed her in places he had imagined in quiet fantasy for years, and they were suffused with an electric charge that revealed a reality far beyond imagination. Their fingers, their arms, their bodies, buzzed with an ignition of ancient fuel, flaming with a warm conflagration of passion. Lucky was burning in a way she had never allowed with her other lovers, and she knew the joy of pleasure deferred then unleashed. She wanted to loose herself on Buck in a way she never had before. She wanted to show him that there was a wealth of love in her for which it had been wise to wait.

Buck was learning that for himself, and he let himself enjoy each moment fully. He tasted Lucky and she was more delicious than he had ever hoped. She was so delicious that he almost did not even care when they knocked glasses off the table, but the noise at least shocked them enough to cause them to pause for a moment.

"Maybe we should go into the room," Lucky suggested.

"I think we should," Buck quickly agreed, thankful that he had taken Buddy's advice and removed all the pictures of Julia. He had gotten over her death, but he did not want Lucky to think that he hadn't. He felt that Julia, in her far off corner of heaven, would be as happy as the kids would be if he and Lucky got together. Julia had been instrumental in them returning to the ranch and maintaining a connection with Lucky, even when Lucky herself did not seem to want it.

They raced into the room, kissing and groping the whole way. They slammed the door behind them, and Lucky had to pause as she realized that this was the first time she had been in this particular room in over 25 years.

"Wow," she gaped. "Mom never had it like this." She looked about what was once a familiar space but was now like some room out of a museum. Buck had hung various exotic gifts and mementos that he had collected over the years in his travels with the kids. Every conceivable sort of object was carefully stowed in every available spot, save for a large bed in the middle with clean bedding (that one had been his own idea).

"I'm sorry I didn't ask," Buck admitted. "I didn't really plan for this day, like maybe I should have. Do you want me to take it all away?"

"Are you kidding? I love it!" she cried, pushing him down onto the bed. She started to devour him, but he held her away.

"Wait a minute!" Buck stalled. "Is this a respectful thing in this room? I mean, what would your parents think?"

Lucky let out the loudest and longest laugh she had had in years.

"What's so funny?" Buck finally squeezed in.

"You actually wonder what my parents would think about us getting together?"

"Oh, right," Buck smiled, and then laughed. "I see what you mean."

"I might just as well ask what Julia would think."

"I see what you mean," he said again.

Lucky raised her voice in a loving way. "Okay, any of you dead people out there mind if a couple of us lonely living people get together tonight? If you do, make a noise or...levitate something." Pure silence.

"No? Well, Buck, the 'ayes' have it." She pulled him down on top of her, and he came down just enough for full contact, supporting most of the weight on his elbows.

Their kisses now were more graceful, less hungry. They knew they had nothing to rush, and they languidly reclined on the porch of passion. Time was rich and slow like molasses, and they vertically danced their way out of the rest of their clothes, and under the blankets.

Their bodies were primed and ready for what they had to give to each other. They blended in such a delightful way that they felt waves of the most pleasing memories from far in their past as well as hints of future climaxes. They mixed into a cleansing swirl of present pleasant feeling, pushing deep within and blowing out the dust of old worries. They loved for pleasure, they loved for each other, they loved for love, for so many reasons, but that they loved, and loved well, was all in all.

They slept in the rest of the day, Buck's new museum like décor and scheme providing a nice dark blanket of cozy. They awoke in the dusk of a new day and dreamily stirred in the golden light of California sunset. They shuffled out, cleaning things up, dreaming things up, singing things up and about the whole house. The evening stretched out with no word from June or Sahi, and Lucky realized that they had not probably guessed their plan would hatch so quickly.

"We should all be having dinner and getting ready for Buddy coming back tomorrow," Lucky said.

"Should we call them?" Buck wondered.

"Oh yeah, call them," Lucky said. "You have their numbers?"

"Yes, of course." Buck pulled out his cell phone and punched a few numbers. "Hey. Where are you? Where? Well, come home. You never said you would be gone all day. You're still grounded, remember? Sahi has to what? No, she can do that on Monday. We need to get ready for Buddy coming home tomorrow. No Sahi doesn't..."

"Here, give me the phone," Lucky said as she took it. "Hi, June, can I talk to Sahani please? Yes, I called her Sahani. No, she is not in trouble. Quit laughing and put her on. Hi Sahi, look, Buck and I want you to come home. We need help moving Buddy's stuff out of your room. No, you won't be interrupting anything. NO, you WON'T be interrupting anything. I can't talk about that now, just get home. All right." She handed him back the phone. "They're coming back."

"I gathered." Buck was smiling. He felt something better than the sex, almost as good as the love. He felt like he finally had an ally. "Thank you."

"For what?" she asked.

"For coming back," he said.

"I should have never left," she returned.

"Don't say that."

"Why not?"

"Because so much has happened, so much might have happened, still might happen. You're here now, and that's enough."

"Then thank YOU."

"You're welcome."

"You're welcome, too." They kissed.

They spent the rest of the evening in happy busy-ness, moving Lucky's stuff into the master bedroom. When June and Sahani came home they were smiling and giggling at almost everything, like when Buck and Lucky scolded them almost identically at different times for staying out so late. Everyone was in a jovial mood, and no one questioned the new arrangements. Lucky was going into Buck's room, Buddy was moving into the apartment, and Sahi was moving into Buddy's old room next to June. Everyone was charged and quickly finding solutions to once intractable problems

During a break over hot chocolate, they set out plans for new buildings at the office site, and for expansion into a larger complex, including a community center and organic farm. At Buck's suggestion they decided to call it "New California," and they drew up detailed plans for which lands to acquire to connect it to other communities.

"They've just installed a system, a sustainable node, called a 1Earth Server, that connects them to others worldwide in a wiki system. M.C. Hager designed it and has the prototype up in Boulder Creek, but the company is called ExpressCasts in Mountain View."

"Most of that was beyond me," Lucky confessed. "I thought M.C. Hager was a rock and roll writer guy."

"Yeah, that's him. He is an entrepreneur too. Did well with Mo-DV and Virtual Venues and some others."

"Oh well, bully for him. Has a new project, does he?"

"Yes, you'd like this one. It's about saving all the local permaculture and sustainability knowledge of the world in one place, or rather, many one places," Buck informed her. "It's that big tech tower in the office, and the solar panels on top."

"Cool. So much to catch up on," Lucky acknowledged.

"I hope none of it is too prosaic, I hope," Sahi said, a bit mischievously.

"Of course not," Lucky said sincerely. "It is the least I owe to all of you...catching up on all that I have missed.

"But we have so much to thank you for, too! Getting Dad out of his funk, mostly."

"Hey!" Buck scolded her, good naturedly. They finished their long range planning and returned to the task of the evening. Sorry, Belle, but that old house had never been so clean.

When Buddy came home the next day, it was the most joyous time in their collective memory. The sun beamed down in glorious gratitude through clouds of majesty in the eyes of the young Buddy as he wheeled up the new ramp into the apartment. He squealed with delight when he saw what his dad had built in the house. Custom bars and rope ladders hung all over, making it look more like a playground or gym than a bedroom. The décor featured pictures of Julia mixed with art by June and Sahi, creating a uniquely Buddy flavored funhouse.

"Almost perfect, Dad," he called out in the midst of his climbing, and he almost slipped and fell, but he caught himself.

"Be careful!" Buck called out.

"I am!" he declared as he swung back to the door. "More importantly, Lucky, where are you staying?"

"Well," she stammered. "Well, until the office is ready for me, I am going to sleep in your dad's room, on the floor."

"You will be much more comfortable in the bed."

The girls laughed, and Buck rubbed Buddy on the head.

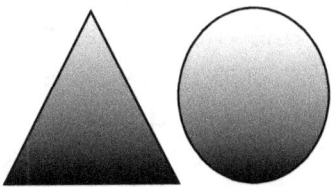

AtruaOna (37) Planted

Lucky began to really enjoy life, despite all the difficulties. She welcomed being pulled outside of herself by the needs and desires of family. She rode with June over the hills, and experienced a familiarity and closeness beyond even what she was experiencing with Buck, and Buck filled her more than had even any man.

She let herself be loved by Buck, and he was ready. She loved more than she had loved anyone. Anyone human, that is. She remembered her old Divine Lover, and spoke to him daily, but came to understand more of what He had been trying to teach her. He was not meant to be her Earthly lover, and she had been the recipient of a veritable miracle by ever having experienced what she had, but it would be presumptuous to think it could ever be like that all the time. She did wonder occasionally if she had left Him, and if she was somehow making a mistake, but the Universe seemed to make it clear that she was meant to be at the ranch.

Buddy was making tremendous progress, but he still needed a lot of constant help. Lucky still felt a little responsible perhaps, but she also loved him like a son, and found herself feeling more for him than she had felt for any of her animal patients. She became a delightful regular fixture at the ranch for the first time in years, and the very land breathed its relief.

She also made herself a part of the organization more than she had been in many years. She learned that many things had changed, and that there were great environmental, social, and economic pressures facing the company like never before. But there were unique and dynamic individuals in her companies that were part of the next generation. Under Sahani's command, they had organized into a powerful force for good worldwide.

Lucky and Buck allied their companies with like minded organizations such as the Sustainable Business Institute in Silicon Valley and 1Earth Media Technologies in Boulder Creek. They centered their own enterprises at the New California Center in Freedom, but would travel about the West promoting various causes. As the 1Earth Server Global Community came online, all the folks at the New California Center became dynamic players in the formation of the network. Sustainable communities all over the world were connected in a social network and wiki that catalogued all the great work and indigenous knowledge from all over the world. Lucky really got it how animal agriculture worldwide could be helped with such a system.

Meetings and workshops seemed to go on all the time at New California, and trips would be made up to Boulder Creek where there was another 1Earth center. The nodes spread out over the world, but local centers provided the contact points with the real world. Lucky and Buck, in some ways, felt a little left behind by it all, but they were the media darlings of the whole movement. They were happy to be a story, happy to be seen together, and almost happy that Buddy was happy for them. Buddy was the sweet sorrowful center of so much they felt, but they were glad to feel most of it. They certainly felt needed, and appreciated, and they hit stride where they felt good keeping pace with each other.

Lucky had a lot more time to spend with Sahi, too, and she became to be truly amazed with what the young executive had been able to accomplish in such a short time. At least, it seemed like a short time to Lucky, but Sahani had been just a little girl when Lucky had last had any significant role in the company. They were driving up the coast one day, Sahani at the wheel, when Lucky asked her to pull over. No sooner had Sahi complied and Lucky was vomiting out the door.

"Oh dear," Sahi gasped. "Are you all right?"

"No!" Lucky spat out. She pulled a towel out of a bag and proceeded to clean herself up. "Okay, let's go."

"Are you sure you're all right?" Sahi questioned her.

"No," Lucky responded in a perfectly normal voice. "Let's get going."

Sahani just stared at her and did not start the car.

"Start the car," Lucky said.

"You seem nonchalant. Did you eat something?" Sahi was on to something.

"Of course I ate something," Lucky snapped. "Probably shouldn't have before this trip. I'm just carsick."

"I've seen you ride the back of an elephant and not get sick," Sahi continued.

"I didn't say I was elephant-sick," Lucky pointed out. "Come on, start the car. I'll feel fine later on." She gesticulated until Sahi finally turned the key.

"When the morning's done?" Sahi questioned her.

"What? You think this is morning sickness? Impossible."

"Did you have sex with Buck?"

"OH! Sahani! None of your business!"

"That would make it possible..."

"It's not impossible for that reason," Lucky suggested.

"Then why? When was your last period?"

"Sahi, I haven't had a period in over ten years!" The reality of it hung in the air and then sunk in. "I couldn't be?"

"Did you?"

"What?"

"With Buck?"

Lucky paused. "Yes."

"Then it's possible," Sahi concluded, and she knew. She sensed the hormones and the change in Lucky. Lucky only began to see it in such a light for the first time. She went through the typical stages of denial, and anxiety, and acceptance.

"I somehow thought it might not be possible," Lucky admitted.

"Oh, it's possible," Sahi pointed out. They continued the rest of the day in a combination of excitement and dread. They were at a permaculture conference at the former Redwood Elementary campus. All of the topics they had to cover that day dealt with such monumental life issues that everything seemed to blend with the cause of the new life growing in her body. Lucky found herself cupping her belly every now and then, imagining the life blossoming inside, letting herself go on mental reveries imagining the Big Bang to be something similar, just on a grander scale. Big Bang seemed like the wrong name for the creation of the universe. Everything she saw came into being in a much slower more gentle way. If time itself were created in the Big Blossom, as she was now calling it to herself, she saw no reason that it had to be hurried.

She suspected that being pregnant may make her more aware on some levels. She could sense more about the people around her. She would find herself intently scrutinizing the other conference attendees, only catching herself when the occasional individual would frown back at her. Everyone seemed oddly famished to her. They seemed like they were on the brink of starvation, although the buffet was amply stocked, with Lucky Star Organics, amongst other things. Everyone seemed hungry, or scared perhaps, proceeding with that sort of intensity that Lucky associated with a pack of coyotes that she had seen in the canyons in back of the ranch.

Some people made her instinctively react defensively, covering her midsection with her arms or crossing her legs. They seemed out of place, even amongst the others, like wolves in coyote's clothing. Although she supported the cause and was very interested in the topic, Lucky found herself tiring quickly, giving Sahi clues that she was ready to go. Sahi hardly needed them, as she was used to being in tune to higher frequencies of priority and need. They had made the appropriate final exchanges and farewells and were soon on their way.

Lucky was quick to lose herself in the beauty of the passing countryside, and was glad yet again that Sahi was driving. She marveled at the towering redwoods as they passed through green tunnels of forested highway. Everything reminded her of birth, seemed, cars emerging from tunnels of dark emerald.

It was natural enough, she figured, for a pregnant woman to become a bit obsessed with the idea, but she merely marveled that she slipped so easily into the feelings. She would have expected that she would be the type to resist maternal urges well into her middle ages, yet she fell ever so gently into the arms of hormonal and genetic inevitability. It was not that she resisted the feelings, or doubted her love for Buck anymore. She just marveled at the passage of great generational shifts within her bosom, waves of progeny yet to be claiming dominion over a willing servant. She felt the waves, and accepted them as a timely part of a natural arc. She rode the waves of feeling with corresponding curls of words, filling the void with endless conversation with Sahi.

Sahi felt the emotional and hormonal tug, and she struggled to remain steadfast in her own path of persistent advance of a specific progressive agenda for herself and her community. She had been so precocious in other parts of her personality that she had allowed her own sexuality to mature at a measured pace only. The proximity of the flowering of her mentor and friend had a catalytic effect on her, however, and Sahi felt herself being pulled deeper into womanhood serendipitously. She welcomed the chance to lose herself in Lucky's life like a girl might with an older sister. Lucky's romance was Sahi's romance, and they savored the opportunity for such seemingly simple yet precious pleasures.

The ride home down the coast was a California dream, the setting suns streaking the evening mist with a fiery brush. The girls conjectured endlessly about how to tell Buck, and when. There was a measure of uncertainty in the situation, but very little uncertainty as to how Buck would react. He would immediately celebrate and start making plans for a wedding, both girls were pretty certain, even before he had asked Lucky properly. Of course, everyone knew she would keep the baby, and willing to have a man's baby might seem equivalent to agreeing to marry him, but there was a key romantic difference. She would definitely have his baby, but she might not, just might not marry him. Not automatically. He would have to ask her. And she would have to consider.

This was the ultimate conclusion made by the two women as they made their way back to the ranch. They had already decided how Buck was to react to news that was only maybe news and of which he had no awareness. He was going about his business working on Buddy's room, minding his own business, unforewarned about the strong female presence about to embrace his entire life. He loved both of these women in different ways, and he had longed many years for the sweet presence of a lover and friend, but he had become accustomed to being a single dad. June and Buddy had been his everything for a long time, and nothing could ever really budge that, he had always thought.

The girls drove expectantly onto the ranch. June and Buddy were down at the pond, saw the truck drive in, and June ran over to meet them. Sahi decided it would be best if Lucky and Buck had a little time to themselves, so she stopped the truck and jumped out to distract the kids.

"Hey Buddy," she said excitedly, "Is all the life gone from the pond?" when she knew very well it was not.

"Gone? Are you kidding?" Buddy was incredulous. "There's more than ever. Let me show you the latest batch of frog eggs," he said, motioning her over and walking with his hands.

June was not so easy. "What's up?" she asked pointedly at Sahi.

"Uh, nothing, new frogs eggs, apparently," Sahi shook her head, and headed towards the pond.

June walked right past her towards Lucky. "What is it Lucky?" June asked her directly.

"Oh, nothing," she tried to be dismissive. "I need to talk to your father," she added, realizing at the end that she had made a mistake.

"You need to talk to my FATHER? What for?" June asked suspiciously. She crept over to Lucky and sniffed the air. "Are you pregnant?"

"JUNE!" Sahi said, "you shouldn't ask that!"

"No, no, it's okay," Lucky said. "I might be. What makes you ask, June?"

"There was something different...I smelled," she haltingly admitted.

"You smelled, all right," Buddy said.

"BUDDY!" Sahi chastised him this time.

"I didn't smell," June corrected herself. "I sniffed something different. Things are changing!" she said as she rubbed her hands together in excitement.

"Well, listen," Sahi dragged them over to the pond, and Lucky could hear them fade into the distance. "That is really for them to discuss amongst themselves before we start deciding everything you..."

She took the stairs like she had so many millions of times, but there was something very different in her now. She could not help but imagine her mother smiling down on her with a certain smug reflexive grin. Lucky found herself tempted to resist this image of her mother even now, against an echo from the grave. She knew that such echoes could hold us, beyond the influence of a single life, pulling everyone towards forgotten destinations. Yet she was carrying herself, and so much more. This life inside of her finally gave her a perfect reason to choose others over herself, and truly be happy about it. She was happy, like she could never have explained to a younger version of herself. She was happy to be walking into this house, this very old friendly house, carrying Buck's baby, ready to do something crazy, like marry him.

In the flash of just a few moments she had spanned a lifetime of feelings between them. She accepted the love he must have felt all those years to have done all that he had. She gushed inside at the thought of the pain that she most certainly must have caused him. She allowed herself to feel all that regret, finally, because she was allowing herself to give in completely to the solution. She would let herself sink into the love that Buck's presence always promised. She would allow herself to be bound up in his net of plenty, harvesting a bounty long in the making.

She walked over the threshold feeling that she was bringing a gift to the old homestead like no other. She could feel the ghosts dance and shimmer with the expectation of new life. She walked through the house but it all seemed empty. She went through each of the rooms, almost ceremoniously carrying her new precious bundle to each of her childhood romps, flashing through memories of the past and future. For a moment she felt that she had missed everyone, for the house was empty in all the old rooms where there had always been a constant bustle. It took her a moment to realize that the new century was different, and that the life of Buck's family had shifted to the extension in back.

What had been the old garage and store room extending into a hill overgrown with blackberries had become the new apartment. Since Buddy's transformation constant modifications and improvements had been happening in the old back area, and now this had become a favorite living spot for the whole family. Buck was drilling something in the ceiling, standing on a short ladder and disappearing into a tangle of bars, only the vibrative scraping notes indicating that he was drilling something up there. As he reached up his jeans hung low as his shirt rode up his torso that extended up into the shadows.

Lucky felt herself moved in adventurous ways that savored a different side of life than she might have explored before. She put her bags down and crept up to Buck working up above. Slowly she put her arms around his bottom and pulled him close, her lips and tongue tracing a warm course down below his navel. His drilling abruptly stopped as if in a hardened woody knot, with a slight trickle of sawdust falling into Lucky's hair, but that was his only reaction at first.

Lucky continued her concentrated attention to Buck's midsection, and he responded with singular movement below the belt. With a slight moan he struggled with the drill up above and pushed his hips into Lucky's face.

"How you doin' up there?" Lucky asked in a slightly muffled manner.

"Better down there," he responded.

"Can I help you with anything?" Lucky asked, looking up.

"Yeah you can help me put my drill away," he answered, fumbling with something above.

"I was just going to take it out," Lucky said as she playfully nibbled at his crotch.

"Okay, okay, hey, help with this one first," Buck said, emerging fully from the ceiling and making his way down the ladder with a drill in his hand. Lucky let her hands, arms, and lips migrate up his bare chest as he made his way down.

"Well, what do I have to thank for this special treatment?" Buck wondered.

"Maybe I'm just coming around," Lucky suggested.

"Well since there may be others coming around let's retire to somewhere more private," Buck suggested.

"I was hoping you'd say something like that. Can you take a break?"

"Oh sure. I've been at it all day. Certainly this has become a never ending project. Labor of love, though." They made their way back to the main bedroom and settled into the shadowed recesses.

"Labor of love, I like that," Lucky said as she pushed her body against his. They wasted no time with further conversation and pressed their bodies together in a deep moving embrace. They allowed themselves a sort of abandon that they had never given themselves before. At one time they might have worried about the kids or visitors, but now they figured they would assume they did more than they would ever actually do so they might as well enjoy themselves.

They knew what to do, and they wasted little time. They had spent so much time in a relatively platonic relationship that a lot of pressure had built up behind the dam when they finally opened the gates. Their energy was of a couple adolescents, but they had a grace and style that came with a lack of desperation and nervousness. There was an ease and pleasantness that had overtaken both of them, and it allowed for tremendous sensual pleasure. They had taken the time to learn exactly what pleasured the other, and so it was a short time before they climaxed together in a warm moist mutual explosion of feeling.

The afterglow surrounded both of them as they reclined in the warm air and let themselves soak in the moment. There was a thick blanket of contentment that covered them and they reveled in the luxury of it.

"Well that was unbridled, even for you," Buck said in an easy sort of way.

"I'm embracing things," Lucky at least started.

"Things?" Buck wondered. "You got something in mind besides this little fun, don't you?"

"Sort of...well, yes," Lucky began.

Buck could sense the momentous nature of what she was feeling, but he could not quite identify it.

"You're not...leaving again, are you?" he ventured.

"No! No, silly," she reassured him. "Just the opposite."

"The opposite? But, you wouldn't..." Buck paused, finally catching up. "You're not...are you...pregnant?"

Lucky's throat closed with the tight smile on her face and she just nodded. Buck hollered and through his fist up in the air. He landed and gently put his hands on her shoulders. "Is this good? Are you happy? Is it mine?"

"Yes, yes, and of course!" Lucky answered. She was genuinely happy as she saw the joy in Buck's face.

"Oh Lucky," Buck affirmed. "I promise you, I will take care of this child for as long as we both live."

"I know that, Buck," Lucky laughed. "I know what a good father you are. That's not what I worry about."

"So you are worried about something? I'd thought you'd be more certain about us after all," he figured.

"No, not us. Buck, I'm worried about the baby is all, and, you know, I've never done this. I'm scared."

"A woman who would climb up the side of a mountain in a storm is worried about having a baby?"

"Well, it's about having another life at stake. Before I was the only one that could get hurt."

"No, others could get hurt, too."

"Yes, I'm sorry. I realize now I did inadvertently hurt people, and I don't want to do that anymore, especially not an innocent little baby."

"Lucky, you won't hurt this baby by giving it life."

"I know, but how do I know?" Lucky reasoned. "And you, I don't want to hurt you."

"And don't worry about hurting me, Lucky," Buck smiled. "I've gotten pretty tough, over the years."

"That's what I'm getting at, Buck. I don't want you to be so tough, so strong, so hard, anymore. I won't hurt you, not with this new life so dependent on us, and I've come to see how I truly feel about you."

"Oh, really? Well, I think I know how I feel about you."

"I hope I do, that's why, knowing how you feel, I say, yes."

"Yes?" Buck asked.

"Yes, I will."

"You will?"

"Marry you."

"Marry me? Woah, I hadn't thought of that!"

"You hadn't thought of that? I figured you would automatically want to marry someone you got pregnant."

"Well, at one time, maybe, but Lucky, you have to realize that I am not just myself anymore. I have Bud and June and a lot of responsibilities. I have already committed to all of them already.   I can't automatically say a woman like you would have to do anything with a man like me, but I do promise that I would take care of our child too."

"I think I understand.   I know that you have a family with Bud and June and Sahi and everyone and this house and everything."

"Oh, I know. I apologize, you are already part of the family. Lucky, will you marry me?"

"Marry you? Woah, I hadn't thought of that."

"Touche.   Can I say yes to your earlier question?"

"I never asked you," Lucky pointed out.

"Okay," Buck thought for a moment. "Can I take your earlier yes as an answer?"

Lucky thought for a moment. "Yes."

"Woohoo," Buck hollered as he jumped in the air once again.

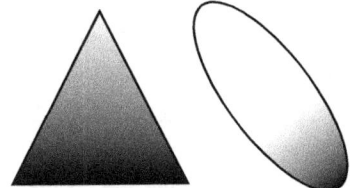

AtruaDua (38) Pushed

Life had a melodic quality for the family in the weeks that followed. There was enough busy activity to make anyone think that they may have been trying to mask a deep uncertainty or uneasiness, but really everyone was quite comfortable in their full schedule. Buddy was an inspiration to all. In a short time he had become densely muscled in his upper body, even as his legs atrophied. Everyone wanted to hope that Buddy would walk again, but he himself seemed driven to approach life triumphantly with or without his legs.

Buck continued to add on to the apartment with abandon, making everything to Buddy's specifications until it all resembled a combination of playhouse and jungle gym. June and Sahi had become inseparable, and had they had taken to following Lucky around as midwives in training. They imbued the ranch and rest of the land with a youthful fecundity that it had not seen in sometime. The operations of the ranch and the foundation reached new heights of success. The rest of the world had caught up with Lucky and Buck and everything they had taught, and now that they had an upcoming wedding to add to the mix, they became media darlings. They even had to deal with paparazzi when they decided to throw a party to announce their engagement. The Lucky Starr ranch became a media circus as over 200 people of various types filled the property with their cars and small groupings spread across the area. Someone, at some point, opened up the milking barns and shooed a small herd of cows into the midst of all the partiers. Even though it was clear that it had to be Buddy or June, because the cows would not easily escape if someone just opened the barn door. Instead, a more knowledgeable assistance would be required, but no one seemed concerned with blame as soon as the cows were back in place.

There had been some bumps in the road. Buck had wanted to just run off and get married, maybe in Vegas. That was too unromantic for Lucky and she insisted that they plan a big wedding. She felt that Belle would have wanted it, even if she was no longer living. The ranch seemed to want it, at least in the minds of the women, and Buck was not one to ever go against the desires of the ranch. This was a favorite topic of daily conversations for everyone seemingly but Buck, and the girls felt it was all public interest number one.

"Two months is not enough time," Sahi said as she folded laundry one day with Lucky and June.

"And it's still winter then," June chimed in. "Don't most people get married in the spring or summer usually?"

"People get married year round these days, especially around here," Lucky reasoned. "And how much time do we need? Whatever we manage in that amount of time will be fine."

"But why do you want to rush and limit things?" Sahi asked. "This is a huge day in your life. Don't you want to make it perfect?"

"Yes, of course," Lucky agreed. "And most of it will be remembered in pictures, and I don't want to look like a marshmallow."

"Oh that's it," Sahi finally got it.

"What?" June asked.

"The baby," Sahi filled in.

"Oh, you don't want people to know you're pregnant?" June guessed.

"No, I'm not trying to hide anything. Everybody will know that I'm pregnant. I just don't want it to be totally obvious, okay?"

"Oh, okay," Sahi granted her. "It will be okay. We will find the best time and place for it all, and just the right dress to make to look nice and unpregnant, even though everyone will know the truth."

"Good. And it's going to be here at the ranch?"

"Here at the ranch?" Sahi gasped. "What if it rains?"

"We can put up tents. Believe me, we have dealt with rains," Lucky said. "I've rescued 2000 cows, pigs, and horses in a typhoon in Bangladesh, I think I can successfully wed Buck Smith."

"Are you going to take his name?" Sahi asked.

"Well, I was thinking about hyphenating, you know, like Lucky Star-Smith, which has its own charm, but it's kind of awkward, you know. Somehow I think I have been Lucky Star for too long to change it now.'

"How romantic," June said with a playful sarcastic twist.

"Yeah, yeah, well we get our romance outside of names," Lucky retorted.

"How quintessentially liberated of you," Sahi commented.

"Maybe.   I think Buck and I are just tired of stressing over surface details.   There is enough to worry about."

"What do you have to worry about?" Sahi asked her.

"Uh, well, you know, details of the wedding, and such things," Lucky tried to recover.

"You just said you didn't want to stress over details," June pointed out.

"I said 'surface' details, like where we have the wedding," Lucky finally recovered fully.

"I think the Ranch is the perfect place," June said.

"I agree," Lucky said, and she gave June a hug. She patted the last folded towel and looked out the window for a moment.   Sahi watched her gaze, wondering, but June just picked up some piles and went out.

"Are you sure you're okay?" Sahi asked her.

"I never said I was okay."

"Are you okay?"

"I'm not sure," she admitted.   "I just don't know...what's it supposed to feel like to be pregnant?"

"Good question.   You should probably ask someone who has been pregnant."

"I know. I miss my mom," Lucky said with flush of emotion in her voice. The irony and the poignancy of so many conversations came back to her, but try as she might she could not hear her mom's voice saying anything new in her mind. She could not coax the walls to give her any advice. They stayed the same neutral and balanced observers they had always been.

"Look, you have the best medical attention in the world.   The doctors would know if there was any problem," Sari tried to be encouraging.

"I know, I know. I don't know, maybe being a little nervous is natural when you're pregnant and about to get married," Lucky said with a smile, and they laughed. They both considered saying more, shuffling a bit with the remaining piles of laundry. The moment drifted away, and they went about the house tending to various chores.

Lucky went about the motions of finishing the day, but she was noticeably distracted. It could have been physical or psychological, or both, and she felt something decidedly momentous drawing near. Natural, of course, as Sahi would say, for one about to get married and have a baby. She decided to turn in early and was quickly asleep even before Buck got home.

She quickly eased into dreamland and found herself walking along the ranch trail that led into the hills. The hills rolled and undulated in that dreamlike way, leading this way and that. Everything had for her that haunting familiarly of a landscape that one has still never seen, floating like a mistaken memory. It was the ranch, but it was more, something else, somewhere else. She recognized hints of the home of her old Love, hiding behind the ancient groves and craggy coves.

"Why don't You come out? Why are You hiding?" Lucky called out into her dream.

A blaze of light flooded her eyes with the blue tint of memory, and Lucky stood before her Ancient Love, stunned by His sudden presence.

"I never hide, but can become obscured," He said, with infinite patience.

"I haven't seen you in years," Lucky lamented.

"Exactly, yet as always everywhere I aM."

"It's You, all right. Same flowery language that evades the point," Lucky ventured.

"I speak simply what is."

"I see. Well, what's the occasion?" Lucky asked. "You haven't come around in years, but You show up suddenly there has to be a reason."

"Lucky, I am always here, available to all, in whatever form you can experience Me. You have been exploring your life, seemingly away from Me, but I am always here. At certain points in life people get closer to things considered out of reach, on the other side, like the fullness of My Love. Yet I am always here."

"What 'certain points in life'? What are you talking about, what's going to happen?"

"Lucky, I am saying that no matter what happens, I am here for you. I am Everything, Everyone, the Whole Universe, and We All conspire to love and care for you."

"What are you saying? What are you going to do?" Lucky stopped wondering. "No. You can't have my baby. You can't take my baby!"

"The child's spirit is it's own, ready in its own time," He told her.

"How can a baby know? How can a baby choose?" Lucky pleaded.

"A spirit can know. A spirit can decide that it is not ready, that the time is not right."

"No, it can't be true. I am ready. I am ready to be a mother. I am ready to have a child. You can't take this from me."

"I do not take, I only give. But it can only be exactly right at the exactly right time."

"You can't do this. You can't take everything like this. You can't have my baby! You can't..." Lucky continued to yell and scream in the dream, shaking herself against the growing awareness of Buck's arms circling her, trying to comfort.

"Lucky, it's okay! It's me, Buck. You're safe. You can calm down," he was saying. Lucky stayed half in the dream.

"Don't tell me to calm down," Lucky said, only slightly more clearly.

"Please, Lucky, please, it's okay," he tried to reassure her.

"I know it's okay, I mean, I'm okay, okay?"

Buck fumbled through the darkness and finally found a lamp switch. The air was thick and the blankets were tangled, and it took a second for them to realize that Lucky was sitting in a pool of blood.

"NO!" She screamed, and that was the only real thing she would say for hours. She said nothing as Buck drove her up to Dominican Hospital, although the steady stream of warm tears certainly spoke of something. She felt gutted, absolutely scooped out, a hollow shell. Buck held her hand, and she appreciated the strength, she felt the love. But she felt it was too late. She had already lost it, lost something dear, deep inside her belly, something horribly fundamental. She missed it somehow.

She said nothing as the doctor confirmed that they had lost the pregnancy. It hardly even seemed liked a baby anymore. It felt like a dark pool of blood somewhere inside, some sticky darkness.

Buck felt things shifting in the silence. Part of him cried inside, cried like a child like when he lost his mother. But another part of him was not surprised, and this part was embarrassed for the part that cried, so no tears reached the surface. He felt the loss, sure, as he always had. He greeted loss like an old bully, same pressure slightly dulled by a not uncomfortable familiarity. Still, he could not help but hope he could kick loss for good someday.

The drive was the longest in their lives, perhaps because so little was said in words.

"Perhaps it's best..." Lucky began.

"Perhaps it's best we call things off, post-pone them maybe," Buck said, sensing it in the air between them.

"Yes, perhaps. But we don't have too," Lucky maintained.

"No. We can do whatever we want," Buck agreed.

"Yes, whatever we want...but," she paused.

"But?" He asked.

"But...perhaps its best," she suggested.

"Perhaps," he countered, and that was the last that they said. They shared hardly a word for weeks after that. Sure, gestures, glances, actions, spoke volumes. The image of the blood in the bedroom pretty much killed their sex life, and the rest soon followed. They shared a bed, but only for sleep, and seldom at the same time. There was love, and tremendous sympathy, but the sap was draining from branches, Lucky remembering what Bud would say when she was a little girl asking about the apple leaves turning color.

June and Sahi circled their metaphorical wagons around Buddy, providing a dense screen to blanket him like a warm fog so that he might continue healing unabated. He, for his part, attacked health with a vengeance. Though control of his legs eluded him, he became impressively strong in his upper body. He refused to acknowledge any amount of pity or doubt, he would insist everything was as it should be. He hardly acknowledged Lucky at all, and was able to send enough love and admiration to his father that it helped them both get through it.

Lucky slowly began a process of consolidating her possessions that made it clear to most involved that she was going to be leaving soon. It is as if the whole ranch knew that a graceful return was inevitable and was best expedited by allowing a graceful escape. Lucky almost began to resent the casual ease with which everyone accepted the growing evidence of her departure. Finally she had to take it up with Sahi, at least, to prepare for details.

"So, Sahani," Lucky began, the formal tone indicating a business topic one evening as they were cleaning up dishes together. "I need you to make some travel arrangements..."

"Oh, finally, business again?" Sahi said with a faintly challenging note.

"Yes, I think we have business in India. I think it will interest you. I need you to arrange flights back," she continued.

"I am very interested to find out what sort of business we have in India," Sahi admitted. "Because you have shown zero interest in either the organics business or the foundation for some time now, while I have been skyping with our offices in Bangalore and Mumbai twice daily, and since we have implemented our new 1Earth cloud system it all can be run from anywhere if you just show an interest, so I am very interested in your business interest in India."

"What I meant to say is I think it would be good if we got back to India amongst the people again."

"I understand now," Sahi immediately softened. "I would be glad to arrange that for you."

"For me? You mean, for us," Lucky suggested.

"No, I just told you," Sahi was firm. "Our businesses can be run from anywhere, and I'm needed here, at the ranch."

"Here at the ranch?" Lucky asked. "Don't you want to go back your home in India?"

"Don't forget, I was an orphan in India when you found me."

"Who is now a hugely famous business woman," Lucky correctly maintained about Sahi. Sahani had become a virtual icon of feminine power throughout the subcontinent.

"Using funds from expatriate Indian entrepreneurs here in Silicon Valley, you know that," Sahi continued. "Global is everywhere and nowhere. This ranch, the Lucky Star, is somewhere. Somewhere real. A place so real that it spilled out to touch the world. There is some magic here, and it needs me."

Lucky had a tear in her eye when she hugged Sahi. Nothing in her could begin to argue with a truth every fiber of her being could understand. Sahi would remain for all the right reasons, and Lucky would leave for reasons of her own.

Buck never could understand those reasons, but he supported them as best he could. He did manage to reach out one last time before she disappeared.

"Lucky," he said, one night under a new moon when she was almost finished packing. His voice betrayed that he was not as strong and smooth as he had hoped. "You know, this is always your home."

She turned, with genuine warmth and compassion. "I know, thank you. Maybe someday I will be worthy of it."

"You already are, maybe just not all ready." And that was it.

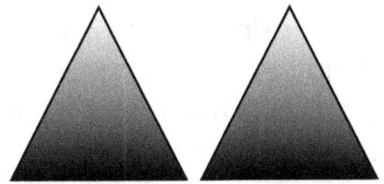

AtruaAtrua (39) Lost

Lucky knew that she would be back to the Ranch. All of Santa Cruz County used to joke that there was a curse that people, once settled there but choosing to leave, could only leave for so long. Lucky took it for granted that she would return. Perhaps that was one of the reasons that she left so easily. For some part of her it was a natural thing, like breathing. Even she would eventually admit that she had taken it for granted that she would always return to the Lucky Star Ranch. She just never expected that it would take 27 years.

"Certain major decisions in life act as bifurcation points. They are quantum axes upon which revolve multiple potential parallel universes," Lucky's friend Pradesh was saying in one of their hilltop workshops in the Himalayas. "When you left California so long ago, the world was facing many such collective quantum axes. Many choices could be made, around global warming, around energy and communication systems, and each would result in some different string of incidents."

Lucky understood that he was trying to comfort her. He was trying to explain why things had happed as they had. Sure, the world could have turned out many different ways. Maybe nothing had to happen at all. But so much had happened. This was her story, her universe, and it was bound to be poignant and thick with agony and ecstasy. The future could have turned out differently, and most likely always will, but she knew now it was about her story, not about what happened. Everything dripped with such meaning for her that she could not but help get it on some level.

She had left California many years ago in what had been considered difficult economic times. Certain parties had strained the system just as certain natural pressures kicked up. Lucky had arrived in India as a celebrity and took a different approach than before. Rather than disappear into the hills she decided to disappear into the masses. She began whirlwind work, whisking about the world. She was called a new Mother Theresa, but she resisted the title. There was too much going on to accept misplaced praise, she thought.

Those first couple years she had regular contact with the ranch, but not really. A few times she had the opportunity to travel back to the states, but she passed always on some ultimately trivial circumstance. Many times later she would regret not immediately going back, not calling every day and talking to everyone. She would always talk to Sahi, but their conversations where so uniformly formal with all that was going on that she really only ever called her Sahani any more.

That all changed abruptly. Lucky would try to figure where in the path she bifurcated, but she never could sort it all. People had always predicted that California would tumble into the sea, and in this string of universe it did. It was not exactly like everyone had pictured it. Climate and geological scientists rarely interacted, but their worlds did. Many had warned that a significant chunk of the Antarctic ice cap could come off with significant consequences, the worst of which would be a global sea level rise of at most ten feet. Well, all things are connected, particularly on a single planet, and when the ice sheet went a great earthquake shot up the eastern edge of the Pacific Ocean. When it hit California it caused massive subsidence of the drained aquifers of the famous valley areas. This caused a relative sea level rise in most of California of almost two hundred feet.

Many millions died in California in the great quakes, but many were dying worldwide even with the smaller rise in sea level. Lucky joined a huge effort that saved millions of people in Bangladesh. Everyone figured that California was gone, forever tumbled into the sea. The media played it that way. All the people gone, the people dead, sunk into the sea. Occasionally the news would show a new map, and islands still persisted, some quite large, and Lucky was certain that one of the largest held the remains of the ranch and its people.

Politically the world changed rapidly. Massive food shortages in the wake of the now huge and undeniable climate change had led the remaining political powers to join together in one great police state. Its grip was weak, however, and Lucky remained a great player within its shadow. She worked to create justice and solace for man and beast both, but she was up against pure corruption. It was pure corruption now without any competition. The people, still in their billions but not growing in population so much anymore, pretty much had to get by on their own.

There were still great technological advances, but they were on a more modest level. Certain global systems, like GPS, had failed, without a replacement except inferior local versions. Global travel was greatly restricted, not even allowed in certain areas like the seas around the former California. All normal citizens could no longer fly, and black market shipping was a dangerous business, especially when the cargo was human. And no ships on record ever went to the Eastern Pacific anymore, with the exception of passing within a few hundred miles of Alaska through the now quite wide Bering Gulf.

Lucky had maintained an extensive network of her own companies through the organic farms she had created in Asia and Africa. Food had become the ultimate commodity and hers enjoyed a special protective consideration from the remaining elites. They knew what was good for them. She had spent years trying to shore up her various forms of capital so that she might finance a secret naval expedition to the islands of California.

Pradesh was one of Lucky's longest and best employees. He was brilliant engineer and financier and was the only person that held top positions in both her official projects and her unofficial grand plan of secret mission to California. He had designed and personally perfected each aspect of the secret mission, which was why he was trying to convince Lucky not to go.

"So, in some very close universe, maybe you never left California, and you died in the earthquake," Pradesh was saying.

"Or lived to help my family and friends rebuild and replant," Lucky quietly stressed. They were in one of the few places they reasonably could expect not to be recorded, but they were cautious. "Or maybe if I had never left, the earthquake wouldn't have happened. Maybe every story is different, and every different thing we do different things happen. Well all this all happened in my story, in my world. My home ranch became islands, and I was told no one survived, but now I see farms and buildings and people..."

"Lucky, that new data from Google could have meant many things," Pradesh argued weekly. A secret connection had sent them Google Earth data of the California Islands, which had been officially completely blacked out since the earthquake.

"Pradesh, you know that data showed new agriculture and new building on those islands. We have been told for so long that no one survived, but it's all blacked out, why?" Lucky demanded, not that he would really know.

"Okay, so even if people survived and are rebuilding, there is no guarantee that any of them are your friends or family," he pointed out.

"I know, but, maybe you don't understand," Lucky persisted as always. In a way Pradesh needed to test her resolve. "You see, even if there is any chance, I have to try."

"Lucky, you may be Lucky, but even after years of trying, we can find nothing about anyone who knows anything about that area. We have some maps made from stolen data from a satellite that isn't supposed to be flying. For all we know it could be fake data."

"It could be fake data," Lucky conceded. "But if there is a chance I still have to try."

"I still have to try to convince you not to go. Everything is uncertain. We can't know what we are meant to do or be for sure."

"Even in an uncertain universe we have to make bold choices, Pradesh," Lucky insisted.

"There is only one thing of which I am truly certain," he said.

"What is that?"

"That if you go away on that boat I will never see you again."

"You don't know that for sure," Lucky said with fading determination.

"Yes of course I do. Either you die trying or you succeed, either way you don't come back, and I don't see you again."

"Okay, I can't even argue that you would see me again, but I can promise you that I will try to get you information back. I will try to send you a message."

"Then I shall always be listening," Pradesh conceded. "You know I have provided for everything." Lucky nodded and kept looking at diagrams. Pradesh had indeed designed an expedition like not other. He had designed the boat, christened "Lucky II" completely out of titanium with solar charging surface and sails, with a hardened electric structure to resist electromagnetic pulses surrounding a hybrid electric and hydrogen system. "You never know what to expect." He had made it completely modular so it could be disassembled and rebuilt after being brought overland to the farthest point in Russia. They could insure relative secrecy on land, and they planned to mimic an ice berg and float until well out of the most traveled lanes. The plan was brilliant, the ship flawless, but it would still probably never work.

"I wish I could go to Russia with you," Pradesh sighed. It was hard to trust underlings with the Lucky II, but their delicate plan required him to remain in India to decrease suspicion. They would say that Lucky was going back into the mountains to pray, and no one would question how long that would take, as long as Pradesh remained to answer questions.

"I am going to go up the mountain a little sooner than you had thought," Lucky let out.

"What are you talking about?" Pradesh began to get nervous again.

"I am going to leave to go up the mountain a month earlier than we had previously planned," she revealed.

"What? Why are you doing this? This is all so finely turned. A small mistiming could change everything..."

"Yes, we know that, don't we? Timing is everything. That is why I have to go up to the mountain early. I have to face this truth, my truth, before I go on this journey."

"So you are going to go into the mountains and fast for a month before you begin this most arduous of journeys?"

"I'm not going to be fasting. I am going to be meditating."

"Are you going to be eating?"

"Well, no, not necessarily..."

"Then you are fasting. You will lose all strength. It is foolish!"

"It's a fool's mission, you already said so yourself. If this thing is going to have any chance at all it has to be in tune with divine intentions. For this thing to go off it has to be one lucky miracle after another, and the only way I can assure that is to go strike a bargain."

"Well, who is the bigger fool, the fool or the fool who follows him, eh? I will do what I can as always." And he did. He always did. Lucky knew she would always try to get a message to him, for just such a little piece of information would be priceless to him.

Lucky, of course, did exactly what she thought she needed to do. It had been a long time since she had seen her own spectacular blue version of God. She knew he was all around, but she had been through such hardship and difficultly that she had come to somehow believe that she had to go through some sort of penance to see Him again. In truth, she had performed enough penance to purify fifty lifetimes of sin, but she felt she needed more. The Universe was happy to accommodate her, and she climbed up to a familiar old hole in the side of the mountain.

She had slipped into meditation so easily before, and had never suffered hunger or thirst, but this time was different. She had expected it to be different, in a way, and had even hoped it would be hard, for she wanted to be sure she earned it. She spent long days on the hard rock. She wanted to truly feel that she had suffered for the right to reach Divinity, and so she fasted and suffered. It was many days, and she felt like it was right. It was cold, and she was hungry, and she was thirsty, until one day, she got it.

She finally saw, once and for all, that she had done enough. She saw how it never really mattered before how much she had done, and it did not matter now.

"Are you here?" she asked.

"Of course," He answered.

"Will you show yourself?"

"Will you see me as I am?"

"I don't know."

"The answer is that you can only see me as I am, if you would but look."

"More riddles. Can you talk plainly, please?"

"What would you have me say?"

"Can't you help me?" she pleaded.

"Okay, I will help. You seek Me in a form you think I must take. I am everywhere. When you chose to take a physical body, for you did choose, you chose to seek me in a physical body in that way. Later, you seek other forms of love in other ways."

"But you came to me in a physical body," she argued.

"You received gift after gift, but received them differently. I am All Things. I came to show you one thing, but to keep Me you had to see Me right in front of you. For that form of love there are ancient ways, and those meant to share in such manifestations."

"You mean, as Buck?" she ventured.

"Sure, as Buck," He allowed.

"And so, does that mean, you give blessing to this mission?" she dared be hopeful."

"It does, and I do. You understand more and more," He blessed her.

"And You will be with me always, because it's all You."

"Exactly"

"Thank you. Bless you. Thank you."

"No, thank YOU, my sweetest child. Fear not, for this life will not leave you without great love."

"Thank you," she said one last time. Thanks was all she felt anymore. She wondered why she did not just feel it all along. But she understood, really. She always wanted to really earn it. She wanted to have understanding, and she wanted to really earn it, so that part of her lesson was not done. It was not done because she was not done. She hit a groove now. She now knew that she made her own future. Her own expectations went in front of her like a seismic ripple.

She came down the mountain early, filled with fire, and did not even think about how it affected the plan. When she surprised Pradesh and the staff with her return, she merely said she was making only a brief visit before going back to meditate. She told them she had caught glimpses of another cave deeper in the mountains and she was going to go deeper in meditation as well. Pradesh made a big point of opposing the idea. She thought he almost opposed it too well, but she could see that he had a lot of feeling in what he was doing.

He had put together a very tight crew out of many secret recruits and had trained them on all aspects of the Lucky II and the mission. For different reasons, the crew included three men and three women, in addition to Lucky. Lucky Number Seven, she called herself. The other six were three couples, one Russian pair, one Chinese pair, and one Indian pair. The Russian pair, Yuri and Irena Uhormsky, were the naval experts of the group, having studied marine science and technology for their whole lives. The Chinese pair, Li Kwon and Mia Ng, were electronic engineers and survivalists familiar with the territory they were crossing. The Indian couple, Sandheer and Meerka Gupta, were the medical experts and food specialists. Together they had the most calculated chance of succeeding.

They certainly felt special as they began together on the journey. Some of the other company members sensed something was going on. Such a group does not train so completely without some sort of word getting out. No one really figured they would be making a secret trip to California. That never really occurred to anyone, for it would have been thought too crazy to even consider.

Pradesh had difficultly accepting as much on faith as Lucky had. There was too much, but he had stopped counting on anything actually working long ago. He viewed it more as an academic exercise. Pradesh wanted to see it succeed, but he felt he never would. He could not even say what success was, but he could at least try to give them the best chance of getting them to California.

Lucky herself knew she would succeed, and she was quite a leader and inspiration for the group. She would travel with them as a hooded monk, but the others were to be a small missionary party. Part of the reasons for having such a diverse group was to have as many language groups represented as possible. Just getting to the new tip of Russia would be no small feat in itself, but then they were supposed to avoid Government gunships in the high north disguised as an ice berg. It was beautiful, but there were so many possible bifurcation points that it was impossible to say what would happen to the entire group.

Lucky tried to explain what guided her, but her young crew could hardly stop to listen. They were well trained, but they had experienced so little in their short lives, or so it seemed to Lucky. She realized then that she knew she would make it, but she could not say the same for any of the crew. They all came on for their different reasons, and with their different destinies. As she accepted the uncertainly of it all, she was left with just gratefulness. She was grateful that such special young people were willing to throw it all in with her for a voyage to a place which supposedly no longer existed. She was grateful to Pradesh for investing so much of his time and effort when he believed he was just sending them all away forever and for good. She was thankful that people could give so much not even knowing where they were headed.

She dared not leave a note for Pradesh, or even look him up the night before they were to leave, so she merely said a prayer, and renewed her promise that she would try to get him a message some day in some way.

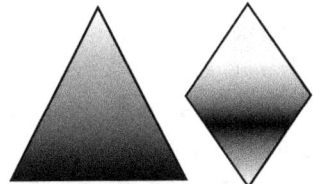

AtruaKatero (40) Renewed

Bud came down over the hill into New Star Cove and peered into the distance over the waves. Luke Hager had said there would at least be a periscope visible, and Bud was renowned for his vision. He rode with his young apprentices who seemed to follow him everywhere these days, so he hardly questioned their presence any more. Sahi was back at the Ranch with their baby boy, Krishna Sky, and his dad with other members of the tribe.

He came down the slope simultaneously scanning the waves looking for some small clue. Around the bend instead he saw something definitely metallic headed their way, but it was not small, nor was it sleek. Luke Hager had been telling him about the new submarine he had been working on, but what he saw coming into the bay barely looked like it could make the last few leagues. It was metallic, and it had a crew, but it rode low in the water, and it seemed quite beat up. It almost looked like some strange mechanical sea serpent was sticking out a large hypodermic nose into the water ahead, creating a strange wake as it sucked its way through the water. Only when the strange mass almost came to shore did Bud realize what he was looking at.

Luke had his submarine towing the larger mass, and the whole thing came to a slow creep in the middle of the lagoon. Dozens of kayaks and canoes now sped out to the floating mass. Some were old fiberglass models in various states of repair, others were newer wood and skin versions. Luke brought the sub to a halt and it came to the surface. His craft was the antithesis of the others, looking more like a spaceship than a submarine. He threw a hatch open and discovered the crowd quickly scrambling all over the two vessels. Luke suddenly climbed out and stood like a giant Viking surveying his haul, immediately taking charge of the scrambling horde.

"Easy with that!" Luke shouted. "That craft has taken on a lot of water. Should've sunk already. Damndest think I ever saw." He called down into the hatch. "Send up the remote, Kai!" A hand held up a small device, and Lukas grabbed it before carefully leaping over to the floating mass. "I have to push it over to the shore!" he yelled out as he saw Bud and his men riding onto the beach.

The hatch closed and the sub sank below the waters again and started pushing on the flank of the mass. Luke jumped to the front and operated his handheld. Fortunately the lagoon of New Star Cove was protected and placid with a long thin beach next to a long pier of recycled materials. Old bits of street signs, light posts and tin roofs were perfectly cut and shaped into the exact new function on a new structure lovingly labeled "WatsonWharf.". The rest of the beach was immaculate and thick with wildlife, sea lions and harbor seals on the rocks at the south end, and kelp beds with sea otter throughout.

"Easy...easy...OK that's good!   Pull out and surface, and get those solar films out fast!" Luke spoke into his device.

"What? I was going to take a shower on the beach first," Kai's voice crackled thinly over a tiny speaker in Luke's hand.   Luke was already jumping down to the beach in front of Bud's horses.

"Nice maneuvering," Bud yelled.

"Thanks, I learned it from a whale."

Bud ignored the comment. "So that is one significant salvage score!"   Bud congratulated Luke as he jumped off his horse and clasped hands with his old friend in the ancient manner.

"More significant that you know. Take a look at this," Luke said, brushing some kelp off a section of the boat revealing the name 'Lucky II.' The surface was battered but the lettering was clear. Bud leapt onto the surface and started to clear it off. He moved with a strange grace on the latest version of the wicker legs that Sahi had created for him. "Careful.   Some parts of it are unstable. What's more, Lucky I is inside, with a couple of passengers, in pretty bad shape."

"What? Come on, let's get them out of there," Bud said, hastily clearing off more debris.

"Hold it!" Luke said, leaping up to the top and grabbing Bud's shoulder. "They're stable.   One of them's a doctor, apparently. They've just went a long time without water.   They need to go to the med center, but we need more help. Go in by the portal over there." He pointed towards the back.

"John, Peter!" Bud called to his men. "Ride up to the Med Center and bring down the ambulance! Hitch up four horses for a heavy load." He turned back to the ship and started to clear off the top.

"Hey careful with that, there is some valuable stuff there...high tech stuff," Luke said.

"Lucky Star has returned and you're worried about salvage!" Bud declared.

"That's what you pay me for," Luke said. He was a special player in the new economy of the islands. He had perfected the art of recovering and rebooting all sorts of gear from the bottom of the ocean. As mayor of New Star, Bud was one of his best customers.

"Where did you find her?" Bud asked, as he searched for a hatch.

"Well, that's just it," Luke said, scratching his head. "I didn't find her, I was led."

"Led?" Bud said, "By whom?"

"By what, really, or whom. Damnest thing I ever saw. We were testing the sub when we were charged repeatedly by a whale, a humpback, to be precise."

"What?" Bud was doubtful, and he was frustrated by not being able to find a hatch.

"I'm telling you this whale came right at us three times before we finally decided to follow it. It swam fast but breached continuously so we could see it, and about 50 nautical miles out we saw the floating mass for the first time, coming straight at us. As we got closer we realized that it was being pushed by a giant blue whale. As we landed the whales just disappeared. There's a recessed handle in that cleared area right there in the back," he pointed.

"What's Malakai doing?" Bud asked as he opened the hatch, noticing the new sub maneuvering around the Lucky II. "Nice sub, by the way. I'll have to take a demo ride later."

"Yeah, later," Luke nodded. "I think he's checking out our latest find. We've hardly checked the outside till now. Go inside."

Bud found the depressed handle and spun the latch, causing a portal to swing open with a hiss of an airtight seal. He climbed down inside and let his eyes quickly adjust. Noticed at first with surprise that the windowless cabin was lit with fiber optics fixtures, and he could see the interior well. There were seven bunks along the wall, three of which were occupied and a fourth figure tended to one of them. In a pool of full spectrum light lay Lucky Star, who looked worn and emaciated, but she beamed in her own particular way as Bud approached. She was being tended by Meerka Gupta. The other bunks held Mia Ng and Irena Uhormsky, the only surviving members of the expedition.

"Am I in heaven now?" Lucky asked, as Bud leaned over her. "Because I think you might be Buddy Smith, and I never thought to see Buddy Smith alive again." Meerka went to tend one of the other women.

Tears welled up in Bud's eyes and he placed his head on her heart. "You're home, Lucky, that's all. Yes its me. And you're home."

"And, your father, Buck...is he still alive?"

"Oh, yes, he is still alive, and well. Many of us survived."

"I bet he will be surprised to see me," Lucky figured.

"Actually, I don't think so. He was the only one who said you'd make it. Others thought for sure you'd died after being betrayed."

"But, wait," Lucky was confused. "How did you know about that?"

"Well, we know about a lot, actually. Basically, we're pretty advanced here. We have special scientists called Data Archaeologists, or DatArchs, and they were able to track you guys all the way up till you apparently evaded the gunships that thought they had destroyed you."

"But...you have been dark, dead islands supposedly, for so long..." Lucky was perplexed.

"That was just by a special agreement made with the UN right after the global quake. The 1Earth Servers here survived, and we kept advancing and rebuilding, and we got an agreement with the global government to keep us silent. Do you know what happened right after you were dest...disappeared?"

"No. We lost all instrumentation shortly after that. Everything electronic shorted out," Lucky said.

"Exactly. Some kind of global electromagnetic burst," Bud informed her. "Some think from the sun, but others think it was some terrorist group against the global government. The hardened 1Earth Servers survived again, hardened and all that, so our technology survived, but the rest of the world went dark. We were tracking everything very closely, and DatArchs have found a plot hatching, but there is evidence for the solar flare, to. Maybe it was both, but you are the first word we have heard of anyone for seven months now."

"But the islands, tell me about the islands."

"Well, you have landed in the Cove of New Star. We are the main city of South Island, which is the largest of the New California Islands. Our capital is now Boulder Creek on San Lorenzo Island."

"New Star Cove, I like the sound of that," Lucky said.

"Yes, you're home," Bud told her. "The Ranch has survived, thrived even. All of Watsonville went underwater and Corralitos and the Ranch became New Star Cove."

"And Sahi?" she asked cautiously, ready for anything. "Did she survive?"

"She did," he informed her. "And she is now my wife, and the mother of our beautiful little boy, Krishna Sky."

"Congratulations!" she shouted, patting him on the back. "And June? Did she make it?"

"Yes, and June. She is married to Skylor Hager up in Boulder Creek, and they are the Governors of New California."

"Governors?"

"Yes, it's part of the New California Constitution. Every ruling position must be held by a man and a woman. Sometimes they are a couple, sometimes not. Sahi and I are the leaders of South Island and..." He was about to continue but they heard hard footsteps on roof and some kind of commotion on the beach."

"Hey, Bud, you better come out here," Luke called down the hatch. "The cavalry has arrived, or the Indians, maybe, from the looks of 'em, whichever side you want."

Bud got up and went towards the hatch. Lucky pulled herself out of the bed to follow him.

"You really shouldn't," Meerka said, coming over. Meerka looked weak and tired herself, but she had somehow kept herself going to take care of the others as they had slowly weakened with thirst. Their water purifiers were electric and had malfunctioned as well.

"Like hell I shouldn't," Lucky said as she briskly pushed her way past Bud. "This is my new damn town, I can do what I want." She climbed out the hatch and sat cross-legged on the hull. It was a beautiful sight for her to see the glorious rag-tag tribe that came down the hill onto the beach. First a strange design hang glider and reclining-cycle floated overhead, accompanied by red-tail hawk circling in tandem. A band of many including 12 people, seven hybricycles, 17 horses, nine dogs, a bobcat and a squirrel accompanied the ambulance wagon down the road onto the beach. Sahi was in the lead, with the baby strapped to her back. She blazed like the sun queen of the island, riding her mount like she was part of it. The team was healthy and strong, of all ages, and Buck brought up the rear. Lucky's eyes watched him, strong as ever, behind it all, stoic yet warm.

"Aaaaaaaaeeeeeeeeeeeeeeeeeeeeee!"   Sahi screamed continuously as she jumped off the horse and scrambled up the craft into Lucky's arms, muffling her cries in Lucky's breast. "It's true, it's true, thank God it's true!" she said between mixed sobs and laughter.

"Dear Sahani, you have done well," Lucky said quietly. They rocked slowly in embrace with Bud as well, while the rest of the greeting party milled about the beach. The pilot landed his craft on the long flat strip on WatsonWharf, while below in the most sheltered but sunny part of the cove Lukas and Malakai laid out floating solar films to recharge the sub.

"We need stretchers! Medics, prepare for two immobilized," Bud said as he pulled away and went back towards the hatch. "What is the name of the Doctor?"

"Meerka," Lucky said simply.

"Meerka?" Bud called down the hole.

"Meerka?" Sahi said hopefully. As a dark squinting head emerged slowly into the bright sunlight, Sahi began to cry out again, "Aaaaaaaaaaeeeeeeeee!" She broke off to give her old friend a hug, and they cried in each others arms. Bud broke off to help the medics now scrambling up the craft with stretchers.

"Hey old man!" Lucky cried out across the crowd to Buck in the back still sitting stoically on his mount. "Not much for teary reunions, are you?"

"I'm waiting for you to come home," Buck answered. "You're still floating on a piece of Asia."

Lucky understood the invitation, and she slowly started to climb down the side of the Lucky II. Bud came over to help, ironically swinging his still paralyzed legs, in his special device created by Sahi, with such grace that no one doubted his eminent capability to help anyone that might need it. "No thanks," Lucky said. "I can do this myself." And she lowered herself down to the beach.

Buck dismounted and started across the stretch of sand. When they realized that now only a small distance separated them, they both broke into a run. They met in the middle in a clap of flesh and clothing, pausing hardly at all before losing themselves in a deep kiss.

A huge cheer arose from all around as work momentarily ceased so the crowd could celebrate the reunion of the two lovers. The shouts echoed off the hills, human voices joining with dogs, horses, and a hawk, to create a cacophony appropriate to announce such an epic occasion. Buck and Lucky slowly came out of their embrace and started towards Buck's horse, smiling coyly like a celebrity couple modestly walking a line of paparazzi. As they approached the horse Lucky stopped.

"Oh my," she said. "It's Luck!"

"Luck II," he corrected her. "You know, your name and it's derivatives have found itself all over this place." They jumped onto Luck's back together as one mass, and they started in light canter back up the road. Buck seemed to be holding back as if in concern for

Lucky, so she soundly slapped the mare's backside and they all took off up the hill in a blur and a yell.

Bud and Sahi worked with Meerka to get the stretchers out with Irena and Mia. Their bodies were so small and emaciated that the well-muscled medics looked liked they hardly expended effort as they lowered the two down to the beach and onto the horse-drawn ambulance. Bud walked over to Luke and Malakai who were now unfurling more apparatus from the sub on the beach.

"Always more inventions, eh Luke?" Bud commented.

"Always," Luke agreed.

"You ain't seen half of it," Malakai said, pulling out some tubing. "This is a solar desalinator. They could have used one of these on the Lucky II."

"I hope to see it all," Bud nodded. "I hope now isn't the only time to get a demo?"

"Now? Are you kidding?" Luke asked. "We have no time now, we want to get to the ranch for the party." With that Bud realized that he was right, that there would be a celebration of several days at the Ranch. It seemed the new citizens needed hardly any excuse for a party, and this homecoming would be the biggest event in some time.

"You're right," Bud agreed. "Did you get a message to Skylor and June?"

"Yep, they're coming down tomorrow by airship," Lukas said.

"Sweet," Bud said. "All right then, it is going to be an awesome party, isn't it?" The ambulance took off up the hill and the rest followed in tandem.

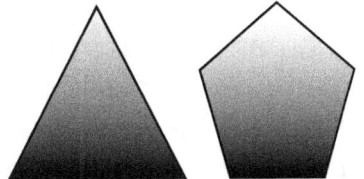

AtruaPentero (41) Released

The air was shining and clear and perfect for flying as the bright new airship came down to the clearing above the ranch house. Several quiet electric motors drove propellers that articulated in every direction to direct the airship down. A crew of four operated the various controls, and June and Skylor were strapped into two lead passenger seats in the nose.

Lucky and Buck were in the heart of the crowd that welcomed the great ship, and everyone cheered as it touched down. June was immediately out of her seat with Skylor not far behind. They ran through the crowd to Lucky and Buck, and June grabbed them both in a giant bear hug, screaming and laughing like Sahi had the day before. She introduced Skylor without pausing her conversation one bit, trying to inform Lucky of everything she had missed.

As was the style of the times, the next couple days were a nonstop celebration at the Ranch. Lucky marveled at the changes that had occurred as the Ranch had become the nerve center of the new society. All sorts of recycled material buildings housed people, animals, and green technology in all various amalgamizations. Music and merriment seeped out from every door and window as the entire population of almost two thousand joined in.

The party was constant and featured several spontaneous transformations, whether it was for a meal or bathing in the river. Lucky and Buck had no trouble finally slipping away into the old ranch house and their old room, both of which were hardly different at all from the day Lucky left. She walked through the whole space slowly and lovingly, caressing old surfaces and admiring old pictures. They ended up in the bed, which was one of the few new items around, being made of a new material fabricated up at Gray Whale Ranch Village at the ruins of the former university campus.

They fell into each other's arms, not saying anything, not knowing what to say, playing with each other like it was the first time, hovering at some boundary because there was really still so much to say.

"Buck, I am so sorry..." Lucky began. "I never should have left..."

"Hush, you don't have to apologize for anything, it's not about that," he said, putting his finger to her lips.

She kissed his finger as she said, "But I missed you so much, for so many years."

"Oh I missed you too," Buck said. "I wanted to go after you, but they wouldn't let me."

"I never expected you to come after me," Lucky said.

"I know, but you must understand, we knew intimately what was going on with you, even as you thought we had disappeared, and I would have, but then I was told..."

"What were you told, Buck?"

"Well, I know we both have had visions, of things, so, once...after the Council ruled I could not try to go for you, in despair I retreated into the Canyon, you know, the crevice way back up in, and just stopped eating. I stayed there day and night, in some sort of vision quest, but I don't know, it was in despair more than any kind of courage, but it happened somehow..."

He went on to describe how he awoke the fourth night in a golden light, bathed in a warm being. He felt great comfort, where he knew there had been sadness and loss, he felt joy. He turned over and saw Her again, the Eternal Mother and Lover, holding him in Her arms. He saw an endless line of women, queens, goddesses, all linked in an endless chain of love.

"Fear not, my son," She had said. "Fear not. Ask and you shall receive."

"I don't know what to ask," Buck managed.

"What do you wish for most in your heart?"

"That Lucky would come home."

"And so she shall. But you must let her come. You must not go to get her, or you may be lost. You must be strong enough to let her return," She had said.

Buck explained how he had promised, and how he had returned to Ranch life with a new vigor. He had worked now with the community for years always with the conviction that someday she would return.

"Oh, Buck," Lucky swooned. "That was why you made me come down off of the Lucky II! But, in all that time, you never took another, you never had another love?"

"I had many loves, but never another woman in this bed, no woman had my body," he told her, and they melted into another passionate embrace. They felt no boundaries this time, no reason to stop, and they let themselves flow deeply into each other. They made love with their bodies like before, but now with their spirits, too, their souls feeling and spinning in the ecstasy of union. Then Lucky knew, and Buck knew, as he became her old blue Lover, and she became his Eternal Lover, they knew. They knew that they were the manifestations in flesh of the great sacred gift that they were seeking. They knew that in sacred union they had found themselves at the beginning of Everything, where all true possibilities sprung forth, a special, holy place that they had never known existed, but for which they now knew they had always longed.

The next few days of celebration turned into weeks, and then finally merely shifted into the Solstice Celebrations. Buck and Lucky were given a grand tour of the new islands by airship. June and Skylor had been building a fascinating society on the islands, aided in no small part by the new technologies that had developed from the 1Earth servers after the Earthquake and EMF blast. They were forming themselves into a culture truly egalitarian and sustainable, taking the best of the old world and combining it with the totally new. Mia and Irena recovered quickly. All the single men of the islands had descended on New Star Cove when they heard that a ship chock full of new women had landed. Great legends were born of their journey and all the heroism and treachery that had transpired.

Time moved more slowly, the peaceful agrarian life lending a longer span, and soon it was the next Harvest season. June, Sahi, and Lucky were making lunch in the old ranch house, each fairly bubbling with life and excitement, anxious in their own ways. Sahi was keeping young Krishna Sky happy in the corner with homemade finger paints.

"So I have some big news," June was saying. She always led the conversation these days. She and Lucky were almost frantically making food in large quantities and varieties. "I didn't want to say anything until we were sure, but, I think...I...am pregnant!"

"All right!" Lucky exclaimed.

"Hurrah!" Sahi joined in.

"You know how much, ever since Krishna Sky was born, I wanted to share in that joy. You know how much I wanted to share in motherhood with you..."

"Well, you know," Sahi had to offer. "We might share in it with more than just Krishna Sky..."

"No way! You're not..." June started.

"I...believe so!" Sahi nodded.

"Unbelievable!" Lucky shouted. The girls hopped and hollered and spun around in each others arms.

"How can it be so?" Sahi asked. "That we should be so blessed, when the rest of the world is...well..."

"Girls," Lucky interrupted. "I don't want to be... uh...pardon the phrase...premature...bless my tongue...but I think I might..."

"What?" both June and Sahi said together.

"Yeah, well, it just might be, so...there."

"Pardon me," Sahi said. "But...is that possible?"

"Sure," Lucky assured them.

"I mean," Sahi continued. "You didn't have a cycle for a long time, right? Did you have one later?"

"Yeah, DatArchs couldn't read that from cyberspace, could they? Yeah, I had really heavy periods regularly ever since I left, right up to about 4 months ago..."

"And that was..." June stuttered. "That was...when you and Dad...okay enough of that!"

"Right," Sahi agreed. "It is possible, even at your age, I'm sorry. Your meditation likely affected all that. You could be."

"Yes, I am, girls. This I know. I am pregnant, and he will live. This I know, just as I know that you both will have girls."

"All right!" June shouted, as she gestured at the table. "My God! That's why we're obsessed with food!" They all laughed, a laughed the walls had waited to hear. They fell into an embrace against the table, and Krishna Sky shrieked in delight.

"The blessings flood over us!" Sahi declared. Both girls delighted in the fact that they all knew Lucky was right, and they were all tremendously blessed. They grew fat and happy together, all the women and their kin, rich in a land and newly reunited with a sustainable Way, through love.

It was hard to say which father was more proud of the growing life in his wife's womb, but everyone granted great reverence and respect for Lucky's child from even before birth. He was born healthy and strong, in the spring, and was named Isaac.

The girls were born on the same night in a new month of the corn planting moon, and were named Gem Star Smith and Lucky Skye Hager, respectively. The Society chose to remake almost everything, including the names of months and the days. They even voted at one point to get rid of Monday and Tuesday, electing on a system that had six five-day weeks a month. The 12 months were all 30 days long, with a two day period at the end of pure celebration, in a system that reflected the true balance of the seasons. All religions were encouraged and explored, and great advances were made in science, particularly with quantum computers and biology.

Sophisticated centers of learning had evolved in several parts of the islands, each around the nucleus of a 1Earth Server. The great knowledge of the Lucky

Star Ranch made New Star Cove one of the most productive agricultural areas and supported a growing population. The years saw great peace and harmony. Animal populations rebounded just as the Society's knowledge of animal communication reached new heights. Luke, Bud, Skylor, and June became great explorers in ever more sophisticated craft, always renewable and efficient. They took to the air, land, and sea, carefully mapping all the new places of their world.

They preserved great amounts of the knowledge of the past. They developed ever more complex quantum systems that allowed them to trace intricate paths into the earth with animals and living neural networks. Their DatArchs traced delicate lines of Data that developed up to the day the rest of the world went dark. They pushed advancing technology beyond singularity, achieving key goals that had been part of the pre-crash technological world. They rapidly made everything completely sustainable, and connected, and open. Life and animals flourished with the people in all the towns. They competed with each other as to where could create the most diverse local flora and fauna. Communication between species became common, particularly after the creation of the Levi/Harley 3000 universal translator, a handheld computer made by Lukas and Skylor that held over 2000 species languages and allowed for communication directly with whales and birds, as well as other mammals. The whales took particular care to tell the people exactly what was up.

On all sides of the main island were theaters and festival grounds, and all tried to outdo the others with the size and extravagance of their events. Another reason they abolished Monday and Tuesday so there could be only three days of work for every two day weekend party. These festivals and holiday celebrations evolved year to year and became great combinations of open market and exchanges and performance concerts. Even the animals had become a part of it as certain researchers had discovered what makes animals "party," like great schools or flocks or herds. The very power to make joy manifest in all creation was explored. It was a great time, and the only shadow was the thought of the rest of the world.

It would not be wrong to say that the search for data on the rest of the world was another primary driving force for the Society. The DatArchs had built a powerful guild on their knowledge, and other Tech guilds had developed afterward. Each worked out a method of value on exchange based on barter and consensus, but everyone valued information on the new world and of the old. Still no messages of any kind came back from the rest of the world, despite all the forms that Lucky tried, from shortwave to messages in bottles. She wanted get word to Pradesh about her success, but she knew not if he even still lived.

Lucky and Buck knew they would never leave the Islands again. Going up to Boulder Creek or Gray Whale Ranch Village by airship was far enough. Lucky satisfied herself that she had tried to reach her old friend. Motherhood had certainly changed her. Isaac was such a surprise that every day of life was a special gift, after that. Lucky had no need to go off exploring for some sort of meaning. Meaning was all around her, and she knew it. She and Buck raised a strong tribe, and Isaac was becoming a leader in his own right.

It was perhaps inevitable that a major movement for a great explorative expedition would eventually take hold and build to great proportions. Isaac, Gem, and Lucky Skye became leaders of a new generation. Too many of the younger folks were clamoring for more data on whatever remnants of civilization might remain out there. Skylor and June wanted to go, but were considered too valuable, and so Luke, Malakai, Isaac, Gem, and Lucky Skye were the leaders of a team of 50 chosen to make the journey. They came to me at every step for advice.

Yes, I am back in the story, just as I said I eventually would be. I had become the official story-teller for the Society. My job had been to gather and scatter the great stories of the new civilization. I had done as much as I could to educate my sons, and grandchildren, and was content to stay at our mountain top paradise over looking the setting sun. I had always envisioned these mountains as islands whenever they would be encircled with fog, from my earliest childhood, so the images were comforting to my aging mind. I had seen great sorrow, and great joy, and had endeavored to share both with my fellow men, women, and children. I could still tell the story, but few more great adventures were to use my own feet. My wife and I were gloriously happy and grateful to watch our own sons become such spectacular men.

Luke and Malakai felt they were meant to go on such an expedition, and they prepared to take their families along. With their new technologies they expected it to be a vacation of sorts, if a working one. No one was prepared to underestimate anything. They were supplying themselves with some of the best gear ever devised by humanity. They assembled an Armada like none ever seen, with self-powered high tech craft that could go above, below, and on the surface of the water at different times. The skills of the crew were unmatched by any throughout time, and Isaac was a shining lead example, along with Lucky Skye and Gem as well. They all would come to me for advice, but what could I tell them but more stories of what had been?

Lucky and Buck grew old together, happy as the hills, till they could hardly remember not being together. We would all gather at Gray Whale Village for the Annual Rite of Spring, and it had grown into the largest gathering of the islands, all spread out on the hills below the ruins of the university. We would have a camp near the very top, were we could watch all the festivities. My wife and I stood amazed at the crowd stretched out before us. Lucky and Buck stood with us to watch this most grand of festivals unfold, for it was to be like no other. On this date the long planned expedition was leaving towards the south, beginning their great journey. It was a splendid chain of silver seeds that stretched out to the distance, some 48 ships in all. They would be in contact the whole time, so it was planned, and they played out to the southern horizon as the people watched and celebrated.

We knew our children were going off to their own adventures. We felt the weight of time, and we feared for their safety. We remembered all the pains that we had suffered for our adventurousness in our lives, and we wondered why our children and grandchildren had the same need to learn through experience. We wondered, and we prayed.

It was my wife that first saw the visitors coming down from the north. It was hard to determine what they were, until they came much closer.

"They're the whales!" Rockelle exclaimed. "They are going to join the expedition."

"That's a good sign," I said, remembering the part the whales had played in our story.

"Look, they're swimming right over where Mission Street used to be!" my wife noticed as we watched them proceed past High Street Beach. The great celebration noticed the great migration of whales, and the crowd of thousands at the festival began to sing, shout, and drum to the whales in honor. The pod seemed to gain strength and confidence and the proceeded towards the silver beads in the distant summer horizon.

I turned to remark on the scene to Lucky and Buck, but I discovered they had gone. They were on a horse together, riding down the long hill. My eyes grew heavy and my mind grew wild, and I swore I saw a herd of cows and horses join them, and all sorts of animals coming along. The mountains rolled an opened up, and the couple were joined by multitudes of creatures, people and animals. There were the spirits of all the animals that Lucky and Buck had ever treated with love and care, all the livestock around the world that they had saved, and all the people that have lived because of the livestock. They all joined in a huge procession, marching off into a part of the southern island that I had never before seen.

Clouds circled around the mountain peaks, and the now great herd of souls followed Lucky and Buck onto some misty bridge that went over to some land of rainbows, where light and time bent bows of heart and mind. It was love that drove them all together, and they pushed higher and faster as they entered the transcendental. Lucky and Buck became themselves arm in arm as they rode back into their Eternal Home, and the Greatest Love was there to welcome them. As they arched through the sky, the grand procession that followed along streaked into the heavens like a star shower in reverse.